Lavish Praise for THE CARETAKER:

"Simpson has fashioned a slick, clever thriller out of an intriguing premise."—*Library Journal*

"A malevolently menacing thriller . . . Grabs readers by the throat and doesn't let go."
—*Booklist*

"An oddball voice and momentum that are hard to beat. The premise is unusual too. . . . A page-turner that will grab even those not addicted to them."
—*Booknews* from the Poisoned Pen

"A curious tale of suspense . . . {with} some pleasant, old-fashioned virtues: a strong narrative, solid pace, and a genuinely surprising ending. Not a bad combination."
—*Chicago Tribune*

"The author has created an elaborate and complex story, full of lies, betrayal, greed, {and} seduction. . . . Someday, you may see this one on the screen."—*Roanoke Times & World-News*

"Kinky-creepy. You won't mind."
—*The Philadelphia Inquirer*

"Wickedly hilarious . . . Simpson can show how generous helpings of passion, sex, and luxury make fools of so many of us mortals. Trashy, nasty, and fun."—*Kirkus Reviews*

Turn the page to read more raves for the novels of THOMAS WILLIAM SIMPSON. . . .

W9-BPK-872

THE CARETAKER

Thomas William Simpson

BANTAM BOOKS

New York Toronto London Sydney Auckland

This edition contains the complete text of the original hardcover edition.
NOT ONE WORD HAS BEEN OMITTED.

THE CARETAKER

A Bantam Book

PUBLISHING HISTORY

Bantam hardcover edition published February 1998
Bantam paperback edition / March 1999

ISBN: 0-553-57805-7

Published simultaneously in the United States and Canada

Bantam Books are published by Bantam Books, a division of Random House,
Inc. Its trademark, consisting of the words "Bantam Books" and the portrayal
of a rooster, is Registered in U.S. Patent and Trademark Office and in other
countries. Marca Registrada. Bantam Books, 1540 Broadway, New York,
New York 10036.

PRINTED IN THE UNITED STATES OF AMERICA

OPM   10 9 8 7 6 5 4 3 2 1

For Susan

Special thanks to Laura Blake Peterson, my friend and agent at Curtis Brown, Ltd., and Kate Miciak, editor extraordinaire, for putting up with me and making sure I got the job done.

And if any mischief follow, then thou shalt give life for life, eye for eye, tooth for tooth, hand for hand, foot for foot, burning for burning, wound for wound, stripe for stripe.

Exodus 21:23–25

Part One

THE OFFER

1 The trouble began with a letter. Actually, the trouble began long before the letter. The trouble began when Carl Patrick Donovan's father received that notice of foreclosure from the bank.

But there's no need to step back quite that far, at least not yet. There will be plenty of time later to sort things out.

The letter arrived certified. Sam had to sign. Gunn should have signed, but he was away, wheeling and dealing, so Lou, the postman, a shy and retiring type who collected old comic books and hiked in the mountains for recreation, assured Sam she could sign. The legal-size envelope was addressed to:

Mr. Gunn Henderson
1271 North Sycamore Drive
Alexandria, Virginia 22313

The return address was simply:

Creative Marketing Enterprises
P.O. Box 424
Amagansett, New York 11930

A quick glance at that return address and Sam decided it must be some kind of sweepstakes notification, a free romantic weekend for two at Leisure Village in the Poconos, some marketing nonsense like that. But then, right on cue, before Lou had even stepped off the front porch, the telephone rang.

Sam picked up in the downstairs hallway. "Hello?"

"Mrs. Henderson?"

"Yes."

"Good morning, Mrs. Henderson. How are you today?"

A salesman, she knew immediately. Married to one, Sam could smell a salesman a million miles away. But what was this one selling? Long-distance phone service? Magazine subscriptions? Swimming pool chlorinators? They didn't even have a swimming pool, though Sam wanted one. Sam loved to swim for exercise.

"I'm just fine."

"I'm sorry to bother you, Mrs. Henderson, but I was wondering if your husband, Mr. Gunn Henderson, was home this morning?"

Sam did not make a point of telling complete strangers the whereabouts of her husband. Many years ago, during a youth some might call sheltered, her parents had instructed her never to talk to strangers. Sam had carried these instructions with her into adulthood, then passed them on to her own well-protected offspring. And as a viewer of the local TV news in the

Washington metro area, she also possessed an irrational fear of men who broke into homes, raped women, and stole children.

This fear was one of the ways Gunn justified the presence of loaded guns in the house: protection from the riffraff. Gunn had quite a collection: handguns, shotguns, various types of hunting rifles.

"May I ask," Sam asked, "who's calling?"

"Ron Johnson. From Creative Marketing Enterprises."

Sam took another look at the certified letter still in her hand. A slight furrow creased her brow. "Yes, Mr. Johnson. What can I do for you this morning?"

"I'm sorry to bother you, Mrs. Henderson. We were just calling to inquire if your husband had received a certified letter recently sent to him by Creative Marketing Enterprises."

"I see."

"Would you know if that letter had arrived?"

Sam had the distinct feeling Mr. Johnson already knew the answer to his inquiry. She glanced for a third time at the envelope. There was nothing special about it: just a plain white envelope, simple lettering denoting the sender, Gunn's name and address typed neatly across the center. She felt the weight. It seemed practically empty; as though it might contain nothing at all, a single sheet of twice-folded paper at the most.

"Yes," she answered. "Your letter arrived."

Sam glanced out the window, thinking she might just see Mr. Ron Johnson sitting in his company Chevy at the end of the driveway talking to her on his cellular phone. But no one was out there except for Lou, slowly making his way across the quiet suburban street to the home of Glenda and Brian Young. Glenda had recently filed for divorce. Emotional abuse. But that's another story.

"Excellent," said Mr. Ron Johnson. "I'm very glad to hear that." He sounded genuinely pleased.

Samantha would find out later, much later, after it was too late, that there was no Mr. Ron Johnson employed at Creative Marketing Enterprises. Ron Johnson did not exist. Nothing but a voice on the telephone. On the telephone we can be anyone we want.

"Actually," said Sam, not really knowing why she was offering unsolicited information, "I'm holding your company's letter in my hand at this very moment. It arrived just before you called."

"That's a coincidence," said Mr. Ron Johnson, without the slightest twinge of irony in his voice.

"I thought so, too."

Ron Johnson made a little laugh.

Sam wondered if she should be scared, wondered if it would be prudent to go into her husband's study and get the revolver out of the top right-hand drawer of his desk.

Before she could decide, Ron said, "I won't take up any more of your time, Mrs. Henderson. I would just ask you to please make sure your husband gets that letter as soon as he returns home."

This request caused the furrow in Sam's brow to deepen. "I don't recall saying my husband wasn't home."

"Oh, I'm sorry," said Mr. Johnson. "I guess I just assumed."

"Yes," replied Sam, "I guess you did."

"So," asked Mr. Johnson, "is your husband home?"

"He's in the shower," lied Sam.

"I see. Then you will be sure to give him the letter?"

"I said I would."

"Thank you."

"So what is this, anyway?" she asked, trying now to sound casual. "Did we win something? A trip to Disney World?"

Ron Johnson laughed again. "Oh, no, Mrs. Henderson, trust me, nothing so trivial as that. This is about a job opportunity. You see, Creative Marketing Enterprises is looking for some very extraordinary salespeople. One person in particular. We feel your husband might be our man."

2 An extraordinary salesman: That described Mr. Gunn Henderson to a T. The man could sell anything. He started out at the age of eight selling newspapers. Door to door. In an affluent neighborhood of Westchester County. He learned early the power of his easy smile. On collection day a toothy grin usually earned him a nice commission from overwrought housewives searching for a bit of levity from their domestic drudgery.

Gunn did not need to sell newspapers; his daddy was a VIP down at Continental Bank and Trust in NYC. Vice-president in charge of home mortgages and small business loans. But Gunn Jr. wanted his own dough. Gunn Jr. did not want to have to ask Gunn Sr. or anyone else for anything. One year Gunn sold more newspapers than any other kid in the entire state of New York. He received a special gold plaque with his name etched across it. Everywhere he ever lived, he hung that plaque on the wall over his bed.

After his son graduated from Colgate University, Gunn Sr. wanted Gunn Jr. to follow in his banking footsteps. Gunn Sr. thought banking, all that power and money, was the pièce de résistance of the business world. Besides, his son had followed him everywhere. Gunn Jr. had gone to the same prep school and the same college. Gunn Sr. had taught his boy how to hit a forehand and how to knock a pheasant out of the sky. A couple peas in a pod, Henderson the Elder and Henderson the Younger had spent countless hours together in duck blinds and deer blinds discussing the ways of the world.

But at the age of twenty-two, Gunn Jr. asserted his independence. He was in too big a hurry to settle for a twenty-eight-thousand-dollar-a-year glorified clerk's position at the bank. Gunn wanted to go after the big bucks straight out of college. So he went to work for Xerox selling copy machines. Again, door to door. More or less. He was given leads as to where he might call, but beyond that he was on his own. Which was just fine with Gunn. That's exactly how he wanted to play the game. Gunn was the master of the cold call. The smooth-talking young Henderson could sell guns to the Peace Corps, battleships to the Swiss Confederation, everlasting love to sweet and innocent young girls.

Gunn could walk in on virtually any business and within half an hour have the right person or persons convinced that a brand new Xerox 8600 super-duper deluxe copier was absolutely essential for the continued growth and prosperity of that company.

Gunn sold an incredible number of copy machines during his first year on the job. By his third year his commissions had reached nearly one hundred thousand dollars annually. This before his twenty-fifth birthday. The company kept wanting to make him a regional sales manager, but Gunn kept putting them off. He knew regional sales managers dealt with back-stabbing company politics. Regional sales managers had to shuffle too much paper. Regional sales managers, Gunn liked to say, had to kiss too much ass. Gunn Henderson did not kiss ass. Gunn Henderson was a lone wolf. Have copier, will sell. Just stay out of his way.

So what's Gunn going to sell now? Cigarettes and chocolates to the other inmates?

3 Sam took one more look at that envelope from Creative Marketing Enterprises, then tossed it on the hall table along with the rest of the day's mail. No way would she have opened that letter, curious though she might be. One did not even think about opening the mail of Mr. Gunn Henderson. Not even if one was Mrs. Gunn Henderson.

Once, early in their marriage, Sam had opened a Christmas card addressed not to the two of them, but just to Gunn. She was not being nosy; she was just opening the Christmas cards, glancing at them, and tossing them into the bowl on the kitchen counter.

Gunn, upon learning of this felonious offense, became furious. "How dare you open my mail!" he demanded the moment he discovered her crime.

"Excuse me?"

"Who the hell do you think you are, opening my mail? You see this card?!" He shoved the Happy Holidays greeting in her face. "This card was addressed to me, not to you! Do you see your name anywhere on this card? *I* don't see your name anywhere on this card. Don't ever open my mail again!"

Sam, that ancient incident always in the back of her mind, tossed the certified letter from Creative Marketing Enterprises onto the hall table, unopened. The letter would have to wait until Gunn's return.

Sam had things to do anyway. She bustled around the house: breakfast dishes in the dishwasher, beds made, bathrooms tidied up, a load of clothes into the washer, another load, from last night, out of the dryer. Normally Sam did not leave things in the dryer, but these were just towels, nothing that would wrinkle.

Next she made some phone calls, most of them regarding Megan's ninth birthday party the following Tuesday after school. Sam always made a big deal over birthdays and holidays and vacations. She loved to see the smiles on her children's faces.

By ten-thirty she was in the Explorer for her first trip of the day. At eleven o'clock she hit the courts for an hour and a half of fairly aggressive women's doubles. The four competitors might not have been the most beautiful shotmakers ever to wield rackets, but they played with a determined ferocity. They bombed around the court, slashing and thrashing at every ball that came their way. They fought hard for every point, even though they seemed utterly unconcerned with the score.

Sam enjoyed her exercise. Practically every day she ran or biked or played tennis. She liked keeping fit. Eighteen years out of high school, but she could still fit into the jeans she had worn senior year. Every now and then she would tug those faded Levi's up over her hips, take a deep breath, close the zipper, and snap the snap. Just for the pleasure of it. Just to prove she could still do it.

After tennis Sam raced home to take a shower. After drying and brushing her hair, she called Mandy to tell her she would be late for lunch.

Mandy, her best friend, became instantly agitated. "Late again! My God, Samantha! How dare you? You're so damn selfish and irresponsible. All you ever think about is yourself!"

Sam giggled. She liked when Mandy imitated Gunn.

"Don't worry," added Mandy. "Take your time. I changed the reservation in anticipation of your tardiness."

Sam's tardiness was a well-known fact among family and friends. She simply did not do well with time. Most people accepted this small quirk in her character. A few, of course, did not. Such as her punctual husband. Gunn always knew the time. Even without access to clocks or watches he could quote the time with uncanny accuracy.

In Gunn Henderson's philosophy of life, tardiness was right up there with rape, murder, and sloth.

"Where the hell have you been?" he would roar when Sam showed up even thirty seconds late for dinner or a movie. "You do nothing all damn day, then you can't even be somewhere on time!"

Sam tried to do better. She really did. She liked to please. She set the clocks in the bedroom and the kitchen five or ten minutes fast. She bought a wristwatch that had its own alarm. She wrote notes to herself so she would be on time for appointments. She even read a couple of how-to books on punctuality. It all helped. A little. Not much. Time and Samantha Ann Quincy Henderson simply did not see eye-to-eye.

On her way out the door, Sam spotted that certified letter resting on the hall table. She wondered about the job offer Mr. Ron Johnson had mentioned earlier on the phone. She wondered if Gunn would be interested. She figured he would at least listen to what the man had to say.

Not that Gunn was a big listener. He preferred to do the talking, dominate the conversation.

But he listened very closely when the judge cleared his throat and passed a sentence of twenty-five years.

Sam hurried out the front door, hopped into the Explorer, and flew across town. She liked to drive fast. Not that fast was much of an option. In northern Virginia, within spitting distance of the District, people, lots of them, were always on the move. It seemed at times as though sitting still, being at rest, had become the eighth deadly sin. Right up there with greed and gluttony.

Sam had a drink with lunch, a rare indulgence. Something smooth and icy and sweet. A strawberry daiquiri. Gunn hated when Sam drank. Especially when she drank when he wasn't around. He hated when she got silly, when she giggled and had a good time with her friends.

The other girls, Mandy and Sally and Judy, split a bottle of wine. The alcohol made them all giddy. This was their monthly let's-get-giddy party. The four women sat around in some fancy restaurant, had a drink, ate some lunch, made fun of their husbands, and joked about running off with the new tennis instructor at the club. Max something or other. Very Mediterranean. Sam actually thought Max was kind of gross, dark and greasy, but it was still fun to fantasize. Sam was, still is, very particular about men. She is not easily attracted. Everything needs to be just right: face, hair, body, hands, voice, smell, temperament— the whole package. Foreign men, men with ponytails, men with beards, scrawny men, fat men, men with whiny voices, men who sweat or swear too much—all these kinds of men turn Sam off.

The girls decided Judy needed to run off with Max. Judy, they decided, needed some excitement in her life. She had the most boring husband in all creation. God must have worked overtime to make a man that dull. Judy complained about him all the time. She complained about the amount of TV he watched, his performance in bed, the amount of food he ate, the way he picked his teeth with his fork after meals, the fact that he only ever talked about two things: his work (stock analyst) and his mother, whom he claimed he despised but nevertheless talked to long distance two or three times a week.

Then, all of a sudden, someone announced it was nearly three o'clock. The girls disbanded in a flash. They quick got the check, divvied up the total, and made their escape. They all had places to be, things to do, people, mostly young ones, who needed their attention.

It was Wednesday. That meant Jason and Megan needed to be picked up at school. Thank God they both went to the same school. Next year they would go to different schools. On opposite sides of town. That would be a transportation and logistical nightmare. Although, Sam had a plan. Dissatisfied with the quality of education Jason and Megan were receiving at public school, she had the pressure on Gunn to send them to private school. She already had one picked out, just across the Potomac River in Georgetown. It would mean even more time spent chauffeuring, but Sam found that a small price to pay for her children's education. Thus far, however, Gunn had refused to foot the bill.

When Sam pulled up to the school, a few minutes behind schedule, Megan stood waiting patiently outside the front door. Jason, on the other hand, was nowhere in sight.

This simple scenario pretty much summed up the personalities of the Henderson offspring. Megan was sweet and generally cooperative. Like her mother, she liked to please. Even as an infant she had enjoyed making her mama smile.

But her older brother had been burdened since birth

with a rather tough disposition. His mother, who had spent untold hours trying to make the boy happy, finally decided Jason had simply been conceived during a bad lunar phase. Of course, she also believed in the power of genetic mutation. The boy was, after all, a direct link to his rather difficult daddy. And that was not really Jason's fault.

So Sam did the best she could. She worked overtime to make her son feel loved and secure. It was not always easy. Her patience and understanding sometimes wore thin.

Like today. She needed almost fifteen minutes to track Jason down. She finally found him in the gym shooting baskets with some other kids. She told him they had to leave. He ignored her. She told him again, in a slightly louder voice. He continued to ignore her. So she yelled at him. He yelled right back. They stood there and argued. Sam knew arguing with Jason was a big mistake. The young man knew how to push her buttons.

Eventually, the three of them climbed into the Explorer and set off on their appointed rounds: Megan to ballet and Jason to piano.

Megan loved ballet. Jason hated piano. Getting him to practice his scales was like trying to catch a greased pig. He was always screeching at his mother and trying to slip away. Still, she made him stick with it. Not because she thought he would be the next Vladimir Horowitz or Elton John, but just because she wanted him to develop his small amount of musical aptitude, even if just for his own personal enjoyment later in life. She had to push him and prod him, coax him

along with sweets and special favors. And still he resisted every step of the way.

Usually with encouragement from his father. Gunn
Henderson, Jock Extraordinaire, wanted his boy out
playing ball, running around, getting dirt on his teeth
and blood on his elbows. Gunn did not want Jason
sitting at the piano like some sissy.

Sam dropped Megan at the YWCA in Alexandria
for her ballet class, then she zipped back to Arlington
for Jason's piano lesson. The whole way he whined, "I
don't wanna go to piano. Piano sucks. I hate piano."

What he wanted to do, Sam knew, was go home,
microwave a bowl of Orville Redenbacher cheese-
flavored popcorn, and watch cartoons and sitcom re-
runs for eight or nine hours.

"Too bad," his mother told him. "You're going to
piano."

For Sam, the toughest part of parenting was forcing
her children to do things they didn't want to do, but
which she believed would be good for them in the
long run.

At the piano teacher's house, Sam had to walk Jason
to the front door. She always had to walk him to the
door and hand him over to Mrs. Wyatt. If she didn't, if
she just dropped him off out front and drove away, he
would wait for her to disappear around the corner,
then he would sprint into the woods behind Mrs. Wyatt's house. He had done it before. And he would, Sam
felt sure, if given the opportunity, do it again.

So she made the handoff to kindly old Mrs. Wyatt, a
woman with the patience of Job, then she raced over to
the market for some fresh tofu and organic veggies.
She and the kids were part-time vegetarians. Now

they're full-time vegetarians. They never ate meat when Gunn was out of town on business. Now Gunn is out of town for a good long time. Gunn was a full-time carnivore. Two and often three times a day he consumed large quantities of dead animal flesh. All kinds of flesh: deer, duck, cow, pig, chicken. Ground, filleted, boiled, or barbecued. It didn't matter. Just give Gunn meat. Lots and lots of meat.

When Sam once suggested they all become vegetarians, for both health reasons and environmental reasons, Gunn roared, "Faggots don't eat meat. This family, goddammit, eats meat!"

With her bag filled with tofu, basmati brown rice, and fresh snap peas, Sam headed back to the YWCA in Alexandria where she got to see exactly two whole minutes of her daughter's ballet lesson. Then back into the Explorer and out onto the clogged arteries of suburban Washington. The lawyers and the government bureaucrats were beginning to swarm. It was a bad time for the innocent to be out on the roads.

Sam didn't care. As they crawled through traffic, she had a nice giggle with her little girl.

As always, eight-year-old Megan overflowed with enthusiasm and smiles and good cheer. Ballet, she informed her mother, had been awesome. "Absolutely awesome."

Sam leaned over and gave her daughter a kiss. She loved her kids. Three or four more would have suited Sam just fine, but Gunn, who had balked at one, had slammed the brakes on at two.

Megan was quite the little ballerina. She loved to dart around the dance floor in her little pink slippers. And at fifty-six pounds soaking wet, she could leap into the air and swirl around in circles with her tremendous hang-time.

All the way over to Mrs. Wyatt's, Megan carried on about becoming a great ballerina, the greatest ballerina in all the world. She was not boasting, just dreaming out loud, dreaming with a wide grin on her face.

Sam dreamed right along with her. She wanted, more than anything else in life, for her children to fulfill their dreams and desires. But she had decided years ago not to push them, only to encourage.

Unfortunately, the moment they pulled into Mrs. Wyatt's driveway, Megan's dreams vanished. She grew mute. Perfectly still and silent. As though some terrifying evil lay in wait just outside the Explorer.

It certainly was not Mrs. Wyatt who brought on this reaction. Oh, no. No one other than her loud and merciless sibling could bring on a stillness and a silence this overwhelming.

Megan could not make a peep without big brother Jason making fun of her, ribbing and ridiculing. It was nothing more than his raging sibling jealousy and his adolescent insecurity, but Megan did not understand any of these twitchy psychological concepts. She was just a little kid.

4 Gunn called home sometime after nine that night, not long after Sam had put Jason and Megan to bed. He called from New Orleans. From the Hyatt. From his suite on the nineteenth floor with a view of the Superdome. This fact impressed Gunn far more than it impressed his wife.

"I'm calling a little early tonight, babe," he said, "because I have to go out again. The client got himself half stewed at dinner on bourbon and port, and now he wants to go down to the French Quarter and listen to some authentic New Orleans jazz."

"The client," said the dutiful wife of the hotshot salesman, "is the boss."

Gunn laughed. "Exactly so. But in this case the client is also a loud, fat, obnoxious, foulmouthed asshole."

Gunn, Sam felt quite sure, did not see the irony in his description. Of course, Gunn was not fat. Not an ounce of fat anywhere on his person. Gunn would never allow himself even so much as a love handle. His self-image depended largely upon his highly honed physique.

"Just remember, Gunn," Sam said, right on cue, "the client, no matter how loud, fat, obnoxious, or foulmouthed, is always right. You taught me that on our first date."

Gunn laughed again. Then he started in. They both knew the drill. He spent the next ten or fifteen minutes slicing and dicing the client, running the client down in every conceivable manner, getting a whole host of ugly and negative attitudes off his chest. You see, Gunn Henderson had a rather unique, if somewhat bizarre, take on the art of salesmanship. Basically, he viewed sales as warfare, and the pitch as his weapon of choice. He used his mouth instead of a gun. The client was the enemy. The client needed to be subdued without mercy. To do this successfully the enemy had to be despised. No way around it. In the Gunn Henderson Guidebook to Successful Sales, the salesman who did not hate his client was a salesman destined to fail, doomed, at the very least, to earn himself a paltry commission.

Gunn did not believe in paltry commissions. He believed in extracting every possible nickel from the client's pocket. "You have to hate the son of a bitch," he had often told his bride, "while at the same time making him believe you love him and envy him, worship the ground he walks on. You have to make him think he's your best friend in the whole world. And you have to make him feel important, a VIP, the freaking Pope if that's what it takes."

Probably Sam should have listened closer to these maxims during the early phase of their relationship. Maybe they would have been a wake-up call. But by the time she had a real handle on Gunn's twisted philosophy, it was, as they say, too late. His good looks and great charm had already cast their spell over her young and relatively innocent soul.

She sat there on the edge of the bed, the phone at her ear, only half listening to him vent. It was just part of her day, like folding the laundry or poking holes in the potatoes or getting the oil changed in the Explorer, part of her duty.

Finally he began to wind down. He said, "I better get going."

Sam snapped back. "Yes, you don't want to keep the client waiting."

"This SOB hates to wait."

Sam asked him when he would be home.

"Tomorrow night," he told her. "Friday at the latest."

"Okay. But remember, we have a dinner party at Mandy and Tad's Friday night."

She heard him sigh. He wanted her to hear him sigh. His sigh was like a lion's roar. "Let's make that Saturday at the latest."

"Gunn!"

"Come on, Sam. Tad's an asshole. All he ever wants to talk about is the goddamn Washington Redskins. Christ, the guy remembers fumbles and pass interceptions from last October. A night with him is like a night with the dead. And his wife's not much better."

"Don't start on Mandy, Gunn."

"I'm not starting on anyone."

But, of course, he was. Gunn could not help himself. He needed to run down others to keep himself running strong.

"Good," said Sam, "because I don't want to hear it."

"Mandy's okay. I like Mandy. She's just not the sharpest knife in the drawer, that's all. I mean, how many people do you know who try to iron a wrinkle out of their shirt after they put it on?"

It's true, Mandy had once tried to do exactly that. She was in a hurry, trying to get somewhere to do something. In her rush to get out of the house, she touched a hot iron to her silk blouse just above her breast in an effort to remove an unsightly wrinkle. For weeks afterward she had a nasty purple burn mark on her chest from the top of her breast to her collarbone. But so what? We all make mistakes. Mandy was Sam's friend. A good friend. Her best friend. She was in no mood to listen to Gunn run Mandy down just to fuel his own flaming ego.

"Friday afternoon at the latest," she told him.

"Okay, Sam, I'll be there."

"And next Tuesday is Megan's birthday. Don't forget."

"I won't. But I better get going. The asshole's waiting downstairs in his long black limo."

"Can't keep the client waiting," Sam muttered again.

"Never a good idea. Gives the bastard time to hate me more than I hate him."

Gunn had always been big on the locker room slang. Even in front of his wife and kids. The swearing made Sam uncomfortable, but she rarely said anything. It would only make him do it more. He loved to do little things, insignificant things, to upset her: cursing, clipping his toenails onto the carpet, not flushing the toilet, putting things away in the wrong place, tracking his muddy shoes across the floor. He would do these things, and then, when she became upset, he would become instantly indignant. "God, Sam, what are you getting so worked up about? It's not like I did it on purpose."

Of course, the classic passive-aggressor never thinks he does anything negative on purpose. They usually have mommies who tell them how sweet and wonderful they are. Gunn was no exception. He had been hearing about his perfectness since popping out of the womb.

At the last second Sam remembered the letter. "Oh, wait! Something else."

"It'll have to wait till I get home. I have to go."

"You received a certified letter today."

"A certified letter? From who?"

"Some company called Creative Marketing Enterprises."

"Never heard of them. What do they want?"

Sam considered telling him about the call from Mr. Ron Johnson, but at the last second decided against it. "I don't know. I didn't open it."

"But it was certified, right? You had to sign for it?"

"Yes. It was addressed to you, but Lou let me sign for it."

"Lou? Who's Lou?"

"Lou's the mailman."

"You know the mailman by name?"

Suspicion: another of Gunn's lovely qualities.

"Yes, Gunn, I know the mailman by name. I've seen him practically every single day since we moved into this house almost three years ago. In three years you usually learn someone's name."

Gunn pictured a big, handsome, strapping mailman

strutting up his front walk, climbing the brick stairs, two at a time. For a good thirty seconds he said not a word. Then, finally, "Yeah, okay . . . so . . . what about this letter?"

"Do you want me to get it? Open it? Do you want me to read it to you?"

"I do . . . yeah . . . but . . ." Gunn was distracted again by Lou, by thoughts of Lou parking his mailbag in the front foyer and having his wife on the plush living room rug. "But not right now . . . Shit . . . I have to get downstairs."

"It would only take a minute."

"No! . . . Goddammit!"

Gunn, peeved and paranoid, hung up without whispering a single word of amour. He did not even bother to say good-bye. Perhaps he figured his small display of anger would be enough to make his wife send Lou away forever.

Gunn Henderson: Husband. Father. Lover. Salesman. And, in Sam's eyes, Mr. Wonderful.

Hey, there was a time she thought so. She really did.

5 Sam did not sleep well that night. She tossed and turned with only a vague notion of the whys and wherefores. Nothing in particular had her upset or off kilter. Just the usual questions one asks oneself at three o'clock in the morning: Who am

I? Why am I here? Is there a God? Do we all possess both good and evil in our hearts? Would I look sexier if I had contact lenses tinted sky-blue? Am I doing all I can for Jason and Megan? Does my husband sleep with other women when he is away on business?

Answers to Sam's musings were not forthcoming, so after another round of tosses and turns, she flipped on the light. She always kept two books, usually novels, next to her side of the bed: a literary classic and a piece of trash. She tried desperately to read the classics, those miracles of fiction she should have read back in high school and college, but rarely did.

The truth was this: Sam slogged through five or six trashy novels in the time it took her to read a single classic. That night, though, she reached for the real thing: Faulkner's *Absalom, Absalom!*. But she made this move not with the purest of intentions. She had high hopes Mr. Faulkner and his plodding prose would make her drowsy after just a page or two. It had done so on several other nights past. But not tonight. Tonight she read and read and read. Until almost four A.M. Finally she got up and took a Xanax. It helped her relax and fall asleep, to dream beautiful, hazy dreams.

But then, unfortunately, she could not rouse herself in time to get Jason and Megan out of bed and aboard the school bus. Cause and effect. Sam slept until ten minutes of nine. She would have slept even later had not Megan wandered into her bedroom and slipped between the sheets for her morning snuggle. One of the best parts of the whole day.

It was closing in on ten o'clock by the time the trio finally headed out of the house. On the way to the

front door Sam stopped in the hallway to pick up the
car keys. They were lying right on top of that certified
letter. So, without really thinking about the consequences, she picked up the letter also. She picked it up
and stuffed it in her purse. She suddenly felt an uncon-
trollable impulse to open that letter. She wanted to rip
open that envelope and read all about this great job
offer Mr. Ron Johnson of Creative Marketing Enterprises had mentioned on the phone the previous morning.

Impulses and their roots are often difficult to pin
down. Everyone has the urge from time to time to do
something better left undone. Occasionally we act
upon our impulses. But most of the time we just let
them fade away. Life, after all, would be a chaotic mess
if we pursued every last bit of stimuli that popped into
our huge but underused brains. So what about Sam
and her impulse to open Gunn's letter? Was she just
bored? Searching for excitement? Teetering toward
skydiving or bungee jumping?

Sam's children were her primary focus in life. She
cared for them, cooked for them, worried about them,
entertained them, did her best to instill them with
kindness and good values. But Jason and Megan were
growing up so fast. They spent most of their time in
school or with friends or participating in one activity
or another. Sam had more and more time to kill, more
and more hours to fill. She'd thought about going back
to work, but Gunn attacked the idea. And frankly,
Sam was not real enthusiastic about it either. Graduate
school had floated around in the back of her mind, but
she had never done more than send for an application.

So here was this letter, this certified letter from

some company up in New York. It represented mystery and intrigue, a potential alteration of a life that had become somewhat routine and predictable. How could she not want to rip it open and see what it said?

It usually took about twelve minutes to drive to school. Sam made it that day in less than ten. She pulled right up to the front entrance. Megan reminded her they needed a note for being late. Jason suggested it might be easier if they just took the whole day off.

The idea appealed to Sam. They could go into D.C., maybe visit the Smithsonian. But she knew it would be an irresponsible move. Jason had enough problems keeping up with his work.

"Not today," she replied as she scribbled them each a note on a memo pad she kept in the small storage compartment between the seats.

A kiss from Megan and a grunt from Jason and off they went to further their educations. Sam watched them go, and as she watched them she hoped they would make it safely through that day and every day. There were so many pitfalls along the way.

More than she knew.

Then, plumb out of patience, she grabbed that certified letter out of her purse and held it between her fingers. She studied the return address: P.O. Box 424, Amagansett, New York 11930. It had a familiar ring, Amagansett, but Sam had no idea where in New York it was. She dug the pocket road atlas out of the glove box and looked it up. After consulting the list of towns and cities in the back of the atlas, she located Amagansett: out near the eastern tip of Long Island, halfway between Southampton and Montauk.

She closed the atlas, and right there in the parking

lot of the grammar school, Samantha Ann Quincy Henderson threw caution to the spring wind. She ripped that envelope wide open and pulled out the contents.

Dear Mr. Henderson:

My name is Arthur James Reilly. I own a small marketing company that has successfully developed several products in the home entertainment field. Last year we grossed in excess of thirty million dollars. This was accomplished with a very small staff. Net on this gross was, let us say, acceptable.

I prefer to keep overhead to a minimum. I do not believe in middle management. But in two areas I deem it absolutely essential to spend and spend well: R&D and sales. Without a good product you may as well pack up and go home. But quite often even the best products fail without the assistance of a first-class sales team. And sales, Mr. Henderson, is obviously why I am contacting you.

I could toot your horn for a page or two, run down your impressive string of successes in office equipment, computers, and now athletic merchandise, but I doubt very much if you are a man who needs his ego stroked. I would prefer to move directly to the bottom line. I am about to release an entirely new product with enormous earning potential. I am expecting one hundred million dollars in sales before the end of this millennium. To accomplish this goal, I need a national sales strategist with guts, vision, and energy. I need someone willing to commit himself one hundred percent.

Base salary for this position, Mr. Henderson, is

$250,000 per annum. In addition, there will be extensive travel benefits, first-class health and dental insurance, a special housing arrangement, private schools for your children, and a long list of other perks as well. And sales incentives could easily triple and even quadruple your base salary in just the first year or two.

Obviously, sir, I am not yet offering you this position, but I am most assuredly offering you the opportunity to meet with me and discuss the future.

I will give you a few days to let this matter digest, then I or someone from my office will contact you to see if we might arrange a date to meet and chat.

All the best to you and yours,

Arthur James Reilly
President and CEO

6 Gunn was, predictably, furious when he found out Sam had opened his certified letter. He ranted and raved for a good ten minutes.

"But, Gunn," Sam did her best to explain, "the other night on the phone you wanted me to go get the letter and read it to you. In order to do that I would have had to open it."

Logic had never played a big part in the life of Gunn Henderson. Oh, he thought it did. He thought he was the most logical man in all the union. He was the purveyor, after all, of Henderson Logic. Henderson males for countless generations had been practicing this special form of logic. Certainly his father, Gunn Sr., had employed the art of Henderson Logic in both his personal and his professional life. As husband, father, and banker, Gunn Sr. had lined up on the side of Right one hundred percent of the time.

So what if Henderson Logic had no foundation in rational or compassionate thinking? It nevertheless gave Gunn and his male predecessors enormous power to justify their actions and opinions.

Gunn would go to great lengths to justify his position on everything from which cereal should be eaten for breakfast to the role of tsunamis in global weather patterns. To argue with Gunn was to argue with God. He knew all. The certified letter provides a perfect example:

"I wanted you to read the letter to me, Sam," he replied that evening to her explanation, his voice right on the edge of irritated. "That does not mean I wanted you to read the letter to yourself."

"Oh," Sam thought silently, "now that would have been a neat trick."

She chose not to utter this bit of sarcasm out loud. She made this decision not because she was afraid of Gunn Henderson; although, she was quite often careful with the words she let flow from her mouth. Make no mistake, she did fear her husband. Probably a lot more than she was willing to admit. Even to herself. But that night she simply remained mute because she did not want to escalate a silly argument moments before a pleasant dinner party with their friends.

They were in the car. Gunn's car. His precious

Porsche. His weapon against middle-age middle-class domestic servitude. His sheet-metal fortress against growing old with a wife and kids. Sam knew the car had a number: 711 or 813 or 969. Something like that. She could never remember. He thought she cared. He thought she thought he was a sexy and wild free spirit because he drove around in that stupid little overpriced car that made so much noise you could barely hear the radio even at full volume.

Gunn always kept the Porsche in the garage. Locked. With a special mesh cover over it. "Dust is the enemy of a fine paint job." He definitely expressed more affection for his car than he did for his kids. And God forbid if anyone touched that fine automobile. The full wrath of the Lord would strike down any person fool enough to lay a finger on that polished red bullet.

Once, a couple years earlier, young Jason had fallen out of the big maple tree in the backyard. The fall had led to a broken arm. The Explorer was in the shop for service that day, so Sam was stuck at home without a car. Well, the Porsche was out in the garage, but Sam did not even have a key. She had only driven the car once. With Gunn sitting right beside her, barking orders every time she'd let the rpm's slip below three thousand.

But suddenly she had an emergency on her hands. Her son, their son, clearly had a broken arm. She could see it hanging there off his shoulder all bent and twisted. Jason was screaming at the top of his lungs and probably getting ready to go into shock. So, in a state of panic, Sam decided to drive Gunn's Porsche to the emergency room. What else would any normal parent do?

It took her more than fifteen minutes to find the stupid keys. Good old Gunn had hidden them. In his underwear drawer. Inside the crotch of one of his jock-straps. Oh, yes, G. Henderson definitely saw that car as a physical extension of his maleness.

Anyway, to make a long and agonizing story short, Sam finally got Jason to the emergency room. A doctor x-rayed the arm and put it in a cast. He assured her it was a clean fracture of the radius that would, in four to six weeks, heal up as good as new. The doctor gave both mother and son something to settle their nerves, then he sent them on their way.

They returned home. Sam put the car carefully away in the garage. She dusted it off and replaced the cover. She then put Jason on the sofa in the family room in front of the television with a bowl of his favorite pop-corn and a large glass of Coca-Cola. Everything went smoothly. No problems whatsoever.

So what did Gunn Henderson, Porsche Club of America member, say that evening after he had lis-tened to their tale of woe, after he had signed his son's cast with his vast, sweeping signature? He said, "You know, Sam, you could have taken a taxi. In fact, under the circumstances, it might have been safer to take a taxi. For all concerned."

"Bastard," Samantha had whispered under her breath.

●　●　●

So THEY were in the Porsche. Zipping along far too fast for Sam's taste in that cramped and noisy little compartment. No legroom. No headroom. Nowhere to even put her purse. Seat narrow and confining, as hard as steel. This, she kept asking herself, is *fun*?

And Gunn, behind the wheel, his testosterone surging, his right foot mashing the accelerator, his right hand ripping through the gears every time they sped up or slowed down more than two or three miles an hour. Of course, Gunn thought he was totally in control, the Mario Andretti of Alexandria, Virginia. And to hell with Sam, sitting there, whining, asking him for the one millionth time to please, Gunn, slow down.

Not only was Sam afraid of being maimed or killed in a car accident, leaving her children without a mother, but she had always been prone to motion sickness, ever since her childhood. And that twitching, jittery Porsche was like being bounced around inside the lunar module.

And Gunn, all worked up, trying every trick in his passive-aggressive book to escalate the argument. "I've said it once, I've said it a thousand times: I don't want you opening my goddamn mail."

"Fine with me," Sam should have said but didn't. "I won't open your goddamn mail." No, instead she held herself steady as they zipped around a corner. "Please, Gunn, will you slow down?"

"Christ, Sam, I'm only doing fifty."

Then, to show his dominance, he pushed that number up closer to sixty, then sixty-five. And then he ranted some more about invasion of privacy and learning to mind one's own business, until finally, very much in character, he grew mute. But you could feel him still fuming. You could smell it. Why? Because

Sam had opened his stupid letter? Because she had asked him to slow down? Because he was basically a control freak and a nut case?

Sam did not know all the reasons for Gunn's foul humor. The letter? A tough week at work? Exhaustion? So many possibilities. She had long ago stopped trying to figure him out. She just knew he fumed all the way across town to Tad and Mandy's house. It would not have been difficult for a stranger to think she had called his mother a filthy rotten whore and his father an abusive pimp, so profoundly noisy was his silence.

But then they pulled into the Greers' driveway. Nice and easy. Not too fast. They pulled in, Gunn shut down the Porsche, and lo and behold, when he stepped out of the car he had miraculously turned himself back into Mr. Wonderful. He was once again Chairman of the Board of Charm. He even had the audacity to take his wife's arm as they strode up the brick walk toward the front door. Someone might possibly be looking out the window. And if they were, Gunn would be ready. His smile was the size of the moon when Mandy pulled open the door and welcomed the Hendersons into her home. He gave her a hug and a kiss and told her she looked stunning, as always.

Mandy swooned.

All night long Gunn the King of Sales had them swooning and smiling and laughing: the Greers, the Lungrens, the Platts. He told them all about his antics down in the Big Easy with the owner of some National Football League team. Some big shot. Worth millions. Billions. Gunn told them how he had snared this gentleman, the same gentleman he had referred to as an asshole on the phone a couple nights earlier, into a major sales deal with his company.

At that time Gunn was a national sales rep for one of the large sporting goods manufacturers. The Just Do It Gang. Gunn just did it. He convinced this owner to outfit his players solely with merchandise from Gunn's company. It was a major coup.

"I kept the SOB up until dawn," he told his fellow partiers. "We must have gone to every bar in the French Quarter. Finally, around three o'clock in the morning we wound up at Preservation Hall, the last great bastion for authentic New Orleans jazz. I gave the guy at the door a hundred-dollar bill to get us up close to the stage. I bought another round of drinks. It must've been like the twentieth round. But I think that round did it."

Gunn paused here to sip his beer. And to make sure he had everyone's attention. He did.

"These old black guys were playing some very funky, bluesy jazz. They were totally into it. So was my mark. He was one-hundred-percent absorbed in the music. So absorbed he actually started to cry. I'm not kidding. That rich SOB started wailing right there in Preservation Hall. The music, the booze, the atmosphere—the whole thing just blew him away. The tune was about this dude who loses his woman to another dude. I had the feeling the same thing had happened to my boy. Worth zillions but some broad must've blown him off. He looked about ready to stand up and start singing the blues. But hell, I don't know. All I know is later, in the back of his limo heading back to the hotel, he says to me, 'I give up,

Henderson. You win. Draw up the papers and we'll make this a done deal.' So that's what we did."

Oh yeah, Gunn the King of Sales had the Greers, the Lungrens, and the Platts in the palm of his hand. He knew how to tell a tale, how to keep his audience entertained. Which was why Mandy Greer could never fully understand what Sam was talking about when she complained about her man. Sure, Mandy knew Gunn had a thing about Sam being on time, and she knew that Gunn, like most men, could occasionally get a little out of sorts with his temper, but considering the competition out there, Mandy generally found Gunn a charming, funny, good-looking, hardworking guy. And he made money, plenty of money. And he wanted to make even more money. Truckloads of money was his dream.

All true, all true. But Mandy and the others had no idea about the scene in the Porsche earlier that evening. That scene and a hundred other scenes just like it. They had never seen the angry, brooding, insulting King of Sales. That was for Sam's eyes only.

After the party, around midnight, heading home, pumped up on beer and tequila and his performance, Gunn continued his role of Mr. Wonderful. It was clear he felt the evening had been a great success. He told Sam he loved her and worshiped her, that she was easily the greatest gal in the world. He drove slowly, didn't shift unless absolutely necessary. Instead of caressing the leather shifter, he gently stroked his wife's thigh. He definitely wanted to have sex when they got home.

And most of the time Sam would have felt the same desire. Gunn and Sam had a very good sex life. Their attraction to one another had hardly waned since their first lustful months together. Gunn was usually a fine lover, an almost perfect blend of romance and pure passion. But sex with Gunn after he'd been imbibing was never particularly pleasant.

"So," Sam asked, his fingertips dancing between the shifter and the inner part of her thigh, "are you going to follow up on this offer?"

He slowed as the car in front made a left turn. "What offer?"

"The offer from Creative Marketing Enterprises."

"Oh, right. I don't know. I doubt it."

"Why not? It sounds like it might be a good opportunity."

Gunn glanced at his wife. He wanted to bark at her. Tell her he would decide the good opportunities from the bad. But not tonight. Tonight his drowsy penis was doing the talking. "You're right," he mumbled. "Maybe it is."

"The money sounds excellent," said Sam. "But I really like the part about private schools for the kids."

Gunn did not give a damn about private schools for the kids. The kids were spoiled enough by their mother already. But the comment did remind him that Sam had opened that damn letter. Again, he almost snapped at her. But he held his tongue in anticipation of what lay ahead.

"Sure, the money's good," he said, "and so are the perks. But what the hell is Creative Marketing Enterprises? Who are they? I've never heard of them. They're not on the stock exchange. They're not a publicly traded company. I couldn't even find them on the NASDAQ."

"Maybe it's privately held."

"Hell, Sam, any jackass can print up some letter-head and spew some glorious bullshit about the millions of dollars that will soon be rolling in. A goddamn homeless bum can afford to buy a first-class stamp to mail a letter."

"I agree," said Sam. But then added, "Still, a quarter of a million dollars a year in base salary is nothing to sneeze at."

Gunn shrugged. "With the deal I'm about to close, I could make a hundred and fifty, maybe a hundred and sixty thou this year. That ain't half bad."

"No," said Sam, "it's not. It's unbelievable. But why not at least listen to what these people have to say? It can't hurt to listen."

Gunn reached between his wife's legs. "Okay, baby," he assured her in his softest, sexiest voice, "I'll listen."

7 Mr. Arthur James Reilly called personally the next morning.

Jason answered the phone. In the kitchen. When he found out the call was not for him, he pretty much just dropped the receiver on the floor. "I think it's for you, Mom. Or for Dad. I'm not sure what the guy said."

Then, before his mother could lecture him for being

rude, he raced out the back door. Sam bent down and picked up the receiver. "Yes? Hello?"

"Good morning. Mrs. Henderson?"

"Yes."

"This is James Reilly. From Creative Marketing Enterprises."

Her whole body perked right up. "Yes, Mr. Reilly. Good morning! How are you?"

"I'm just fine, Mrs. Henderson. I hate to bother you on Saturday morning, but I thought this might be a good time to reach your husband."

"No," Sam fumbled. "I mean, yes. It is. This is an excellent time to reach him. But right now he's out. Jogging. Running actually. He hates when I say he's jogging." She was beginning to babble. She glanced at the clock on the wall: 9:56. Gunn had been gone for almost an hour. "I expect him back any second."

"I see," said Mr. Reilly. Then, "May I assume the two of you have had an opportunity to read and perhaps discuss my letter?"

His voice sounded friendly, but formal; the voice of an older man, distinguished, well educated.

"Oh, we have, yes," Sam answered, "briefly. Gunn was out of town until yesterday. On business, of course. Probably he is the one you should talk—"

Gunn took that moment to stride through the door. Sam cut herself short, stared at her husband. Even after nearly fifteen years of marriage she still enjoyed looking at her guy. Sweat poured off his brow. His gray gym shirt was soaked through, showing off his broad shoulders and thick chest. Closing in on forty, Gunn still gave off an aura of youth and power and fitness. His six-foot-one-inch frame stood ramrod straight.

Sam covered the mouthpiece. "It's Mr. Reilly."

"Who?"

"Arthur Reilly. From Creative Marketing Enterprises."

Gunn did not look impressed. If anything, he looked annoyed. He grabbed a dish towel off the counter, wiped the sweat off his face. "What does he want?"

"He wants to talk to you."

Gunn wiped off his arms and neck with the towel. "Pushy son of a bitch, ain't he? Calling on the weekend."

Sam shrugged and shoved the receiver in his direction.

Gunn turned away. "Tell him I'll call back."

Sam shook her head. "No, talk to him."

Gunn crossed to the sink for a glass of water. "Get a number and I'll call him back."

Sam scowled at her husband.

Gunn ignored her.

Still scowling, Sam spoke into the telephone. "I'm sorry to keep you waiting, Mr. Reilly. Gunn just walked through the door."

"I understand, Mrs. Henderson. Perhaps it would be more convenient if I called another time?"

"Oh, no," she assured him, fearing a quick end to Gunn's job opportunity. "He'll be right with you."

Gunn snarled at her.

She covered the mouthpiece. "Would you talk to him? Please?"

By begging just a little bit, Sam got Gunn to relent. He grabbed the phone out of her hand. Immediately he turned on the charm. "Good morning, Mr. Reilly. Gunn Henderson here."

Sam was not privy to Mr. Reilly's end of the conversation, but it was clear from Gunn's long silences that Mr. Reilly was doing most of the talking. Gunn gave brief, mostly affirmative answers, and, much to Sam's amazement, he also did quite a lot of smiling and even laughing. And the laughter sounded genuine, not something phony to appease the mark. Apparently this Mr. Reilly also knew how to turn on the charm.

Finally, after eight or ten minutes, Gunn said, "That sounds like an excellent plan, Mr. Reilly. First class. But I'll need to clear it with my wife. She's in charge of our social calendar."

Then another brief pause before Gunn said, "No, I don't think that'll be necessary, Mr. Reilly. Let's just ask her. She's standing right here."

Gunn covered the mouthpiece and turned to Sam. "He wants us to go up to New York for a meeting."

"Both of us?"

"Right."

"New York City?"

Gunn shook his head. "No. Out on Long Island someplace."

"When?"

"Next weekend. We'll fly up on Saturday morning, come home Sunday afternoon."

"This is about the job?"

"Of course it's about the job."

Gunn could be so ugly, so rough. But this time Sam chose to ignore it. "I think we can go. But what about Jason and Megan? Are they supposed to go?"

"No kids."

Jason's baseball game and Megan's ballet rehearsal flashed through Sam's brain. She hated to miss either one. "I guess I'll see if they can stay with Mandy."

"The kids," he reminded her, "are your department."

And then Gunn turned away. But he did not immediately turn his attention back to the telephone. No, he wanted to make this Mr. Arthur James Reilly wait a little while longer. Gunn scribbled something onto a piece of paper lying on the counter. Nothing important. No cancer cures or strategies for economic revival or solutions for world hunger. Just some nonsense about Quinn the Eskimo, the mighty Eskimo, the mighty Eskimo Quinn.

Then, after a sufficient amount of time had passed, Gunn brought the phone back into play. "Yes, Mr. Reilly, we have a go. The tower has cleared us for takeoff. We'll be there next Saturday morning."

Sam had seen Gunn use this simple ploy many times before. If there was something he was unsure about, something that demanded a few extra seconds or days of deliberation, he would offer up his wife as a possible stumbling block, a kind of social sacrificial lamb. He'd told Reilly he needed to clear the invitation with his wife. But this was nonsense, nothing more than a smokescreen. Gunn Henderson always did exactly as Gunn Henderson pleased.

8 The Hendersons took the nine o'clock shuttle from National to La Guardia. A man was there to meet them as they came off the plane. He knew who they were without asking. Sam found this a bit unsettling, but Gunn just shrugged it off. Strangers picked him up at airports all the time. Sometimes he was recognized, sometimes not.

The man took their bags and led them through the terminal to a long stretch limousine waiting just outside the exit. He swung open the rear door and ushered them inside. "Have an excellent weekend, Mr. and Mrs. Henderson." He closed them into the spacious cabin. As soon as they got settled, the limousine pulled away from the curb.

The driver welcomed them through the intercom. "Morning, folks. My name's Stan. I'll be your driver today." Stan seemed miles out in front, separated by a thick pane of glass. That limo was as long as a bus. "There's fresh juice in the fridge, fresh croissants in the warmer. Help yourselves. If you would like to watch TV, you'll find the remote located on your armrest. CNN is channel fifty, the Weather Channel you will find at forty-two. But I've checked and can tell you it's supposed to be a beautiful weekend: mostly sunny with highs in the upper fifties to low sixties. We have about a two-hour drive ahead of us, but I'll do my best to shorten that. Traffic here on Long Island is always unpredictable. So just sit back, relax, enjoy the trip. If you need me, just press the intercom button on the remote."

Stan clicked off the intercom and accelerated smoothly into the flow of traffic exiting the airport.

"Wordy son of a bitch," mumbled Gunn.

Sam poured herself a glass of freshly squeezed orange juice and settled into that plush leather seat. The time had come to relax. Maybe they were only going away for one night, but it nevertheless demanded some of the same preparation as a two-week holiday. And, of course, those preparations had fallen to Sam. She had to make arrangements to get Jason to his baseball game and Megan to her rehearsal. She had to pack. In fact, she had been up late doing exactly that. And then she had gotten up at the crack of dawn, rousted the kids and driven them over to the Greers' before she and Gunn left for the airport.

She sipped the juice, closed her eyes. She had decided to use this weekend as a minivacation. No arguing, no fighting, no running around in the Explorer, little or no movement at all once they reached their destination. She just wanted to cruise along, catch her breath.

Sam had never been out to the end of Long Island before. A college friend, Brenda Jones, had lived on the North Shore in Cold Spring Harbor. Sam had visited Brenda there a few times, and each time they had talked about driving out to Montauk and the Hamptons, but it never happened.

Sam thought about Brenda as they drove east through a rush of traffic on the Long Island Expressway, about some of those late nights at school when they would stay up into the wee hours studying and talking and giggling. Brenda had a wicked sense of humor. Especially when it came to men. Barely twenty years old, but that girl did not trust the male species. "Beasts," she liked to call them, "controlled by two primitive triggers: food and fucking."

Remembering, Sam laughed. Her laughter echoed through the limo. Gunn immediately needed to know what was so funny. He could not stand his wife finding something humorous which did not originate from his mouth.

"Nothing," she told him, without bothering to open her eyes.

He badgered her for a minute or two, but finally his attention shifted and she fell fast asleep.

She awoke sometime later, groggy and disoriented, to the sound of Stan's voice on the intercom. "That was Bridgehampton we just passed, folks. Next up will be East Hampton, although we'll be turning off just before we reach the village. Well worth a visit, though. Lots of nice shops, good restaurants. Main Street's an excellent place to scope for celebrities, but being April it's a little early in the season."

"Who's this joker?" Gunn wanted to know. " 'Scope for celebrities.' "

Sam shrugged. She had once seen Dustin Hoffman

outside the Ritz-Carlton in Boston. It had given her a small thrill.

Stan turned off onto Stephen Hands Path about a mile west of East Hampton village. The road wound past several wood frame homes with well-kept lawns and white picket fences.

Gunn looked out the window at the scenery but addressed his wife. "You had yourself a pretty good nap."

Sam could tell he was still irritated about her laughter. "I was out cold."

"For over an hour."

"I guess I needed it. I didn't get enough sleep last night."

The limousine swept past a large working farm. Horses and cows grazed in a lush pasture. Then Stan turned off onto Old Northwest Road. Farmland gave way to sandy soil and scrub pines. Stan made another turn or two. There were very few homes, just the occasional gravel drive penetrating the pines.

A few more minutes passed before Stan slowed and turned into one of those gravel drives. A pair of wrought-iron gates blocked their way. Scrolled into the gates was the name of the estate: PC Apple Acres. Stan worked the code box and the gates swung open. They passed through and continued on.

The driveway ran straight for almost a hundred yards through thick woods. Then, awash in late morning sunlight, the land opened up. The drive turned to smooth macadam. And dead ahead, surrounded by shade trees and an abundance of azaleas and rhododendrons, stood the mansion. An enormous brick mansion of the classic Georgian style with a slate roof and draped with thick vines of English ivy.

The Hendersons stepped out of the limousine and gawked while Stan took care of their luggage.

* * *

INSIDE, they learned on their tour, there were twenty-three rooms, including eight bedrooms (most with their own bath), two libraries, a den (the differences had something to do with windows and bookcases), an immense sunken living room, a sitting room, a game room, a sun room, a family room, all kinds of eating rooms and reading rooms and just relaxing rooms. Rooms, basically, for every possible mood, desire, or function.

And virtually everything throughout every room, at least in Sam's humble interior design opinion, was aesthetically pleasing and tastefully decorated. Nothing tacky or overdone. Everywhere she looked she saw the right curtains, the right carpets, the right paintings, the right beds, the right tables, the right chairs. Some of the rooms might have been a tad dark for her essentially lighthearted taste, but throw open a few windows and splash some antique white on the walls, and presto, the place would brighten right up.

She kept expressing her sheer, unfettered delight as they passed from room to room. She could not contain her pleasure as one lovely space ran into another. Gunn tried to remain aloof, as though all this architectural splendor had no effect on him whatsoever. But it was obvious from his body language and by his wide-open eyes that he, too, was favorably impressed by those enormous rooms and high ceilings.

Gunn was always impressed by what money could buy. As they walked through that magnificent Georgian home, Gunn felt an almost rabid desire to make the mansion and all of its exquisite furnishings his own. Gunn needed to possess. Possession was a big part of the Henderson psyche.

Their tour guide for this ramble through the manor house was a tall, impeccably dressed white-haired gentleman named Mr. Duncan. They never learned Mr. Duncan's first name. He told them he worked for Mr. Reilly in a variety of roles. "Whatever Mr. Reilly needs done," Mr. Duncan explained, "I do." He had a faint English accent and he carried himself like a proper English butler. He was polite, and utterly formal. He insisted on calling them Mr. and Mrs. Henderson even after Sam asked him several times to please use Gunn and Sam. "Yes, Mrs. Henderson," he'd replied, "I'll do that," and then he would give her a brief, shy smile.

He knew quite a few details about the Hendersons: where they lived, what they liked to do, the names and ages of their two children. Sam was, at first, mildly alarmed by the extent of his knowledge. It seemed, somehow, an intrusion, a violation of her family's privacy. But it soon became clear that Mr. Duncan meant no harm; he simply wanted his guests to relax and feel at home, as though they were all just one big happy family and maybe he was some distant uncle Gunn and Sam were meeting for the first time.

Moments before he left them alone in their bedroom, a vast space dominated by an antique canopy bed, Mr. Duncan threw out a few details that upset Gunn but did not bother Sam in the least. By this time she had other things on her mind. Like the huge, elevated Jacuzzi waiting for her in the bathroom with its gold fixtures and marble tile.

"Lunch," Mr. Duncan informed them, "is available anytime. Feel free to go down to the kitchen and see Mrs. Griner. She will prepare anything you might desire. Don't be shy. She'll be hurt if you don't ask for something."

Gunn thought immediately about meat, red meat, rare. Sam thought a salad with some fresh greens and red peppers would hit the spot after the long trek from Virginia.

"Dinner," continued Mr. Duncan, "will be served this evening at seven-thirty in the main dining room. Jackets and ties for the gentlemen would be appreciated. If you packed light, Mr. Henderson, I feel confident I can find you something both pleasing and appropriate for the occasion."

"Thanks for the offer, Duncan," said Gunn Henderson, "but I always travel prepared for any contingency." Gunn, quite the fashion plate, had told Sam to pack him both a dark suit for formal wear and a sports jacket and slacks in the event things turned more casual.

"That's fine," replied Mr. Duncan. "Now, as for your meeting with Mr. Reilly. He will be arriving late this afternoon. He has requested individual thirty-minute meetings with each of his prospective salesmen, just to get acquainted."

Gunn jumped all over that. "What are you talking about, Duncan? What prospective salesmen?" A note of irritation had quickly slipped into his voice. "I thought I was the only prospective salesman invited to this gig."

"I'm sorry, Mr. Henderson, I thought you knew. All five candidates for the sales position have been in—"

"Stop right there, Duncan. I'm not a candidate for anything. I don't know what gives, but your man Reilly invited me up here to talk a few things over. I wasn't planning on taking part in some damn sales competition. I think it would be wise for you to get this Reilly on the telephone so we can get this thing sorted out."

Patiently, calmly, hands held perfectly still against his abdomen, Mr. Duncan replied, "I will most certainly do that, sir. I believe Mr. Reilly is already en route, but I will make every effort to contact him."

"That's a good fellow, Duncan. You tell Reilly I would like to speak to him at his earliest possible convenience. Otherwise, my wife and I might find it necessary to blow this joint."

By the time he finished his assault, Gunn was giving a pretty accurate but nevertheless insulting imitation of Mr. Duncan's proper English accent. Sam, embarrassed, tried to shut her husband up, but Mr. Duncan did not seem to mind. On the contrary, the white-haired man departed with a smile on his face.

Did he know something they didn't know? Was he privy to a few facts beyond their grasp?

● ● ●

THE HENDERSONS did not leave in a huff. The Hendersons did not leave at all. They stayed the whole weekend. They no doubt would have stayed longer had they been able.

Sure, Gunn stomped about the room, spreading some profanity in his wake, babbling about being misled. Sam did her best to keep him calm and steady. Fortunately, within three or four minutes, a knock settled upon their door.

"You see," Gunn said to his wife, "sometimes you have to act like a horse's ass to get results." Then, to the door, "It's open, Duncan."

The door opened, but Mr. Duncan did not enter. Tom entered. Tom the tennis pro. Tom had on his tennis togs: white shirt, white sweater, white shorts, white socks, snazzy white sneakers with a blue stripe. Tom wanted to know if Gunn maybe wanted to play some tennis, hit a few balls.

Of course Gunn wanted to play tennis. Tennis and hunting were Gunn's two primary distractions from his relentless quest for money. Give the man a gun or a racket and watch him jump for joy. G. Henderson never turned down a tennis match. He would kill to engage in the competitive combat waged between the white lines. The big question now is: Will Gunn be able to get a game in the prison yard? It's clear he will not be getting his hands on any guns.

So Gunn played tennis with Tom on the red clay court in the mansion's backyard while Sam retired to the Jacuzzi for a bit of R&R. Moments after striking his first forehand, Gunn forgot all about his little hassle with Mr. Duncan. A late afternoon meeting with Mr. Reilly sounded just peachy.

After her bath, Sam went down to the kitchen and met Mrs. Griner. The cook wore a few extra pounds, but she was a pleasant woman with a round, red face. She obviously liked to eat. She ate all day long. A steady supply of food ran from the cupboards and counters to her mouth. Mrs. Griner never actually sat down and ate a meal; she simply consumed steadily while she prepared meals for others. While putting together a salad for Sam, she gobbled down some red leaf lettuce, some carrot, celery, artichoke, shredded cheddar cheese, and several fistfuls of homemade croutons.

In between chews, Mrs. Griner talked. She loved to talk almost as much as she loved to eat. Sam thought the cook had an English accent, but actually Mrs. Griner had been born and raised in Northern Ireland.

"So, Mrs. Henderson, tell me about your children. I hear you have two. A boy and a girl. They must keep you busy. Do you have any help? Lots of young mothers today have help. Nannies and all that. When I was bringing up my kids we never had any help. I had to work my fingers to the bone. I . . ."

Sam nodded and ate her salad and half listened to Mrs. Griner ad-lib her way through a lifetime of child-rearing and hard labor. In the background, through an open window, Sam could hear the sound of a tennis ball being hit back and forth, back and forth.

Gunn was out there, beyond the swimming pool and the formal gardens, playing with Tom. Tom was an excellent player. He had all the shots, as well as speed and stamina. But Tom had been instructed by his employer to ease up, to throw the match, to play to his opponent's strengths. So that's exactly what Tom did. He kept the ball short to Gunn's forehand side, thereby allowing Gunn to blast winners down the line.

Tom's employer had done his homework. Tom's employer knew how much Gunn Henderson liked to play tennis. And even more important, he knew how much Gunn Henderson liked to win. Gunn, raised in an intensely competitive family environment, led by the great banker, Gunn Sr., needed to win at all cost. It was essential to his very being to come out victorious. Tom's employer understood this perfectly. And so, he had instructed Tom to let Gunn win.

And win, Gunn did. But not too easily. Six-four in the third. And never for one second did Gunn think Tom was tanking the match. Tom was too skilled a player to let that cat out of the bag.

So Gunn won. And after the win he relaxed. Just as Tom's employer knew he would. Gunn relaxed, had a couple of cold ones with Tom, then settled back to enjoy his weekend in the Hamptons.

9 Gunn was scheduled to have the fifth and final get-acquainted meeting with Mr. Reilly at seven o'clock. By quarter of seven Gunn had himself shaved and showered and groomed. In his dark blue Armani suit, he looked like a million bucks, like a man who could sell anything to anyone.

Sam made sure she told him so. She knew her man liked praise, that he flourished under its flag.

A few minutes before seven, Mr. Duncan arrived to accompany Gunn down to Mr. Reilly's private study. Gunn told Sam he would meet her in the dining room for dinner. Mr. Duncan, the consummate gentleman, assured her he would return to accompany her down-stairs.

After Duncan and Gunn departed, Sam called Megan and Jason at the Greers'. Mandy and Tad had two children also, a boy and a girl about the same ages as Jason and Megan.

The kids didn't have much time to talk. The whole crew was on its way out the door for pizza. Jason wouldn't even get on the phone, but he did pass on the message through his sister that they'd lost their base-ball game and the coach was a jerk. Megan said she was nervous about tomorrow's ballet rehearsal.

"Don't be nervous," Mom told her. "Just relax and have fun."

"Will you be back in time for the recital next week?"

"Next week?" Sam's heart almost broke. "Megan, sweetie, I'll be back tomorrow night. Just a couple hours after the rehearsal."

That made Megan feel much better. She told her mother she loved her and missed her and couldn't wait for her to get home. Sam assured Megan she loved her too.

Megan said bye and hung up.

Sam sat on the edge of the bed. She wondered if it was weird to miss your kids after only being away from them for a few hours.

● ● ●

DURING THE pre-dinner cocktails Sam met the compe-tition. The four other couples had already gathered by the time Mr. Duncan escorted her into the large and lavish living room. Gunn was still behind closed doors with Mr. Reilly.

Mr. Duncan made the introductions. Sam met Rich and Betty from Atlanta, Georgia. Rich sold pharmaceuticals. Lots and lots of pharmaceuticals. For one of the J&J companies. Rich had a big, phony laugh and enormous hands he kept wrapped around Betty's waist. Sam next met Bob and Rose from Greenwich, Connecticut. Bob sold insurance for the Hartford. Lots and lots of insurance. Of various types. He specialized in Group Health and Whole Life but enjoyed dabbling in Homeowner's, Auto, Boat, and Disability. Within mere moments of meeting Sam, Bob had worked a new Life Plan for Young Execs into the conversation. Sam smiled and waited for Mr. Duncan to lead her away. Next she met Mike and Stacy from Philadelphia, Pennsylvania. Mike sold high tech computer hardware and software to governments and multinational corporations around the world. He must have determined Sam was not a prospective buyer because he had absolutely nothing to say to her after a cursory hello that sounded more like a caveman's grunt. Finally she met Troy and Constance from Chicago, Illinois. Exactly what Troy sold was never stated, but Sam thought he might have been in gems and precious stones. His wife, dark, sullen, and snobbishly silent, wore an exotic array of bracelets, necklaces, and rings the size of grapes. Constance looked like a walking jewelry store. A little gauche, thought Sam, not at all tasteful.

After the introductions, Sam stood around the well-appointed living room with her chilled glass of chardonnay and did her best to make small talk. Normally she enjoyed trading tales with strangers at cocktail parties and other social settings. She enjoyed meeting new people, finding out what they did and where they lived. But this evening she felt different. She felt a kind of hostility toward the people in that room. After all, they had not been invited out to that fancy mansion in the Hamptons to get chummy with each other. This was a competition. They were there to engage in a nice, civilized cat fight. Only one salesman, Sam knew, would be left standing after the final bell.

Sam took the time to size up suits and dresses, shoes and hairstyles, voices and mannerisms. She concluded that all four of these couples circulating around the living room looked like carbon copies of one another. All their parts were easily interchangeable. You could have put Bob's head on Mike's body and no one would have known the difference. Stacy could have traded places with Rose and no one would have been the wiser. All were in their mid to late thirties. All looked healthy and reasonably fit, still under the illusion they had total control over their emotional and financial lives. All wore fashionably conservative evening wear. All were white. In fact, all were quite possibly white Anglo-Saxon Protestants.

Including Sam. Oh yes, she recognized the irony. She knew all about irony. At Smith, the study of literature had been mandatory. So she was not for one second unaware that she looked very much like the others. She wondered how Mr. Reilly would be able to tell them apart. Maybe he would give them numbers and name tags.

At precisely seven-thirty the door to the study opened and Gunn emerged with Mr. Reilly. Together they strode confidently into the living room. Sam

could see immediately that Gunn had held up his end
of their marital bargain. His end being to provide a
strong financial backbone for the family. Her end being to raise the children and make their home life
pleasant and cozy. Old-fashioned, yes, but the unwrit-
ten, even unspoken, agreement had been working reasonably well up until that time.

Up until Creative Marketing Enterprises crept into
their lives.

When Mr. Reilly entered the living room, all voices
grew mute. Mr. Reilly had his hand on Gunn's shoulder. They were both laughing. Sam felt sure Gunn had
hit Mr. Reilly with one of his slightly off-color salesman's jokes. Mr. Reilly must have enjoyed it. Sam felt
her chest swell with confidence. Suddenly she no
longer looked like all the others. She now had a separate identity. That was her husband over there across
the room; the one in direct physical contact with the
main man, the man with the power to make and break
lives. The others in that room suddenly looked small
and insignificant.

Gunn made every effort to guide Mr. Reilly directly
to his wife's side, but Mr. Reilly was a perfect gentleman. He knew his role as host and purveyor of the
big offer. He did not want to show favoritism this
early in the game. So he broke away from Gunn and
greeted his guests as a whole. Then he went around
the room and met the wives one by one. They obedi-
ently stood quietly by and waited their turn. There
was, after all, loads of money on the line. And Mr.
Reilly held the keys to the vault.

Arthur James Reilly probably stood a hair under six
feet tall. But he played taller, much taller, like a man

six three or four. He had an impressive bearing. He stood perfectly erect. Like a Marine. And yet he managed to appear relaxed. His elegant blue suit, made of cashmere and silk, fit like a fine glove. It had obviously been tailor-made by someone who knew how to measure and cut and stitch.

Arthur James Reilly was a handsome man in his early sixties. He had a ruddy complexion under a short crop of silver hair. His manners were exquisite, his self-confidence supreme. Sam watched him move about the room. He looked to her like an actor she had once seen in some movie. She could not recall the name of the film, but it seemed to her, as she stood there watching him chat with the other wives, that the actor's role had been that of a high-powered business executive, a CEO of some Fortune 500 company.

At dinner he easily dominated the conversation. And he did so without the slightest show of bravado. This was a man who did not need to talk about himself. He told jokes and stories. He easily made his guests laugh and listen. And never once did he talk about work or business or why he wanted to pay a salesman a quarter of a million dollars a year, for starters. He saved all that for the intimacy of his study.

The meal came in many courses: tomato and basil soup, a fresh garden salad, a black bean appetizer with just the right amount of jalapeño pepper, both a meat entrée and a fish entrée, plus a variety of choices in the wine and dessert and coffee departments. It all tasted exceptionally fine and was served by a staff of three extremely good-looking young men who whisked in and out of the dining room with nary a sound. They seemed able to anticipate the needs of the guests even before those needs arose.

Sam had a second, and then a third glass of wine.

After the meal Mr. Reilly asked for another round of meetings. This time he wanted to meet with both the husbands and the wives. One couple at a time. The Hendersons were fourth in line, next to last.

Sam and Gunn sat in the living room along with the other hopefuls waiting their turn. They sipped coffee and port and endured an uncomfortable silence. All attempts at polite conversation quickly petered out.

Just before they went in to chat with Mr. Reilly, Gunn herded Sam into a corner. He was tense, only a few sips of port away from becoming hostile. "This is such bullshit," he grumbled.

Sam, startled, prepared herself for a lengthy harangue. "What do you mean? What's the matter?"

"Throwing us all together like this. Like the freaking Christians awaiting the lions. And it's so damn obvious it's being done on purpose. Reilly's doing this just to increase the competitive atmosphere between us."

"Maybe," suggested the innocent wife of the battle-weary salesman, "it's just simpler and more efficient for Mr. Reilly to handle it this way."

"Give me a break, Sam. This guy Reilly knows exactly what he's doing. He's a pro, a very cool operator. And the thing is, the thing that really ticks me off, is the fact that the SOB has my number. I know he has it and he knows I know he has it, but I'm helpless to do anything about it. He knows damn well I don't want one of these other assholes being offered this job over me. He knows I'll put up with this crap, that I'll do whatever it takes to make the right impression. That's why, Sam," and Gunn got right up in his wife's airspace for this one, "that's why I want you to charm his socks off when we go in to see him. He has to want *both* of us, baby. This is a team effort."

And so, with Gunn's pep talk ringing in her ears, Sam went into that study and did her best to help the Hendersons' cause. She tried especially hard after Mr. Reilly threw a teaser into the mix about halfway through their little chat. The three of them spent a few minutes just jawboning, talking about this and that, about kids and schools and education and parental responsibility. Mr. Reilly expressed his view that child-rearing was clearly the most important job a mother or father would ever have.

Sam jumped right in. "I agree, Mr. Reilly. Absolutely. And I know Gunn does too. As soon as our firstborn came along, Jason, I stopped working so I could be a full-time parent. It was a bit of a financial strain, but Gunn and I felt that money was far less important than a good strong family unit."

"That's exceptional, Mrs. Henderson," replied Mr. Reilly. "You should be applauded for putting aside your vocational ambitions and your material desires."

Sam smiled. "Samantha, please."

Reilly smiled back. He had fine straight white teeth. "Samantha, yes. I wish more young parents felt as you two do. Your generation seems, in general, at least in my humble observance, to be overly caught up in the hasty struggle for money and material goods. I believe ambition is fine and healthy, but not at the expense of sacrificing the moral and emotional needs of our children."

Sam, into it now, gave Gunn's hand a squeeze. "I couldn't agree more, Mr. Reilly. And I'm afraid we are going to pay for our selfishness in the long run. I'm afraid this next generation of children might be so poorly raised that it could threaten the very fiber of life as we know it."

Gunn, a man with a finely tuned ear for, excuse the expression, bullshit, gave his wife a quick, curious glance; one that seemed to shout, *Ease off, Sam! You're beginning to babble.*

Sam had indulged in three glasses of chardonnay. Two glasses of wine had a tendency to make her giddy. Three glasses and all manner of verbal inhibition came tumbling down. Especially when she started talking about something close to her heart. Like her children.

But Mr. Reilly was downright touched by her eloquence. At least he acted like a man moved. Of course, neither Sam nor Gunn had the slightest idea at the time that the whole thing was an act. A scam. A live and extremely convincing performance by a first-rate player.

Reilly nodded with sincerity, his hands clasped across his lap. After a moment, he said, "I'm glad this subject came up. The job I have in mind will undoubtedly entail quite a lot of sacrifice. Not only on the part of the husband, but on the part of the wife as well. It will demand extensive travel. Gunn, you can expect to be out on the road several days each week, especially in the early phases of the operation. Even an occasional weekend might come into play."

Gunn seized his cue. "We're used to the travel, Mr. Reilly. It's tough on the family sometimes, but we manage. I guess you could say it goes with the salesman's territory."

"That's a fact, Gunn. But still, I wanted you to know up front. Just in case it poses a problem."

"No problem," Gunn assured his potential boss. He said this even as Sam sat in that plush leather armchair wondering exactly what *several days each week* meant. Did it mean two days a week? Three days? Five days? Six days? How much would her husband be gone? Sacrifice was fine, to a point. Jason and Megan needed a father.

Mr. Reilly continued. "I also want you to know that this job will demand relocation. If you come on board with Creative Marketing, the Hamptons will be your base of operations. In fact, this house will be your base."

Sam did not understand. Neither did Gunn. "You mean," he asked, "I would be working out of your home?"

That's when Mr. Reilly hit the Hendersons with the clincher. That's when he threw his home run pitch. That's when Samantha Ann Quincy Henderson redefined sacrifice.

"Oh no, Gunn, you'd be working out of *your* house. I mentioned in my original letter that this job would include housing as one of its perks. I believe in making my top salesman king of the roost. I want him living at the top of the heap. I want him feeling potent and powerful. That's why, if we decide to work together on this particular project, this estate—PC Apple Acres—Samantha and Gunn, will be your home for as long as you are employed by Creative Marketing Enterprises."

"This house will be our home?" Sam asked, her eyes wide, her emotions swirling, her thoughts confused. "This house we're sitting in right now?"

Mr. Reilly smiled. "That's right, Samantha. This house we're sitting in right now."

10 The Hendersons made love that night. Twice. Gunn was sweet and tender. They lay there afterward and talked about what it would be like to live in that grand house, that brick Georgian mansion.

"I wonder if Mrs. Griner comes with the deal," Sam whispered into the darkness. "She's an excellent cook. And she seems really sweet."

"And what about Tom?" added Gunn. "The guy I played tennis with earlier? I wonder if he's available for a match on demand."

"And let's not forget Mr. Duncan. Does he stay on as our social secretary and general confidant?"

They had a good giggle over the possibility of having their own domestic servants. Gunn rubbed his hard, muscular legs against the thin and sinewy legs of his wife. "Pretty wild, hey, Sam?"

Sam nodded. "It would be like living like royalty."

"I don't know about that. A guy offers as much as Reilly is offering, you can be damn sure he'll expect results. No half-ass efforts will be tolerated. It'll be produce or take a hike."

"He knows you'll produce, Gunn. That's why he invited you here in the first place."

"Maybe so . . . but I can feel the pressure building already."

That brief moment of insecurity from her husband caused Sam to run her fingers through his thick brown hair. She wanted to keep her man relaxed and confident. "Pressure has never bothered you before."

He took a second before responding. "And believe me, Sam, it won't this time either." But then he moved his legs away, rolled over to his side of the bed. "You want to know the weird thing?"

Sam could feel his mind working overtime. "What?"

"Twice now I've asked Reilly to tell me what we'll be selling, give me the lowdown on the product line, and twice he has subtly changed the subject without giving me an answer."

Sam thought about it. "Maybe he just wants to wait until he's made a decision on who to hire. No use spilling the beans to all five of you."

Gunn nodded. "That makes sense."

"Of course it does. And besides," she added, "exactly what he has to sell doesn't really matter. He knows you can sell anything."

Gunn seemed satisfied with that. Sam had stroked his ego nicely. So they kissed, and soon thereafter Sam fell fast asleep. Gunn stayed awake awhile longer to brood and scheme and search for new and exciting ways to win.

● ● ●

IN THE MORNING, after a hearty breakfast served in their room, Gunn had another meeting with Mr. Reilly. He came back from this third encounter all charged up and raring to go. "Reilly tells me we're definitely in the hunt for the job offer."

Sam, still lolling around in her nightie, grabbed him by the arm and pulled him toward the bed. "I'm not surprised."

Gunn, too worked up to sit or lie down, broke free. "Two of the others have already been eliminated. And Reilly says a third will probably back out because the wife doesn't want to move."

"So we have a fifty-fifty chance."

"Better than that, baby. Better than that. Always give me better than even odds against any man."

Sam had to smile. She knew her husband could be difficult, loud and bossy and obnoxious, occasionally even abusive, but sometimes, when things were going good, she liked his cockiness. She had married him, at least in part, because of that cockiness. His cockiness made her feel strong and secure. It made her feel significant.

Gunn paced around the room. "Reilly went over some of the perks in more detail."

"Such as?"

"Such as the house. It's definitely in the game plan. I get the job, we get the house."

Sam's smile broadened. "The whole house?"

"The whole house, Sam. And Mrs. Griner goes with it. Duncan doesn't, but there's a woman who cleans."

"What about schools for the kids?"

"Reilly says the local school system is the pits. So the company's willing to foot the bill for private school."

Sam had been thinking about this ever since she had read the letter. "For both of them? Private schools for both Jason and Megan?"

"That's what he said."

"God, Gunn, it's like a dream."

"It's no dream, Sam."

"Maybe not. But it almost sounds too good to be true."

Gunn started taking off his shirt and pants. "Hey, you work hard, you reap the rewards."

Sam, a mass of different emotions swirling inside her brain, nodded.

Gunn pulled on his tennis togs. "Listen, Sam, I have a match with Tom in a few minutes."

"That's too bad," she said, smiling. "I had something else in mind."

"Later, baby. Can you find something to do for a couple hours?"

"Of course. You go ahead. Does Tom come with the package?"

Gunn laughed. "I don't think so. He's the pro over at the local club. He was just brought in for the weekend. But Reilly assures me there are plenty of good players around." He sat on the bed to tie his sneakers. "And oh yeah," he added as he stood up, "that's another thing."

"What?"

"Membership in a couple of the local country clubs. A golf club and a tennis club. Reilly says the tennis club has grass courts. That's as close to Wimbledon as I'll ever get."

Gunn's enthusiasm ranneth over. He kissed his wife hard on the lips, grabbed his racket, and tore off to find his friend Tom the tennis pro. Sam stood there in the middle of that fancy bedroom with her mouth hanging open. She felt dizzy and mildly disoriented, a feeling she would have quite often in the days and weeks and months ahead.

11 Half an hour after Gunn ran off to play with Tom, Mr. Duncan knocked on the door. He asked Sam if she would like to take a stroll around the grounds. "It's a fine day," he told her, "but still a trifle chilly. You might want a sweater."

They descended the wide front stairway with its elaborate walnut banister, walked through the formal living room, and went into the rear library lined with leather-bound books. French doors led outside onto a large slate terrace. At the edge of the terrace was the swimming pool, an enormous body of water with a black liner and shaped to look like a woodland pond. A man-made mountain stood at the far end of the pool. It stood over thirty feet high at its summit. It looked like a perfect scale replica of the famous Matterhorn. A stream ran down the mountain and then waterfalled off the edge into the pool. At the top of the mountain a ten-meter diving platform stuck out over the water.

Sam took one look at that platform and saw danger. "I'm not sure I'd want Jason jumping off that."

Mr. Duncan smiled and nodded. "It's a bit high, yes, but the pool below is deep enough for both jumping and diving."

They walked around the side of the pool and out onto the lawn. An ivy-covered wrought-iron trellis led the way into a formal English garden beginning to show signs of renewed life. Everything was neat and tidy and ready to bloom. Sam kept thinking the terrace and the pool and the garden would be the perfect place to pass the summer. Change, she decided, was in the air. Good, clean, positive change.

Beyond the garden rose a tall hedge of boxwood. They walked through an opening in the hedge, and there, before them, lay the red clay tennis court. Gunn and Tom battled between the white lines. After the point Gunn waved and smiled. He must have been winning again.

"Your husband is a very strong player," said Mr. Duncan.

"Yes," said Sam, her eyes following the ball back and forth, "and he very much likes to win."

They watched the match for several minutes from a teak bench just outside the doubles line. Sam was a reasonably good player in her own right; not up to Gunn's level, but she certainly knew the game. And after watching several points, most of which were won by her husband, she began to think something was amiss. This fellow Tom was clearly quite skilled with the racket. He moved around the court with speed and agility. He swung effortlessly and made contact with the sweet spot on virtually every stroke. But he kept putting the ball exactly where Gunn liked it most: a bit short, waist-high, and almost always to the forehand side. Tom kept playing to Gunn's strength. Sam wondered if he might be doing so on purpose. She was about to ask Duncan his opinion, when Duncan suggested they continue their tour down to the water.

The sun was beginning to warm the air. Sam removed her sweater, tied it around her waist. They followed a red cinder path around the back of the tennis court. At the end of the path they came upon a small orchard of apple and peach trees. Fresh spring buds looked ready to burst wide open.

Beyond the orchard stood a group of buildings clustered in a clearing: a five-bay garage, some storage sheds, and a large red barn. The barn stood three full stories high.

"Many years ago," Mr. Duncan explained, "this was a working farm. The property contained over two hundred acres. There were fruit trees, hay fields, cornfields, pasture for horses and cattle, even a cider mill. Then real estate prices began to skyrocket, and little by little the land was sold off."

Sam took a long, slow look around. Everything was so well kept, in perfect repair. "How much land," she asked, "is left?"

"About sixteen acres. It reaches down to the Sound."

"Long Island Sound?"

"Actually, Shelter Island Sound." Mr. Duncan took her arm and led her past the barn. "Come, let me show you."

They followed another red cinder path. This one was wider, wide enough for a car or a tractor to pass. More boxwood, nearly six feet tall, lined both sides of the lane. Straight ahead Sam could see the water.

The hedge ended and the land opened up. A large swath of lawn led to a narrow strip of sandy beach. A wide expanse of water reached out for as far as Sam could see.

"Shelter Island Sound," said Mr. Duncan. "Off to the right is Gardiner's Bay. Beyond the bay is Long Island Sound. The landmass straight out in front of us is the south shore of Shelter Island."

They stood at the edge of the beach. The sand was strewn with smooth, round stones and a few large boulders. To the right Sam could see a high, sandy cliff. The water, dark blue, almost black, glistened under the bright sunshine. For a minute or more Sam just let her eyes soak up the beauty. She breathed in the salt air.

"It's magnificent," she said, finally. "Absolutely spectacular."

"Yes," replied Mr. Duncan, "I would have to agree."

Her eyes continued to wander. Off to the left, perhaps a hundred yards down the beach, at the back of a small cove, she saw a dock jutting out into the water and a large stone building standing right at the water's edge.

Mr. Duncan sensed her interest. "That would be the estate's boathouse, Mrs. Henderson. All kinds of floating equipment inside there. At last glance I seem to recall a speedboat for water-skiing, an old mahogany runabout for cruising and fishing, a lovely wooden sailing skiff, a rowboat, maybe a canoe or two, a couple of kayaks. . . ." He slowly petered out.

Sam immediately wondered if those boats would be available for the family's recreation if Gunn got the job with Creative Marketing Enterprises. But she decided it would be best to keep her curiosity to herself, at least for the time being. She did not want to sound pushy.

They headed back in the direction of the mansion along another narrow cinder path. It cut straight across the swath of green grass and came out behind the large red barn. As they walked past the barn, a side door suddenly swung open. A man, apparently in a bit of a hurry, stepped out. He bumped smack into Samantha.

"Easy there, Brady," said Mr. Duncan. "We don't want to be knocking Mrs. Henderson to the turf."

Brady stepped back quickly and gathered himself. He wore leather work boots, brown work pants, a T-shirt, even though it could not have been more than fifty-five degrees, and a canvas baseball cap. In one hand he held a large hammer, in the other, a box of nails.

"Very sorry, ma'am," he said, as he touched the brim of his cap. "I wasn't watching where I was going. It's just an excuse, but I guess I wasn't expecting to see anyone out here."

Sam smiled at him. "No harm done."

He glanced at her shyly, then let his eyes fall to the ground. He had wonderful blue eyes, penetrating blue eyes, maybe the bluest eyes Sam had ever seen. He was about her age, she thought, maybe a bit older. His face had started to show some wear and tear, a few lines and creases. And that morning, because he obviously had not shaved in two or three days, he looked pretty scruffy. But those eyes; those eyes made the world light up around him. Those eyes, thought Sam, made him look like a little boy.

"Well," Brady said, kicking at the dust, still staring at the ground, "I best be getting back to my work." He stood there for another moment or two, looking uncomfortable and uncertain, then he once more tipped his cap before hurrying off in the direction of the garage.

They watched him go.

"Who was that?" Sam asked Mr. Duncan.

"That would be Brady. He takes care of things here on the estate. A fine fellow. Extremely pleasant. Perfectly harmless. Anything breaks or goes wrong, you just call Brady. He'll fix it in a jiff."

"So he lives here? On the estate?"

"Yes," replied Mr. Duncan. "Out in the boathouse, actually."

They walked on, back toward the tennis court. Sam could already hear the strike of the ball beyond the boxwood.

Her thoughts had started to wander when she heard Mr. Duncan say, "You should hear him sing sometime."

"Hear who sing?"

"Brady!" answered Mr. Duncan. "The caretaker. He has the most amazing and melodious voice. Truly splendid. No formal training that I know of, but God gave that lad the voice of an angel."

Sam turned and glanced over her shoulder for another look, but the caretaker was gone.

12 Sam and Gunn reluctantly departed PC Apple Acres shortly after lunch. Stan drove them back across Long Island to La Guardia Airport. He asked them along the way if they'd had a good time. Indeed they had. So good, in fact, that they wanted to stay for another week or two. Maybe another year or two.

That, of course, was exactly how those who had staged their pleasant little weekend retreat in the country wanted them to feel. They wanted the Hendersons to want more.

Give people a few creature comforts, make them feel like important cogs in the social wheel, and they can be so easily manipulated.

Sam and Gunn went home and settled back into their routine. Gunn went to the office Monday morning while Sam got the kids off to school, vacuumed the house, did the food shopping, picked up the dry cleaning, started dinner, took Jason to baseball practice, and ran Megan over to her flute lesson. Just another day on the run.

Mr. Reilly had told Gunn he would call either Tuesday or Wednesday with his decision. Gunn had told Sam not to hold her breath, but she was holding it nevertheless. She wanted to make the move to PC Apple Acres. At least she thought she did.

All this despite the fact that Gunn had not definitely decided to take the job even if Reilly offered it.

"Sure, the job's selling," had been his refrain all the way home on the plane, "but selling what? I need a few more clues as to what the hell I'd be peddling. Plus the fact there has to be a catch. I can't believe this guy Reilly doesn't have some hidden agenda."

"His agenda," insisted Sam, "is making money. And he wants you to help him do it."

"Maybe. But I'll have to hear more before I accept any offer."

●   ●   ●

MONDAY TOOK FOREVER to pass. Tuesday even longer. Tuesday evening crept by as though time had been suspended, and still the whole day came and went without a call from Mr. Reilly or anyone else from Creative Marketing Enterprises. Gunn, Sam noticed, paced around the family room for more than an hour after dinner. Several times she saw him glance over at the phone. Once she even saw him pick up the receiver and check for a dial tone.

The two calls that did come through that evening were both for Sam. Just girlfriends calling to chat. Nothing important. Gunn glared and hovered during these conversations. He hated when Sam talked on the phone. He always figured she must be talking about him, more than likely in a negative way. So here was a bona fide reason for him to tell her to cut it short. Bona fide in G. Henderson's mind anyway.

"I don't know what the problem is," Sam said after she'd hung up. "We have call waiting."

"I don't give a damn," came the chilly response. That old Henderson Logic churning once again. "Let's just keep the damn line open."

Oh yes, Gunn wanted Reilly to call. He definitely wanted Reilly to call and make him an offer. Even if just to placate his enormous Henderson ego.

Wednesday was more of the same grind. The waiting game. Wednesday evening the telephone did not ring even once. The silence from those phones made all the Hendersons anxious. Even Jason and Megan. And they didn't even know what all the fuss was about. They knew something about Dad maybe getting a new job, but kids don't pay much attention to that kind of stuff.

By eleven o'clock, getting ready for bed, Gunn had lost his cool. "Son of a bitch, I hate people who don't do what they say they're going to do. If you say you're going to do something, you should damn well do it. You agree with me on this point, don't you, Sam?"

Sam sat on the bed leafing through a copy of *Architectural Digest*. "Yes, Gunn, I think people should do what they say they're going to do." She hoped he would not fume for long.

"So tell me if I'm wrong. Didn't Reilly say he'd call me by tonight?"

"That's what you told me he said."

Gunn stomped around the bedroom trying to look busy, trying to look like he had something to do. He had nothing on but a pair of boxers. Black silk boxers.

He looked good in those boxers with his muscular thighs and his hard, flat stomach. Real good. Gunn still had the body of a college senior.

"Yeah, well, that's what he said. Screw him. The moron must've given the job to one of those other turds. . . ."

Other turds? Sam wondered. Did this make Gunn a turd also? She kept her smile to herself and decided not to find out.

"His loss. Not that I really give a damn. I just wanted the offer, not the goddamn job."

Sam sat propped up on the bed and listened to her husband bark and growl. He sounded like a rabid dog. The entire performance was strictly canine. It all had to do with his silly male ego, his all-consuming need to win, win, win. Here he was, calling a man who was considering him for a quarter-of-a-million-dollar job a moron, and he didn't for one second see the irony or the disrespect.

Sam did not care to listen further. She snapped off the light beside her bed and buried her head in her pillow.

● ● ●

THURSDAY NIGHT the phone rang in the middle of dinner. Sam happened to be walking by at that moment carrying a basket of warm rolls, so she picked it up. "Hello?"

It was him. The man. Arthur James Reilly. He asked after the family, then apologized profusely for not calling sooner. "A sudden and unexpected family emergency," he explained.

"It's not a problem," Sam assured him. "I hope everything is all right."

"All is well, Mrs. Henderson. I mean Samantha. Thank you."

Then Gunn got up from the table and more or less grabbed the phone out of his wife's hand. He had to act like a tough guy. The strong, silent type was his role this evening. But about all he said for the next eight or nine minutes was, "Yes, sir," or "I see," or "That'll be fine." His expression did not change. It remained stern and stoic.

"What's going on?" Jason asked his mother.

"It's the man who might hire your father."

"Will we have to move again?"

Sam did not want to get into that, not right now. "Let's just wait and see what your father finds out."

Jason thought this over for a second or two, then said, "Well, just so you know, I'm not moving. I'm staying here."

"Good," Megan told her brother. "You can stay here and we'll move."

"Shh," insisted their mother.

Gunn finished his call a few minutes later. He hung up the receiver and marched back to his seat at the head of the kitchen table. He made Sam wait. He made Jason and Megan wait. He made them all wait.

He made Sam ask. "Well?"

Still the face did not change. "Well what?"

"Well everything? What did he say?"

Another second or two passed. Ten seconds. Fifteen seconds. Finally, Gunn's whole face relaxed into one big wise-guy grin. Almost a smirk. Sam knew right away Mr. Reilly had made an offer.

Gunn clenched his fist and slammed it against the tabletop. "I got it. I knew I had it. So did Reilly. He knew from the beginning I was his man."

Sam felt the skin on her cheeks flush, the way it does after you eat too much chocolate. "So, what did he say? What did you say? What did you tell him?"

"Easy, Sam. Just take it easy. I have to fly back up there on Saturday and talk a few things over with him. I'm not one-hundred-percent satisfied yet this is in our best interest. Sure, the money's good, but there's some details Reilly and I need to iron out. Like I still don't know what he wants me to sell. After I get a few more facts, I'll decide."

"You mean, *we'll* decide," Sam quickly inserted into the exchange. "I think we all have some say in this." She looked around the table at Jason and Megan. "All four of us."

"Right, Sam," said Gunn, as he raised a fork filled with gravy-soaked red meat to his lips while the children looked on, *"we'll* decide." Then he stuffed the food into his mouth and said not another word.

13

They did not decide. Gunn decided for them, for the whole family. For Sam and Jason and Megan.

When he returned home from his meeting with Mr. Reilly on Sunday night, a deal had been struck. Sam could not actually say she was unhappy a deal had been struck, but it would have been far more pleasurable, to say nothing of equitable, had Gunn consulted with her before signing a contract with Creative Marketing Enterprises. A contract, she found out later, which more or less made him a handsomely paid indentured servant.

They talked it over on the way home from the airport. Gunn, of course, did most of the talking. His enthusiasm for Mr. Arthur James Reilly and Creative Marketing Enterprises suddenly knew no bounds. He was sky-high with the possibilities of the future. You would not have been able to bring him down with a ground-to-air missile.

"This is an unbelievable opportunity, Sam. One that I'd be a fool to let slip away. This could make us rich. Rich! I've seen the numbers on paper. If I do my job, if I bust my butt, if I get this product to fly, I could make a couple million bucks in the next two or three years. A couple *million,* Sam."

Large round numbers like that caused Sam's enthusiasm to begin rising by leaps and bounds, too. She immediately envisioned living in the lap of luxury. She saw herself shopping at the best stores, dining at the finest restaurants, attending the most lavish charity benefits and balls, vacationing at the most exclusive resorts. She came back to earth long enough to ask, "So what's the product, Gunn? Did you find out what you'll be selling?"

"Of course I found out. Do you think I'm an idiot? What do you think I went up there for?"

This ugly little blast of reality caused Sam to recoil. But only for a moment. "So," she said, "tell me."

"The actual product," replied the supersalesman,

"doesn't matter. This guy Reilly is a marketing genius. He knows people will buy virtually anything if you can make them think they need it. This product will sell, Sam. With me at the helm, I know this product will sell."

"I'm sure," she agreed. "But what is it?"

Gunn ignored her. Or maybe he simply did not hear her. He was fully occupied with what had happened up at PC Apple Acres.

"Reilly and I agree we need a national sales strategy. Something that will hit coast to coast all at once. We need to saturate the market. I gave Reilly the analogy of the movies. You know, the way they put a flick in eight million theaters at the same time. You do that, you get exposure. You get exposure, you sell seats. You sell seats, you make money. It's simple. Reilly loved the analogy. He couldn't get enough of it."

Sam was getting plenty of it, all she could stand. "Okay, so tell me, what's the product?"

Gunn came back to her, slowly. "The product? Hell, Sam, it's a goddamn work of art."

"A work of art?"

"It's so simple it's almost scary."

"Tell me what it is!"

Sam had the feeling Gunn didn't really want to tell her, but finally, not looking at her, he said, "It's basically a piece of wood."

"A piece of wood?"

"A round piece of wood."

"I don't understand."

"Jesus, Sam, I don't know. Reilly showed me one. A prototype. It looked like a wooden coaster. You know, one of those things you set a glass on to protect your furniture."

"I know what a coaster is, Gunn."

"Yeah, well, this thing looks like one of those. It's round. It's maybe three-eighths of an inch thick, four inches in diameter. Reilly hasn't really decided on the exact dimensions yet."

They were driving south on I-395. Heading for home. Sam was behind the wheel. It suddenly felt mildly surreal to her inside that glass and leather cabin. Like the Explorer might actually be floating rather than rolling on its radials. Sam had a picture of this "coaster" in her mind. It struck her as utterly absurd. She wondered if it all might be a joke, a kind of practical joke on Gunn, on her, on her entire family. The whole thing: the certified letter, the fancy week-end at PC Apple Acres, Duncan, Reilly, Mrs. Griner, the two-hundred-and-fifty-thousand-dollar-a-year of-fer . . .

"Sam! What are you doing? Where the hell are you going? You went right past our exit!"

Gunn was right: she had. Preoccupation can often lead to distraction. And worse.

Gunn ranted about her spaciness and stupidity while she got them back on track. Eventually she re-turned to the subject. "So, what do you do with this coaster? This round piece of wood?"

Gunn glared at her. He did not care for her sarcastic tone of voice.

"It's a toy, Sam. You hold it in your hand. You spin it. You try to stop it. You play games with it. Games you invent yourself. It's a creative toy. But it's more than a toy. It's a personal device."

"A personal device?"

"That's right. It'll help you relax. Help you concentrate. Help you meditate. You can use it to calm yourself in this crazy and hectic world."

Oh yes, no doubt about it, Gunn Henderson had definitely shifted into supersalesman mode.

"Americans will buy this product by the millions. By the tens of millions. It will be the next craze. Like the Hula Hoop and the Pet Rock and the Hacky Sack. Every kid in the country from four to ninety-four will have to own at least one of these products."

"What's the name of this product?"

"It doesn't have a name yet. We have to be extremely careful with the name. The name is vital. It's as important as the product itself. Maybe even more important. We have a whole team of researchers working around the clock on the name."

Gunn's zeal did not surprise his wife. He always became obsessed with the products he sold: newspapers, copiers, computers, basketball shoes, gym shorts. It was this passion that made him a top-notch salesman. Still, she felt an ongoing skepticism concerning this piece of wood. She even had a brief premonition that this piece of wood could lead to the downfall of her family. But the premonition passed. She could only assume Mr. Reilly knew what he was doing. After all, the man was incredibly wealthy and successful.

Gunn continued. "Reilly figures in mass numbers it will cost about thirty cents per product to manufacture, package, and ship. Maybe forty cents per product for the deluxe model. Retail price, on the other hand, will run between three ninety-five and nine ninety-five, depending upon the model and where you shop.

Now that," and Gunn looked his lovely wife dead in the eye, "is a very sweet markup. Never in all my years as a salesman have I been involved with markup like that."

Feelings of dizziness and disorientation once again began to creep into Sam's psyche. The idea that some little round piece of wood was going to make them wealthy had her brain spinning. Still, she cleared her thoughts long enough to reply to Gunn's pronouncement. "That's like a thousand percent."

"At least," cheered Gunn. "I tell you, Sam, the profit margin on this thing will be enormous. And I signed on for a cut of each unit sold."

"Like a commission?"

"Better than a commission."

"Better?"

Gunn nodded. "It's more like being a stockholder. A stockholder lucky enough to get in on the ground floor. Trust me on this one, Sam, we're going to make millions."

Millions. Right.

Sam's emotions swung back and forth between ecstasy and doom.

14 Gunn had a few other surprises for his wife as their Sunday evening drive home from the airport progressed. Sam slowly began to realize Gunn and Mr. Reilly must have had quite a time for themselves up at PC Apple Acres. They seem to have made all kinds of decisions far and beyond Gunn's future employment. Decisions that would profoundly affect Sam and her children. Decisions Sam had no say in whatsoever. Decisions that would ultimately change everything. Decisions that would eventually lead to disaster.

For instance: Creative Marketing Enterprises needed Gunn's services ASAP. Meaning that Gunn, who was gainfully employed by a large and financially secure sporting goods manufacturer, would essentially have to say sayonara to that company as early as Monday morning. There was no time for long good-byes, for thirty days' notice. Mr. Reilly had told Gunn he could close his deal with the owner of that National Football League team, but after that he wanted Gunn full-time on the first team at Creative Marketing. Gunn already had in his possession a thick portfolio detailing the company's financial picture: its research and development arm, its product line, and its earning potential.

"Bedtime reading," Gunn called it. The portfolio was thicker than the D.C. business-to-business yellow pages. Too bad it was all a lie, a fiction, a fully detailed fabrication.

And then there was this tiny detail that Gunn lobbed into the air as Sam steered through the suburban streets of Alexandria: "Reilly really needs me to make the move out to Long Island without delay."

Sam's foot eased off the accelerator. "What do you mean, without delay?"

"Now look, Sam, don't get all bent out of shape about this."

"I'm not getting bent out of shape. I just want to know what *without delay* means."

Gunn hesitated, then said, "It means we still have a little time."

Sam had to brake, hard, as first a cat and then a dog darted across the street.

Gunn grabbed the opportunity to change direction. "By the way, I called my parents last night. After I finished up with Reilly. I wanted to get the old boy's take on the job offer." The old boy, of course, being Gunn Sr..

The mention of her in-laws altered Sam's focus immediately. "I've been meaning to call your mother for weeks. How are they doing?"

"Not too good."

"Your father is still using the wheelchair?"

Gunn nodded. "My mother says he uses it more and more."

Gunn's parents still lived up in Westchester County, near Armonk, just north of the Kensico Reservoir on Whippoorwill Road. They were only in their mid-sixties, but in recent years their health had deteriorated badly. Gunn Sr. had to spend most of his time now in a wheelchair. And his wife barely had the energy to walk up and down the stairs.

"You know," said Sam, "we should really go see them. We haven't been up there since Christmas."

Gunn had been hoping the conversation would take this turn. "I figure with us out in East Hampton we'll only be a couple of hours away. I can get up to see them a little more often."

"That'll be good. Your mother will like that."

"It was one of the reasons," Gunn told his wife, "that I decided to take the job."

"Yes," replied Sam, her focus returning, "let's get back to the job. What kind of time frame are we talking about?"

"Sam, you have to understand, Reilly needs me to get the ball rolling."

"Meaning?"

"Meaning we might as well just do it and be done with it."

"Be done with what?"

"With the move. The company's taking care of all the details: packing, shipping, the whole nine yards. You won't need to do a thing. Just throw some clothes in a suitcase and go."

"Go! Go when, Gunn?"

"We're thinking two weeks. Well, today's Sunday, so actually a week from Friday. Twelve days."

"Twelve days! You want me to pack up and move my whole family out of my house in twelve days?"

"That's the idea."

"You can't be serious."

"It's the plan."

Sam slowed, switched on her left blinker, and turned the Explorer into the driveway. "Well, it's a ridiculous plan. It's ludicrous. I can't do it."

"Sam, I think—"

"We've been here for three years, Gunn."

"I know, but—"

"I can't move in a week. I can't move in a month. I need time to think, time to prepare, time to—"

"Don't start, Sam. You pushed for this. You wanted this to happen. So I did it. I got it done. I made it happen. Don't start backing out now."

He was right, of course. She had pushed for it. She had been pushing for it ever since the certified letter first arrived in the mail. She wanted it all right: the money, the mansion, the maid, the private schools. But maybe she did not want it quite so fast. She needed a second to catch her breath. Somehow, in the back of her mind, she had assumed all of this would take weeks, maybe months, to evolve and grow and eventually happen.

"I'm not backing out," she told him. "I'm just wondering about a few things is all. Like the kids. What about the kids? What about school? We're right in the middle of the school year, Gunn. We can't just pull Jason and Megan out of school."

"Give me a break," railed Gunn. "You think it'll be the end of the world if we take the kids out of school before the end of the year. But it won't be the end of the world. It's only a couple months till summer vacation. Believe me, Sam, they'll survive. They might even be better off for it."

"Oh right, I've heard this line before. Make them rougher and tougher and more resilient and all that nonsense!"

"Sam, this is not a big deal. We don't need to sweat this school thing." And then, without thinking, Gunn added, "Reilly's taking care of it."

"Reilly's taking care of *what*?"

"He's getting them enrolled at some private school not too far from the estate."

"What! Why is Reilly doing it? Why aren't *we* doing it?" This loss of control was beginning to make Sam slightly hysterical.

"It's one less thing for us to worry about. Reilly assures me it's one of the best private schools in the state."

"Oh, well, if Mr. Reilly says so, I'm sure it is."

"Look, Sam, two weeks from tomorrow Jason and Megan will walk into their new classrooms. Easy as pie. So just try and relax. Look at the big picture. It'll all work out."

Sam parked the Explorer in front of the garage, threw an evil eye at her husband, then stepped out onto the driveway. "You can drive the babysitter home." And with that, she slammed the door.

On her way into the house she told herself to stay calm, to take things one crisis at a time. The next few weeks might be stressful, but before long, she reassured herself, their lives would be better than ever. Much better.

True enough, but first Gunn had one more little

announcement to make. He made it later that night, as they were getting ready for bed. He made it only under duress, following a direct question posed by his lovely and practically naked wife.

"So what," she asked, "are we going to do about the house?"

Gunn considered telling a little white lie, but then sighed and said, "It's all taken care of."

"What do you mean, it's all taken care of?"

"The house is already sold, Sam."

"Sold? What do you mean, sold? How can it be sold?"

"I sold the house."

Sam's voice went up an octave. "No, it's not sold! It can't be sold. I don't want to sell the house. I love this house!"

"What do you mean, you love it? You've been talking about moving into a bigger house for a couple years now."

"Yes, but that's different. That's just kind of . . . dreaming. What if this job doesn't work out? What if you don't like it? What if we don't like living in East Hampton?"

"There are lots of other houses, Sam. I'm sure we can find one that's—"

Then it dawned on her. "Wait a second. How could you have sold the house? It's not even on the market."

Gunn hesitated, then, "Reilly bought it."

"Reilly!" She suddenly began to fear this Mr. Reilly.

"Well, the company, actually."

"Creative Marketing Enterprises bought our house?"

"That's right. Reilly wanted to make this transition as quick and easy for us as possible. He made me an offer I couldn't refuse."

"Meaning what?"

"Meaning we made a nice profit over what we paid. And you know as well as I do, Sam, that the market is pretty flat right now. It could take us a year or more to sell this place."

Gunn was right, of course. The market was flat, dead flat. They had friends whose homes had been for sale for months.

But why? wondered Sam. Why would Reilly offer such a sweet deal?

It registered in the back of her brain as nothing more than a dull blip, but Sam sensed something foul lurking in the shadows.

Which, of course, there was. Something quite foul. Evil even. Too bad Sam was blinded by the money and by that fancy Georgian mansion.

As for her husband, well, he, too, was overwhelmed by the quantities of cash that he felt certain would soon be flowing his way. For a reasonably intelligent and sophisticated young man, Gunn Henderson certainly took on the role of the fool as he prepared to move his family lock, stock, and barrel out to the eastern tip of Long Island.

Part Two

THE JOB

15 PC Apple Acres—Sam learned what it meant on moving day.

Initially she had assumed P. C. Apple was somebody's name, perhaps the previous owner's, or maybe Mr. Reilly's partner or best friend.

Later she had thought maybe PC stood for Politically Correct. One hears the term so often lately. Politically Correct Apple Acres.

She could not have been further off track.

Mr. Duncan was on hand to greet the family when they arrived. At least when Sam and Jason and Megan arrived. Gunn had flown off to Houston or Miami or some such place to begin selling what he had labeled "The Toy of the Century." He would be joining his wife and kids later.

"How much later?" Sam had wanted to know.

"Not long. Maybe a day or two."

"Make it a day," Sam pleaded. "Please. This is stressful enough without having to do it alone."

Mr. Duncan immediately called the children by their first names, as though he had known them for years. Megan did not seem to mind. Jason scowled and turned away. He was irritated and upset about this sudden move to a new place, about being yanked away from his friends. Irritated and not about to hide it. Sam did not blame him. This was the boy's third move since starting school. She hoped it would be his last. She had talked to both children for hours, explaining to them why they had to move, assuring them they would be very happy in their new home.

Duncan took them on a tour of the house. The sheer size of the place caused Jason to perk up. "We're really going to live here?" he asked his mother.

"That's right."

"Where's my room?" he asked Mr. Duncan.

"Upstairs," came the answer. "Do you want to see it?"

Of course he wanted to see it. But first they had to finish touring the first floor. As they crossed the living room and headed for the front foyer, Jason asked, "So who's this P. C. Apple guy?"

At just that moment, Brady, the caretaker, entered the house through the front door. He had several suitcases under his arms and in his hands. "Sorry to interrupt, sir," he said to Duncan. "I just wondered where to put these bags."

"Brady," said Mr. Duncan, "this is Mrs. Henderson."

Sam smiled, almost shyly, at the caretaker. "Yes, we've met."

"Oh, right," said Mr. Duncan. "That morning out by the barn."

"Good morning, ma'am," said Brady, meeting her

eyes for only a moment. "Please don't think me rude, but I'd like to lighten my load."

"Of course," said Sam. "I believe those are mine."

"Master bedroom suite, Brady," ordered Duncan.

"Yes, sir." Brady, heavy load intact, steered across the foyer and started up the wide sweeping stairway.

The others watched as he reached the landing and disappeared down the long hall.

"Who was that, Mommy?" Megan tugged at Sam's hand.

Sam gave her a hug. "That was Mr. Brady, honey. He takes care of things around here."

"What about this P. C. Apple guy?" demanded Jason. "Who is he?"

Mr. Duncan smiled. "Well, Jason, it's not a person. It's more of a . . . well, more of a thing."

"What kind of thing?"

"The name has to do with computers."

"Computers?" asked Sam, as Jason lost interest and darted ahead.

"Yes," answered Duncan. "PCs and Apples. I'm not really up on this computer business. I'm far too ancient. But I gather the world is divided into PCs, or personal computers, and Apple computers."

Sam knew the difference. She and Gunn had bought the kids an Apple Macintosh computer a couple of years earlier. Jason, to her surprise, had mastered the machine in no time.

"So what's the significance?" she asked. "Why PC Apple Acres?"

They started across the foyer in the direction of the stairs. First Megan, then Sam, then Mr. Duncan. Sam had a moment to wonder what had happened to Jason, when suddenly the boy came roaring down the stairs riding that thick mahogany banister.

They made way as he whisked past. He flew off the end of the banister and landed on the floor of the Italian marble foyer. He made a smooth and graceful landing. Very athletic. The boy was definitely his father's son.

Nevertheless, Sam felt she had to reprimand him. "Jason! What do you think you're doing?"

"Just taking a ride, Mom."

"You could have killed yourself. Besides, this is not our house."

"But you just said it was our house."

"I never said it was our house. I said we'd be living here. Now do not, do you hear me, do not slide down that banister again!"

"Jesus, Mom, don't make such a big deal. You make such a big deal about everything." He sulkily rejoined the little tour as they started up the stairs.

Sam made an embarrassed apology to Mr. Duncan.

Duncan brushed the whole thing aside with a wave of his hand. "Anyway," he continued, "getting back to PC Apple Acres. Both the name and the property came about because Creative Marketing Enterprises first made its mark in the field of computer software."

"For PCs and Apples?"

"Yes, exactly. Several years ago the company released a computer game called Battle Zone."

"Battle Zone!" cried Jason. "We got Battle Zone a few months ago. It's awesome."

"I understand it is," agreed Duncan, as they made their way along the wide upstairs hallway.

"It has everything," said Jason. "Tanks and planes

and ships and machine guns and land mines and guys that get blown to smithereens and everything. A very cool ride."

Mr. Duncan smiled. "And an exceptionally popular game. For both the PC and the Apple. The company has sold millions of copies. Battle Zone has been an international best-seller since it was first released."

The quartet entered the master bedroom suite. Sam's suitcases were arranged neatly in the center of the room. But there was no sign of the caretaker. "I wonder what became of Brady?"

"Yeah," said Jason, "he like disappeared."

"Brady's a rather shy and quiet fellow," answered Mr. Duncan. "He may have slipped away along the back stairway."

"Back stairway! Awesome! Where is it?" Jason did not wait for an answer. He took off to investigate on his own. Megan followed close at his heels.

Sam watched them go. And as she watched, she wondered if her children would be happy here, if she and Gunn had made the right decision in bringing them to PC Apple Acres.

She felt sure they had.

16 Gunn did not show up at PC Apple Acres for almost a week. Sam had a pretty good head of steam going by the time her husband finally walked through that fancy front door.

"It couldn't be helped," he started explaining before she could even open her mouth. "Reilly had me visiting every damn toy store and five-and-dime between Houston and Dallas. You have no idea how many toy stores and five-and-dimes there are out there, Sam. I had no idea how many there were. Thousands of them, I tell you. Millions. Every little podunk town in America has a place to buy zippers and staplers and Monopoly sets. I thought it would take me a couple days to cover that territory. It took a little longer. Sorry, baby."

Sam just stood there in that vast front foyer, arms crossed, and glared at her husband. The apology helped, but not much. Her anger and stress levels had blasted off the charts several days earlier. A quickie explanation followed by *sorry, baby* was not enough to pull everything back into equilibrium.

Unfortunately, Gunn, not the model of patience and sensitivity under the brightest of circumstances, had been put through the wringer his first week on the job. First of all, his former employer, the sporting goods giant, was royally ticked off about his hasty departure; so ticked off, in fact, that a lawsuit for breach of contract had been threatened. Gunn doubted the lawsuit would ever materialize, but he felt pretty certain future recommendations from the firm would not be particularly glowing. Actually, he would probably need to strike those four and a half years from his résumé altogether. Not that he was worried about his résumé. He felt confident Creative Marketing Enterprises would make him a wealthy man.

All he had to do was survive the war. Six different motels in as many nights. All but one of them cheap interstate ramp motels with nary a creature comfort beyond an ice machine and maybe an extra blanket in the cheesy dresser drawer. Gunn was used to better. He was used to first-class Marriotts and Hyatts and Radissons where you could get your suit cleaned and pressed overnight without ever leaving your room. But the crummy motels were just the tip of it. He could handle the motels. And the lousy fast-food restaurants. And the long pulls on the interstate. But the morons who owned and managed those toy stores and those five-and-dimes, my God, dealing with these idiots from dawn till dusk was enough to make Gunn contemplate criminal action.

Like Billy Lee down in Silver Creek. Billy Lee ran the Newberry's over on Main Street. Billy Lee was the man to talk to if you had a product you wanted displayed in the Silver Creek Newberry's. So Gunn talked to him. Gunn gave Billy Lee his initial pitch, the pitch he and Mr. Reilly had put together as a starting point for their new product, now code-named The Disk. Gunn did not actually tell Billy Lee about The Disk. No, he simply told the man that his company was about to market a simple, inexpensive toy that would sweep the nation. Then he told Billy Lee that Billy Lee's store had been selected as a test site for this new product.

"So what you got to show me, boy?" Billy Lee wanted to know. "Lemme see one of these here simple, inexpensive toy things."

"I can't show you one just yet," the salesman replied. "We need to keep it under wraps for another month or so. But trust me, you'll be one of the first to get a look."

"So then what the hell you doin' here, boy?" Billy Lee stood about five feet six with his big-heeled cowboy boots on. "Ain't you got nuthin' better to do than go 'round sellin' somethin' you ain't even got?"

Gunn did not enjoy being called boy by a man half a foot shorter than himself. Especially a man as ugly as Billy Lee. Billy Lee had a ragged scar running from the outside corner of his left eye down across his cheek to his upper lip. The scar pointed directly to the missing tooth in his mouth. And the way he dressed: cowboy hat, cowboy boots, black denim jeans, black denim shirt, and one of those stupid rope ties with a silver clasp holding it together. Who, Gunn kept wondering, made this clown the manager of anything?

"I'm just making a friendly call, friend," answered Gunn. "Just to get the ball rolling."

Billy Lee gave Gunn a study. "That's an awful fancy suit you got on for a boy sellin' junk toys."

The suit Gunn had on had cost him twelve hundred and fifty bucks. It had been tailor-made by a Hong Kong tailor who visited the D.C. area every spring and fall. Gunn had a dozen or more tailor-made suits. He handed Billy Lee his business card, smiled, told the man he would be in touch, and got the hell out of the Silver Creek Newberry's lickety-split.

Most of Gunn's calls had not fared much better. Some had been worse. In Slow Lick Hobbies 'N Crafts, the owner, a dyed-in-the-wool redneck who hated Yankees, foreigners, and Catholics, drove Gunn from his store with a snub-nosed .38 that he claimed had killed "a dozen of them dirty Mexicans and almost as many darkies."

At that moment Gunn wondered if maybe he had made a bad career move.

But he mentioned none of this to his wife. Gunn rarely brought the job home with him. Instead he brought home a sullen mood and an irritable disposition, and it was usually up to Sam to figure out what had happened.

So Sam felt abandoned and Gunn felt exhausted after his week down in East Texas.

Gunn set down his bag and took off his coat. "So," he asked, "how's the house?"

Sam did not waste a second. "I can't believe you had to be gone all this time. You at least could have been here when we moved in."

"You're right, Sam, I should have been here. But Reilly wanted me to get started. The job——"

"I don't care about the job, Gunn. To hell with the job! The job could have waited a few days."

Gunn sighed and tried to give his wife a hug. Sam blew him off, pushed him away. So he headed for the living room, threw himself into the first easy chair he could find. She followed close behind.

"Okay," he asked, "what has you all riled up? And don't tell me nothing because I know damn well it's something besides my absence."

"I'll tell you what has me all riled up." And she did. "First of all, that Mrs. Griner, the cook, has turned out to be some kind of creature from hell. She's an absolute monster. When we came up here for the weekend I thought she was so nice and sweet."

"I remember you saying that. I thought so, too."

"Well, she's not sweet at all!" Sam was practically screaming. "She's like some sadistic Marine Corps drill sergeant. She runs the house like a military camp. Especially the kitchen. Breakfast is served from seven till exactly seven-thirty. Lunch from twelve-thirty till one. Dinner from seven till seven-forty-five. If you don't make it on time, show up even a few minutes late, you go hungry."

"I'm sure she's just getting used to us."

"She orders Megan and Jason around like they're her servants."

Gunn sighed again and rubbed his eyes. He needed a scotch and then a long, hot bath. "I'll talk to her."

"I mean it's like Doctor Jekyll and Mrs. Hyde. I can hardly believe it's the same woman."

"She has a bunch of new people in the house, Sam. I'm sure it'll be okay after things calm down. I'll talk to her."

"Fine, Gunn, you talk to her. But before you do that I want you to get our furniture straightened out."

"Our furniture? What about it?"

"It arrived the day before yesterday."

"Yeah?"

"I expected to bring some of our own things into the house, to help us feel at home. Maybe not everything, but at least a few pieces to make this house feel more like our own."

"So what's the problem?"

"Well, Mr. Duncan, perfectly polite as always, informed me, and I quote, 'It might be better, Mrs. Henderson, if you did not disturb the overall design character of the household.' Design character! Meaning he did not want our junk mixing in with all this fancy antique stuff."

Gunn did not really care about the damn furniture, except, of course, for one item close to his heart: his cherry gun cabinet that had been in the family for four generations. "Okay, so where's our stuff?"

"It's still on the moving truck."

"And where is the moving truck?"

"It's parked behind the barn."

"Behind what barn?"

"The barn out back."

"And all our stuff is in there? Including my gun cabinet?"

"Including your gun cabinet."

"And what about my guns? You brought them, right?"

"I brought them up in the Explorer, just like you told me. They're upstairs in the bedroom."

Gunn nodded, then sighed for a third time. More times than he usually sighed in a month. "Okay, Sam, let's just take it easy. I'll talk to Duncan. I'm sure we can work something out."

"We better work something out. About Mrs. Griner, about the furniture, and about Megan and Jason."

"What about the kids?" Gunn asked. "Where are they anyway?"

"Exactly," answered Sam, harsh and icy. "Where are they? I'll tell you where they are. They're still in school."

"Still in school? It's after five." Gunn glanced at his Rolex. "Hell, it's almost quarter of six."

"They'll be home any minute."

"Why so late? Do they always get home this late?"

"The limousine picks them up around seven-thirty and drops them off between quarter of six and six."

"But why so late?"

"Because, Gunn," answered Sam, her voice raspy and sarcastic, "this wonderful private school that your boss insisted our children attend is halfway back to Manhattan. It takes over an hour each way to get there."

"Over an hour? There's nothing closer?"

"I asked Mr. Duncan that same question. He smiled at me, his hands folded against his stomach like some kind of British Buddha, and assured me he would talk to Mr. Reilly as soon as he could get in touch with him."

"And?"

"And that's it. I haven't heard back from him yet."

Yet another sigh, followed by a second eye-rubbing,

and then, "All right, Sam, I can see you've had your hands full."

"More than full."

"So let me apologize again for not being here to help you with some of this mess."

"Don't bother. I don't want your useless apologies. I just want some help."

"Sam, you know it's always tough when we first move to a new place. We've been through this before."

"Not this bad."

"It just seems bad."

"It is bad."

"Look, I promise this weekend we'll talk everything over with Mrs. Griner. I'll talk to Duncan. I'll—"

"You'll never find Mr. Duncan. He's disappeared."

"Okay, I'll call Reilly. I'll get everything straightened out. Now let's just try and relax. It might take a little time, but this will all work out for the best. I mean, look at this place. We're living in the lap of luxury."

Sam let go of a sigh of her own. She was glad to have Gunn back. It was so much easier when they did things together, as a team.

Gunn motioned for her to come over. She hesitated, not wanting to let go of all that suppressed anger too quickly. But finally she went, and along the way a small smile spread across her strained face. She sat down on Gunn's lap. They had a long hug and a kiss. Several of each.

And that night, up in their elegant new bedroom, with a canopy of stars shining through the windows, they made love passionately and aggressively after their long and stressful separation.

So completely absorbed were the Hendersons in their lovemaking, that they failed entirely to behold the human eyes watching them through yonder bedroom window.

17 Time passed: a few days, a couple of weeks. Sam settled into life at PC Apple Acres. Mr. Reilly apologized for sending the kids so far away to school. He insisted he had their best interests at heart. Sam accepted his apology and agreed it would be best to leave them there for the remainder of the school year. After all, summer vacation was just a month or so away. And in September, after some research, maybe they would make a change. Or maybe not. Sam had learned that the school was, in fact, one of the finest in the state. Jason and Megan could flourish there.

Mr. Duncan reappeared and apologized about the furniture. He told Sam she could bring any pieces into the house she desired. After thinking about it for several days, she settled for the kids' beds, desks, and bureaus. She thought the familiar furniture would make Jason and Megan feel more at home, even though they both said they didn't really care, the new stuff was excellent.

The rest of their household belongings, with the exception of Gunn's cherry gun cabinet, went over to a long-term storage facility in Riverhead. Sam finally had to admit, at least to herself, that the furnishings in the Georgian mansion were far superior and much more interesting than the sofas and chairs and tables she had collected over the years. As for Gunn's gun cabinet, it took up residence in his office off the living room. He filled it with his collection of revolvers, pistols, shotguns, and rifles.

The final apology came from Mrs. Griner. The cook apologized to Sam for her obstinate manner and short temper. She explained that her nephew, who was her responsibility, had gotten himself into some trouble, and that his troubles had caused his Aunt Greta to become ill-humored and out of sorts.

Sam accepted her apology, then asked, "Is everything all right with your nephew now?"

"Oh, yes," answered Mrs. Griner. "Everything's fine."

Sam and Greta Griner became pals after that. They chatted up a storm while hanging around the kitchen preparing and eating meals. With Jason and Megan gone all day and Gunn gone all week, Sam had plenty of time to kill. She and Mrs. G., as the kids called her, traded life stories.

Mrs. Griner told Sam that she'd been born and raised in and around East Hampton. "The family has been here for generations. Fishermen mostly. My grandfather was a fisherman, my father was a fisherman, and my husband, God rest his poor soul, was a fisherman. Drowned he did, off the Montauk Point, on a stormy night about a decade back."

Sam expressed her sorrow for such a terrible tragedy, but Mrs. Griner shrugged it off. She wanted to know how Sam had met Gunn. She wanted to know if it had been love at first sight.

Sam laughed. "Maybe not love at first sight. But right from the first time I laid eyes on him I thought he was the best-looking guy I had ever seen."

"Well," replied Mrs. Griner, pastry flour on her hands and a smile on her plump face, "I'd give that award to my late husband, but your Gunn is powerfully handsome."

Sam nodded in agreement. "I first saw him when he came into the law office where I worked as an intern. I was a year or so out of college, deciding whether to go to law school or business school. I planned on being a successful career woman. Marriage and family were the last things on my mind."

"Until you met Gunn."

"Really until we had kids. When Jason came along I knew I'd found my true calling. But anyway, Gunn came into the office selling copy machines. He came on real strong. Everything about him was big: big shoulders, big smile, those big blue eyes, big handshake. I thought he was aggressive and obnoxious. I didn't like men who were aggressive and obnoxious. I still don't."

Mrs. Griner mixed the flour in with the sugar and butter. She kept her own thoughts about the male species to herself. "So what happened to change your mind?"

"He spent an hour in with the managing partner. A grumpy, tightfisted lawyer named Mr. Savage. And boy was he savage. Always grumbling about money, a scowl on his face."

"I know the type," allowed Mrs. Griner.

"Exactly. Why are so many men so uptight about money?"

"It's in their genes, honey. Power and money and sex. It's all they know, all they care to know."

Sam laughed. "So, after their meeting, Gunn stops at my desk, gives me this big wink, and asks me if I would like to have a drink sometime, maybe that very same night."

"The forward sort, huh?"

"Totally cocky. I had no choice but to tell him no, thank you."

"Even though you wanted to say yes."

"Let's just say I was feeling ambiguous about it."

"So what did you tell him?"

"I told him I'd think about it."

"And?"

"And he gave me another big wink and left. Later that day I found out he had sold not one but two brand-new expensive copiers to Mr. Savage. You have to understand that this was incredible news around the office. At the time we had one old copier that spent at least half its time broken down. For this salesman to waltz into the office on a cold call and leave with two orders in his pocket was considered something close to a miracle."

"So that made you decide to have a drink with him?" Mrs. Griner mixed in the oatmeal and the chocolate chips. A time or two she took a little taste.

"That and the fact that every other girl in the office thought I was crazy not to at least go out on a date with him."

"So you did?"

"I did."

"And how did it go?"

Sam smiled, remembering. "Two things about that night I'll never forget. The first was the way he was dressed. I mean most guys I went out with had on blue jeans and scruffy sneakers and maybe a shirt with a collar. But Gunn Henderson, not yet twenty-four years old, had on this beautiful suit that fit perfectly. With the right tie, the right shirt, the right shoes. He looked great. And he was a gentleman. He opened doors for me, never tried to dominate the conversation, listened carefully to everything I said."

"Sounds almost too good to be true."

Sam gave Mrs. Griner a look. "Well, we won't go into that."

Mrs. Griner smiled. "So what's the second thing about that first date you will never forget?"

"Oh, yes," said Sam, her brain working on the past. "We were sitting at this small table in this intimate little Italian restaurant, eating by candlelight. I was telling him something, probably babbling because I was nervous. He sat there listening, smiling, his elbows on the table, his face resting in his hands. Then, out of nowhere, when I was right in the middle of a sentence, he said to me, very softly, 'I swear to God, Sam, you have the most beautiful eyes I've ever seen.' I couldn't think of much to say after that."

Mrs. Griner plopped spoonfuls of cookie dough onto the cookie sheet. "Not to say you don't have lovely eyes, honey, but your boy Gunn sounds like quite a salesman."

Sam hesitated for just a moment, then sighed. "Oh yes, quite a salesman. Gunn is a man with a golden tongue."

18 On the seventeenth of May, a Monday, at approximately ten minutes after eight o'clock in the morning, Samantha Ann Quincy Henderson started down the road to damnation. Some might say it was not her fault, the Devil made her do it. But others believe our individual fates are ours and ours alone, that we have only ourselves to blame for both the good and the bad that invade our lives.

That Monday started like any other day. Sam closed Jason and Megan into the limousine and waved goodbye right around seven thirty-five. Then, as per her routine, she poured herself a cup of coffee and went back upstairs to her expansive bedroom suite. She washed her face and brushed her hair. She tidied up and made the bed. The housekeeper, a tiny Puerto Rican woman who spoke only a few words of English but sang constantly in Spanish while she worked, would have done these chores for her, but Sam preferred to have only family in her bedroom. Once a week she allowed Saida in to clean the bathroom.

While Sam fluffed the pillows and pulled the down comforter up over the king-sized bed, she heard what sounded like splashing coming from the swimming pool. But who, she wondered, would be swimming on a day like this? It was cool, almost blustery outside, more like March than May. She knew because she had waged a small battle with Jason over whether or not he needed to wear a jacket to school.

She heard the splashing again as she crossed the bedroom to have a look outside. A large bay window with a cozy window seat occupied nearly half of the rear wall. The window provided a lovely panoramic view of the back of the estate. In winter one could see clear across the grounds to the Sound. But now, with the leaves beginning to fill the trees, Sam could see only the slate terrace, the swimming pool, the formal gardens, and the boxwood hedge surrounding the tennis court.

Sam carefully drew back the lace curtain and peered out the window at the pool. At first she saw nothing. Her eyes needed to adjust to the bright morning sunlight. But after a moment she saw someone in the pool, swimming laps, a man. He swam fast, practically at a sprinter's pace. His body moved swiftly and powerfully through the water. When he reached the end of the pool, he executed a perfect turn. He slipped momentarily below the surface, coiled, then shot off the wall before resuming his stroke. Sam watched as he completed six, eight, ten laps at that exaggerated speed. Finally he slowed and moved into a steady but still powerful breaststroke. He completed half a dozen laps that way, then he exploded again, this time into a butterfly that brought the entire top half of his body clean out of the water.

Sam could see his face clearly as he came up for air, his mouth big and round and wide-open in a gasp for oxygen to feed his lungs.

It was Brady! The caretaker. Sam had hardly laid eyes on him since that morning he had walked through the front door carrying her suitcases. Two or three times she had seen him briefly from a distance. He seemed to pull back if he sensed people nearby. She had asked Mrs. Griner about him, but Mrs. Griner had been mostly silent. She would say only that he was a first-class gardener and fix-it man, but rather peculiar in most other ways.

"How do you mean, peculiar?"

"Just a bit odd is all. Nothing demonic or anything."

Sam had let that settle, then said, "Mr. Duncan told me Brady was a fine singer."

"Like a songbird," had been Mrs. Griner's reply. "A voice that can take your breath away."

"But peculiar?"

"Yes, a strange sort of fellow. I would say he prefers to keep his own counsel. You're talking about a bonanza week when you coax more than a few words out of Brady."

And now here was Brady in her swimming pool, doing lap after lap after lap like some athlete in training for the next Olympic Games. And in this chilly weather. Sam knew the water was heated, but still. . . .

She could not take her eyes off him.

And then her eyes widened. Brady went under to

make a turn, and when he surfaced he had turned over to perform the backstroke. For the first time since looking out her bedroom window, Sam realized that Brady was naked, stark naked. Every time he arched his back to make another stroke, his pelvis rotated up and out of the water, thereby exposing his private parts to anyone who might be watching.

Sam squinted and looked a little closer, just to make sure of her sighting, then she scowled and turned away. Feelings of anger and embarrassment made her face flush crimson. She felt violated. She wondered what she should do about this . . . this . . . this exhibition. Open the window and holler at Brady? Tell him to make himself decent? Call Mrs. Griner and have her do it? Call Mr. Duncan and complain? Call Mr. Reilly? Call Gunn? Just close the curtain and pretend she had not seen him?

After at least a minute of procrastination, however, she found herself edging back to the window. She found her eyes lifting and looking through the glass. She found her focus reaching out beyond the glass to the swimming pool below. But now she did not see him. He was no longer in the pool. She glanced around, her eyes darting quickly. He was not on the deck or on the grass or on the patio. He had disappeared. Her eyes kept moving. Was that disappointment filtering through her thoughts?

And then she saw him: dead ahead, almost at eye level, less than a hundred feet away. Brady stood on the diving platform high atop that miniature man-made Matterhorn. Still in the buff, he stood perfectly still with his toes hanging over the end of the platform, his arms straight out at his sides, his eyes closed in complete concentration.

Sam did not turn away. Oh no, not a chance. She had her eyes and mouth wide open. Brady looked like a Greek sculpture. His muscles were long and hard and sinewy. He had the shoulders and torso of a swimmer, along with a thin waist and a rock-solid stomach.

His eyes suddenly opened. His knees bent. He sprang into the air. For what seemed to Sam like an eternity, Brady hung there in midair before plunging toward the pool. On his way down he executed a very polished two-and-a-half with a twist, then slipped through the water straight as an arrow. Sam had to hold herself back from offering applause. A small gasp spluttered from her mouth. She continued to watch as Brady surfaced, climbed out of the pool, and headed back up the mountain for another dive. She wondered how he could stand being out in that cold air with absolutely nothing on.

"Mrs. Henderson? . . . Sam? . . . Samantha?"

Vaguely, in the back of her brain, Sam thought she heard someone calling her name. The thought had been with her for a minute or more, but mesmerized by this naked man out in the backyard, she had been unable to respond. But now the voice was coming nearer, closing in, growing louder. She blinked and turned away from the window. And there, on the threshold of her bedroom, stood Mrs. Griner.

"I'm sorry to bother you, Mrs. Henderson, but I've been calling, and when you didn't answer, well, I just wanted to make sure you were all right."

"I'm fine," replied Sam, her voice brittle.

Mrs. Griner kept right on coming, straight into the bedroom.

Sam, a jumble of emotions swirling around in her head and belly, reached out and grabbed the drawstring that operated the lace curtains. She gave the string a fierce tug. The curtains swayed and closed.

Mrs. G. arrived at her side, all smiles and concern, a tiny smear of orange marmalade at the corner of her mouth. "Oh, Mrs. Henderson, don't draw the drapes on a morning as lovely as this."

Sam still had the drawstring in her hand. Mrs. Griner gently took it away and began to pull the curtains open.

Samantha's first instinct was to grab the drawstring, violently, if necessary, and keep those curtains closed. No way did she want Mrs. Griner to know what she had been staring at outside the window. But Sam had been taught as a youngster never to grapple or grab. And she was not, by nature, a violent or hasty person.

So what did she do? She did nothing. Nothing at all. She stood there and watched Mrs. Griner open the curtains.

"Ah yes!" rejoiced the cook. "A somewhat cool but otherwise perfectly lovely morning. Soon we'll be able to throw open the windows as well as the curtains."

Mrs. Griner stood there and surveyed the scene. Sam waited for her to spot Brady in the buff, and then, perhaps, to shriek. But half a minute passed and Mrs. Griner just continued to silently absorb the scene.

Sam took a cautious look out the window. She

glanced down at the swimming pool, at the terrace, at the summit of the Matterhorn. No sign anywhere of Brady. The caretaker had slipped away. Sam breathed a sigh of relief.

19

Every morning that week, soon after Jason and Megan departed for school, Brady showed up and swam his laps in the buff. And every morning, after she had washed her face and made the bed, Sam Henderson watched him through the bay window. She watched with a wary eye. She watched while pretending not to watch.

On Friday she decided the time had come to stop watching. She'd watched long enough. She felt childish and stupid, like some cheap voyeur. Watching had become her morning entertainment. It had become a fetish. And Sam definitely did not see herself as a fetishist. She was not the obsessive sort. She simply had a little extra time on her hands now, what with the children being limoed to and from school, Saida doing the cleaning, and Mrs. Griner in charge of the cooking. Nevertheless, Sam felt she had better things to do than watch the caretaker swim laps and execute perfect dives. She had planned a flower and vegetable garden, and now the time had come to plant. She had also decided the time had come to get out and about, see the surrounding countryside, meet some of their neighbors. Yes, she definitely had better things to do.

And besides, Gunn would be home later in the day. He would spend the night with her in bed. He would, she hoped, make love to her. And in the morning he would undoubtedly get up, stretch, yawn, scratch himself, and look out the window. If he spotted Brady out there parading around in the nude in front of his family, swimming and diving, he would not stop to watch. He would not wonder what to do or how to handle the situation. No, Gunn, Sam knew, was a man of imminent action. He reacted, then thought about the consequences later. If he saw Brady out there with his rather substantial member flopping against his thigh, Sam knew Gunn would fly down the stairs, sprint across the terrace, and dive into the pool. He would grab Brady by the neck and hold Brady's head below the surface until Brady stopped breathing and died.

Sam did not want that to happen. She decided the time had come to have a little chat with the caretaker. But when? And where? And how would she approach him? Mrs. Griner had called him peculiar. What if he was rude to her? What if he told her to mind her own business? But this was her business. After all, he was swimming naked right outside *her* bedroom window. She would just ask him to please wear a suit. She had no problem with him using the pool, if only he would cover his loins.

Yes, that's how she would handle it: on the up and up, adult to adult. He seemed like a reasonable enough man. That day out by the barn when he had accidentally bumped into her, hadn't he apologized immediately? Hadn't he been a perfect gentleman?

Sam sighed. Then she took one last look out the

window. There he was again, atop the Matterhorn, with his back to her this time. He balanced on the balls of his feet, as still as a statue. His arms reached high over his head. He bent his knees and flew backward off the platform. He performed a simple inward swan dive, but his long and graceful body coupled with the perfect arch in his back caused the breath to catch momentarily in Sam's throat. He sliced through the water with barely a ripple. Sam turned away.

Enough was enough.

●　　●　　●

SAM DRESSED in old jeans, a T-shirt, a cotton sweater, and hiking boots that doubled as work boots. She intended to get outside, dig in the dirt, get some of that dirt under her fingernails. And while out there, with her spade and garden fork, she would have her talk with Brady, laborer to laborer. But first she needed a bowl of Mrs. Griner's homemade granola with all those oats and pecans and raisins.

She went down the wide front stairs and along the hallway to the kitchen. Mrs. Griner, who rarely left the kitchen except to sleep, was nowhere in sight. But Sam was not alone. Brady sat at the small round wooden table over in the breakfast nook, his hands wrapped around a large mug of steaming hot coffee. He had his clothes on, all his clothes: sweatshirt, overalls, baseball cap, and boots. Sam wondered how he could have dressed and gotten into the house so quickly after his morning's swim.

He stood and removed his cap as Sam entered the room. His hair, Sam noticed, was still wet.

"Good morning, Mrs. Henderson," he said, his eyes

meeting hers for only an instant. "Mrs. Griner told me to come around and see if you could use some help. She says you might want to plant some flowers and some herbs, maybe some vegetables." Brady kept his eyes averted. He mostly looked down at his boots.

Sam could hardly believe the man's modesty. It seemed almost impossible that this was the same man who strutted naked around the swimming pool. Here in the kitchen he looked so shy, almost vulnerable.

"Yes," she replied, "I would like to plant a garden. In fact, I intend to start today. But really, I didn't expect your help. I'm sure you have a million and one things to do around a place like this."

Brady glanced up at her, met her eyes, but not for more than a fraction of a second. "I'm here to do what you want me to do, ma'am."

She smiled at him. "Well, I would like to get a few plants in the ground. I enjoy watching things grow."

"Yes, ma'am." Brady studied his boots. Then, "Lots of formal gardens on the estate, Mrs. Henderson, as I'm sure you've noticed. We have the roses out back, and perennial beds just about everywhere you turn. Now that it's finally beginning to warm up, I've started getting the annuals in the ground: begonias, zinnias, petunias, geraniums, impatiens, marigolds. If there's anything special you like, just let me know."

"I'd like to plant some vegetables, Mr. Brady."

"That would be fine, Mrs. Henderson. I know just the spot. It's been a few years since we grew any vegetables around here. Which is a shame, if you want my opinion."

Sam began to relax. "Nothing better than vegetables fresh from the garden. Green beans and tomatoes are my favorite, but if there's room I wouldn't mind some peas and some peppers, maybe some cucumbers."

"Already a bit late for peas, ma'am. But if we get started right away we could give them a try." Brady looked her in the eye again, and this time he even managed a hasty smile.

Sam felt herself blush. "I had planned," she said, after a moment, "to start right after breakfast."

"That would be fine, Mrs. Henderson. I'll be out in the rose garden. Come out when you're ready and I'll show you a sunny piece of ground that should be perfect for what you have in mind."

Brady grabbed his mug of coffee, came out from behind the breakfast table, and steered himself for the set of French doors that led out onto the back terrace. As soon as he reached the terrace, he slipped his cap back on his head. Sam watched him amble across the terrace, past the swimming pool, and through the trellis leading to the rose garden. Only after he had disappeared did she shake off the effects of his presence.

Such a gentleman, she thought, so polite and considerate. How, she wondered, could this be the same man who had been diving into the pool in his birthday suit less than half an hour earlier? It did not make sense.

After her granola and a couple of telephone calls, Sam headed outside. The sun had risen high into the sky and the air had turned almost mild. Sam knew she would not have to keep her sweater on for long. She found Brady carefully pruning some dead stems in the far corner of the rose garden. He hummed quietly while he worked.

"They tell me you're a fine singer, Mr. Brady."

"You can just call me Brady, ma'am. Everyone else does."

"All right, Brady. And what about your singing?"

He visibly blushed. "Once in a while I guess I belt one out. When the mood strikes me."

"How's your mood this morning?"

"Kind of quiet, Mrs. Henderson. I usually sing when I'm pretty sure no one can hear."

"Why is that, Brady?"

The caretaker took a moment before offering an answer. He made a few more surgical cuts with his razor-sharp pruning shears. He was prudent and deliberate with that all too often destructive gardening tool.

Then, not much above a whisper, he answered. "I guess I sing mostly sad songs, ma'am. Laments, we used to call them in Ireland. I don't suspect people want to hear sad songs much."

Sam wanted to ask him why he sang sad songs, but feared it might be too personal a question. So instead she asked, "I thought I heard a slight Irish lilt in your voice. Are you originally from Ireland?"

"No, ma'am," he lied. "Born and bred right here in the States. But as a young man I spent a few years in Dublin and Belfast."

"I spent a week once in Ireland," said Sam, and right away she felt stupid and wished she hadn't said it. Her announcement sounded so trite and touristy. But when Brady did not reply she kept right on going. "I thought the countryside was so beautiful. . . . So green and fresh . . . And the people were so, I don't know, friendly . . . Always smiling and wanting to help. . . ." She wanted to slap herself across the mouth to make it stay closed.

Brady helped her out. "Yes, ma'am, a very beautiful country. But an angry country as well. Plenty of suppressed anger in Ireland, ma'am." He straightened up. "Why don't we go see about those vegetables, Mrs. Henderson? No time like the present to get the ground ready for planting."

Relieved he had subtly changed the subject, Sam fell in behind him. As she followed Brady through the rear trellis of the rose garden, she wondered why Mrs. Griner had called the caretaker peculiar. He did not seem to her in the least bit peculiar. He seemed quite normal, as well as sensitive and sweet. Mrs. Griner had also called him silent and uncommunicative. Sam thought he seemed quiet, but perfectly willing to chat.

Brady led her to an open piece of ground out behind the barn. The ground was already fenced, but it had not been turned over for several years. Quite an array of weeds had taken hold.

"We've grown vegetables here in the past," Brady told her. "The earth is airy and nutritious. Plus it gets plenty of sunshine and at least a little protection from winds coming off Shelter Island Sound. Your beans and tomatoes will flourish here."

"It looks perfect. Do you think we need to till the soil?"

Brady went in through the gate, bent down, and ran the earth through his fingers. "I don't think so. It's plenty loose. I'll turn it over for you with a shovel and a fork. That should be enough."

"No," said Sam. "I want to do it. Really. I like to get my hands dirty. You must have other things to do."

"Are you sure? It won't take but an hour."

Sam insisted she could handle the job herself.

It might have taken Brady an hour with his wide shoulders and strong back, but it took Sam the rest of the morning to turn over half the soil inside the wire mesh fence. Within a few minutes, she had her sweater off. Within half an hour she had her T-shirt well soaked with perspiration. Every drop of sweat made her feel wonderful. There had been a serious lack of exercise since arriving at PC Apple Acres. But now, each time she thrust the spade into the earth, she could feel her muscles working and her heart pumping. They were muscles in her arms and back that she did not use very often, muscles that would undoubtedly be stiff and sore in the morning. But so what? Sam loved to use her body, every fiber of it. She loved to feel its power and its strength. While she dug in the dirt she thought about Brady. And about Gunn. Gunn had an excellent body, strong and solid from a youth filled with athletics and an adulthood filled with fitness programs and calisthenics. But Brady, he seemed to have a body chiseled from a piece of granite by a master sculptor, Rodin or Michelangelo.

When she stopped to rest she looked for him. After fetching her the spade and the fork, after telling her once again that he would gladly turn the soil, Brady had headed off in the direction of the boathouse. She could see the boathouse in the distance across a long sweep of grass. She knew Brady lived in the boathouse. Mr. Duncan had told her so. She wondered why he wanted to be called Brady. Just Brady. Not Mr. Brady. Maybe Brady was his first name. She would have to ask him; perhaps before she suggested he swim with his suit on. She hoped he would not take offense.

Early in the afternoon Brady returned. He approached so quietly that Sam did not hear him coming until he said, "You've been working so hard, I thought you might like something refreshing to drink."

Sam stopped her digging and turned around. Brady stood there at the fence holding a pitcher of lemonade in one hand and two glasses in the other. Sam smiled, then wiped her brow with the back of her hand. "You must be a mind reader. I've been dreaming about an ice-cold glass of lemonade for at least an hour. I was just getting ready to go inside and get one. Mrs. Griner makes a fresh pitcher every day."

"My pleasure, ma'am. I think you should come out, relax for a bit in the grass, have some lemonade, and let me take a turn at that dirt."

Sam leaned the garden fork against the fence. "I might just take you up on that. If you do me one favor."

"Yes, ma'am."

"No more Mrs. Henderson, Brady. My name is Samantha. Most people call me Sam."

"All right, Samantha. I think I can do that." Brady held the gate open for her, then went in as soon as she came out. He immediately picked up the spade and went to work.

Sam sat down in the lush grass and poured herself a glassful of lemonade. In one greedy swig she emptied the glass. "That was wonderful. So fresh and tangy."

"Have some more."

"I think I will." Sam drank the second glass more slowly. She savored the lemony sensation sip by sip while she watched Brady work. He worked with speed and precision: knees bent, elbows cocked, back straight. Sam had the impression of him literally tearing through the earth. He moved the soil like a human Rototiller.

The physical exercise, the high hot sun, the icy lemonade—it all started to make Sam feel a little tipsy, a little dizzy. For a moment she thought Brady had removed his clothes and was in the garden digging with nothing but his boots on. She laughed.

Brady slowed but did not stop working. "What's funny?"

"Oh, nothing. My mind was just playing tricks on me." Then, before he could ask her what those tricks were, she asked, "Why do you like to be called Brady? Is it your first name?"

Brady increased his pace. "First name. Last name. I don't know. I just like Brady."

"Fair enough." Sam sipped some more lemonade. She'd suddenly started to feel tired, exhausted even, as though she could easily just lie back in the grass and drift off to sleep. But she did not want to sleep. She wanted to talk to Brady about this swimming pool thing. She had to talk to him about it, before Gunn got home and the time arrived for another morning workout.

"Mr. Brady? I mean, Brady?"

"Yes, ma'am?"

"I really need to talk to you about something."

"Yes, ma'am?"

Sam finished her second glass of lemonade. "Yes, well, I'm afraid it has to do with, well . . ."

"Yes, ma'am?"

"I'm so tired all of a sudden."

"Probably all the sun, ma'am. And the shoveling."

"Yes . . . I   guess. . . . But . . . but . . . but . . ." Sam was unable to finish the sentence, or even remember the thought. She suddenly rolled over onto her side and fell fast asleep in the grass.

Yes, it was the physical exertion and the hot sun and the cold lemonade and the fact that Sam had not slept well the night before because she had Brady naked on the brain—all of this had something to do with why she just toppled over and fell out right on that soft green lawn. Something, but by no means everything. Oh, no, the biggest factor, by far, was the Halcion the caretaker had deliberately added to the pitcher after he had squeezed all those fresh lemons for Mrs. Henderson's oral delight.

Back at the boathouse, Brady had considered using Dalmane or Restoril, but had decided Halcion was the best drug for the job. Brady always did his research. He rarely left a stone unturned.

Now he went out through the gate, bent to Sam's sleeping body, and took her pulse. Yes, she was doing just fine, slow but steady. He crossed the field and went into the barn. Half a minute later he returned carrying two folded carriage blankets. One of the lightweight blankets he placed very carefully under Sam's head. The other blanket he shook loose and draped over her legs and waist.

Satisfied she would rest comfortably for at least the next couple of hours, the caretaker returned to the garden. He finished turning the soil and breaking up the ground. Next he went through with a hoe and worked the ground until it was fine enough to sift easily through his fingers. He removed all rocks and roots and weeds. Then he added some compost and two large bags of peat moss. He worked the mixture into the soil. Finally he dug furrows for bean seeds and peas, then holes for tomato plants and cukes. It was the middle of the afternoon by the time he finished his labor.

It was a job well done: thorough and conscientious.

The caretaker was hot and thirsty. He went out into the grass and poured himself some lemonade. But he did not drink, not right away. First he pulled a thin cellular phone out of his pants pocket and made a call.

Satisfied with the information he received, he settled down in the grass a few feet from Sam. She was still out cold, and would be for another hour or so. Brady drank half a glass of lemonade and surveyed the scene: the garden, the finely turned earth, the spade, the fork, the hoe—it all had the feel of a good day's work. The caretaker lay back, put his hands behind his head, and stared up at the deep blue sky. He turned and looked at Sam. She looked serene and peaceful. His head was just a foot or two from her head. Perfect.

The hard swim, the day's labor, the hot sun, the Halcion in the lemonade—they all began to take their toll. Brady's eyes grew heavy. He smiled as his eyes closed. Soon, the caretaker, too, was fast asleep.

20 Gunn had the limousine driver stop at the florist's on Newtown Lane in East Hampton. He went in and bought a dozen yellow sweetheart roses, Sam's favorite cut flower. She did not expect him until dinnertime, but he wanted to surprise her with an early arrival. His first weeks on the job had been a strain—working sixteen hours a day, leaving his wife and kids late Sunday afternoon, not getting home till Friday evening, sometimes Saturday morning. It often seemed futile, all this grueling preliminary work, but Gunn knew that with any new product you had to lay the groundwork, you had to get out there and pound the pavement. Of course, he did it for the dough, for the base salary, good God, almost ten grand on payday every other week. Although Gunn did not actually bring home anything close to ten G's. Not only did a hefty chunk of every paycheck go to Uncle Sam, but Gunn put at least a third and sometimes as much as half of his gross pay straight back into the company's private stock offering. Mr. Reilly assured him that when The Disk hit the stores and Creative Marketing Enterprises went public, every share of stock would increase tenfold.

Gunn's limousine pulled through the gates of PC Apple Acres just a few minutes before three o'clock. Gunn knew Jason and Megan would not be home until at least five-thirty. Plenty of time to give Sam her flowers and coax her up to the bedroom for an afternoon frolic. He went in through the front door, set his briefcase on the marble floor of the foyer, and immediately began calling her name: "Sam! Are you here? Are you home? Samantha!"

Sam, of course, could not hear her husband's call. She was off in La La Land out in the back forty with Brady and the garden tools. But Greta Griner heard. The cook came out of the kitchen and down the hallway to the foyer. "Welcome home, Mr. Henderson. They told me you'd be along a bit earlier than usual. I have a tall Beefeater and tonic on the rocks waiting for you in the kitchen."

Gunn scowled. "Who told you I'd be home earlier than usual?"

"Oh, well, your driver, of course. He called ahead to let me know you were coming."

This bit of news did not give Gunn any pleasure at all. In fact, it seemed to visibly irritate him. "Have you seen my wife?"

"Yes, sir," replied Mrs. Griner cheerfully. "She's been out back working all day, practically since sunup. Digging the garden, she is."

"And where would this garden be?" Gunn moved toward the rear of the mansion, his box of yellow sweetheart roses tucked under his arm.

Greta did not hesitate. "I would guess out beyond

the tennis court, Mr. Henderson. We used to grow vegetables back behind the barn. Brady, the caretaker, probably chose the same site."

Gunn went out through the kitchen and onto the terrace. He stopped and took a look around, assuming he would see his wife. The sheer size of PC Apple Acres had not yet registered in Gunn Henderson's brain. Sure, he knew the place was big, but he hadn't even visited all the rooms in the house yet. Nor had he ventured beyond the tennis court. He hadn't even been as far as the tennis court since his two matches with Tom the tennis pro back during their initial visit. All Gunn had really done since taking the job with Creative Marketing Enterprises was work. Work, work, work. When not out on the road selling, he was holed up in the office off the living room scrutinizing project reports, statistical data, and comprehensive sales analysis for various regions of the country. And, of course, he had to deal with Mr. Reilly, who called several times a day with questions, requests, and to just chew the fat. So, everything considered, Gunn felt more than a little out of the loop. For several weeks now he had been telling himself to relax, take it easy. But standing there on the terrace, box of roses in his hand, he just wanted to see his wife, give her the roses, give her a squeeze and a kiss, and then get her up to the bedroom.

Gunn marched across the patio and past the swimming pool. And he kept marching right through and out the back of the rose garden. He was wound up now, stressed out, feeling the pressure building behind his eyeballs. All morning during his sales calls, then waiting at the airport in Oklahoma City while that goddamn United Airlines fixed the goddamn engine of their goddamn 737, then the flight to JFK that circled New York City so many times they could have flown all the way to London. Through all of it, Gunn stayed calm and cool. Did so with the help of Johnnie Walker. But his fuse was burning, oh, so slowly, but burning nevertheless.

Gunn came around the back of the tennis court and followed the neatly raked cinder path that ran behind the barn. Behind the barn, he remembered, was where Mrs. Griner had told him he would probably find this garden Sam was busy digging. So that's where Gunn marched.

Now, it does not take the vivid imagination of Aristotle to conjure up Gunn Henderson's reaction when he spotted his bride lying in the grass with some man he had never laid eyes on before. Gunn instantly freaked. He completely missed the garden, the gardening tools, the obvious display of hard labor. He saw nothing but his wife's head lying inches from the head of another man.

Gunn practically kicked his wife in the ribs in his manic drive to bring her wide-awake. Only the final thread of his civility kept his leg at his side.

"Sam! For chrissakes! Sam! Wake up!" Gunn held nothing back. The fuse had reached its target. "Goddammit, Sam! *Wake the fuck up!*"

Poor Sam. Normally the tenor of her husband's voice at that exaggerated pitch and roll would have had her on her feet in a split second. But the hot sun and the cool lemonade and the splash of Halcion caused Sam no small amount of difficulty in prying her eyes open. She came around very, very slowly.

Much too slowly for Gunn. Gunn wanted action and a damn good explanation. Gunn wanted his wife on her feet. Now.

That took some time. He more or less had to peel her off the ground and stand her up. Even then she looked a little shaky.

And the caretaker, he just kept lying there, his eyes closed, snoring lightly, the vague trace of a smile on his tanned face. Gunn wanted to erase that smile with the toe of his Cole-Haan cordovan loafers.

"What the hell is going on, Sam?"

Sam rubbed the sleepiness from her eyes. "Huh?"

Gunn gave her a shake. "What the hell is this?"

Sam yawned, a big one, right in Gunn's face. "Oh! Gunn! Hi, honey."

"Who the hell is this?" Gunn demanded, pointing at Brady.

"*Who?*" asked Sam, wobbly on her feet.

"What do you mean, who? *Him,* goddammit!"

Sam took a long, slow look. She saw Brady lying there, really, for the first time. "What do you mean, who is it? You know perfectly well who it is."

"I said," raged Gunn, "who the hell is it? And why are you lying here in the grass with him?"

The nasty tone in her husband's voice reached Sam's brain. Her thoughts finally started to clear. A survival thing. She began to focus. "That's Brady, Gunn."

"Who's Brady?"

"Brady's the caretaker, silly. He takes care of the estate." The Halcion caused Sam to slur her words. "What's in the box?"

"Never mind the damn box. Have you been drinking?" He sniffed her breath. "You sound like you've been drinking."

"Not a drop."

"So why are the two of you lying out here in the grass damn near right on top of each other?"

"He was helping me dig the garden."

"It doesn't look like either one of you is digging anything."

Sam glanced over at the garden. "Look!" she said to her husband. "He finished getting the soil ready. It looks beautiful."

"I thought you said you were doing it together."

"Yes, we were. Together. But then I grew tired, so I lay down here in the grass, and before I knew what hit me, I fell fast asleep. Look, he even gave me a blanket to rest my head."

"How sweet."

Sam heard the venom and the sarcasm in Gunn's voice. She knew her husband did not really think the blankets were sweet. Then she remembered she had never had her conversation with Brady about his choice of swimwear. Or lack thereof. Tomorrow morning, she realized, could make this little scene feel like a picnic.

Gunn did not actually kick Brady, but he gave the caretaker a pretty good shove with his right foot. Brady stirred. His eyes opened. He took in the sights, then pretty much sprang to his feet.

"Oh! Mr. Henderson, sir. Excuse me. I . . . I must have fallen asleep."

"You fell asleep with my wife, goddammit."

"With your wife? No, sir."

"Who are you?" Gunn demanded.

"Brady, sir."

"Brady who? And who do you work for?"

"I'm the caretaker, sir."

"I don't give a shit if you're the Count of fucking Montecristo. Who do you work for?"

"For the estate, sir. I work for the estate."

Sam could see Brady was extremely nervous and upset. He seemed almost to be shaking in his boots.

"For the estate, my ass!" Gunn roared. "Who the hell do you work for? I want a name! Duncan? Reilly? A name, goddammit!"

"Well, sir, Mr. Reilly. But it's not necessary to call him. Really, sir, I just fell asleep for a moment. It won't happen again."

"You're goddamn right it won't!" Gunn roared once more. Then he turned his attention to his wife. He did this by grabbing onto her arm and issuing her a direct order. "Come on, Sam! I came home early today so we could spend some nice time together. I wasn't expecting to walk in on this bullshit."

Sam took a deep breath. She knew she should defend Brady, that he had done nothing, but she did not have the strength. Or the courage. She also knew Gunn would only escalate the entire issue if she opened her mouth. So instead she fell in at her husband's side. Before they disappeared around the side of the barn, she did take a quick peek over her shoulder. She saw Brady standing there, his broad shoulders slumped forward, his face looking forlorn and dejected. She tried to reassure him with a smile, but he only dropped his eyes.

21 Gunn finally handed over the yellow sweetheart roses, but he did so with a heavy scowl on his puss and black crossbones tattooed across his heart. The frolic in the bedroom did not come to pass. In fact, before Sam even had those dainty little roses in water, Gunn had stomped off to his office, slammed the door, fondled a few of his armaments, and buried himself in next week's itinerary: Minnesota, the Dakotas, and maybe Nevada, if he had time. The thought of spending a week in Bismarck and Pierre and Rapid City did little to improve Gunn's mood.

Just before dinner, Mr. Reilly called. He wanted to know how things had gone in Kansas and Oklahoma. Gunn filled him in on all the details. He told the boss everything the boss wanted to hear: number of potential stores and outlets visited, response from owners and managers, Gunn's gut feeling on the level of enthusiasm for their new product. Gunn painted a rosy picture, a land of rinky-dink retailers just standing around salivating for this megahit from Creative Marketing Enterprises. But the truth was this: Gunn needed the product. The owners and managers wanted to see the damn product. They wanted to put their fat little hands on it. Without the product, Gunn was out there naked, downwind of his own verbal gas. It was far too early in the ball game to lay this rap on Reilly, however. Reilly liked good news and good news only. So Gunn just spun the positive spin, something he had mastered way back when he sold newspapers as a kid.

Only after all issues had been discussed in minute detail did Gunn turn the conversation to the caretaker.

"Mr. Reilly, before you go, there's a man here on the estate. I believe his name is Brady."

"Brady, right. I know Brady."

"He's the caretaker?"

"Yes, he oversees the grounds and the gardens, makes sure the buildings are properly maintained."

"I see."

"No problem with Brady, I hope," said Mr. Reilly. "He has always been a very dependable man."

Gunn hesitated, then, "I don't know if we have a problem or not. He's been bothering my wife."

"I don't like the sound of that, Gunn. Bothering her how?"

Gunn had not foreseen this simple question. He suddenly felt stupid and petty. But stupidity and pettiness were not a couple of character traits to slow down Gunn Henderson. He plowed on. "Look, Mr. Reilly, I don't mean to drag you into this, but, well, my wife is in a period of adjustment here and I would like to keep things on as even a keel as possible."

"I understand perfectly, Gunn."

"It would probably be best to just let this Brady go."

"Fire Brady?"

"Yes, sir."

"Sounds a little drastic, son."

"I don't think so, sir. There must be plenty of people out there who can cut grass and wash windows."

Mr. Reilly laughed. "I think Brady does a bit more than cut grass and wash windows. But I can tell you're upset, so why don't we do this? Let me have a chat with Brady over the weekend. Maybe I'll try to get hold of him tonight. He's really a pretty reasonable and decent fellow. I'm sure he will bend over backward to accommodate you."

"Yes, I'm sure, but—"

"Gunn, trust me on this. Let me talk to him. He deserves that much. He's ten years on that property. Maybe more. But rest assured, if he gets out of line, he'll be gone. No one is going to throw my best salesman off-kilter."

● ● ●

GUNN STEWED all day Saturday. He barely uttered a word to his wife. His jealousy kept him at bay. He skulked around the mansion with his shoulders hunched and a nasty scowl on his face.

Reilly called back on Sunday afternoon. He and Gunn discussed Gunn's upcoming midwestern swing. Throughout the entire conversation Gunn waited for Reilly to say something about the caretaker. Gunn had seen neither hide nor hair of Brady the entire weekend.

Sam had not seen him either. Much to her relief, Brady had not appeared for his morning laps, suited or otherwise. But both Friday and Saturday night she had slept poorly, fearing the sound of an early A.M. splash. Probably his encounter with Gunn out by the garden had caused him to keep his distance.

Gunn could tell Mr. Reilly was getting ready to wind up their conversation, and without a word about Brady. He hesitated bringing the subject up himself. The other night he had very nearly made a jackass of himself, running off at the mouth the way he had. He did not intend to do that again. Still, he wanted to know if he could personally can the caretaker.

"Oh, Gunn, by the way," said Reilly, just as they were saying good-bye, "I spoke with Brady."

"Right," said Gunn. "I'd almost forgotten."

"Brady explained to me what happened."

"He explained?"

"Yes. He told me he fell asleep in the grass, I guess not too far from your wife, but he assured me it would certainly not happen again."

Gunn had to think fast. "There might be another side to the story, Mr. Reilly. There usually is."

"Oh, I'm sure there is, Gunn. But why don't we just chalk this one up to a misunderstanding."

"A misunderstanding?"

"Yes. I feel confident we can all get along."

"But, Mr. Reilly—"

"I think we should just leave it at that for now, Gunn. If he steps out of line again, we will have to take action. But personally I don't think there will be any more trouble. . . . Okay?"

Gunn had no choice. He did not want to push it. "Okay."

"Great. Now when are you flying out to Minneapolis?"

Gunn hesitated, then, "Tomorrow morning."

"Tomorrow morning? I thought you might be heading out tonight. Be ready to roll at first light."

"I have a six-forty-five flight out of La Guardia." Which meant he would have to be up and out of the house by four-thirty at the latest. Swell. "My first appointment is at eleven-fifteen."

"Waste of a good morning, Gunn. Waste of a good morning."

Gunn felt the need to explain. "I have meetings right into the evening."

"Okay, son, but let's stay on top of it."

"Absolutely."

"And Gunn?"

"Yes, sir?"

"Knock 'em dead. I'm counting on you. Creative Marketing is counting on you. Your wife and kids are counting on you."

22 So, did Brady show up Monday morning, after the family had scattered, gone their separate ways, for his daily swim? He certainly did. And right on time. Right around eight o'clock. Just as Sam began to pull the down comforter up over the bed. She jumped straight off the floor the instant Brady's body hit the water.

After debating the pros and cons, Sam slipped over to the window for a quick look. She assured herself this glimpse was simply to verify the caretaker's stripped appearance.

But the way she lingered brought some doubt upon this assurance. Yes, Samantha Ann Quincy Henderson took a leisurely look, long enough that she witnessed the platform diving as well as the swimming events. But then, with the exhibition obviously winding down, Sam turned away in anger. She was angry with herself, even if she directed her anger at the caretaker.

She dressed quickly and marched down the front stairs. The time had come to give this Mr. Brady . . . this Brady . . . a piece of her mind. She could not allow his behavior to continue for even one more minute. But by the time she exited the house and reached the pool, the caretaker had taken his leave. She spotted his wet footprints on the slate heading off in the direction of the tennis court.

Sam walked at a brisk clip past the tennis court, down the cinder path, and around the back of the barn. She pulled up in front of the garden. Several flats of tomato plants and pepper plants and various other vegetables in early stages of growth sat along the fence waiting to be planted. She wondered for just a moment how the plants had gotten there. But she knew the answer: she knew Brady was responsible.

Then she looked up and saw the caretaker, in the distance, across the expanse of grass, on his way to the boathouse. He had a towel wrapped around his waist. She set off after him, her pace a bit slowed by the appearance of all those fresh vegetables, of all that innate goodness. Still, her anger had not entirely dissipated; she fully intended to set things straight in regard to proper swimming pool etiquette and attire.

Brady disappeared through the door of the boathouse. A minute or more passed before Sam arrived. She pulled up short, took a deep breath, tried to calm her zealous heart, then she reached out and rapped on the door.

Brady pulled the door open within seconds. He had on a T-shirt and overalls, no shoes or socks yet. His brown hair was wet and slicked back.

"Mrs. Henderson!" He both looked and sounded surprised.

"Mr. Brady, I mean Brady, I'm sorry to bother you, but we need to talk. It won't take long."

Instead of inviting Sam inside, Brady stepped out, pulling the door closed behind him. "Yes, ma'am. If it's about the vegetables, I'm sorry I didn't consult with you on exactly what you wanted, but I was at the nursery yesterday so I took the liberty of picking up a few things. If there's anything else you—"

"Yes, Mr. Brady, thank you, I saw them, but—"

Brady smiled as he interrupted. "Just Brady will be fine, ma'am."

Sam was momentarily distracted by his shy smile, but she fought through it in an effort to make her long-overdue point. "Yes, Brady. I'm sure the vegetables you chose will be just fine. But it's not the vegetables I want to discuss."

"No? Well, the garden is ready to be planted. Just give me the word and I'll be at your service. We could start this morning. Or whenever you have some time. I thought about letting you know yesterday when I returned from the nursery, but I figured it was Sunday and you were probably busy with your family."

Sam sighed. "Don't worry about planting the vegetables, Brady. I can take care of it."

"You're mad at me for what happened Friday afternoon, aren't you, Mrs. Henderson? I apologize. I was out of line. I never should have—"

"I'm not mad at you for falling asleep, Brady."

"Your husband was mad."

"He got over it. Besides, he's always mad about something. Gunn's not happy unless he's mad at someone."

"He called Mr. Reilly."

This was news to Sam. "He did? About you?"

"Yes, ma'am. He wanted Mr. Reilly to fire me."

"What? When did this happen? I had no idea."

"Mr. Reilly called me Saturday night. He was kind of upset. He told me your husband told him that I'd been bothering you. I'm sorry, Mrs. Henderson, I was just trying to help."

Sam felt confused, and mildly light-headed. She wanted Brady to shut up, to give her a chance to talk. "Of course you were just trying to help, Brady. I know that. Gunn, my husband, he's the jealous type. He saw us sleeping in the grass and he right away got all bent out of shape, probably jumped to some ridiculous conclusions. I'll call Mr. Reilly right now and tell him that you did absolutely nothing wrong. I certainly do not want to be responsible for getting you fired."

"Mr. Reilly told me I could have another chance."

"Well, thank God this didn't escalate out of control."

"Yes, ma'am, I agree. I love this job. Now would

you please let me help you plant those tomatoes? It's the least I can do, ma'am."

• • •

BRADY GOT STARTED in the garden while Sam went back to the house, ate some breakfast, and changed into her work clothes. She assured herself several times that the swimming pool subject would be brought up before the sun went down on another day.

They worked together in the dirt for the rest of the morning. Brady, Sam soon found out, had gardening skills and knowledge superior to her own. She quickly acquiesced to his suggestions. He was extremely patient and meticulous in his methods. Sam was used to gardening with Gunn. Gunn hated getting his hands dirty and he always worked at a frenzied and agitated pace. In his mind, the sole objective of virtually all physical labor was to get finished as rapidly as possible. The idea that even some small morsel of satisfaction might be attained from the chore at hand never entered Gunn's mind. He was not a big believer in the ancient adage that established the journey firmly above the destination. Gunn wanted to eat luscious and tasty tomatoes. But he preferred to let somebody else do the dirty work.

Sam watched as Brady carefully removed one tiny plant at a time from the flat. He treated each plant with care and tenderness, as though that plant were a newborn baby. If the fresh young roots were knotted and bound together, Brady used his Swiss Army knife to gently trim them and cut them loose.

"A little extra time now," he told Sam, "will make for a much happier and therefore healthier plant later."

Then he looked at her, smiled shyly, and added, "And, of course, we will be the ones to ultimately reap the benefits when we sink our teeth into happier, healthier vegetables."

Sam loved this kind of talk. In her younger days, before she married Gunn, Sam had read a lot of Oriental philosophy in an effort to better understand her feelings and her surroundings. She had tasted bits and pieces of Taoism, Zen Buddhism, and Shintoism. The whole mysterious notion of happy, healthy vegetables reminded Sam of those days when she had been more in harmony with her inner self, more in touch with the world around her. She knelt there in the garden thinking she would like to get back to that place again.

Most of the time they worked in silence; Brady at one end of the garden, Sam at the other. She could feel him keeping his distance. He obviously did not want any more misunderstandings.

Each plant went in the ground with a pinch of nitrogen-rich compost made entirely from grass clippings, dead leaves, banana peels, potato skins, and other nonmeat food matter. Brady was a great believer in natural compost. He had a large compost heap, he told Sam, out behind the garage.

Next, the earth around the new plant was carefully tamped down using only the palms of their hands. And finally, the plant received a drink of water from a hose running at barely a trickle.

"We don't want anyone drowning today," Brady told Sam.

This notion of drowning caused Sam to think yet again about the swimming pool. She worked away for the next several minutes while wondering if the time had come to broach the touchy subject. Brady made the decision for her when he stood up, stretched his back, and told her he had some other duties to take care of, but that he would return later in the afternoon. He made no other explanation, just turned and departed.

Sam watched as he left the garden and headed for the boathouse. He went inside, and for the next half an hour or so he did not come out. Sam finally decided she needed a break also. She went back to the house for a sandwich and a glass of Mrs. Griner's mint-flavored iced tea.

After lunch she made some phone calls. Summer was fast approaching and several people had voiced interest in coming out to the Hamptons for a visit. Sam's calendar was quickly beginning to fill up with the names of impending visitors. She could hardly wait to see the faces of her family and friends when they pulled up the drive of PC Apple Acres and got a look at the new digs of Gunn and Samantha Henderson. They would be most impressed.

Of course, certain visitors, such as her mother and father (good, stiff Protestants from the Massachusetts Bay Colony), might not enjoy seeing the help skinny-dipping first thing in the morning. All the more reason why Sam needed to set Brady straight as soon as possible. She intended to do so as soon as she got back out to the garden.

And maybe she would have, but Brady was nowhere in sight. So Sam went back to work on her pepper plants. She worked into the late afternoon, slower than ever, because every few minutes she looked up in search of the caretaker. Finally, about four o'clock, her vigil paid off. She saw Brady come out through the boathouse door. She was surprised when he turned around, inserted a key into the door, and locked it.

Why, she wondered, would he do that? Mr. Duncan had assured her the neighborhood was extremely safe; rarely did they bother to even lock up the mansion. She decided Brady simply enjoyed his privacy; that was his business and really none of her concern. But then she wondered if he had been inside all afternoon. In the boathouse. Nearly four hours had passed since he'd left the garden. What could he have been doing inside all that time? Shouldn't he have been out cutting grass or pruning shrubs or dragging the tennis court? But again, Sam decided this was no concern of hers. She was not Brady's boss. She really had no idea what Brady's responsibilities were at PC Apple Acres. She liked Brady; she just wanted him to stop swimming naked in the pool. At least she thought she wanted him to stop swimming naked in the pool.

Brady reached the garden. "Mrs. Henderson, you've almost finished with the planting. It looks great. I think, with a little care, we will have an excellent harvest."

Sam decided to push ahead, not to get bogged down. "Mr. Brady . . . I'm sorry, I mean, Brady?"

"Yes, ma'am."

Sam thought about reminding him to please call her Sam or Samantha, but she did not want to get off track. "Brady . . . it's come to my attention that you, well, that you like to swim."

"Yes, ma'am, I do. Very much. It's excellent exercise. It works all the major muscle groups, gets the heart pumping, and it's great for my lower back trouble."

Sam could see them beginning to drift, but lower back trouble was a big part of her life, what with Gunn occasionally suffering for a week or more with severe pain and spasms. He could be most unpleasant during these episodes, like a wounded grizzly in a bear trap, screaming and growling, making demands. Sam would do just about anything to make sure Gunn never suffered with a back injury again.

"You have lower back trouble?"

"Yes, ma'am," Brady lied. "Scoliosis. That's a fancy name for curvature of the spine. Mine's pretty well twisted. It can give me a bad time if I don't keep close tabs on it. Every day I do these special exercises to keep my back limber and my abdominal muscles firm." In fact, Brady had an exceptionally strong and healthy back. No problems whatsoever.

True enough, Sam thought, Brady has excellent abs. She wanted to hear all about his exercises. Maybe she could get Gunn to try them. But no, the exercises would have to wait; she needed to stay the course.

"So swimming is good for your lower back?"

"It's perfect. No pressure on the back or the hips or the buttocks or the thighs. In the water you're virtually weightless."

Now's the time, Sam decided, to broach with a joke. "So is that why you swim naked? To make yourself even lighter?"

Brady glanced at her, then his eyes shifted directly to the ground. He blushed deeply, nearly to the color of the beefsteak tomatoes that later in the summer would hang on the vines inside the garden.

Sam, her maternal instincts twitching, had no choice but to immediately reassure him. "It's okay, Brady. Really. I want you to use the pool. I just think it would be better for all concerned if you wore a suit."

Brady kept his eyes down. "Mrs. Henderson, I'm so embarrassed. I—"

"It's okay. Really."

"I had no idea you knew. I thought . . . God, Mr. Reilly will definitely fire me now."

Sam did her best to laugh. "No one's going to fire you, Brady. No one's going to hear a word about this. At least not from me."

Brady gave her assurances some thought. Then, "Mrs. Henderson, I would be forever in your debt if we could keep this quiet."

Sam nodded. "I think it's best if we just pretend the whole business never happened."

Brady lifted his head long enough to make split-second eye contact with Sam. "Again, Mrs. Henderson, let me apologize. I had no idea you were aware of my presence in the pool."

This time Sam laughed for real. "Brady, I don't mean to be facetious, but you were difficult to miss."

Brady took a deep breath. He again made eye contact, albeit briefly. "But I always waited until after you left. I always—"

"After I left? For where?"

"For school. And I always made sure I was out of the pool and gone before you returned home."

Sam looked confused. "What school are you talking about, Brady? I never go anywhere first thing in the morning."

Brady looked more than confused; he looked

shocked. "You mean you've been home all these mornings? But I thought you went in the limousine when Jason and Megan were taken to school?"

"In the limousine?"

"Yes."

"No, never."

"My God! I feel like such an idiot. All this time I thought you went with them. I didn't think for a second you were even in the mansion at eight o'clock in the morning."

Sam felt an incredible sensation of relief. The entire issue was nothing but another stupid misunderstanding. Which made sense. Brady always came for his swim soon after Jason and Megan departed for school, soon after the limousine pulled out the driveway. So he'd made a mistake. Everyone makes mistakes. She had feared he was simply rude and inconsiderate. Traits the rest of his behavior did not support.

"Believe me, Mrs. Henderson," Brady said, "I won't go anywhere near that pool again."

"Don't be ridiculous, Brady."

"I'll swim somewhere else."

"You'll swim in the pool."

"No, I'll swim in the Sound."

"The Sound is freezing."

"It'll warm up."

"No," Sam insisted, "I definitely want you to use the swimming pool. You are a wonderful swimmer . . ." She hesitated, but then it came out: all the evidence either of them needed to know she had indeed been watching from her bedroom window. ". . . And an excellent diver." Then, hastily, she added, "I just want you to wear a suit."

Head still down, Brady assured her he would. "I don't think you need to worry about that anymore, ma'am."

Only later, back at the house, waiting for her children to arrive home from school, did a moment of doubt creep into Sam's thoughts. The doubt arose from Brady's appearance in the kitchen last Friday morning. He had been there, drinking coffee at the kitchen table, when she'd come downstairs. How, she wondered, could he have thought she was in the limousine with the kids if she had been upstairs?

But what, really, she asked herself, did this one small point, this one minor inconsistency, prove? It was not Brady's job to keep track of her comings and goings. He thought she was out of the house in the morning, driving to school with Jason and Megan. That was his perfectly reasonable explanation. An explanation that was good enough for Sam. After all, he hadn't been out there swimming in the buff over the weekend when he knew everyone was home. And besides, the matter had now been discussed and resolved. The subject was closed. Brady, Sam felt sure, would from now on wear a bathing suit. He was a good man, an honest man. She looked forward to seeing him around the grounds as spring slid into summer.

23 Summer arrived. School ended. The kids gained their freedom.

Sam was excited and elated, but she also had mixed feelings about Jason and Megan being home all day. She was happy to have them around, filling the vast house with their energy and their young voices. Their presence cut easily through the loneliness that had started to creep into her mornings.

But because they went to school so far away, Jason and Megan had not really made any friends in the neighborhood. They therefore had to rely on each other for companionship. This inevitably meant trouble. They had the ability to play together nicely for only so long. Then the fighting would begin. Jason would get bored with the friendly big brother act, so he would tease his little sister and push her around until she cried. And boy, could Megan cry. Her screams would rattle the walls of that mansion. Then Sam would have to come running, the cavalry to the rescue. She would yell at Jason. He would deny all accusations. Sometimes he would become downright belligerent; the "F word" had suddenly become one of his favorites. Sam would have no choice but to slap him a good one across the behind. This would bring Jason immediately to tears, and then both kids would be rattling the walls with their torments. Peace and harmony shattered.

By the first of July, Sam was beginning to wonder how they would survive the summer. She did her best to keep them occupied, but there were simply too many hours in the day. Jason demanded constant stimulation. Sam suggested wilderness camp, but Gunn, from some motel in Arkansas, nixed the idea. He insisted PC Apple Acres was a privileged wilderness camp and the boy could damn well find something useful to do besides beat up his little sister.

Brady, of all people, saved the day. It started out by the swimming pool. The children were swimming. Sam acted as lifeguard, but mostly she concentrated on a gardening book she had found in the library. The book, oddly enough, was by a man named Brady. It contained the most beautiful color photographs of roses and peonies and geraniums and all different varieties of flowers. Sam had her eyes glued to a full-page shot of a giant purple tulip, when suddenly she heard Megan scream. A normal scream would not have caused Sam to do more than stir, but this scream came very close to sounding like a shriek. The gardening book went flying into the air, and in a flash Sam had her body off the chaise longue and on the move. Megan lay on the brick walk on the far side of the pool. She was into a full-fledged howl.

And Jason? He was already on the hoof, sprinting at full speed in the direction of the rose garden.

"Jason!" his mother shouted, even as she made haste to her sobbing daughter's side. "Get back here!"

Jason was not a stupid child. He had no intention of returning to the scene of the crime. He might take some lumps for thumping his sister as she climbed out of the pool, but those lumps would come somewhere down the road. Jason believed firmly in putting punishment off for as long as possible. So the lad kept right on running, through the trellis and into the rose garden.

Sam knelt at Megan's side. The little girl's sobs had not subsided. Sam soon found out why. Megan's knee and shin were gashed and bleeding where the leg had made contact with the concrete edge of the pool.

"Jason," Sam screamed again. She loved her son, but she became furious with him when he mistreated his little sister. He was a bully, just like his father was a bully.

Sam held her daughter against her breast, stroked her long coppery hair, and assured her everything would be all right. Once she had Megan reasonably calm, she eased the girl to her feet. "Come on, sweetie, let's go inside and clean this up. We'll make it all better."

Megan, sobbing and trying to get her breath, allowed her mother to steer her toward the house. The duo did not get very far.

"Mrs. Henderson, ma'am, not to bother you, but I thought I heard you calling for this green recruit."

Sam turned around. And there stood Brady, framed by the rose-covered trellis. He held Jason by the scruff of his neck.

"Let me go!" the boy demanded.

Brady ignored him. "I found him tearing through the rose garden, trying to escape. What would you like done with him?"

"Throw him in the dungeon!" shouted Sam.

"No," demanded Megan, "throw him to the wolves."

"I said," screamed Jason, "let me go!"

"The dungeon sounds a might damp, ma'am," said Brady. "And the wolves a bit gruesome. But if I could make a suggestion?"

"Anything."

"Well, just passing by the house from time to time in the past week or so has led me to suspect that young Jason here gives his little sister a pretty rough time on a regular basis."

"Several assaults every day."

"Yeah!" agreed Megan, whose eyes had finally started to dry. "He beats me up all the time!"

"I know a thing or two about big brothers," lied Brady, who, in fact, had grown up with two sisters, one older and one younger, "having had one myself, and I know one of the big reasons they pick on the younger ones is because they get bored, and when they get bored they get ornery, and when they get ornery they often get mean."

"All true," agreed Sam.

"So the key is to keep this young buck from getting bored."

Jason did his best to break loose, but Brady's hand gripped his neck like a vise.

"And how do we do that?" the boy's mother wanted to know.

"Only one way," said Brady.

"Which way is that?" asked Sam.

"We put him to work."

"Work?" queried Jason, the word like an evil curse upon his tongue.

"Work?" questioned Sam.

"That's right, ma'am: work. Good, hard, honest work. Cures most all the ills that plague mankind."

● ● ●

SO BRADY put Jason to work, with Sam's blessing. Jason fought tooth and nail against the sentence, insisting he would tell his father and his father would beat up everyone in sight. Gunn's possible reaction had indeed been of some concern to Sam, but in the end she felt something had to be done or Jason might maim Megan before summer gave way to fall and the pair went back to their private school.

The promise of three dollars and fifty cents an hour put an end to Jason's protests. Like his daddy, the boy loved money. But this hefty wage for such a young whippersnapper came with a few strings attached. Every time Jason swore, he would be docked an hour's pay. Every time he hit his little sister or abused her in any way, he would be docked two hours' pay. If he made her cry or bleed, three hours' pay. And if he became ugly, belligerent, or rude to his boss or to his mother, he would forfeit a whole day's wages.

Much to his mother's amazement, Jason liked working. Probably he enjoyed the structure. But also, Brady made it entertaining. When the time came to mow the fields, Brady taught Jason how to operate the tractor and the brush hog. Brady could see Jason liked the power equipment, so he showed the boy how to clean the filters and change the oil and tighten the fan belts.

And then, when the novelty of lawn work began to fade, Brady took Jason down to the boathouse. The boy's eyes grew wide with wonder the moment he walked into that watery garage. Four bays wide the boathouse was, and every bay filled with recreational vessels. A whole new world of sights and smells greeted Jason's senses: not just the boats but the oars, the sails, the motors, the gasoline, the oil, the leather, the wet canvas.

Brady put Jason to work cleaning and polishing. As a reward for a job well done, Brady would hand Jason the oars so he could row the dory, or a paddle so he could take a spin in one of the kayaks. These simple self-powered craft, along with the canoe and the rubber dingy, kept the boy occupied for a couple of weeks. But, as Brady knew the lad would, young Henderson soon turned his attention to the power craft. That brand-new pair of Kawasaki Jet Skis floating in the far bay looked especially interesting to Jason. He eventually got up the nerve to ask Brady if he could take one for a spin. Jason had come to view Brady as a pretty cool guy by this time, casual and laid-back, nothing like his uptight, high-strung parents. Brady just kind of floated through the day; nothing seemed to bother him. Jason thought he probably smoked dope. He had seen some kids at school smoking dope, and he figured he might want to try it before long. Maybe he would ask Brady if he could get him some.

"Listen, kid," said Brady, "I'd show you how to operate the Jet Ski and turn you loose in a second, but

I can't do it. Your parents would hand me my head on a silver platter."

"My parents suck."

"You just lost an hour's pay."

"Brady!"

"Them's the rules, dude."

"But *suck* isn't even a swear word."

"Is in my book. Look, kid, most anything goes around here, but violence and profanity don't work for me."

Jason moped, but swiftly recovered. "So what about the Jet Ski?"

"I said no way."

"What about we take them out together?"

"No problem. But Mom and Dad will have to give their okay. Those babies are fast. And dangerous. You have to be careful. And my gut tells me that you're a wild and reckless kind of guy."

Jason had never thought of himself as wild or reckless, but he liked the sound of it, liked thinking of himself as a wild man. He couldn't wait to get one of those babies out on the water. He would make it fly.

"So if I get their permission, you'll go out with me?"

"Absolutely."

That night at dinner Jason started hounding his mother. As adolescent and preadolescent males are prone to do, Jason stretched the truth some in an effort to get what he wanted.

"Mom, Brady says tomorrow I can take out one of the Jet Skis."

"He does, huh?"

"Yeah."

"And what's a Jet Ski?"

"It's this thing you ride around on the water."

"What kind of thing?"

"It's no big deal. It's just this little boat."

"What kind of little boat?"

Megan answered that one. "A fast little boat."

"Shut up, big mouth!"

"Don't tell your sister to shut up."

Jason decided it would be wise to apologize, so he did.

"That's better," said his mother. "Now what about this Jet Ski?"

Jason gave his little sister a look that said she'd be smart to keep her trap shut, then he turned to his mother. "It's just this little one-man powerboat."

Sam did not like the sound of the word *power*. The kid should have left that one off his description.

"No powerboating," said Sam, "without your father. You can just wait until he gets home this weekend. He can decide whether or not you can operate this Jet Ski thing."

Jason battled and whined the rest of the way through dinner, but Sam would not budge. "You can use the canoe till Saturday. No motors."

To enforce her decree, Sam informed Brady first thing in the morning that Jason was not, under any circumstances, to use any boats with motors until he had his father's permission.

24 Gunn arrived home from Nevada late Friday afternoon. He had spent his week pushing The Disk, or at least the idea of The Disk, in such provocative burgs as Ruth, Cherry Creek, Palisade, Battle Mountain, and Lovelock. He had finished up his swing in Reno.

Gunn Henderson was a bad boy in Reno. In town less than twelve hours, asleep half of those, he nevertheless managed to commit two of the seven deadly sins in that brief snippet of time. First he lost five hundred bucks playing blackjack, then he had sex with a woman who was definitely not his wife.

Was this woman a whore? No shortage of whores in Reno, but she did not demand payment from Gunn for her quick turn between his sheets.

The situation unfolded something like this: Gunn dropped the five hundred in a little under an hour, then he retired to the bar to nurse his ego. After his first Beefeater and tonic, a decent-looking brunette wearing a short skirt and a low-cut silk blouse sat down all alone a few stools away. She ordered a glass of champagne, then, when the bartender brought the bubbly, she told him the roulette wheel had been kind enough to pay her almost one thousand dollars in a couple of lucky spins. The bartender, a big burly guy with a ponytail and several hoop earrings, who sometimes earned as much as four hundred bucks a night in tips, congratulated the brunette on her winnings. He right away hoped to see some of that money come his way. It would help line his coffers for that double-wide trailer he had his eye on out in the desert south of town.

Gunn ordered another Beefeater and tonic, then he turned to the brunette and offered his congratulations also. She smiled, polished off her champagne, and said thanks.

Gunn thought, oh, what the hell, and asked her if he could buy her another glass. It had been a long week.

"You married?" the brunette asked.

"Yes, I am," Gunn answered, after only the briefest hesitation.

"Good," said the brunette. "Because tonight I'm definitely not looking for any long-term commitments."

The bartender overheard all this, and because he was kind of an angry and sullen guy, like a lot of guys, he made Gunn's drink with the cheap gin rather than the good stuff because he had the dude in the slick suit pegged as a chump who wouldn't know the difference.

He was right. Gunn did not know the difference, didn't have a clue. Gunn ordered the expensive stuff because ordering the expensive stuff made him feel important and sophisticated.

Gunn pretty much poured that second gin and tonic down his throat in one greedy gulp. With thoughts of infidelity dancing around in his head, he needed something to ease his conscience.

Gunn and the brunette sat cozied up to that Nevada bar, side by side. They talked a few things over: Reno, the weather, the joys of gambling. Their exchange was strained and not particularly witty. After his third and her fourth, they retired to his room. Things did not go real well up there, either. The guilt and the booze made Gunn a very limp lover.

To his surprise, the brunette, whose name he never learned, hung around for quite a while anyway trying to get a rise out of him. And finally, after much pulling and prodding, she did. Within just a few frenzied minutes they both had an orgasm, although the brunette's was entirely phony. She had not been in the least bit erotically aroused.

She hung around in bed for eight or nine minutes afterward, cooing and stroking, then she got up and pulled on her skirt and blouse. Just before leaving, she walked over and gave Gunn a peck on the cheek. "God," she whispered in his ear, "you were great. What a night! First I win a thousand bucks, then I run into a stud like you."

She turned and swept out of the room without another word. Gunn suspected a touch of sarcasm in her voice, but his opinion of himself was far too lofty to let that sarcasm stick in his craw. Moments later he fell sound asleep, a satisfied man.

Gunn may not have slept quite so soundly had he seen what took place down in the bar soon after he closed his eyes. The brunette sat alone in a booth enjoying yet another glass of champagne. She loved champagne. It made her feel tipsy and giggly and dizzy.

A man joined her. He wore an inexpensive blue suit and a fedora like the kind men used to wear back in the forties. He had the fedora pulled down so it covered his eyes.

"How did it go?"

The brunette smiled at him. "No problem. A piece of cake."

"He bought the setup?"

"Absolutely."

"No troubles at all?"

She thought about the mark's erection, or lack thereof. "None at all."

"How did he seem? Cooperative? Reluctant?"

"What do I look like? A fucking shrink? He seemed like a horny guy who wanted to get laid and couldn't believe his great good fortune running into a beautiful and willing lady like me."

"Okay. So you left him happy?"

"I doubt he'll file any complaints with the sex police."

The man in the fedora nodded, took an envelope out of his jacket pocket, and slid it across the table. Before the brunette had a chance to even pick the envelope up, the man stood, turned, and left the bar.

The brunette opened the envelope and pulled out the contents: ten crisp one-hundred-dollar bills. The roulette wheel might have been a fake, but this was the real thing. All in a night's work. Another day on the job. She smiled again and sipped her champagne.

25 Sure, Gunn felt guilty. A little bit anyway. Enough to give it some thought. He did not enjoy cheating on his wife, but God, it wasn't like he had been in love with the bimbo or anything. He just had a quick roll in the hay. Another form of physical exercise, like tennis or running or squash. It happened every now and then, maybe two or three times a year. It went with the territory, always being on the road. Hell, a little extracurricular sexual activity was practically part of the traveling salesman's job description.

He drove away his guilt by being extra especially nice to his wife and kids all weekend long. He was even pleasant and charming to Sam's ditzy friend Mandy and her goofy husband, Tad, and their two silent, humorless brats, Tad Jr. and Danielle. The Greers arrived early Saturday morning with enough gear, Gunn thought, to pass the rest of the summer. Actually, they only planned to stay for a week. Which was just fine with Gunn. Come Monday morning he would be back on the road, someplace decent for a change: northern California and Oregon.

Saturday afternoon Gunn agreed to give the Jet Skis

a go. Jason had been bugging him ever since he'd walked through the front door the night before. So he and Jason and Tad and Tad Jr. all headed down to the boathouse after a fine lunch out by the swimming pool. They found Brady tinkering with the huge Chrysler inboard on the old mahogany runabout.

Gunn moved directly onto the offensive. "Brady, we want to give those Jet Skis a run. Are they fueled and ready to go?"

Brady, his face hidden beneath the engine cover, allowed himself a slight smile. So the man wanted to treat him like a servant. He could handle that. That was not a problem. In fact, he rather enjoyed it. He ceased his labors and wiped the grease off his hands. "Yes, sir, Mr. Henderson, they should be all ready."

Gunn brushed past Brady without saying another word. He led his small troupe to the end of the boathouse where the two Jet Skis bobbed on the water in the far bay.

Brady thought about remaining silent, but decided to allow himself one small jab. "Mr. Henderson, sir, would you like a quick overview of the STX's controls and operation?"

The question did not please Gunn. Actually, it very much displeased him. Not only did Gunn loathe instruction of any kind, but instruction from the goddamn caretaker? "I don't think so, Brady."

Brady went back to tinkering with his engine. He knew it was just a matter of time.

Gunn hopped aboard one of the Jet Skis. He had been on a Jet Ski once, several years ago, when he and Sam had spent a week in Jamaica. Nothing to it: turn the key, wind the throttle. So that's what he did. Unfortunately, not much happened. Just a few clicks. He took a look at the controls, found nothing else that needed doing, gave the key another turn. Still nothing. He shrugged. "I don't know. Sounds to me like maybe the battery's dead."

"Try the other one, Dad."

Gunn climbed aboard the other Jet Ski. Same outcome.

Jason said, "Let me ask Brady."

"Wait a second," insisted his father. "I'm sure it's no big deal. We can figure it out."

Tad and Tad Jr. stood up on the dock. They did not really care if the Jet Skis started or not. Neither was particularly fond of loud, high-pitched engines or harsh noises of any kind. They would have preferred to take a spin in one of the sailboats.

Gunn, however, was not into wind power; he preferred horsepower. Vast quantities of horsepower running at high rpm's. But first he had to get the damn thing running. He did his best to maintain a cool facade, but inside the gears were beginning to grind.

Then his kid said, "I'll get Brady. He's a whiz with this kind of stuff."

Gunn tried to stop him, but too late. Brady came right over. Without uttering a word, the caretaker climbed aboard the Jet Ski not occupied by Gunn Henderson. He reached down underneath the console, flipped the safety switch, pulled out the choke, and turned the key. Instantly the motor turned over and the engine began to idle. Slowly Brady pushed in the choke. "They run better if you let them warm up for a few minutes."

"Christ," grumbled Gunn, "how did you get that damn thing started?"

"You have to make sure the safety switch is down. Then choke it."

Gunn mumbled an obscenity under his breath.

Brady ignored him. He climbed back onto the dock and handed out the life jackets. Jason, Tad, and Tad Jr. willingly put on the jackets. Gunn insisted he did not need one. Brady told him the United States Coast Guard required the use of life jackets by all persons when operating gasoline-powered equipment on the open water.

Gunn got right up in Brady's face and said, not all that quietly, "Fuck the United States Coast Guard, pal."

So, that situation cleared up, the Hendersons and the Greers set out on their Jet Skiing adventure. Gunn and Jason went together on one craft, while Tad and Tad Jr., somewhat reluctantly, ventured out on the other one. Gunn drove the good ship Henderson first. He wanted to show his boy how to handle the vessel.

Gunn steered straight for open water, passing through as quickly as possible the small inlet that protected the boathouse and the stretch of sandy beach from the harsh northwesterly winds that often blew across Long Island Sound. The Greers followed at a far more conservative pace. Gunn showed Jason how to speed up and slow down using the throttle, how to stop, how to steer. "Not much to it," he assured his son, "but I want you to take it easy. Especially at first."

After a few minutes father and son switched places. Jason took the controls. He proved a little twitchy on the throttle, and he tended to oversteer, but otherwise he caught on pretty fast. He kept asking his father if he could go faster, increase their speed.

"A little bit," Gunn kept telling him. "A little at a time."

Pretty soon Jason had that Jet Ski zipping along the surface of the water, bouncing and banging over the small swells. The Henderson ship kept running circles around the Greer ship. Tad Jr. had declined to take the controls, and Tad Sr. was plenty happy just puttering along not much above an idle.

Back at the boathouse, Brady had finished tuning the inboard. He had the engine cover back in place and all of his tools stored away. He was a methodical and tidy mechanic. His work done, he cleaned his hands, then climbed the steep set of stairs to his living quarters. A locked door was unlocked with a key he kept in his pocket. The door opened out onto a wide deck overlooking the water. The deck provided a beautiful view of the inlet and Shelter Island Sound beyond. A pair of high-powered binoculars sat on a glass table situated in the middle of the deck. Brady picked up the binoculars, brought them up to his face, and peered through the expensive glass. It took a moment or so, but soon he found the Hendersons. Young Jason was still at the helm. No good. Brady wanted the boy's old man back at the controls. The boy would not do. Too risky. Brady just wanted to terrorize, not maim or kill.

So like a big cat on the prowl, the caretaker waited. He had developed incredible powers of concentration over the course of his adult life. Given the proper stimulus, he could keep his mind focused for hours on end. Gunn Henderson was all the stimulation Brady needed.

For almost twenty minutes he stood perfectly still up on that deck. The only thing that moved was his head as he followed the course of that Jet Ski through the binoculars. Brady knew Gunn Henderson would have another go at the controls. No way would he return to shore without first spinning a few circles around that dullard, Tad Greer.

And sure enough, Brady watched closely as Gunn tapped his boy on the shoulder. The time had come to once again switch positions. Gunn got behind the controls and jacked the throttle. He did a few 360's to show Tad Greer how a real man handled a Jet Ski. Gunn also knew the women would be coming down to watch from the dock, so he wanted to put on a show, just in case they had arrived.

And right on cue, there they were: Sam and Mandy and Megan and Danielle, all lined up on the dock below Brady's perch. Brady felt confident they could not see him, but he nevertheless stayed motionless and silent.

Gunn showed off for a good ten minutes, circling and zipping through his own wake, but finally he had enough. He turned the Jet Ski around and made a beeline for the boathouse.

Brady calculated Gunn's distance offshore at approximately half a mile. He waited seven seconds before he calmly reached down and picked up the remote control device resting on the glass table. The device was about the size of a paperback book. On its front console it had several switches and two large black dials. A flexible antenna protruded from the top. Binoculars still in place, Brady switched on the remote control device with his free hand. A red light blinked on the console.

The Jet Ski moved closer, perhaps a quarter of a mile now straight out from the boathouse. Brady saw it begin to slow. He put down the binoculars and stepped to the front of the deck. Directly below, the female contingent had all eyes focused on the action out beyond the inlet. Brady held the remote control device out in front of him with the antenna pointed directly at the Jet Ski. He flipped a few switches and slowly began to turn one of the large black dials.

Immediately, the Jet Ski began to pick up speed. At first Gunn Henderson looked confused. But his confusion quickly gave way to concern, and then to panic. Brady watched as Gunn tried to slow his machine as it sped across the water on a direct course for the boathouse dock. Gunn's right hand frantically jerked the throttle back and forth. His left hand tried in vain to turn the Jet Ski off, to cut the power.

Brady turned up the dial a bit further. The Jet Ski increased its speed even more. Brady could now see Gunn screaming over his shoulder at his son. He could not actually hear Gunn's words over the whine of the engine, but it did not take a rocket scientist to know that "Abandon ship!" or something along those lines was spilling from Gunn's mouth.

Below, the women had started to panic, too. Samantha looked visibly shaken. "My God, what is he doing? He's so close! Why doesn't he slow down or turn around?"

And then they all watched as Sam's young son threw himself off the back of that Jet Ski. Gunn fol-

lowed close behind. Brady felt a small twinge of satisfaction as the two bodies bounced and skidded along
the smooth surface of the inlet. The Hendersons, father
and son, Brady knew, would be plenty sore, but otherwise okay. The Jet Ski had not been traveling that fast.
With another turn of the dial he could have made it go
much, much faster. Of course, the speed had seemed
incredibly fast to Gunn and Jason, what with land
looming less than a hundred yards in the distance.

Brady slowed the Jet Ski as soon as the Hendersons
hit the water. Then, when it neared the boathouse, he
flipped off all the switches. He watched as the Jet Ski
slowed to an idle and began to circle. Circling was its
normal operation whenever the driver wound up in the
drink.

Gunn and Jason slowly swam toward shore. Below,
the panic-stricken wife and mother breathed a trembling sigh of relief.

Brady put away his remote control device and went
downstairs. "I saw what happened from up above," he
said to Sam. "Is everyone all right?"

Sam had her arms wrapped around her little girl.
Both looked pale and anxious. "I hope so."

"They must be okay," said Brady. "They're both
swimming."

"Gunn must've had some kind of mechanical problem."

"Come on," said Brady, "let's go see."

They all walked quickly to the end of the dock.
Gunn and Jason reached the dock at the same time.
Brady helped Jason out of the water. The boy, visibly
upset, went straight to his mother. She hugged him to
her breast.

Gunn insisted on getting out of the water on his own.

Next came Tad Sr. and Tad Jr. Tad Sr. puttered up to the dock and cut the engine. Brady helped them disembark. The caretaker tied the Jet Ski off to a piling. "So," he asked, "is everyone okay?"

Jason and Tad and Tad Jr. nodded. Not so Gunn. He looked ready to blow. His face was flushed red with anger and embarrassment. And even redder were his chest and his abdomen where he had made contact with the water after abandoning ship.

Too bad, thought Brady, a life jacket would have prevented that.

"Goddammit to hell, Brady! Did you see what happened out there? My son and I were almost killed! What the hell went wrong with that damn machine of yours!"

Brady stayed calm. He paused for just a moment, then he shrugged and shook his head. "I saw you coming in, sir. It looked like you had a bit too much speed."

"Too much speed!" Gunn lost it. "Fuck you, too much speed!"

The Tad Greers glanced at one another. And then, in unison, they cupped their hands over the ears of their offspring.

And a good thing too, for Gunn Henderson had more to say. "The son-of-a-bitching machine has something wrong with it! The throttle must be broken. The piece of shit wouldn't slow down. It almost killed both of us, for chrissakes! Isn't it your job to keep this stuff maintained?"

"Yes, sir, it is," answered Brady. "But I can assure

you, Mr. Henderson, these machines are practically brand-new. Not more than a dozen hours of use on either one of them. They haven't been troublesome before."

"Well, they're troublesome now, goddammit!"

"I'm sorry about this, sir." Brady sounded downright conciliatory. But then, in the next breath, he asked this question. "Are you sure you know how to operate the craft safely, sir? I only ask because, well, sir, because you showed some inexperience earlier when first trying to get the craft up and running."

Gunn just about took a swing at the caretaker. Only the presence of his wife and kids and friends held him back. "Okay, Brady, you know so damn much—let's see you take that piece of shit for a spin around the bay."

In his wildest dreams Brady could not have asked for a better response from his adversary. He did not hesitate. He pulled off his boots, his socks, his overalls, and his T-shirt. Beneath his overalls, to Sam's astonishment, Brady had on a swimsuit, one of those tight little spandex jobs, not much more fabric than a jockstrap. It looked brand-new.

Brady paused for a just a second or two at the end of the dock. All eyes took a gander at his long, lean, muscular frame. Then, satisfied, he bent his knees and launched himself into the air. He made a shallow racer's dive into the water and came up stroking hard. His powerful crawl had him out to the still-circling Jet Ski in a flash. He climbed aboard, checked the controls, and revved the throttle. The Jet Ski raced forward. Brady put the craft through its paces right there in the inlet, right in front of the Hendersons and the Greers. He accelerated and decelerated, he did circles and figure eights, he handled that machine with skill and consummate precision.

Finally, after five or six infinitely long minutes, Brady brought the machine back to the dock. He made a soft landing against the bulkhead and cut the engine. "I see what you mean, sir," he said without hesitation. "That throttle does seem to be sticking just a bit. The cable might have stretched. I'll take care of it immediately."

Perfect silence on the dock. No one moved or said a word. Everyone waited for Gunn's response. All those present fully expected big bad Gunn to explode. Sam especially. She had her arms around her children. She held them close.

But Gunn Henderson found himself in a quandary. He did not know what to do. While awaiting the caretaker's return, Gunn had fortified himself with several lines of attack. But when the caretaker acknowledged Gunn's assessment of the situation, Gunn found himself speechless. The caretaker had given Gunn an out. Gunn thought it over and decided to take it.

"Good," said Gunn Henderson, "you do that. And do it now. We certainly don't need anyone getting injured around here."

Then Gunn turned away from the caretaker and led his wife and kids and guests from the boathouse. Gunn did not like the caretaker, this Brady. He had every intention of exacting some form of revenge against the caretaker at the earliest possible opportunity. Exactly when and precisely how would need to be determined, but in Gunn's mind anyway, the deed was as good as done.

Nobody fucks with Gunn Henderson, was Gunn Henderson's thought as he marched away from the boathouse. And those who do, pay.

26 The mansion was filled with guests all summer long. Every old acquaintance from even way back when came crawling out of the woodwork once word spread the Hendersons had themselves some fancy digs out in East Hampton. Sometimes there were people sitting around the breakfast table Sam had never laid eyes on before.

More than once she had to answer the question, "Who are you?"

And once when she answered, "Gunn's wife," the questioner asked, "And who, perchance, is Gunn?"

Sam hated to do it, the man seemed pleasant enough and he had excellent table manners, but really she had very little choice. After all, she had young children wandering around the house. The man could be a psychopath or a child molester or a kidnapper. So Sam let the man finish his coffee and croissant, then she politely asked him to leave. He went without debate, smiling and thanking everyone as he headed for the front door.

Friends came. Parents came. Siblings came. Aunts and uncles, nephews and nieces came. They all came and, of course, all they wanted to do was play. They were on vacation. They didn't want to do any work. They wanted to hang around the pool and swim and play tennis and drink gin and eat Mrs. Griner's endless platters of tasty hors d'oeuvres.

After a while Sam became quite sick and tired of having visitors in her house all the time. It seemed like all she ever did was work. Even with Mrs. Griner in the kitchen and Saida doing her best to keep the big house clean and the beds made, Sam put in several hours a day simply trying to keep the whole enterprise running in a reasonably smooth and orderly manner. Almost every day she had to run out to the market for something: milk, bread, butter. And at least twice a week she had to go out and do a major shopping in order to keep the shelves stocked. She was spending three and four hundred dollars a week on food and drink and paper products. Not that her guests noticed. They were too busy having a good time on the beaches and the golf courses to pay attention to the labors of their hostess. Besides, they figured anyone with the dough to live in such a fancy mansion no doubt had the funds to keep it running in first-class fashion.

But the fact was this: Gunn gave his wife just four thousand a month from the nearly twenty grand he received in salary. Sure, four G's is nothing to sneeze at, but it goes fast when you're spending fifteen hundred of it on laundry soap and paper towels.

One afternoon, it must have been the middle of August, Sam loaded herself into the Explorer and drove into town. Two of Gunn's sisters and their husbands and their kids were visiting. They consumed more food than a small army.

Sometimes she drove all the way up to Riverhead where there was a large supermarket that had relatively reasonable prices. But with summer traffic, the trip to Riverhead could consume most of a day. So usually she just went into the A&P in East Hampton where the prices were inflated almost beyond reason. Three bags of groceries could easily suck two hundred dollars out of her wallet. A gallon of premium orange juice was six dollars, a small bunch of grapes five dollars, a head of broccoli three ninety-nine. And, of course, the long narrow aisles were jam-packed with happy and smiling vacationers in their swimsuits and tennis togs and biking shorts who seemed positively joyous at the prospect of spending seven dollars and forty-nine cents a pound for scrawny-looking chicken cutlets.

Sam vowed she would not allow this to happen again next summer. Next summer would be different. Next summer she would limit the number of visitors, control the duration of their stays, and inform all upon arrival that meals were a luxury, not a privilege, at PC Apple Acres.

Of course, Sam might think these thoughts but she would never actually be able to find the courage to implement them. She was a kind, softhearted, and generous person who loved to please and make people happy. Thoughts of cracking the whip slipped into her brain, but an enormous abyss separated Sam's thoughts from her actions.

She loaded the groceries into the Explorer and steered for home. Traffic along Main Street was clogged, as usual, with what seemed like every motorized vehicle in the state of New York. It took her almost fifteen minutes to creep less than half a mile to her turn for home. Once off the main drag, traffic began to thin. By the time she reached Old Northwest Road, it had virtually disappeared. Sam hit the gas. She longed to get back, finish her chores, and relax, maybe take a swim or just lie in the sun. But near the corner of Old Northwest and Mile Hill Road, she heard a sudden explosion. One of her tires had gone flat. She swore under her breath and pulled off the road. A flat tire was more than Sam wanted to deal with at this point. She sighed, climbed out of the Explorer, and slammed the door. Both front tires looked fine, but the right rear was dead flat. She kicked it and swore again.

Changing a flat tire was not Sam's forte. In fact, she could not remember ever changing one. She had watched her father change one when she was a kid, and another one Gunn had changed in the middle of a rainy night on their way home from a party. That time she never even stepped out of the car. Gunn had insisted she stay warm and dry. He could be like that: kind and chivalrous, the perfect gentleman.

But now what? Where was the spare? Where was the jack? How did the jack work? Damn.

Not to worry. And why not? Because Brady came to her rescue. Brady? Was this a coincidence? Not likely.

Very early that morning, before dawn, before anyone else at PC Apple Acres had even opened their eyes, Brady had been out in the drive attaching a small explosive device to the right rear tire of Sam's Explorer. Brady had the power to detonate that device via remote control anywhere at virtually any time, thereby guaranteeing a flat tire wherever and whenever he chose.

Brady chose Old Northwest Road about a mile and a half from the entrance to PC Apple Acres.

Now he pulled up behind the Explorer and climbed out of his old and battered pickup. "Trouble, ma'am?"

Sam did not think it strange for even a moment that Brady had suddenly appeared out of thin air. She ran into him quite often while out and about running errands. There were hordes of visitors in East Hampton, but basically it was a very small town. The same faces popped up everywhere: at the grocery, the drugstore, the post office, the vegetable stand. Besides, Sam felt overjoyed to see the caretaker; he would fix her flat tire.

Which, of course, he did. While she stood by and watched. Liberation has its limits.

Then, just in case she had another flat, Brady followed her back to the estate. He parked behind her in the driveway and helped her tote in that load of groceries. Brady: a good, decent, honest fellow.

"When you have a few minutes, Mrs. Henderson," he said to Sam after he had hauled in the last bag, "I would like to show you something."

"I have a few minutes right now."

Sam followed Brady out the back door and across the terrace. Several family members, including Jason and Megan, frolicked in the swimming pool. Gunn's sister Marjorie, not Sam's favorite person in the world, was on lifeguard duty. She sort of acknowledged Sam in passing with a roll of her eyes. But those same eyes followed Sam, and her friend, all the way through the rose garden and out the other side.

Every family of any size has a Marjorie in its midst. She's the one with a smile on her face and a dagger hidden behind her back. Relentlessly dissatisfied and unhappy, these disgruntled sibs thrive by spreading dissent. They are like a human cancer upon harmonious family life.

Marjorie, once divorced and twice married, was in big trouble with hubby number two. The reasons why could no doubt fill many pages, but it all came down to the stark reality that Marjorie was a nag and a witch and a back-stabber, and number two had finally reached the end of his tether. Number two wanted out. And Marjorie knew he wanted out. Which only made matters worse, caused her to reach for new levels of bitchdom.

It also made her appoint a new lifeguard, abandon her chaise longue, and make a beeline for the rose garden. She knew the good-looking guy with her sister-in-law was the caretaker; her brother had pointed him out and run him down several days earlier. Marjorie wanted to know where they were going and what they were doing. She had found it odd that Sam disappeared for an hour or more almost every day. Errands and grocery shopping were invariably the stated reasons, but Marjorie, her paranoid little mind always looking for grit and grime, rarely accepted simple explanations. Marjorie was an ulterior motive kind of gal.

So what did Brady want to show Sam? The garden, of course.

Vegetables were sprouting up all over that patch of earth and Sam had not paid a visit for weeks. Too busy with her guests. But for the past fortnight Brady had been delivering fresh green beans to Mrs. Griner. And now there were peppers on the vine and the first tomatoes had started to turn red.

"My God!" cried Sam. "Unbelievable! It seems to have happened overnight."

"I think, Mrs. Henderson, you've just been occupied."

Sam sighed. "You can say that again. Sometimes I feel like I'm running a hotel."

"A lot of people coming and going."

"Too many."

"It always happens in the summer. Things will calm down before long, after Labor Day."

"I'm looking forward to that."

Sam knelt in the dirt to get a closer look at that first luscious red tomato. It looked wonderful to her, absolutely beautiful.

How, she wondered, had she missed the garden growing? In the spring it had been one of her top priorities. It seemed just a few short weeks ago that she and Brady had turned over the soil, dug the tender young plants into the warm, moist soil.

Time moves too fast, she thought, and then she heard herself say it softly out loud, "Too fast."

Brady heard the melancholy in her voice, but at the same moment, out of the corner of his eye, he saw movement over near the barn. At first he thought it must be some of the kids, running around, maybe playing hide-and-seek. But no, when a head poked out from around the corner, Brady saw immediately it belonged to Gunn Henderson's younger sister, Marjorie. She had obviously abandoned her position at poolside to follow and spy on her sister-in-law. Brady had exceptional hearing. Now he heard opportunity knocking.

"Don't you wish," he said to Samantha Ann Quincy Henderson, "that we could have back all the time we've ever wasted."

Sam turned and looked into his eyes. She had been thinking almost exactly the same thought. "I do wish that sometimes, yes."

Brady knelt beside her. He cupped one of the small, still-green tomatoes in his open palm. "I think it's part of the reason I love gardening. It gives me a firm handle on time as the plants take root and mature and produce. My own life often seems so fragmented and distracted, but the life of a pepper plant or a tomato plant has purpose and vitality."

Sam nodded as she considered his words. She was moved by their depth and their sincerity. "But Brady," she said, "you strike me as neither fragmented nor distracted. You seem incredibly balanced and centered."

Brady caught another glimpse of the sister-in-law peering around the corner of the barn. "I suppose," he said, "these things are relative. I know ultimately I seek stillness."

Sam nodded. She had been into this stillness thing, along with Oriental philosophy, in her younger days. Not much stillness once Gunn arrived. And then the kids. No, not much stillness at all.

Sam reached down and picked up a handful of dirt. It felt cool and moist against her palm. She held it for a few seconds, then she spread her fingers and let the soil escape, back to the ground.

"You've done a wonderful job with the garden," she

told Brady. "The plants are healthy, the soil is loose, there is not a weed anywhere."

"It takes only a few minutes a day," he replied.

"Yes," agreed Sam, "but every day. Day after day."

He nodded. "I usually come out first thing in the morning. Like with a lot of things in life, if you allow the garden to get away from you, ignore it for any length of time, especially during growing season, then you usually wind up with a mess on your hands."

"Neglect," said Sam, again nodding, her thoughts working feverishly, "is a terrible thing."

Their faces were only a few feet apart. Sam raised her head and met Brady's eyes, but she could not hold his gaze for long. She glanced away and prepared to stand.

Brady, one eye still on the sister-in-law, beat her to it. He moved quickly to his feet, held out his hand, and helped Sam up. "Can you give me just a few more minutes of your precious time, Mrs. Henderson?" he asked. "I'd love to show you one more thing."

Sam knew she had responsibilities waiting for her back at the house, but those responsibilities could wait; she needed some time to herself. And if she wanted to be honest with herself, which she did not, she enjoyed Brady's company. He made her feel calm. And still.

Brady led her across the sweep of lawn to the boat-house. As they stepped out onto the dock, Brady took a quick look over his shoulder. Sure enough, the sister-in-law was in hot pursuit, doing her best to remain anonymous by darting from shade tree to shade tree as she made her way across the scandalous battlefield.

Brady and Sam walked slowly out to the end of the

dock. The old mahogany runabout with the huge Chrysler inboard engine floated there on the placid water against the bulkhead. The long, beautiful antique wooden boat had been cleaned and waxed and buffed. The dark wood glowed so brightly, Sam could see her reflection in the smooth, rounded bow. The brass cleats and chrome seat stays were polished to a high shine.

"We've been working on her," said Brady. "Your son and I. Jason's done an outstanding job. He's a hard worker when he has some incentive and he puts his mind to it."

Sam ran her palm along the wide mahogany gunwale. "It's gorgeous. God, it's exquisite. Jason really helped?"

Brady nodded. "He worked his tail off to get her looking this good. Step in and have a look around."

Marjorie arrived at the corner of the boathouse just as Brady took hold of Sam's hand and helped her step over the gunwale into the runabout. Marjorie's eyes grew wide and happy. This feeble excuse for a vacation had finally taken an interesting turn.

The runabout was twenty-six feet from stem to stern. It had plush leather seating for eight and plenty of standing-around room for at least that many more. Brady showed Sam around: the captain's seat, the fully stocked bar, that shiny Chrysler inboard. He purposely stayed close by her side during the entire tour. From a distance the whole affair no doubt looked rather intimate. The fact that almost all of the conversation revolved around young Jason's contributions to the runabout's appearance did not reach the corner of the boathouse. Marjorie filled in the audio details any old way she wanted.

"If you have the time," said Brady, pushing his luck as their tour wound down, "I could take you for a little spin around the bay. She cruises even better than she looks."

Sam smiled. A little laugh even spilled from her mouth. "Thank you, Brady, both for the offer and for helping out with Jason. This summer would've been a disaster had you not intervened. As for a cruise . . . well, maybe another time. I have guests. . . ."

"Of course," said Brady. "I understand. I didn't mean to monopolize your afternoon. Another time, then?"

"Yes."

Then, as he helped her out of the boat and back onto the dock, Brady took another quick look over at the boathouse. And sure enough, Gunn's meddlesome but unwittingly helpful sister was still at her post, her spiteful eyes narrowed and squarely on the prize.

27 Gunn arrived home on Friday to begin his summer vacation. Mr. Reilly had at first balked at two weeks off after less than four months on the job, but Gunn convinced him that everyone else in the country was on vacation anyway. Besides, the time had come to put phase two of the sales operation into motion. It made sense to wait until after Labor Day to unveil The Disk. Mr. Reilly and Gunn agreed to meet at the Plaza Hotel in Manhattan on Tuesday morning following the long holiday weekend.

Gunn needed a break. It had been only four months, but ninety percent of that time he had been out on the road working fifteen and sixteen hours a day. A family vacation in Maine and Nova Scotia had been planned, but at the last minute, to the great displeasure of Sam and the kids, Gunn had nixed the trip. He was whipped. He just wanted to hang around the estate, play some tennis, get to know his neighbors, enjoy his kids, make love to his wife.

Well, the best-laid plans and all that malarkey.

Gunn had been home less than a day when little sister Marjorie cornered him in his office. Saturday, late morning, that downtime between breakfast and lunch. The various visitors had dispersed on foot, on bike, and on water. Sam had gone off to run some errands. The mansion was empty except for Gunn, his sister, and, unbeknownst to either one of them, the caretaker. Brady, suspecting sister Marjorie might have some beans to spill, had been keeping a close eye on her movements ever since Gunn's return the night before. When she failed to leave the house after breakfast along with the rest of the troops, Brady slipped into the basement and made his way up the secret stairway to the main floor.

The mansion had secret passages leading everywhere. Almost all the rooms in the great house could be spied on if you knew how to access these hidden arteries tucked behind the walls. Brady knew every nook and cranny. He could find his way blindfolded to the library or the study or one of the distant bedrooms. The house had been built back in the twenties by a filthy rich industrialist who was both a voyeur and a paranoid. The industrialist enjoyed watching people engage in sexual acts, and he trusted absolutely no one: not his wives, not his mistresses, not his kids, not his servants, not his employees, not his competitors. So he had his architect design the house with his own personal eccentricities in mind.

Brady stealthily made his way to Gunn Henderson's office. He arrived behind the wall and silently opened the small, waist-level peephole just as sister Marjorie slipped into the office and closed the door.

"Hey, sis," said Gunn from behind his desk. He sat filing some papers, winding a few things up before starting his vacation in earnest. "What's up?"

"Oh, nothing," she said. "Just easing my way into another tough day here in the Hamptons."

"Not a bad spot, huh?"

"It's incredible," replied sister Marjorie, her little brain churning, "but you don't seem to have much time to enjoy it. All you do is work."

Gunn closed his file drawer. "The price of fame and fortune, sis. But no more work. I'm now a man of leisure. Two weeks with no worries."

"I guess you'll spend some time with Sam."

Here we go, thought Brady.

"Hope to," said Gunn. He pulled open the center drawer of his desk.

Marjorie hesitated, but not for long. Familial duty, her own brand of it anyway, called. "Look, Gunn, I know it's not my place to pry, but you're my big brother and I just, well, I just want to know."

"Know what?" Gunn, only half hearing his sibling, searched the drawer for his bank statement.

"If everything is, you know, okay between you and Sam."

Gunn looked up at his sister. "Reasonably good. You know. Sam whines some about me being gone so much. But hell, she knew the travel was part of the deal. Why do you ask?"

"No particular reason," Marjorie lied. "She's just been kind of snippy and distant ever since we arrived. I've barely seen her."

"I think she's pissed off having so many people in the house. She claims all she does is work while everyone else plays."

Marjorie guffawed. "My God, Gunn, it's not like she doesn't have plenty of help. She has a cook, a maid, a lawn man."

"Hell, Marjie, you know Sam. She can be moody sometimes. Maybe she has her period. That always weirds her out."

Sister Marjorie paused, tried to decide how best to proceed. Caretaker Brady waited. While he waited he popped a grape-flavored gumdrop into his mouth.

Brother Gunn closed his desk drawer and stood. He had a tennis match at noon. "By the way," he asked his sister as he headed for the door, "have you seen Mom and Dad lately? We invited them out here, but Mom says Dad's too weak and feeble to go anywhere."

Marjorie was not ready to change the subject, but she had to answer her brother's question. "He doesn't go anywhere except to the doctor's."

Gunn stopped in the doorway. "So now they claim

it might be this Lyme disease? This thing with the tick?"

Marjorie shrugged. "That's what the doctor says. They both have a lot of the symptoms."

Gunn shook his head. "Hard to believe, the old man with all these health problems. I don't remember him being sick even once the whole time we were kids."

"He wasn't," replied Marjorie. "Neither of them was."

Gunn looked concerned. He sighed, hesitated, and then, "Sam and I plan on driving up to see them sometime in the next couple weeks. I don't really know what else to do."

"There's not much we can do."

Gunn squeezed his sister's arm, then turned again for the door. "Anyway, I have a tennis match in a little while. I better get my stuff on."

Marjorie did not want him to go, not yet. She had to pull the conversation back into focus. Before Gunn could cross the threshold, she said, "I don't mean to beat a dead horse, but I really am a little worried about Sam."

"Worried? How come?"

"I don't know. Her mood, I guess. But also I've noticed that she seems awfully tight with the lawn man."

Gunn stopped in his tracks. Slowly he turned around. The concerned look on his face became instantly hostile. His voice took on a razor's edge. "Tight with the lawn man? You mean Brady?"

"I think you called him the caretaker."

"Yeah, the caretaker. Why do you say she's *tight* with him?"

Brady sucked his gumdrop and listened as Marjorie spun her web. And he watched as Gunn's body grew rigid and his blood pressure soared into the stratosphere.

"I'm sure it's nothing," Marjorie insisted. "But I know that yesterday they arrived home from somewhere together. Then they spent at least an hour in each other's company, first out by that garden behind the barn, then down by the boathouse. Probably I should mind my own business, but you are my brother, Gunn. If there is anything going on, well, I'd hate for you to be the last know."

"Christ! I knew that son of a bitch was trouble. I knew it the first time I laid eyes on him."

"Gunn, really," said sister Marjorie, her voice soothing and concerned even while her nerve endings twitched with delight, "I'm sure it was all perfectly innocent."

"Innocent my ass. He's had his beady little eyes on her ever since we moved in here."

"I didn't know that."

"Well you know it now," snarled Gunn.

"So what are you going to do?"

"I don't know. Maybe I'll kill the bastard!" Gunn thought about grabbing a gun from the solid cherry gun cabinet, maybe taking a quick hunt around the grounds. But a glance at his watch reminded him that he had a date between the white lines in less than half an hour.

●　　●　　●

HAD GUNN found the caretaker that day, he might well have committed a homicide. Certainly he would have inflicted some damage on the caretaker's physical being. But the caretaker was no dummy. The caretaker was, in fact, quite brilliant. He had an IQ in the one-eighty range. And he definitely had a big enough brain to slip out of the mansion and keep himself scarce for the remainder of that day and most of the next. Scarce, but not entirely absent.

Gunn did not catch up with his wife until late that afternoon. With a dozen people in the house, she had decided to make the trek into Riverhead. Three hours, three hundred and eighty-eight dollars, and fifteen bags of groceries later, Sam arrived home to find her husband in a jealous rage. Gunn came storming out the front door of the mansion even before she had put the Explorer in park. He charged up to the vehicle and peered through the windows, as though expecting to find the caretaker lying in the back, perhaps naked.

"Where the fuck have you been all day?"

"Excuse me?"

"You've been gone since breakfast."

"You're right, I have," said Sam, not yet apprised of her husband's finicky emotional state. "It's been another exciting day in the Hamptons." She sighed.

"I asked you where the hell you've been."

"Actually," countered Sam, "I believe you wanted to know where the *fuck* I'd been."

"That's right. Where the fuck have you been?"

Sam stared at her husband. "What are you all worked up about? Your face is as red as a beet."

"This is not about my face, goddammit! This is about where you've been."

Sam was tired. And irritable. And she had a headache, a dull throb behind the eyes. The traffic on Route 27 had been brutal, the number of shoppers in the Riverhead supermarket roughly equal to the number of people living in the greater New York metropolitan area. She had no taste for battle, especially with Gunn. So what did she do? She dug up some sarcasm and gave her man an answer.

"Well, let's see. Where have I been? I stopped at the post office and bought some stamps to pay some bills. I licked some of the stamps and stuck them on the envelopes. Then I went to the bank, where I know all the tellers personally because I stop in at least once or twice a day. Then—"

"It doesn't take all damn day to go to the stinking post office and bank."

"Very good, Gunn, it doesn't." Sam had heard enough. She pushed open her door and stepped out onto the asphalt. "But it does take all damn day to drive into Riverhead and buy enough damn groceries to feed your damn fat sisters, their fat husbands, and their demanding, ungrateful children!"

Sam's outburst brought Gunn's attack to a momentary impasse. Her words, plus the enormous number of brown paper bags shoved into the back of the Explorer, made it difficult for Gunn to pursue his attack. Especially after he became aware of several family members gaping at his actions from various windows and doorways. He had no choice but to retreat. Hefting four heavy bags into his arms, Gunn, looking rather apelike, lurched toward the kitchen.

● ● ●

HOURS PASSED before Gunn was able to go back on the offensive. All through the rest of the afternoon and all through the evening, through cocktails and dinner and family chitchat out under the stars, Gunn scowled at his wife and gave her dirty looks every chance he got. He had this rather peculiar habit of folding his tongue between his teeth whenever he became angry or agitated. On several occasions that night, Sam saw Gunn's tongue clenched firmly between his teeth. Unfortunately, she still did not know the reason why. She assumed the lovely Henderson disposition was simply stepping out after a long hard stretch of work. Too bad she was not privy to sister-in-law Marjorie's morning meeting with big brother Gunn; like the caretaker, Sam too might well have made herself scarce.

The entire incident no doubt escalated way out of control due to the large quantity of alcohol Gunn consumed over the course of the evening. Eight to twelve ounces of Beefeater's would be a pretty good guesstimate.

Gunn arrived up in the bedroom after Sam had already changed into her nightgown, washed her face, brushed her teeth, and climbed into bed. She did not expect to have a real swell time with Gunn that evening, certainly no giggles or lovemaking were in the mix, but nor did she expect to take a beating. He had only ever hit her twice before, and those blows had been relatively harmless slaps, no physical damage done. Emotionally, however, those slaps had not exactly deepened the bond Sam felt for her spouse.

He came into the bedroom looking relatively calm. And inside he actually felt calm. Probably because he knew what he had to do. There was really very little choice.

Gunn paced for just a moment or two, then he sat in the armchair over by the window. He kicked off his loafers. He leaned down and pulled off his socks. He unbuttoned his shirt and loosened his belt.

Sam watched over the top of her gardening magazine. Her husband's silence alerted her to the reality that all was not well in Hendersonville. He pulled off his shirt and his chinos. Sam decided to make a move in the hopes of cutting Gunn off at the pass.

"I'm whipped," she said softly. "I can barely keep my eyes open."

Gunn said not a word. Instead he shot her yet another evil eye, then, being a very fastidious fellow, he placed his shoes carefully in his closet, hung his chinos on a hanger, and threw his shirt and socks into the laundry hamper. Gunn's ultraneatness was all part of his controlling personality.

Sam put down her magazine and switched off the light. Maybe, she thought, just maybe we'll get through this without a scene.

Not a chance, honey. Gunn was on the prowl. She knew it when he left the door to the bathroom wide-open while he relieved himself. Normally he shut the door in accordance with her oft-stated wishes. But tonight he left the door open, then proceeded to take a long, aggressive pee right smack into the center of the bowl. This meant, Sam knew, that the gloves were off. Gunn was ready to rumble.

Still, she fluffed up her pillow and made a show of going to sleep as he came out of the bathroom with his encumbrance not yet fully garaged inside his silk boxers.

"Just one question before beddy-bye," he announced.

Sam sighed. This one question, she knew from experience, could take hours to answer and lead to all sorts of vile skirmishes.

"Yes?"

Gunn sat on the edge of the bed, his demeanor still calm. "What the fuck is going on between you and this goddamn caretaker?"

Okay, so at least she knew now the reason for all the hostility and the dirty looks. Sometimes with Gunn it took hours, even days, to find out why the man was upset. Sam knew it would be tough to nip this one in the bud, but still, she had to try.

"What are you talking about?" she asked.

"I'm talking about you and this son of a bitch Brady."

"But why do you ask if there is something going on between us? What do you think is going on?"

"That, dear, is what I want you to tell me." Gunn: still calm, still in control.

And Brady: behind the wall, sucking on a butterscotch candy, following the action as though watching a movie down at the local three-plex.

"Don't be ridiculous, Gunn. There's absolutely nothing going on between Brady and me."

"That's not what I hear."

This made Sam sit up. "What does that mean? What do you hear?"

"Things."

"What things? And from who?"

"Who doesn't matter. Who has nothing to do with it."

"Oh, I think it does. I think it has everything to do with it. I think that busybody sister of yours is behind this. I think—"

"Don't drag my sister into this. She has nothing—"

"She just wants to stir up trouble."

"That's crap."

"If it's crap then I suggest we march down to her bedroom right now so I can hear, firsthand, what slimy accusations she's been making against me."

"Bullshit, Sam! I don't need Marjorie to tell me when something foul is happening in my house. I have eyes and ears. Now tell me what the fuck is going on with this jerk-off who cuts the grass!"

Cool, calm, collected Gunn had finally taken a hike. Up and over the hill. In his place had stepped a man similar in appearance but working himself into a rage, and preparing to go ballistic. This man, because of his jealous, guilt-soaked nature, actually believed his wife was clandestinely bedding the caretaker.

The accusations and denials, the attacks and counterattacks, went on for most of an hour. The master bedroom suite was set off by itself at the far end of the mansion, so even when their voices began to screech, no one else, except, of course, for the caretaker, could hear.

Gunn did not stay long on the bed. As was his habit when fighting with his wife, he paced. Back and forth across the bedroom he marched, wearing a path in that expensive Persian carpet. Occasionally he detoured into the bathroom for a quick suck on the cold water faucet. All the yelling and screaming gave Mr. Gunn a dry mouth. He usually went in to drink whenever his wife began to drone on for too long.

After one pit stop, somewhere not long after midnight, Gunn emerged from the bathroom. The animal inside had taken full control. He kicked the bedpost and roared, "All I know is this: I work my ass off for you! I bust my butt out on the road sixty, seventy, eighty hours a week, and for what? So you can lie around this goddamn palace humping the shitbag who pulls the weeds and sucks the dirt off the bottom of the damn swimming pool? Well, I've had it! I ain't doing it anymore!"

Sam, momentarily blindsided by Gunn's reference to the swimming pool, was nevertheless nearly as wound up by this time as her hubby. She flung off the bedclothes and practically leapt to her feet. "*You've* had it? What about me? I've heard all I care to hear tonight! I refuse to listen to one more word!" With that, Sam pulled on her robe and headed for the door.

Gunn, loud and massive and vibrating with hostile energy, blocked her way. "Where the hell do you think you're going?"

"I'm going to look for an empty bed where I can get away from you and your craziness and hopefully get some sleep. Maybe by morning you will have come to your senses and be ready to apologize."

Gunn, his big frame filling the space in front of the door, did not budge even a millimeter. Arms folded across his chest, he just stood there and glared at his wife.

"Get out of my way, Gunn."

"Fuck you."

"Don't say that to me."

"Fuck you!"

Sam sighed. "Look, you've said a bunch of ugly things to me. Now I suggest you back off before you do something we'll both regret."

That's when he shoved her.

Brady had his eye mashed right up against the spy hole.

"You bastard! Don't push me!"

Gunn shoved her again. "I'll *push* you, goddammit. I'll *push* you until you're straight with me about what the hell is going on around here!" And then, strike three, he shoved her one more time.

Sam stumbled. She fell back against the bed. Her brain told her to stay calm, but at the same time some primal instinct deep down in her gut told her to strike back. She struck. Surprise allowed her to slip in one good shot to Gunn's jaw before that huge masculine presence reasserted itself.

A split second of shock registered on Gunn Henderson's face, and then he retaliated. "Don't you hit me, you bitch!" Gunn raised his hand and slapped his wife hard across the jaw.

Sam screamed. Gunn hit her again, this time with his fist. His closed and angry fist. The blow knocked her to the floor. His rage way out of control, he kicked her a good one in the ribs.

"You bastard!" she screamed. "You'll pay for this!"

Brady popped another butterscotch candy, his eyes as big and red as ripe tomatoes.

Sam struggled to her feet. She did her best to strike another blow upon her husband. But, of course, her best was nowhere near good enough. Six inches taller and nearly seventy pounds heavier, Gunn easily cast aside her pitiful blows. Then, because he had not yet expelled all the demons gnawing at his insides, he nailed her again with his fist, this time right between the eyes.

Down went Sam. This time she did not get up. This time she decided to just stay on the floor. Not that she really had much choice.

Blood flowed from her nose, tears from her eyes.

Part Three

THE SEDUCTION

28 Sam's nose was swollen to twice its normal size, but it was not broken. She had a pretty nasty shiner around her left eye, and some discoloration under her right. Her cheeks and lips were puffy. All in all, Sam did not look good, not good at all. She looked bad. She looked like a battered wife. Her ribs hurt where Gunn had kicked her. She had bruises on her chest. Quick little breaths were all she could manage.

Immediately after inflicting his final blow, Gunn had transformed himself into Mr. Remorseful. Seeing the blood and the damage done, he fell upon his wife and begged for forgiveness. Not so fast, Gunny. Sam may have been down, but she definitely was not out. Stronger and tougher and more resilient than most people gave her credit for, she told him to get off of her and to get the hell out of her room.

"Get out!" she screamed. "Get out or I'll wake up your sisters and show them what a monster their big brother really is!"

Gunn, after some begging and pleading, got out.

Sam slammed the door on his back and threw the lock. After a good, long cry she mustered the courage to face the bathroom mirror. One look led to another round of tears. But eventually, around two A.M., she picked herself up off the floor, ran a hot bath, cleaned the dried blood from her face, and took two Xanax tablets with a tall glass of cool water. She soaked for half an hour in the steamy water, then, her tears and her thoughts finally vanquished, she crawled into bed, pulled the comforter up over her shoulders, and fell asleep.

She did not leave the master bedroom suite for three days. When Gunn returned the following morning, she told him to get lost.

From the other side of the door, he whispered in his kindest, gentlest voice. "I just want to make sure you're all right. My God, I can't believe we let things get so out of hand."

"*We?*"

"Okay, me. I know I'm to blame. I'm sorry, Sam. You know I love you. You know I would never mean to hurt you."

"Go to hell. Go away."

"Can't you let me in? Please, just for a minute. I need to make sure you're okay." Gunn was not really sure he wanted to go into that room. He was afraid of what he might see.

Sam did not care what Gunn Henderson did or did not want. She just wanted to go back to sleep. She did not want to think or talk or listen. "Go away, damn you, or I'll scream."

"I'll go, but can't I bring you something? Coffee? Toast? One of Mrs. Griner's homemade sticky buns?"

Sam thought about it. "I'll take a cup of tea. Herbal tea. Mrs. Griner knows the kind I like."

Gunn, happy he had made some progress, sprinted down the back stairs to fetch the tea. When he returned with it a few minutes later, Sam told him to leave it on the floor outside the door.

"Okay," he said, "I will, but . . . well . . . what should I tell them? Mrs. Griner wanted to know if you weren't feeling well."

"Tell them whatever you want, you bastard," answered Sam. "Tell them I have a headache. Tell them you're a raving fucking lunatic who beats his wife. I don't give a damn what you tell them."

Gunn told them Sam had some kind of bug, "hopefully of the twenty-four-hour variety, but we're not quite sure yet. She feels really lousy and doesn't want to see anyone. Not even me," he added.

Sam's twenty-four-hour bug turned into a forty-eight-hour bug and then into a seventy-two-hour bug, and still she did not venture out of her room.

The time came for Gunn's sisters and their families to depart PC Apple Acres, but even then Sam failed to appear. Sam muttered, "Good riddance," when Gunn informed her they were leaving, but downstairs Gunn said, "Sam feels really bad about not coming down to say good-bye, but her stomach and her head still hurt. I think I might have to call the doctor."

They all said that sounded like an excellent idea, and then they all left. Even Gunn was glad to see them go. He had been on pins and needles for three days and three nights thinking about his wife waltzing into the kitchen with her face all bruised and banged up. Several times a day he had been making room service calls. Whatever Sam had demanded, he had brought: food, drink, aspirin, cold compresses. Each time he had to leave the goods at the closed door.

Jason and Megan were allowed one brief visit in the evening. Sam wanted her children to know she was alive and reasonably well. But she kept the drapes drawn and the lights out, and even then she kept her face pretty much hidden down in the sheets. No way was she going to let her two lovely, innocent kids see that she had been battered at the hands of their father.

●　　●　　●

THE DOMESTIC HELP began to whisper about Mrs. Henderson's lengthy convalescence. Mrs. Griner and Saida had several discussions about what might be wrong with the Missus. Even Brady got in on the act. Of course Brady got in on the act. He had to set the record straight. He had to take full advantage of this very unfortunate situation.

He ran into Saida one afternoon at the farmstand out on the Sag Harbor road. Well, he didn't actually run into her; he followed the Puerto Rican housekeeper there one day after work, then acted like the whole thing was a coincidence.

"How is Mrs. Henderson doing?" he asked after they exchanged greetings.

"I guess not so good," answered Saida. "I no see her all week long. She not come out of her room."

"You know why she hasn't come out of her room, don't you?"

"She sick."

"Not really," said Brady. "It's because she's all beat up."

Saida looked confused. "All beat up?"

"Listen, Saida, promise me you won't tell anyone I told you this, but her husband beat her up."

"Mr. Henderson? No! He kind of loud and rough sometimes, but I no see him beat up his wife."

"I saw her, Saida. Her face is a mess. That's why she won't come out of her room."

"I no believe it."

"You just wait," said Brady. "Eventually she'll have to come out. The bruises might have faded by the time she does, but they won't be gone. You have a look for yourself."

"I feel so bad for her."

"Me, too," said the caretaker.

●　●　●

BRADY WAS RIGHT: eventually Sam did come out of her room. By the time she did, the swelling had pretty much gone down and the bruises had started to fade. She did her best with makeup to cover the black-and-blue marks that had turned green and yellow and orange. And, even in the house, she wore a large pair of very dark glasses, "because," she explained to a curious Jason, "my eyes are all red and sore from the *bug* I had."

But try though Sam did, she could not cover up the truth from anyone taking a closer look. Like Mrs. Griner. A victim of spousal abuse herself in her younger days, Mrs. G. knew after just a split-second glance that Mrs. Henderson had been beaten by her husband. Of course, Brady had already related the particulars of the incident to her. But the actual sight of Sam bruised and battered brought back some ugly memories and caused Greta no small amount of consternation. She considered saying something to Sam, but finally decided to keep silent.

Others, however, allowed their lips to flap. Before long it seemed like anyone even remotely connected with PC Apple Acres knew that Gunn Henderson was a wife-beater. Soon the entire village of East Hampton knew the dirty secret. People who had never laid eyes on either of the Hendersons knew the husband beat the wife. The situation was discussed in the cold cuts line at the grocery store, at posh cocktail parties, under umbrellas on the beach, in golf carts, on catamarans and water-skiing boats, anywhere and everywhere people congregated in groups of two or more.

All the hushed gossip flew right by the man accused. Gunn, his massive ego insulated against all negative vibrations, held his head as high as ever. He figured a little time, some good behavior, and a few expensive gifts would buy back his wife. Sure, she was silent and angry and sullen right now, but that would pass. He just had to be patient, bide his time.

Gunn had also figured out a way to spread around some of the blame for his wife's condition. In fact, by the end of the week he had managed, at least in his own brain, to shift virtually all of the responsibility onto the shoulders of Brady the caretaker. If that son of a bitch, he told himself, had just stayed out of our affairs, kept clear of my wife, none of this would have happened.

Late one night, with Labor Day fast approaching, Gunn descended on the boathouse to confront the caretaker. He had been avoiding Brady ever since his anger and jealousy had abated following the debacle with his wife, but now he was on the prowl again. Not only would he be returning to work soon, once again leaving Sam alone with this home-wrecker, but he also had himself utterly convinced that her bruises were Brady's fault.

His loud knocks upon the boathouse door went unanswered. He peered in the windows but saw no one. In fact, he saw nothing. All of the lights were out. The boathouse was as dark as a tomb. But Gunn, his adrenaline pumping, needed this confrontation. He decided to wait. If necessary, he would wait all night long.

Had Gunn turned around and looked across the field to the barn, he would have seen plenty of lights glowing up in Brady's third-floor retreat. That's where Brady had his telephones and computers and fax machines and modems. That third-floor retreat was where Brady kept in touch with the rest of the world. He had daily communications with London, Paris, San Francisco, Hong Kong, and Tokyo. A man who needed only three or four hours sleep per night, Brady could work practically around the clock with his incredible powers of concentration. If it had not been for a notebook he needed from the boathouse, he might well have kept Gunn Henderson waiting until dawn.

It must have been about one A.M. when Brady, lost in a world of assets and bottom lines, crossed the field and unlocked the boathouse door. Gunn, dozing in the shadows, heard the key hit the lock. The sound pierced the quiet summer night and brought him instantly awake.

Gunn stepped out, directly behind the caretaker. "Brady."

Brady flinched. He rarely flinched. But he had not

expected this. All week long he had been keeping close tabs on Gunn Henderson, but tonight, because business beckoned, he had dropped his guard. Never a good idea, Brady knew, to drop your guard. Do it once too often and you'll pay the piper. But not tonight. Tonight would be a breeze. Tonight Gunn Henderson would be full of nothing but hot air. After leaving his wife a mess, he would be all bark and little, if any, bite.

Brady pushed open his door, reached swiftly inside, and turned on the outside spotlight. The light exploded against the darkness, directly into Gunn Henderson's eyes. Gunn recoiled. He closed his eyes against the brightness, then covered his face with his hands.

Brady addressed his momentarily blind accuser. "Mr. Henderson? Is that you, sir? You gave me quite a surprise. I wasn't expecting anyone. Can I help you with something, sir?"

Gunn had no choice but to move to the defensive while his pupils adjusted to the sudden burst of intense light. If Gunn had been toting a piece, say one of his rifles or revolvers, Brady could have easily disarmed him at that moment. But Brady knew the man did not have a weapon.

"Yeah, Brady," replied Gunn, his vision returning, "you can help me with something."

"I'll do my best, sir. What is it?"

Gunn had Brady pretty much in focus now. "Stay the fuck away from my wife."

"Your wife, sir?"

Brady stood in the doorway, where the spotlight did not shine. But Gunn stood out in the open, awash in brilliance. Incredibly, he made no move at all to alter this defensive situation. Like a jackrabbit caught in the headlights, Gunn stood there frozen, nothing moving but his mouth.

"That's right, lawnmower man, my wife!"

"Excuse me, sir, but I've really only had contact with your wife a handful of times since your family moved here to PC Apple Acres in the spring."

"Don't bullshit me, caretaker."

"I wouldn't do that, sir." Brady's responses remained gentle and polite. But maybe, he thought, maybe the time had come to spook this arrogant son of a bitch, this chip off the old block of the great and powerful moneylender, Mr. Gunn Henderson, Sr. A slight personality twist might do this wife-beater some good.

"I don't give a damn what you would or wouldn't do, caretaker. You just listen to me, and listen good. If I so much as catch you glancing at my wife, I'll gouge your fucking eyes out with my thumbs. If I get wind that you're bothering my wife, I'll be on your ass so fast you won't know which way to shit."

Brady offered a wry smile. "I'm quaking in my boots."

Gunn paused, frowned, then, "What did you say?"

Brady reached in and turned on the hall light. He wanted to make sure Henderson could see him now. "I said, friend, that your threats have me quaking in my boots."

"Yeah?" Gunn had definitely not expected belligerence. "Well, my threats should have you quaking, because step out of line just one more time and you'll be off this estate the second I snap my finger."

Brady mimicked quaking, then, "My God, Gunny, you must have enormous power around here."

Gunn frowned again. "What did you call me?"

"Gunny."

Only Gunn's mother called him Gunny. "I suggest, caretaker, you not call me that again."

"What would you like me to call you, Gunny? Mr. Henderson? Or perhaps you would prefer it if I called you *sir*?"

"Are you looking for trouble, Brady?"

On the contrary, Brady felt like telling Henderson, I *am* trouble. I am your worst nightmare. And you don't even know it. But he didn't; he held himself in check. Better to just let things simmer. He had already said enough, maybe too much. No good bringing the pot to a boil. He had waited years; a few more days or weeks or months amounted to nothing at all.

"No," said Brady instead, "I don't want any trouble." And with that Brady beat a hasty retreat. He did not care to let the situation deteriorate further. He stepped into his foyer. Gunn tried to follow him inside. Brady closed the door. Gunn tried to open it. Brady threw the dead bolt.

"Where the hell are you going, caretaker?" Gunn demanded. "Open the damn door, you son of a bitch! I'm still talking to you!"

Gunn stood there making demands and shouting obscenities for twenty minutes or more. He pounded on the door and even kicked it while insisting that Brady come out and act like a man.

Too bad Brady missed most of Gunn's performance. Brady grabbed the notebook he had originally come for, then departed the boathouse through the back door. He went down the steep flight of stairs to where the boats, almost invisible against the black of night, bobbed on the still water. From there Brady went around the boathouse and up through the field to the barn. As he entered the barn, he could still hear Gunn Henderson's shouted curses. The psychological absurdity of the whole affair made Brady smile. He was always amazed at the predictability of human behavior. But he did not dwell on his amazement for long. No, Brady had work to do, deals to cut, products to push, money to make. Gunn Henderson was merely one of his many projects.

29 Gunn stewed for the rest of his vacation. He tried repeatedly to get hold of Mr. Reilly so he could have the caretaker fired and thrown off the estate. He had decided, as he trudged back to the mansion after his midnight encounter at the boathouse, to draw a line in the sand: either Brady goes, he would tell Reilly, or I go. But Reilly was out of town, on vacation, incommunicado.

So who could Gunn turn to? Certainly not his wife. Sam hissed at him every time he dared to even glance in her direction. There was absolutely no way she would listen to his tale of woe concerning the caretaker.

Sam would not even acknowledge his departure when he went back to work early on Tuesday morning.

Lying in bed, she simply turned over and pretended that the flow of words coming from his mouth beyond the bedroom door had no impact whatsoever upon her ears. For Sam, at that time, Gunn Henderson did not even exist.

It took three hours and a half for the limousine to make the trip from PC Apple Acres to the Plaza Hotel. Traffic was all a-snarl as the limo drew closer to the Big Apple. The throngs living out on Long Island had their commuter vehicles pretty much parked out on the LIE and the BQE. Gunn, in the back, his head buried behind a sales analysis projection chart Reilly had faxed him over the weekend, tried not to fret. But fret he did. Gunn loathed waiting, especially in traffic. Somewhere in the back of his twisted brain, he truly believed traffic should part as he approached, make way for G. Henderson.

By the time the driver pulled up in front of the Plaza, Gunn could feel the tension in his neck and lower back. The muscles felt tight, ready to spasm. Sam had never bothered to tell him about Brady's back exercises. She'd feared, and rightly so, that any mention of the caretaker would only send Gunn into a terrible rage.

So now, aching and irritable, he climbed out of the limo and stretched right there on Grand Army Plaza, right in front of the hotel with taxi horns blaring, cop car sirens wailing, and humans of every race, creed, and color pushing and shoving for position in the vicious fight for fame and fortune. Right there Gunn did some deep knee bends, some neck rolls, and some hip twists. Then he took a few deep breaths, grabbed his briefcase, and headed for the entrance to the hotel. At the front desk he asked for Mr. Arthur J. Reilly's room. The clerk looked up the room number, made a call, and soon Gunn found himself in an elevator soaring skyward to one of the luxury suites.

The door to Arthur J. Reilly's room, however, was not opened by Arthur J. Reilly. No, the door was opened by a gorgeous blonde who, had this been a cartoon, would have caused Gunn's eyes to triple in size and pop right out of his head on springs. She had all the tools: the blond hair, the blue eyes, the high cheekbones, the full rosy red lips. And that was just the face. She had the body to go with it: thin and curvy in a tight knit dress with a hemline not too far south of her belly button. Gunn thought she looked like one of those sexy beauties you find in the glossy lingerie catalogues; the ones you want waiting for you in the sack after a long, rough day on the job.

"Gunn Henderson, I presume?" Even her voice radiated sex appeal: husky but sweet.

Gunn managed not to swallow his tongue. "Yes . . . uh . . . I'm . . . uh . . . Gunn Henderson. I was looking for . . . uh . . . Arthur Reilly."

"Of course, yes. Come in."

The blond bombshell swung the door all the way open, leaving plenty of room for Gunn to pass. He entered the suite with a couple of uncertain steps, fearing, perhaps, that he might do something stupid like trip in front of the sexiest woman he had ever seen this close up.

She held out her hand. "I'm Nita," she said. "Nita Garrett."

Reilly's wife? Gunn wondered. Kept her maiden

name? No way. She was young enough to be his daughter. His granddaughter, for chrissakes. But you never know, Gunn knew, guys with money get all the best babes. Maybe his mistress? His executive secretary? With special carnal duties, of course.

Then he noticed she still had her hand out. He took it, very carefully, and gave it a gentle shake. "Gunn Henderson."

She smiled. Perfect teeth. Every single one straight and true and pearly white. "Yes," she said, "I know. I've been expecting you."

He had already forgotten her name. Gunn never forgot a name. It was the salesman's first commandment to never forget a name. Hear it, remember it, use it. But this time he drew only blanks. Mesmerized by her physical presence, her name had never registered in his brain. He swallowed hard, tried to think of something snappy to say. Finally came up with, "You have?"

"Mr. Reilly said you'd be here between nine and ten this morning. He told me to wait for you. He should be back any—"

At just that moment Mr. Reilly swept through the still-open door. He wore tan slacks, a light blue Brooks Brothers blazer, and a pink dress shirt open at the collar. "Ah, Gunn, I see you've arrived. Sorry I wasn't here to greet you. A breakfast meeting went a little late."

"No problem," Gunn told him. "I just walked in a minute or so ago."

"Good, good. So I can safely assume you've met Nita?" Mr. Reilly turned to the blond bombshell. "I mean Ms. Garrett?"

"Yes," answered Gunn, "I have." But again, the name did not register, just those luscious lips.

"Excellent." Mr. Reilly closed the door and moved into the middle of the large suite. It looked like a well-appointed living room in an affluent home: deep sofas and chairs nicely arranged on a plush rose carpet. There were Tiffany lamps on the tables and original oil paintings on the walls.

"Let's relax, get comfortable," said Reilly. "Coffee and croissants over there on the sideboard, Gunn. Help yourself. I have a twelve-thirty lunch down at World Trade, so I'd like to jump straight in. There'll be time enough later for chitchat."

Gunn did his best to get a grip on himself. He knew Reilly, who had incredible powers of recall, demanded total immersion in the details during meetings like this, but Gunn's eyes and thoughts kept drifting in the direction of Ms. . . . Ms. . . . damn, what was her name? Gunn, his hand actually shaking, poured himself a cup of joe, no cream or sugar, and took a seat where the blond bombshell would not be directly in his line of vision.

Nita sat on the love seat, her long and lovely legs crossed. And a good thing, too, because once seated, that already short dress barely covered her hips, much less anything lower. Gunn took a deep breath, gulped his too hot coffee, and stared straight ahead at Mr. Reilly.

"All right, Gunn," said Reilly, "you've done a tremendous job these past few months laying the groundwork for The Disk. I know you were sometimes discouraged out there, wondering if all those visits to all those small towns really had any value. But let me assure you, they did."

"Don't worry, sir," replied Gunn, "I don't get discouraged."

"I know. That's why I hired you." Mr. Reilly turned his eyes to the blond bombshell. "You're looking at one of the best, Nita. I mean, Ms. Garrett. One of the very best in the business."

Gunn's brain clicked on the name: Nita Garrett. Nita Garrett. Nita Garrett. He figured Nita must be short for Anita. He decided he liked Nita better. Sexier, more class.

"You want to succeed in sales," Mr. Reilly continued, "here's the man to keep your eye on."

Gunn beamed. But still, he kept his eyes averted. He feared if his gaze latched onto those legs, he would not be able to let go.

"Okay," said Mr. Reilly, "enough with the kudos. We're here to make money, people. And we're going to do that, Gunn, by hitting the large wide-open markets: the big cities and the major metropolitan areas. No more small towns, at least for the time being."

Gunn looked momentarily confused. "Then why—"

"Because, Gunn, we needed those small town bases covered. Once The Disk hits, all those toy store owners and five-and-dime managers will remember when Gunn Henderson came in to make his pitch. They'll remember and they'll be excited to realize they're part of this phenomenon sweeping the country. They'll order Disks by the millions and push them on every customer who strolls through the door. Trust me, Gunn, people want to be part of the action, part of the big events, the successful campaigns. You may not believe it now, but not one of your many stops was in vain."

Gunn nodded. He could feel himself getting pumped up. Mr. Reilly had that effect on him. Gunn wanted to get out and sell. He wanted to get out and hustle. All the crap of the past two weeks, all the crap involving his wife and that lowlife caretaker, abruptly drained out of his system. He felt free again, as light as air. Well, almost free. As soon as the opportunity presented itself, he wanted to talk to Reilly about Brady, about once and for all canning his ass. But not now, not yet, not with Nita in the room.

"So," Gunn asked, rubbing his hands together, "where do we start? I'm ready to rock and roll."

"That's the spirit, Gunn." Mr. Reilly could sense Gunn's excitement and enthusiasm. He reached into the pocket of his light blue blazer and pulled out a small royal blue velvet bag. The bag had a gold-colored drawstring. Reilly loosened the drawstring and pulled out a round wooden object exactly four inches in diameter and three eighths of an inch thick. He held it up between his thumb and index finger. "Here it is," he announced. "The Disk."

The three of them marveled for a moment at its beauty, its symmetry, its simplicity. This was the Basic model: made of oak with a large *D* stamped on one side, in an unadorned velvet carrying case. Reilly brought out the two other models as well: The Deluxe was made of cherry, with the *D* carved directly into the wood and in a velvet carrying case emblazoned with the single word DISK across both front and back. And at the top of the line was the Premium model. Made from solid mahogany, it also had the *D* carved into the wood. But on the opposite side, right in the center, it contained a small number etched into The Disk. This number indicated that this particular Disk was of a limited edition and could be replaced with one of precisely the same weight and density if the original was ever lost, damaged, or stolen. The Premium model also came in the fancy royal blue velvet carrying case, but in addition it had a smooth and lovely mahogany box to protect it from the ravages of life on earth. All three models also came with a story explaining the history and the purpose of The Disk. This story was, of course, a complete fiction, but it made an excellent selling tool. The Disk, so went the story, had its roots in the Orient where, for more than two thousand years, it had been used to stimulate creativity and reduce stress.

"What about pricing?" Gunn asked, after all three models had been studied and stroked.

"Nothing absolutely set in stone yet," answered Mr. Reilly. "But I think we can safely say retail will start at about three bucks for the Basic and go up as high as twenty-five bucks for the Premium, at least in certain high-end stores and retail catalogs."

"But we can make money at three dollars a hit?"

"Absolutely, Gunn," said Mr. Reilly. "If we get the volume. Volume is the key to this whole project. We have to have volume. To get production costs down, I need the power to order a million units at a time. To have that power, Gunn, I need you to go out and get the orders."

"Like I said before, sir, I'm ready to rock and roll."

"That's what I like to hear, Gunn."

Gunn smiled. And so, too, did Nita.

• • •

Ms. Garrett accompanied Mr. Reilly to the lunch meeting down at the World Trade Center in lower Manhattan. Gunn stayed behind at the suite to go over his upcoming itinerary. Reilly had the next month of his life planned out almost to the minute. It looked as though he would be home just four days over the next four weeks.

Sitting there on the eighteenth floor of the Plaza, eating his filet mignon sandwich and endive salad ordered from room service, staring out the window at the vast expanse of Central Park, Gunn had mixed feelings about all that time away from home. On the one hand, he was glad; glad to be away from all the hassles, glad he did not have to see Sam's bruised and somber face, glad he did not have to deal with all the bullshit of trying like a dog to make everything better. He would just send flowers and jewelry from every port, and all, in time, would work out. But on the other hand, Gunn knew his wife was a proud and stubborn woman. Half English, a quarter German, and a quarter Scot, Sam had the blood of warriors coursing through her veins. Gunn knew what had happened up in their bedroom would not fade quickly. And his absence might only prolong the troubles between them. But what could he do? Reilly was the boss. Reilly pulled the strings. If Reilly told him to go to Seattle, Portland, San Francisco, Los Angeles, and San Diego for a fortnight without even so much as a day with the wife and kids, well, he just had to buck up and do his duty.

●　　●　　●

MR. REILLY RETURNED late in the afternoon. Without, to Gunn Henderson's intense disappointment, Ms. Nita Garrett.

Reilly saw Gunn looking over his shoulder for the blond bombshell. The boss laughed, slapped his salesman on the back. "Don't worry, Gunn, she'll be back."

"No, I—"

"A pretty fair looker, huh?"

"Unreal."

"She's on the payroll now."

Gunn wondered in what capacity, but decided he better not ask. "That's good to know."

"As your assistant."

Gunn felt pretty sure he had not heard that right. "What?"

"Nita will be your assistant, Gunn. Now I know you prefer to work solo, but I think she will be an enormous asset."

Gunn's brain suddenly felt like it had been bombarded by a zillion tiny thought stimulators. The blond bombshell, my assistant? My God, he wondered, what'll be the ramifications of that?

"I'm sure she'll be an asset, Mr. Reilly, but, as you know, I usually work alone."

"Here's the way I see it, Gunn. Men turn into drooling, jabbering idiots in the presence of a woman like Nita. They immediately want to rip off her dress and have sex with her. But since they can't do this without going to jail, they settle for simply looking and daydreaming. And while they look and daydream, my friend, you sell. You sell like crazy. Like a madman. They'll want to buy because they'll want to make Nita happy. They'll want Nita to give them a big smile."

"Jesus, Mr. Reilly, I don't know. It sounds kind of . . ." Gunn wanted to use words like *sleazy* and *crude* and *whorish*. But he knew the sales game, no matter how you played it, was sleazy and crude and whorish. It was just a matter of semantics. The blond bombshell had taken his breath away. Why not the client's breath?

"Sounds kind of like what, Gunn?" inquired Mr. Reilly.

"Like a stroke of genius," answered Gunn.

"Exactly," said Mr. Reilly.

By this time it had occurred to Gunn that Ms. Nita Garrett and he would be traveling together, staying in adjoining rooms, sharing meals and drinks and maybe a few laughs. That would certainly not be all bad. Although, it could cause a small problem. On the home front. With Sam.

"Now listen, Gunn," said Mr. Reilly, "I want you to know I called this meeting in the Plaza for a reason. I thought about coming out to the house in the Hamptons, but decided it would be better to rendez-vous here. I know you love your wife and that Sam's a very fine woman, but experience has taught me that an assistant like Nita Garrett can turn wives into crazy people. No matter how up front and professional the relationship might be, wives can conjure up all kinds of jealous and paranoid scenarios."

"I appreciate your concern, Mr. Reilly," Gunn tried to sound convincing, "but I don't think it will be a problem."

"That's fine, Gunn. I didn't think it would be. I just like to draw a line between business and pleasure, between what goes on at home and what goes on at the office."

"I agree, sir. One hundred percent."

"It's better that way," continued Mr. Reilly, "for you, for me, and for Creative Marketing Enterprises. As titillating as she might be, Nita Garrett is your business associate. Nothing more. Understood?"

"Of course, sir. Absolutely."

"Good," said Mr. Reilly, "just so we understand each other."

Gunn nodded.

Mr. Reilly moved to the sideboard to pour himself a scotch and soda. After offering Gunn a drink and Gunn declining, Mr. Reilly returned to his place on the sofa. "Now, Gunn, I have one more matter to discuss with you before we bring this meeting to a close."

"Yes, sir?"

"It's kind of a touchy issue. It concerns Brady, the caretaker out at PC Apple Acres."

"Yes, sir. I'm glad you brought that up. I've been wanting to talk to you about that situation."

Mr. Reilly sipped his scotch. "Now's your chance."

"Well, I don't want to sound like I'm complaining, but the truth is, that man has upset the delicate domestic balance in our family."

"Meaning?"

"Meaning he has several times upset my wife. And with me gone so much it makes things . . . it makes things difficult."

"Difficult how, Gunn? Be specific."

"He's always around. Inflicting himself."

"Are you sure he's not just trying to be helpful?"

Gunn did not particularly like the way this was going. Nor did he like the condescending tone he could hear in Reilly's voice. "I don't know. That could be it. But he's definitely upsetting my wife."

"Is Brady upsetting your wife, Gunn?" Reilly eyed his salesman closely. "Or is Brady upsetting you?"

That one gave Gunn pause. He paused so long to contemplate the anatomy of the question that Reilly chose the moment to bring the matter to a head.

"Look, Gunn, let's be frank with each other."

"Excuse me?"

"I know you beat the hell out of your wife a couple weeks ago."

"Huh? What! I never—"

Mr. Reilly held up his hand. "I think it would be best if you said nothing at all from here on out. It behooves you to say nothing. I know you quarreled with your wife. I assume it was over the caretaker. I know you struck her, hard enough to leave bruises. I do not condone this kind of behavior, Gunn, but I know it happens. The question is: Will it happen again? And the answer is: Not on my watch. Not while you're working for me. Not while you're working for Creative Marketing Enterprises. I can't have my top salesman going around with a badge on his chest proclaiming him a wife-beater. It's not good for business, Gunn. So here's the deal. Plain and simple." Mr. Reilly took a moment to sip his scotch and soda. Then he leaned forward, homed in on Gunn's eyes. "Make nice with your wife and leave the fucking caretaker alone. Got it?"

"But Mr. Reilly, I—"

"I told you not to talk, Gunn. Now do what I tell you. Or you'll be out on your ass. This is your one and only warning."

30 Jason and Megan went back to school; the same school they'd attended the previous spring, the one halfway to Manhattan. Sam had tried to find something closer, but summer had come and gone so fast, barely time to catch her breath, much less research and visit new schools for the children. And then Gunn had beaten her up, throwing her whole world into a tailspin.

"Nothing much good out here anyway," Brady told her one morning as they watched the limousine head out the drive. "Not in the way of private schools anyway."

"What about the public schools?" Sam did her best to stay out of Brady's direct line of sight. She looked much better than she had immediately after her lopsided battle with Gunn, but she still had some vague traces of puffiness and discoloration around the eyes.

Brady, out front early cleaning up the rhododendron beds, kept his eyes on his work. No need to even take a peek, for he had seen the damage done. "I don't think you want your children going to the public schools around here, ma'am."

"No? Why not?"

"From what I hear," lied the caretaker, who had absolutely no knowledge of the East Hampton public school system whatsoever, "they're pretty atrocious. The quality of both students and teachers is quite low. You're talking mostly about the offspring of fishermen and handymen and bartenders. Not exactly the cream of the crop. Probably not the breed of fish you want your children swimming with. And the teachers aren't much better, what with salaries the lowest of almost anywhere in the state."

Brady may have pushed a bit too far on this last point. Sam frowned and looked surprised. "Really? Low salaries? In East Hampton?"

Brady snagged some weeds, shoved them into a canvas sack he had looped around his belt. "Yes, ma'am," he replied. "I know it's hard to believe with all the affluence out here, but you have to remember, the rich folks who own these fancy homes don't live here year-round. They live back in the city where they send their kids to private schools."

Sam saw the logic. "That's true."

"The rich folks," continued Brady, the fibs falling fervently from his lips, "don't give a toot about the local schools. On a conscious level, they want their tax dollars spent on cops and firemen to protect their expensive real estate. And on a subconscious, and more malevolent level, they have no interest in educating the cook's kid. In fact, they'd just as soon keep the cook's kid ignorant in order to maintain the status quo for generations to come. We may be a democracy, but a certain amount of social suppression still exists."

All this while he weeded and cultivated beneath the lush green leaves of the rhododendrons.

Sam, her eyes wandering back and forth between Brady and the limousine that had disappeared through the gate at the end of the drive, wondered about the caretaker's education. She wanted to ask, but decided it might be improper. So instead, she settled for, "Yes, I see what you mean."

The caretaker smiled to himself. He always marveled at how gullible even intelligent people could be, how easy it was to lead them down the primrose path. He kept weeding, but went right on talking. The time had come, however, to shelve the social dogma, to turn back to a more personal approach. "I know it's tough," he commented, "both on you and on those kids, the two of them being gone all day, but it's a sacrifice well worth the price. You can't pay too much for good education. I think Jason and Megan will one day do great things."

This final pronouncement caused Sam to stop moving her eyes. To anyone else, Brady's remark would have sounded sappy and conspicuously manipulative, but Sam was the mother of the children being complimented. Say something nice about their kids and mamas the world over become the easiest creatures on God's green earth to control and beguile. Sam smiled, then trembled ever so slightly at the notion of her two offspring doing great deeds.

"Right now," she said, "Megan wants to be a ballerina, but I think she'll be a painter or a sculptor or maybe a writer. She's so observant and sensitive."

"Yes, ma'am," agreed the caretaker. "I see that sensitivity in her."

"And Jason, he's so intelligent and strong-willed.

He's a natural leader. I think he'll run a large company. Or maybe even the whole country."

"At their age," said Brady, "everything is possible."

Sam, living in her fantasy, nodded. "So yes, they have to travel a long way to get to school. But a bit of sacrifice now will pay huge dividends later. We can't always expect instant gratification."

Brady, content with the knowledge that the two whiners would be out of his hair from dawn till dusk Monday though Friday, immediately filled in the next cliché. "Nothing worthwhile comes easy, ma'am."

"You have to work long and hard to get what you want in life."

Lady, thought Brady, you have no idea. "You can say that again, ma'am."

"Please, Brady, call me Sam."

"Yes, ma'am." Brady chuckled. "I mean *Sam*." And then the caretaker chuckled again. Lightly. As though in mockery of himself.

Oh yes, Brady felt good, really fine. All his worry had been for naught. All summer long he had feared Samantha Henderson might do something extreme and unpredictable, like enroll her brats in the local grammar school, so they would leave home as late as eight-thirty and return as early as three in the afternoon; or maybe something really ugly like hire a tutor and keep the little monsters home all day; or worst-case scenario of all: insist the family move out of the mansion altogether.

Any of these decisions on Mrs. Henderson's part would have thrown an enormous monkey wrench into the caretaker's long-range plans. And that would have been most unpleasant. The caretaker loathed having to count on others, especially such emotional beasts as mothers. No predicting what they would do to protect their little chicks.

31

Gunn did not have sex with Nita during their West Coast swing. But for some reason a pair of her panties, lacy lavender ones, wound up in his suitcase. That same suitcase sat at the foot of Sam and Gunn's king-size bed for over twelve hours before the mysterious goods were finally discovered.

The situation unfolded like this: Early one Saturday morning in the middle of September, after being on the road for nearly a fortnight, Gunn arrived home for a brief thirty-six-hour respite. He could have arrived home the night before, but Gunn had a plan: he took the red-eye from L.A. to La Guardia, arriving in New York just after five A.M. At six-thirty he climbed out of the limo, grabbed his suitcase from the trunk, and headed for the front door. Slowly, quietly, he entered the mansion so as not to disturb any of the still-sleeping occupants. Up the stairs he crept in an effort to deflect even the faintest squeak or creak.

Gunn was convinced this hushed early morning entry had everything in the world to do with his desire to mend fences with his wife. Every night during his absence he had called her on the phone. The first week

Sam had barely uttered a word to him before passing the receiver off to Jason or Megan. But early in the second week she began to thaw. Gunn was on his absolutely positively best behavior: sweet, subdued, occasionally silly, attentive, charming but not too charming. He was the way Sam wished he was always. And every single day he FedExed gifts, overnight priority. Gifts for Jason, gifts for Megan, gifts for Sam. Pears from Portland, cashmere sweaters from Seattle, a tiny gold streetcar necklace from the city by the bay. It all worked wonders in putting the black eye and swollen cheeks behind them. And just a few nights before he arrived home, Gunn actually got Sam to laugh. Right out loud. Just some stupid joke about Catholic priests and the true purpose for their long black robes (to hide the altar boys), but Sam could not help herself; she had herself a good yuck, her first one in weeks.

Still, Gunn knew he would not be entirely successful with his latest campaign until he crawled into bed with his wife and pressed his manliness up against her naked flesh. This would be the ultimate test. And this is why he planned to arrive home very early in the A.M. He feared if he arrived in the evening Sam might be perfectly agreeable, but when the time came for bed she could easily tell him to hit the road, or at least the sofa. But by slipping silently into the bedroom with just a cast of dawn peering through the windows, Gunn could bypass the evening performance and go straight to the quiet whispers and soft caresses. He would just slip between the sheets and strut his stuff. Sam would not, he felt sure, be able to resist.

So Gunn carried out his plan. But do not be misled.

His early morning bedroom raid had another side to it as well, a side riddled with insecurity and paranoia. Oh, yes, Gunn Henderson also snuck into his wife's boudoir at the crack of dawn just in case she might be in there spooned up naked against that no-good immoral caretaker. Gunn may not have bedded Nita, but he had definitely thought about it. Quite frequently, in fact. Night and day. Sitting beside her on the plane flying south from Seattle to San Francisco, he had practically ejaculated into his underwear, so intense were his sexual deliberations. A man with this kind of infidelity rolling around in his brain had no trouble at all conjuring up a sex scene between his bride and this Brady character. It takes a mediocre imagination at best to imagine others doing to us what we would have little problem doing to them.

Alas, Gunn found Sam all alone. Well, almost all alone. Brady, an early morning cup of steaming hot joe cupped between his hands, stood nearby but well hidden behind the wall, eye to the open peephole, watching and waiting for events to unfold. Maybe Sam knew nothing of Gunn's imminent arrival, but Brady knew all about it. He had actually terminated an international teleconference in order to witness this loving reunion.

And loving it was. Gunn's calculations proved extraordinarily accurate. Sam, sleepy-eyed and dreaming of sun-drenched island beaches and fruit-flavored tropical drinks, welcomed her husband into their bed with nary a second thought. The fact that Sam rarely had any coherent thoughts this early in the A.M. aided Gunn's plan enormously. But give Gunn credit: He knew his wife extremely well.

He placed his suitcase, the one containing the lavender lace panties, at the foot of the bed, stripped down to his silk boxers, crawled between the sheets, and pressed his chest up against his wife's back. She moaned softly and melted into him. "You're home so early."

Gunn cooed in her ear. "I couldn't wait any longer. I've been missing you like crazy."

Sam smiled softly. Despite everything, she was happy to have him back in their bed.

Brady, in perfect position just a few feet and a wall away, saw her smile. He breathed a sigh of relief. For weeks, ever since Henderson had inflicted himself physically on his wife, he had been hoping for a reconciliation. It would have been no fun at all to succeed so easily, to bring wrack and ruin to this marriage after just one small intrusion. That would be like taking the gold medal after performing just a single perfect dive. Brady had been planning and plotting for years. He had all sorts of adventures in store for Henderson and his pretty bride.

"Do you have a pot of coffee up here?" Brady heard Gunn ask Sam. "It smells powerfully like freshly brewed coffee."

"Coffee? No. No coffee. But I could use a cup."

"Don't you smell it? God, it smells like there's a pot brewing right over on the dresser."

Brady, smile on his face, sipped his joe. He loved moments like this. They made the whole dreary prospect of everyday life worth living.

"Hush," said Sam. "Maybe Mrs. Griner is down in the kitchen. Just be quiet and hold me. I want to go back to sleep with your hand cupped lightly around my breast."

Gunn did as ordered. He wanted to check out that smell of coffee wafting past his nose, maybe get himself a big mugful. But spousal responsibility beckoned. So he gently cupped his hand around his wife's breast. And as he did, he tried to repress a groinal desire to feel his hand cupped firmly around Nita's breast.

Brady, satisfied all was momentarily well, finished his joe and retreated. He had pressing business back at his command center on the third floor of the old barn. But, no problem. If the need for further surveillance arose, he had other means of keeping tabs on the Hendersons.

● ● ●

THE HENDERSONS, husband and wife and kids, spent all of Saturday together. And a gorgeous late summer Saturday it was. They visited the beach, splashed through the still-warm surf, ate clam rolls and ice cream cones at Yummy's Seafood and Summer Treats out on Highway 27 in Amagansett, cruised out for a look at the Montauk lighthouse. Gunn longed for a hard, sweaty, competitive game of tennis under that deep blue sky, but this desire, he knew, demanded suppression. Today, like it or not, was family day. Today he needed to appease his wounded wife, entertain his annoying son, and wipe the double-chocolate-peanut-butter-cup ice cream off his little girl's chin. Gunn loved his kids; he just didn't like them very much.

Back at the mansion, Greta Griner chopped mushrooms in preparation for Gunn Henderson's favorite supper: bloody filet mignon piled high with mushrooms sautéed in butter and surrounded by a halo of mashed potatoes whipped up with heavy cream. Greta could easily have poisoned those mushrooms and brought Gunn Henderson's abusive life to a grinding halt, but that scenario was not part of the plan. Despite her rather fiery and independent nature, the cook found herself in a very delicate position. She needed to be very careful about what she said and did. Greta loathed Gunn Henderson for the bruises he had inflicted upon his wife's pretty face, but she nevertheless had to keep herself in check. There was the Big Picture to keep in mind. Besides, she knew Henderson would sooner or later get his due.

In the meantime, she had a small chore to perform. It would take only a moment, but she nevertheless took a peek out the front door to make sure the coast was clear before slipping upstairs and into the master suite. Greta was, at times, a wary accomplice in this unfolding drama. But money and luxury and security are powerful stimulants, so up the stairs she bounded on still strong and spindly legs.

The moment she entered the master bedroom she spotted the suitcase. It sat on the floor at the foot of the bed. She picked it up, placed it on the comforter, and zipped it open. On top lay a heap of dirty socks and silk boxers. Greta had to plunge her hand into the mess of soiled laundry and fish around to find that lovely pair of lavender lace panties. But find them she did, under a wad of smelly T-shirts. As per her discussion with Brady, she relocated the panties to the top of the heap, only partially concealing them beneath a gray, smelly, and still-sweaty sock.

Then, satisfied with her handiwork, she quickly withdrew, back to the kitchen and her thick slabs of marinating flesh.

The caretaker, from his post up on the third floor of the barn, observed Mrs. Griner on closed circuit TV. Some months earlier, in anticipation of the Hendersons' arrival, several of the rooms in the mansion, including the master bedroom suite, had been hard-wired for surveillance. Tiny cameras not much bigger than pinheads had been unobtrusively located in out-of-the-way corners so as not to disturb the occupants of the room. The caretaker preferred a live performance, either through the peepholes in the walls or through a window, but, in a pinch, when time was tight, TV cameras served a useful purpose. Especially when just checking to make sure others did as they were told. And, of course, for making videos.

● ● ●

THE HENDERSONS ARRIVED home from their family fun day in the sun late in the afternoon. Long shadows reached across the grounds of PC Apple Acres, clear evidence of the days growing shorter, of autumn and then winter on the wax.

Mrs. Griner greeted the family at the front door, asking immediately if a good time had been enjoyed by all. A chorus of semienthusiastic yeahs echoed through the marble foyer as the quartet filed over the threshold.

"I need a shower," announced Gunn, once again secure he was head of the household and master of his own fate. He headed directly for the stairs.

Greta moved quickly to intercept him. "Mr. Henderson, before you go up, could I have a word with you in the kitchen?"

"Can't it wait?" questioned Gunn. "Say half an hour?"

"I promise it won't take a minute," countered Mrs. Griner. "It's about dinner."

That caught Gunn's attention. The mere utterance of the word *dinner* was music to his stomach. A man who truly loved a good meal. That prison chow must be killing him.

Gunn followed the cook down the hall to the kitchen.

"I'll be upstairs," called Sam.

Greta took a deep breath and dabbed at the perspiration that had collected on her forehead. Mission accomplished, she thought to herself.

Sam climbed the stairs and headed for the bedroom. Mrs. Griner led Gunn into the kitchen. Sam entered the bedroom and crossed directly to the bathroom. She did not even notice the suitcase; her bladder was bursting, screaming for relief. Greta showed Gunn the large slabs of filet mignon marinating in a glass pan on the counter beside the sink. Sam took a pee and washed her hands and face. Gunn bent down and lavished his olfactory glands with the pungent vapors of raw flesh. Sam patted her cheeks with a soft towel. Greta asked Gunn if he would like his filet mignon cooked under the broiler or out on the barbecue. Sam went back into the bedroom for a fresh shirt and maybe a cotton sweater to ward off the evening chill. Gunn told the cook to barbecue the meat out on the grill, medium rare, then added, "And remember, Mrs. Griner, as my grandfather used to say, 'It's rarer where there's none.' " "Yes, sir," replied Mrs. G., "indeed it is." Gunn winked at the cook and left the kitchen. Greta watched him go, then flashed the bastard the bird behind his back. It made her feel a little better. Sam sat on the edge of the bed. Just for a moment, just to give her weary feet a brief rest. Gunn started up the stairs. Sam took note of her husband's suitcase, of the dirty laundry that would need to be washed and dried and folded. She wished he did not have to travel quite so much. The traveler reached the top of the stairs and headed down the hallway. Sam spotted something lavender beneath a dirty sock. She could not recall Gunn owning even one piece of lavender clothing. Curious, she reached over and picked it up. Gunn, his stride long and confident, closed in on the doorway of the master bedroom suite. Thoughts of a hot shower and then tooling his wife danced around in his head. He felt sure Sam was ready for a roll beneath the sheets. But Sam no longer sat on the bed. Sam was on her feet now. Gunn spotted her the instant he passed through the door. She had a pretty fair scowl etched across her face. And a pair of lavender lace panties dangling from her fingers.

"What the hell," she demanded, her voice ice cold and raspy, "are these?"

32 Gunn, physically if not morally innocent, denied any and all knowledge of the lavender lace panties. "Sam, trust me, I have absolutely no idea how those things got in my bag."

Those things continued to dangle from Sam's fingers. "So you don't deny they were in your bag?"

Gunn shrugged. "You said you found them in there, so I assume they were there."

"Yes, Gunn, I found them in your bag. Right on top. So I assume you must know who they belong to."

"You assume wrong. I've never seen the damn things in my life. They're not yours?"

Sam held the panties up a bit higher. They were, thankfully, fresh and clean. "Have you ever seen these on me?"

Gunn shrugged again. "Maybe they're new."

"Sorry, darling, they're not my style."

Gunn, the old mouth moving before the brain could keep it closed, chose this retort: "Maybe you should change your style. Those are kind of sexy." The panties, the arguing, the innuendo—the whole package had in fact given Gunn an erection. Luckily for him, that reality was safely hidden inside his roomy cotton shorts.

Sam screamed her next question pretty much at the top of her lungs. "Who the hell do they belong to, Gunn?"

Behind the wall, the caretaker winced at the shrill inquiry.

Gunn made some hasty calculations, decided to take a new tack, go on the offensive. "Like I said, Sam, I don't know who they belong to, but I would like to know what the hell you were doing in my suitcase."

"I wasn't doing anything in your damn suitcase. It was just lying wide-open on the bed." Sam's voice reached a screech. "And these were lying on top!"

"I never opened my suitcase, dear," Gunn replied. "I left it closed at the foot of the bed."

"Well," said Sam, the sarcasm like poisonous darts upon her tongue, "I guess the Lilliputians must have snuck into the room while we were at the beach."

"I guess so."

"Bastard!"

Brady snickered.

Gunn's mouth once again moved with a bit too much haste. "I think you opened it."

"Excuse me?" asked Sam. "Are you calling me a liar? I told you I found that suitcase open on the bed."

Gunn's tongue kept wagging like the tail of some overheated mutt. "I think you opened my suitcase and slipped that pair of frilly underwear in there just so you could get something started."

Brady, chewing furiously on a handful of Junior Mints, laughed right out loud at Gunn Henderson's ability to rationalize and justify. Fortunately, for Brady anyway, the volume in the bedroom easily snuffed out his impromptu chuckle.

"Don't try and twist this, Gunn!" shrieked Sam. "I won't have you twisting this like you twist everything else. I didn't open your damn suitcase! I didn't plant these damn panties!" She balled up the lavender lace and hurled it at her husband. The panties struck him on the shoulder without physical harm and dropped benignly onto the plush wool carpet. "I didn't do anything, dammit! I didn't do anything!" Sam began to cry. Big wet tears spilled out of her eyes and careened off her cheeks. "Nothing," she screamed between whimpers. "Nothing at all. I just tried to love you, to be your wife and the mother of your children. And what do you do? You beat me. And cheat on me. And lie to me. You bastard! You filthy bastard!"

"Mommy?"

Sam moved her wet, bloodshot eyes across the room. Megan stood in the doorway looking small and frightened and confused.

"Mommy, what's wrong?"

Sam crossed quickly to her daughter, shoving her husband out of the way. "Nothing, sweetheart. Nothing's wrong." Sam put her arm around Megan's shoulder and led the little girl down the hallway to her bedroom. "Mommy's just upset about something," she explained as they walked. "But it's nothing, nothing at all. Everything's just fine. We're going to wash up and then go have some dinner."

Behind the wall, Brady actually felt a twinge of emotion. He probably could have shed a tear, but popped another handful of Junior Mints instead.

Gunn, husband and father, turned and watched his wife and daughter stroll down the hallway. After they had disappeared into Megan's bedroom, he bent down and picked up those lace panties. Where, he wondered, had they come from? And how the hell did they get into his suitcase? He ran the waistband between the thumb and index finger of his right hand. The material was soft and erotic. The horniness that had overcome him moments earlier hit him again. Until that morning, it had been weeks since he'd had sex. Masturbation, though a pleasant, if brief, release, really only caused an increase in his carnal desires. Suddenly, and somewhat absently, he raised his right hand and began to rub those panties against his cheek. His thoughts wandered away, far away, not to his wife, but to distant lands and foreign pussies, one pussy in particular, that belonging to Ms. Nita Garrett. Oh yes, Ms. Nita, in a string bikini, diving into the heated swimming pool at their hotel out in Westwood. Diving in and stroking effortlessly across the surface of the water. Far, far away. Gunn rubbed those panties all over his face as he felt the pressure building down inside his boxers.

"Dad?"

Gunn, startled, dropped those panties and looked up. There stood his son, Jason, in the doorway.

Gunn frowned, growled. "What is it?"

Jason stared at his father, mouth agape.

Gunn roared. "I said, what is it?"

Jason, eyes huge and wide open, said, "Wow, Dad, like that was really weird."

"What the hell do you want, Jason?"

"I mean, you were like in a trance or something. What were you doing playing with Mom's underwear? Is it like some kind of erotic play thing you guys do before sex?"

Gunn, anger his sole remaining weapon, snarled at his son. "Mind your own business, dammit!"

"Hey, I'm sorry. I just wanted—"

"What do you want?"

"Oh, right," answered Jason, pulling back, "it's Mr. Reilly. He's on the telephone."

Gunn had not even heard the telephone ring. He cracked himself on the side of the head, told himself to stay in control. Then he crossed to the table beside the bed and picked up the receiver. Reilly wanted to talk business, dollars and cents. Gunn needed a few moments to gather his thoughts, but once ready, he gave the boss an earful.

Jason lingered for a moment, then he retreated to his room where he decided the time had finally arrived to smoke that joint he'd bought for two bucks a couple weeks earlier in the boys' room at school. Nervous, paranoid, giddy with anticipation, he lit up and blew the smoke out the open window. All efforts to inhale caused him to choke and sputter. But he kept at it anyway, determined to cop a buzz. Halfway through the reefer he spotted Brady the caretaker emerge from the basement and stroll across the lawn. Jason thought nothing of it. He was far too busy trying to keep that smoke in his lungs.

While down the hall Sam and Megan sat on

Megan's bed. They held each other close. Sam did her best to hold back the tears.

And so it went with the Hendersons, another middle-class American family, on that lazy late summer Saturday afternoon.

33 On Monday morning Brady sang. He began singing not long after Gunn departed for Chicago and Jason and Megan headed off to school. He sang in his clear and melodious tenor, a touch of the Irish lingering on many of the vowels. Brady sang from the trees, from the oaks and ashes and maples, sometimes from the uppermost branches.

Back in the kitchen the women chatted and sipped their coffee sweetened with sugar and dappled with cream. Greta Griner did most of the talking; Samantha felt far too low to string together more than a word or two at a time. Not only was Gunn off again for at least another fortnight, but the appearance of the mysterious lavender panties had not been resolved. All day Sunday Gunn had insisted he knew nothing whatsoever about that unidentified undergarment, but Sam could not bring herself to believe him. She wanted to believe him, even if just for her own peace of mind, but sitting there at the kitchen table, pouring even more cream and sugar into her coffee, she felt those distressing jitters of marital distrust. Suspicion blotted out all other stimuli. Greta's rapid flow of words flew past Sam with the speed of a cosmic meteor shower. She imagined Gunn, ensconced in some fancy Chicago hotel room, telling the owner of those lavender lace panties to please toss her lingerie with a bit more decorum. And she further imagined the owner of those panties laughing, then draping a naked, waxed leg over her husband's hard and hairy abdomen. The imagination can be a terrible burden to bear.

"Listen," commanded Mrs. Griner.

The single word, announced so boldly, tugged Sam from her meditations on the art of infidelity. She stared at Mrs. G. and asked, "Listen to what?"

"I thought I heard something." In fact, Greta had heard nothing at all. But the clock on the wall struck nine, the witching hour. She and Brady had planned this the night before.

"What did you hear?"

Mrs. Griner crossed to the French doors leading out to the terrace. "It sounded like singing."

"Singing?" Sam, proud of her hearing, perked up her ears.

"I'm sure I heard something." Mrs. G. threw open the doors. The cool morning air rushed inside. The cook stuck her head out. "Yes, I knew I heard it."

Sam, ambivalent about the distraction, stood. "Heard what?"

"Brady," came the answer. "The caretaker. He must be in a mood. He's singing."

Sam still heard nothing. She crossed to the French doors. Mrs. Griner stepped out onto the terrace. Sam followed.

"Listen carefully," said the cook. "It comes and goes. Probably with the shifting winds." She cupped her ear and listened. "But I heard him. I'm sure I heard him."

Sam stood still and listened. She wanted to hear Brady singing. She needed to hear him singing. She wanted his singing to pull her away from her wretched imaginings. And then, for an instant, coming from a good distance away, she heard it, just a few notes, high and scattered. "You have incredible hearing, Mrs. Griner. You heard that from inside. With the door closed."

Greta smiled, but thought, Poor, dear. Poor, poor dear.

They listened for the voice again. After half a minute or so they heard a few more threads. Then more silence. Mrs. Griner said, "I need to take care of something in the kitchen. Why don't you go out and try to find him? But be careful, dear. Don't let him hear you coming. He gets spooked, like a warbler. If he hears you coming he'll probably turn into a mute."

Sam took Mrs. G.'s advice. She grabbed a jacket and went looking for the caretaker. She heard him for a long time before she actually found him. His voice seemed to come from nowhere and everywhere all at once. It seemed to reverberate and echo throughout the grounds of the estate. Sam walked in circles in an effort to locate the source.

His songs were mostly sad laments, one rolling directly into the next, as though each had no beginning or end, just refrains. They sounded to Sam like ancient songs from the Old Country, songs about the sea, songs about the beautiful Irish countryside, songs about love won and love lost and love never declared, songs about dying and about death. Sam decided

Brady must be a very sad man. Proud but sad, and probably lonely, and most definitely in need of someone to love.

A dead limb from an old maple creaked, then fell, came crashing to the ground about thirty feet in front of where Sam walked. The fallen limb caused her to glance up into the tree. And there, at least fifty feet in the air, in the high branches of that maple, mostly hidden by an abundance of maple leaves, small pruning saw in hand, stood Brady balanced precariously between two gnarly branches. Like some wild woodlands songbird, the notes continued to flow from his mouth: "Out on the sea, in that ancient wooden dory, He pulls up his nets, searching for food and glory. But gale winds from the east, thunder and lightning from the sky, He turns and heads for home, hoping now only not to die, hoping now only not to die. . . ."

Sam stayed perfectly still so as not to disturb him. All the while he sang, he worked. His pruning saw never stopped humming. It sliced through even thick limbs with powerful strokes. The dead branches fell and crashed to the ground, often providing natural rhythms for Brady's melancholy songs.

Sam, mesmerized, watched and listened and in no time at all forgot all about Gunn and his infidelities. After several minutes Brady began to descend, singing every step of the way. Sam thought about running and hiding, but his glorious voice kept her feet from moving.

And then, quite suddenly, he jumped from one of the lower branches and hit the ground lightly. "Ahh, Mrs. Henderson," he said, his voice still carrying a melody, "I had no idea you were nearby." This comment despite the fact that he appeared not in the least bit surprised to see her.

"Oh, yes, well, I was out for a walk and just happened to hear you singing."

Brady blushed and kicked at the dirt with his boots. "Sorry to disturb your peaceful morning stroll, ma'am. Probably sounded like fingernails scraping across a chalkboard."

"Hardly that, Brady. On the contrary, it was quite wonderful. You have a beautiful voice."

Brady blushed again. "Thank you, ma'am. You're far too kind. But I guess any gift I have I owe to my mother."

"Your mother was a singer?"

"Well, she sang. All the time. Day and night. She taught me how to carry a tune."

This was not entirely true. Brady's mother never taught him to sing. In fact, she never sang a note in her life. A quiet and humble woman, widowed before her son reached his tenth birthday, music played no role in her life whatsoever. Brady came by his golden vocal cords naturally, a gift from the Almighty. But he knew the story of his mama's gift would play well with this sweet and sentimental mother of two.

"She taught you well," said Sam. "I'm not a critic or anything, but I think you're good enough to sing professionally."

The caretaker forced himself to blush one more time, no easy task. "Now, Mrs. Henderson, I can't be listening to that kind of talk. I'll get a swelled head over it. And a swelled head is no good for a man climbing into tall trees to cut out dead branches."

● ● ●

THAT NIGHT, after she got the children to bed, Sam called Mandy down in the suburbs of D.C. After the obligatory How are you? How are the kids? Sam said, "I think Gunn's cheating on me."

"Why do you think that?"

Sam told Mandy about the panties.

Mandy thought it over for half a second or so. "Panties in the suitcase ain't good, honey. No, not good at all."

"Especially right on top," added Sam. "As though I was meant to find them."

"So what does the bastard say?"

"He denies knowing anything about them."

"Typical male response: Deny it and maybe it'll go away. God, they're all the same."

"So what should I do?"

"Hire an assassin. Have him shot. Maybe tortured first."

"Mandy!"

"I don't know, Sam. What do you want to do?"

"Cry."

"Oh, right. That'll solve everything."

"It might make me feel better."

"Believe me, it won't. It'll only make you feel worse. It'll only make you feel used and abused."

"Then what do you suggest?"

"Hey," replied Mandy, a lot more bark than bite, "do as the Romans do. The bastard cheats on you, you cheat on the bastard."

The caretaker, up in his business billet on the third floor of the old barn, snickered. He liked this friend, this Mandy something or other. She had an attitude right up his alley. He listened to the ladies on speakerphone with one ear as he listened to the Tokyo stock prices with the other ear. Oh, yes, Brady had the telephone lines over at the mansion well tapped. Not a call came in or went out without his knowledge.

"Mandy, you're horrible."

"Hey, honey, why should he have all the fun?"

"I don't think," said Sam, even as her spirits began to brighten, "it would necessarily be fun to cheat on my husband."

"Now, that depends."

"On what?"

"On who's available."

Brady could hardly believe his ears. This gal Mandy could easily be part of the team. He wondered if he should make room for her on the payroll.

Sam decided to play along with Mandy's rough and tumble advice. In fact, she wanted to play along, just the way she had done hundreds of times before when she and her friend had fantasized about having affairs with the tennis pro at the club or the fitness trainer at the gym or the UPS man who brought the packages to the front door. It was fun to fantasize. She had been fantasizing all her life. Once, years ago, even Gunn had been a fantasy.

"There's always," Sam murmured, "the caretaker."

Brady's ears perked up big-time. Tokyo faded.

"The who?" asked Mandy.

"The caretaker. Here on the estate. He takes care of the place."

"Perfect," said Mandy. "He could take care of you, too."

The girls giggled. Brady marveled at life's imponderables.

Sam said, "He's the sweetest guy."

Mandy groaned. "Sweet can be boring, honey. Sweet can mean simple."

"Oh, no," insisted Sam, "this one is definitely not simple. He's intelligent and sensitive. And he can sing."

"My God, Sam, you sound smitten already. Is he cute?"

"You might call Brady cute, but I wouldn't. I'd call him ruggedly handsome."

"Ruggedly handsome. Sounds like a mix of the Marlboro man and a Ralph Lauren model."

"Something like that."

"So tell me what he looks like."

"You know what he looks like."

"I do?"

"You met him."

"I did? When?"

"He was the one down at the boathouse that day Gunn had the trouble with that Jet Ski thing."

"Him! Sam! He was a dream. Those broad shoulders, that tight little butt. Maybe I'll come up and have an affair with him myself. It's boring down here without you."

"He's a swimmer."

"A swimmer?"

Sam told Mandy about the caretaker swimming naked in the pool. She also told her friend about the diving, and planting the garden, and the flat tire, and his Zen-like approach to life.

"It sounds to me," said Mandy, "like you two are having an affair already."

Sam started to tell Mandy how Gunn thought so too, had believed it so strongly, in fact, that he had hit her and beaten her. Women cry and call their friends when their mates are unfaithful, men swing their fists. But Sam slowed herself down. She said nothing about being battered. She was too ashamed.

"Trust me," Sam told her friend, "I am definitely not having an affair with the caretaker."

But that night, in bed, lights out, the huge room dark and lonely and silent, Sam thought about Brady, about his quiet strength and his tender manner. Thinking about Brady helped her to not think about Gunn. And about why Gunn hadn't called her. And about what he might be doing in Chicago. And with whom.

34 Actually, Gunn had tried to call. Several times. He called when he first reached his hotel room early in the evening after a long but invigorating day promoting The Disk. He called, but the line was busy. He showered, called again, but the line was still busy. He phoned Mr. Reilly, went over the day's action, then called home a third time. Still busy. Busy signals annoyed Gunn. He did not think he should ever have to hear a busy signal. After the third try he smashed the receiver down onto the cradle. All day long he had been wanting to apologize to Sam for this whole ugly misunderstanding with his suitcase and those damn panties. But now she was on the phone. She was always on the damn phone. Jabbering away with her mother or her sister or that twit Mandy. He dialed the number a fourth time. Still busy.

"Fuck it," he announced, and then he went across the hall to see if Ms. Garrett might like to go down and get some dinner.

Nita, as always, looked hot. She had changed out of her short and provocative business suit into tight jeans and a loose cotton rugby jersey. "I'm not much in the mood for a restaurant tonight, Gunn. I'd just like to relax, maybe even watch some TV. I thought I'd order room service: a sandwich and a glass of wine. It was kind of a long day."

"Yeah," said Gunn, standing in her doorway, trying hard to keep his eyes up, "I know what you mean. I'm kind of beat myself. I guess I'll just mosey on down to the lobby, have myself a steak and a beer at the bar."

Nita, as is the case with truly beautiful women all over the globe, knew she had complete control over the situation. "I might be kind of dull company tonight," she said, her voice low as she swept those long blond locks behind her ear, "but if you don't feel like doing the bar thing, you're welcome to join me here."

Gunn, his male brain fumbling with a jumble of contradictory messages, simply could not, in the end, help himself. He crossed the threshold into Nita's suite. He might just as well have entered Lucifer's lair.

For dinner they ordered garden salads and London broil sandwiches and cheesecake layered with fudge. "I like a little something naughty every day," Nita cooed. And a bottle of champagne, "to celebrate," Gunn declared, "our great success today in peddling The Disk."

Yes, Gunny "Don Juan" Henderson turned on the charm the moment he made the decision to enter Nita's turf. During their West Coast swing he had kept his distance, stuck to business, a splendid study in professionalism. But my God, he thought, look at her, sitting there on the carpet, back propped up against the foot of the bed, legs long and lean in those tight jeans, smiling and laughing at all his little jokes and quips, her fine white teeth carnivorously ripping into that sourdough and bloody flesh, a dab of horseradish clinging to the corner of her pretty mouth. He wanted to reach down and stroke that horseradish away with his linen napkin. Too bad those mysterious lavender panties kept getting in his way. They hung there in that Chicago hotel room as high and forebidding as the Berlin Wall. Gunn tried to climb over, but he kept hearing a voice in the back of his head, "Down, boy, down! Easy, soldier. One more step and we'll be forced to shoot."

Nita, privy since just a youthful teenager to the wanton desires of both men and boys, let Gunn suffer. She did, however, thrice excuse herself for trips to the little girls' room. Once there she locked the door, turned the faucets on full power, leaned over the toilet, and stuck her index finger down her throat until she gagged and threw up. No way did she want that foul and disgusting cow flesh entering her digestive system. It was one thing to turn Gunn on with her display of meat-eating, but quite another to actually force her body to process the carnage.

•   •   •

AT ELEVEN O'CLOCK, after watching some boring TV news show, Nita showed Gunn to the door. She told him she needed her beauty sleep. He thought about making a move, but that wall was still far too high to climb. He went back to his room and, after pacing around for a few minutes, brushing his teeth, hanging up his clothes, he called Sam. By the time he called it was well after midnight back on the East Coast. Nevertheless, the phone still gave off that incessant busy signal. Gunn, immediately irritated, tried three times in less than a minute, then he tried, unsuccessfully, to break the receiver over his knee.

Horny, half lit on champagne, pissed off at his wife and her flagrant phone habits, Gunn went back to pacing around that lavish hotel room. Who the hell, he wondered, could she be talking to at this hour? For chrissakes! Then, still pacing, he wondered if Nita was naked. Christ, he thought, I should have made the moves on her. She was ready, I could see it in her eyes. I could be over there screwing her right now. Gunn became suddenly and powerfully aware of his loins. A massive erection stretched the soft material of his boxers. He flipped on the TV, punched a few buttons, found the adults only channel, just $7.95 from midnight till dawn, All-Night Fun and Fantasy. A not particularly attractive couple copulated on a not particularly clean-looking couch. Their movements looked stilted and utterly unerotic. Gunn thought about the cameraman and the soundman and the director and all the lackeys standing around watching these two lowlife thespians fake fucking. It disgusted him. The whole thing disgusted him: the pornography, the bitch in the next room, the bitch back home in her mansion babbling day and night on the telephone, The Disk, Reilly, all the bullshit. Gunn sat on the edge of the bed. He pulled down his boxers and grabbed his semierect member. Another woman joined the TV couple. A ménage à trois. Finally, the erotic element Gunn needed.

35 Sam, dreaming of tall trees swinging in the breeze, thought she heard the phone ring. One of her eyes opened slightly. Still dark outside. Not even dawn. No one would be calling at this hour. She closed her eye. But the ringing persisted.

So, half asleep, groggy from the arrival of Megan in the middle of the night, Sam slipped her arm out from under the sheet and groped around on the nightstand for the phone.

"Hello?"

"Sam!"

"Yes?"

"It's me!"

"Gunn. What time is it?"

"Your time? I don't know. Around five."

"Five A.M.?"

"Yes, dammit. Five A.M. Did I wake you up?"

"I guess you did. But that's okay. I'm glad you called."

"I tried calling last night."

"You did?"

"Yeah, I did. Like about a hundred damn times."

Sam had herself wide-awake now. But she kept her voice low, just above a whisper. Little Megan lay at her side, her head against Mom's shoulder. "That's strange. We were home. The whole night."

"I know you were home. You were on the damn phone."

Sam tried to remember. Sometimes the night before seemed days, even weeks away. "On the phone? I don't think so. Jason might have been on for a while right after dinner, but only for a few minutes. Something to do with his homework."

"A few minutes my ass. The phone was busy all goddamn night."

"Oh, wait, no, I did make a call. Around ten o'clock. To Mandy. But that wasn't for very long. Half an hour at the most."

"Don't bullshit me, Sam!" Gunn made some kind of weird breathing snarl, thus indicating his disbelief in his wife's assessment of time. Gunn had not slept well after his frantic and solo sexual release. That event in conjunction with the champagne, the busy signal, and the girl next door had all blended together to produce a pretty nasty case of insomnia. This sleeplessness led to the four A.M. call to his slumbering bride. "The phone was busy at least until after midnight."

"I don't think so."

"You don't have to think so. I know so. I'm the one

who was trying to call, goddammit. So don't bother fucking lying to me."

Sam sighed. She knew better than to argue with him, but this was totally ridiculous. "I'm not lying to you, Gunn. I wasn't on the phone. Maybe Jason was, but I don't think so because I remember him being plugged into some TV show until it was time for bed."

"Then why was the damn phone busy?"

"I don't know. Maybe there was some problem with the line."

"That doesn't wash." Gunn's suspicious instincts kicked into high gear. "If there was a problem with the line you wouldn't've been able to call Mandy." Gunn uttered Sam's friend's name with a remarkable combination of sarcasm and disdain.

Sam glanced at Megan. The little girl was still fast asleep. "I told you I wasn't on the phone, Gunn. Now can we please talk about something else?"

"Yeah, we can talk about anything you want. I just don't like being lied to."

"I'm not lying to you."

"So then I guess that phone just jumps on and off the hook at its own convenience."

Exasperated, Sam gave up. She had been through this kind of thing too many times in the past. Once the man began to obsess over something, it became virtually impossible to slow his momentum. Over the years Sam had tried everything: arguing, explaining, ignoring. But nothing really worked. Gunn Henderson would not be distracted from his appointed rounds.

"Yeah," agreed Sam, "I guess it does."

Too bad, of course, the Hendersons didn't know the real story behind that busy signal. The truth can be such a source of freedom. The truth, in this case, lay at the feet of the caretaker. A wiz at all things electric and electronic, Brady not only had the phones over at the mansion tapped, he had total control over all incoming and outgoing calls. If he wanted to block all incoming calls with a busy signal, he could so with the flip of a switch. This switch allowed calls to go out but none to come in, thus permitting Sam to call Mandy but not permitting Gunn to call Sam. Brady had figured Gunn, his guilt festering, would try to call his wife. But he did not want them to make that connection. He wanted Gunn to get nothing but a busy signal, thereby causing Gunn to go into the slow burn. And so, the switch had been flipped. Brady didn't flip the switch back until he went to bed a little after one. And he was still sleeping a few hours later when Gunn, battling his demons in that Chicago hotel room, dialed up his wife in the predawn hours. But no matter. Brady had their conversation on tape, all that ranting and growling about busy signals. He would review the tape later in the day, see if anything even remotely interesting had been uttered. He doubted there had been. The Hendersons, husband and wife, were almost tediously predictable.

36 Chicago, St. Louis, Kansas City—Gunn and Nita wooed the buyers wherever they landed. Gunn had the pitch down cold, and Nita, well, Nita struck a corrosive combination of fear and desire into all who came within her potent female aura. Reilly had called it right: Men wanted to make Nita happy. Owners of toy stores and hobby shops, of five-and-dimes and 7 Elevens, of warehouse outlets and suburban malls, wanted to see Nita smile. And since the vast majority of them could not bring joy to Nita's gorgeous face with their great good looks or Olympian bodies or clever wits or charming personalities, they had to resort to pulling out their wallets. To impress Nita they bought readily into Gunn's spiel concerning the phenomenal powers of The Disk, of the millions and millions of Disks that would soon be purchased by American consumers from Augusta to Anaheim, from Savannah to Seattle. Gunn spoke with the confidence and enthusiasm inherent in all great American salesmen, from the fast talkers of the Old West peddling useless elixirs out of covered wagons to the modern-day hucksters pushing used vehicles and junk bonds on a suspicious but still gullible and greedy public. G. Henderson had a golden tongue, and a golden girl at his side. It was a tried-and-true method in American salesmanship: James and Dolly, Hugh and his playmates, Pat and Vanna.

The orders, needless to say, poured forth in prodigious numbers: thousands, tens of thousands, over a hundred thousand Disks in less than a week.

Reilly sounded pleased, but not overly inspired. "A good start," he remarked, "but to make this a viable endeavor we need real numbers. Huge numbers."

Gunn, through the power of fiber optics, assured Mr. Reilly the future looked bright.

"I damn well hope so," replied Reilly, an uncharacteristic edge to his voice. "I've invested millions in this thing." And then, without so much as a farewell, he hung up.

Gunn put the receiver back on its cradle and turned to Nita. "I gave him the numbers. He didn't sound all that impressed."

Nita brushed it off. "Don't worry about him. He can be such an old fuddy-duddy. Worries all the time." She smiled, a big toothy smile that lit up the room. "Besides," she added, "the sales numbers are great. They're amazing! I think we should celebrate."

And with that announcement, Nita threw her arms around Gunn's neck and kissed him full on the mouth.

● ● ●

THAT NIGHT, after pasta and chianti and Caesar salad for two, the sales team of Gunn Henderson and Nita Garrett had sex for the first time. They feigned concern, Gunn being a married man and all, but once up in Nita's suite in the Kansas City Hyatt, fleshly lust intervened and took control. With a few noisy moans and groans, all matter of civility and wedding day vows flew out that fourteenth-story midwestern window.

A few hours later, after the postcoitus stroking and kissing and dozing, Gunn and Nita had sex for the second time.

And a few hours after that, as dawn flashed its early morning brilliance over the dull gray Missouri River, the damp and sticky twosome had sex for the third time.

Gunn had not performed sexually three times in less than twelve hours since his collegiate days up in Hamilton, New York. Lying there beside his carnal cohort, her clear creamy complexion and absolute gorgeousness sucking the oxygen from the room, Gunn knew, without question, that he was a man in love. No, not lust; love, sweet and true.

They did not sell many Disks that day. In fact, they sold no Disks at all. Nor the day after. For forty-eight hours they lolled about her suite, naked and incorrigible, room service trays on the floor, half-eaten croissants on the bureau, cold coffee on the nightstand, the Do Not Disturb sign dangling from the exterior doorknob, the bedclothes all a-tangle.

They called no one: not Reilly, not Sam, not Nita's mother down in Fort Worth sick with some rare tropical disease after a trip to the South Seas. No, these two lovebirds had no time and no patience for the outside world. Their world revolved around events, almost entirely sexual in nature, taking place within the wallpapered walls of that luxury suite. Responsibilities and commitments be damned. They could live on love. And when not actually fornicating, they thought about it and talked about it and played at it: in the bed, on the floor, in the huge, oversized tub. Gunn and Nita were consumed with each other's flesh. They could not begin to satisfy their cravings.

When they grew weary, they did not sleep. They feared sleep. Sleep might break the spell. They would doze, but only briefly. Instead they talked, in hushed whispers and dramatic tones, as though every word they uttered had legitimacy and significance. They spit out the important events of their lives, the defining moments, the crowning achievements. Mostly they exaggerated and fabricated. Outright lies spilled easily from their mouths. Time moved slowly forward.

Finally, on the third day of their affair, they ventured out beyond the walls of the suite. The world looked different: kind of dreamy and surreal. They went down to the dining room for breakfast. They even made a sales call. It did not go particularly well, however. Less than half an hour into the meeting, Nita goosed Gunn under the conference table, causing Gunn to lose his concentration and break into a most unwholesome grin. The potential buyer, a fat cat with over one hundred retail outlets throughout the Midwest, and a very conservative born-again Christian to boot, noted this display of public lewdness, lectured, and then bolted from the room. First Nita, followed soon after by Gunn, giggled as the fat cat stormed out. And as soon as the door slammed closed, killing the sale, Gunn lifted Nita onto the conference table, hiked up her quite short skirt, and mounted her. Instantly she spread her lovely legs. For the next several minutes the winsome duo simulated the sex act. But before Gunn could actually pull down her hose and achieve penetration, Nita suggested they return to her suite. Which they immediately did.

* * *

EARLY FRIDAY AFTERNOON, after having a most productive week physically and sexually, if, perhaps, a somewhat lackluster week commercially and financially, the lovers had no choice but to go their separate ways. At the domestic terminal of Kansas City International Airport, they parted company after a lengthy and tender good-bye. They inserted all sorts of lustful yearnings into one another's ears, including their wet tongues which darted in and out licking and lapping. This public display of affection caused them no discomfort whatsoever; they had no idea anyone else even existed.

"I'll miss you," she said.

"I'll miss you too," he said.

"Thank God it's only until Monday."

"Monday morning."

"Bright and early."

Their voices low and whiny, like a couple of lovesick teeners longing to reunite in first-period French.

Finally, after an interminable kiss and a long, forlorn gaze, they parted: Nita to the Lone Star State to see her ailing mama, and Gunn to the eastern end of Long Island to deal with his wife and kiddies.

All the way back on the plane Gunn told himself to just act nonchalant once he arrived home, as though nothing out of the ordinary had transpired. Just another week on the job.

Back at the hotel, before closing up his suitcase, Gunn had checked and double-checked its contents. It definitely contained not a single pair of lace panties, or, for that matter, any other female attire. He had even removed and discarded a couple pair of his own silk boxers, boxers that wore the labors of his love for Ms. Nita. Sam probably never would have noticed, but why, Gunn asked himself, take chances? Better safe than sorry.

37 While Gunn flew east, Sam took a boat ride. Sam's week had not been quite as rewarding as her husband's. Not only did she continue to bear the marital burdens of her ongoing row with Gunn, but she had other problems as well. Her normally smooth complexion had broken out with several unsightly pimples, a sure sign of stress combined with an overindulgence in greasy potato chips and chocolate. Ordinarily, she stayed clear of such foods, but with Gunn angry and distant and incommunicado, she found her hand in both the chip bag and the candy bag far too often. Salt and sugar, sugar and salt: a disastrous way to try and drive away the blues. One afternoon in the middle of the week she watched soap operas for nearly four hours. At her side at the end of this melodramatic film fest sat an extra-large and totally empty bag of Ridgies and a whole pile of tiny, crumpled tinfoil wrappers. Her complexion revolted that same evening.

And then there was Jason, suddenly acting up at school, picking fights with his peers, disrupting classes, being sassy with his teachers. The principal had called. Sam had to go see him, sans Gunn who was busy in K.C. diddling Ms. Nita. A tall, serious fellow with a prominent set of jowls, the principal lectured Sam on the responsibilities of sound parenting. Sam, makeup doing a poor job of covering up her blemishes, acquiesced with nary a word. She mutely accepted whatever the principal doled out. By the end of the meeting it had been decided that young Jason would not be suspended from school for his behavior, but one more offense and the boy would be taking a mandatory vacation. Sam thanked the principal meekly, then slunk away. It upset her greatly to have her parenting skills under siege. She prided herself on being a good mother.

Friday afternoon found her back in front of the tube. *All My Children* had become a daily obsession. Life at PC Apple Acres had not turned out as expected; Sam needed the lives of these fictional characters to help ease her through the boredom and anxiety of another day. She assumed Gunn would be returning that evening, but since he had not called since the whole busy signal fiasco, she was not sure. She could have called him, she had his itinerary, but every evening she had resisted lifting the receiver. She believed Gunn owed her an apology as well as an explanation. He should be the one to call, not her. If nothing else, she would hold on to her pride.

Then, about halfway into the program, Sam had a visitor. Mrs. Griner stuck her head through the doorway and said, "Someone's here to see you, Sam."

"Someone to see *me*?"

"Yes. Should I send him in?"

"Him?"

But Mrs. Griner did not answer; she had already turned and gone. Sam reached for the remote, switched off the TV. She practically jumped out of her chair, raced across the room, and peered into the small antique mirror hanging above the table on the far wall. She ran her fingers through her hair, dabbed at her makeup, sighed at the sight of those red craters on her chin and cheeks.

"Mrs. Henderson. Hello."

Sam turned. "Brady!" She sounded, much to her consternation, almost breathless, as though she had run a long distance to utter his name.

"How are you today, ma'am?"

"How am I?" Sam had no idea how she was, not real swell if the truth be told. "I'm well, thank you."

"I'm sorry to bother you, Mrs. Henderson, but I had this idea, and . . ." Brady held his baseball cap in his hands. He tugged at the brim to defuse his nervousness, his make-believe nervousness. He was, in fact, not nervous at all, as rock-solid and confident as Washington crossing the Delaware. ". . . and, well, back over the summer, in August, you expressed an interest in taking a ride in that old runabout, and, well, it's such a beautiful day, warm and sunny with the Sound as calm as a bathtub, and, what with fall coming on and the fine days now few and far between, well, I guess I just thought you might like to—"

A big smile had spread across Sam's face. Her first genuine smile in over a week. "Say no more, Brady. I'd love to take a ride in that runabout." Sam recalled her conversation with Mandy. "In fact, I can't think of anything I'd rather do."

● ● ●

HALF AN HOUR LATER they rendezvoused down at the boathouse. Brady already had the mahogany runabout gassed up and ready to go. He took Sam's hand and helped her into the boat as she stepped over the gunwale.

"Have a seat, ma'am," said Brady, "and I'll cast off the lines."

"Enough of this ma'am business, Brady," replied Sam, as she made her way forward. "We've been through this before. I want you to call me Sam."

Brady untied the stern line and tossed it into the boat. "Yes, ma'am."

"Brady!"

Brady gave her a shy smile.

It was one of those perfectly benign late summer days when you say, "I wish it was exactly like this every day." The temperature: about seventy-one degrees. The wind: light, maybe five knots, out of the south-southeast. The clouds: just a few, high and billowy. The seas: smooth and glassy, only the wake from the runabout cruising just above an idle causing any ripple at all.

They crossed Shelter Island Sound and rounded Cedar Point. Gardiner's Bay, vast and as peaceful as a pond, spread out to the north and east. Brady pointed out some landmarks: Ram Island, the north shore of

Long Island, Gardiner's Island. The sky was so clear, Sam thought she could see forever. Had the world been flat, she felt sure she could have seen the coast of Normandy. Without thinking, she uttered this frivolous thought aloud.

Brady smiled and said, "I remember, when I was a kid, I thought the earth was flat."

"Really?"

Brady nodded. The boat, large and stable, chugged along, its enormous Chrysler V-8 engine buried beneath several layers of thick soundproofing. At this leisurely speed the passengers could speak in normal tones, no shouting or straining necessary.

"My father had a map of the world on the wall of his office," explained the caretaker. "It was flat, of course. I remember staring at it for hours when I was a kid. I just assumed the real world was also flat."

This was not entirely false. Brady's father did have an office, and he did have a map on the wall of his office. But it was not a map of the world; it was a detailed street map of the borough of Staten Island with gold stars showing the locations of the houses Brady's father had constructed. But before Brady ever even got out of the fifth grade, his father, Michael Donovan, threw himself off the Verrazano-Narrows Bridge into the Narrows of New York Bay.

Sam smiled at his story of the map. She liked Brady. He was so calm, so steady, so unpretentious. Unlike her husband, he seemed to possess no ego, no desperate and unrelenting need to impress and inflict. "So," she asked, "how old were you before you realized the world was round?"

Brady, his eyes fixed on the horizon ahead, allowed

himself a brief glance at his passenger. The glance gave him time to consider his response: light and witty or thoughtful and provocative? He chose the latter. "Oh, I don't know," he said, his eyes wandering away, "when the sea is this peaceful I sometimes still think the world might be flat."

Sam nodded and tried to imagine Gunn making such a response, something so ironic, something so sensitive and unguarded. He never would, not in a million years. He would have been short and intolerant the instant she offered her wayward glimpse of the Normandy coast. "Normandy," she could hear him saying in his condescending tone, "don't be ridiculous, Sam." And then he would launch into some dire mathematical explanation about the curvature of the earth and the maximum distance the human eye can see before the horizon slides away. God, she thought, what a bore!

Sam wanted to squeeze Brady's arm. Just to let him know she was happy out there on the water. But instead she just relaxed, leaned back into the soft leather seat and felt the light breeze touch her cheeks. She glanced over at him. He kept his eyes dead ahead. She wondered why this man, so strong and handsome, so passive and enlightened, did not have a woman in his life. A good and wholesome woman. A woman who deserved a man with such excellent qualities. She decided he must have been involved with the wrong woman, perhaps, over the years, the wrong women. She decided he had suffered at the hands of spiteful, demanding, and aggressive women. Women who took but did not give. And so now, battered and gun-shy, he had opted for a solitary life.

Brady, his highly complex and somewhat twisted brain firing on all cylinders, could feel Samantha Henderson relaxing, dropping her guard, happy and content in the presence of a secure and steadfast pilot. So vulnerable, he thought, so trusting and foolish. For a very brief moment he actually regretted doing what he had to do, but regret, he reminded himself, was for losers. It was a weak and useless emotion, better left to the pitying multitudes. Still, she was simple and sweet. And very pretty.

Brady piloted the runabout around Mashomack Point along the south shore of Shelter Island. He then headed north for Majors Harbor. At an old and dilapidated pier, he docked the boat.

"I thought we might go ashore," he said to Sam. "There's a beautiful beach I'd like you to see on the other side of Sachem's Neck."

Sam followed without the slightest hesitation. She felt perfectly at ease with the caretaker. Not for one second did she think this man could possibly cause her harm.

Brady held her hand as they crossed the rotting and rickety pier with its warped planks and scrawny pilings. In his other hand Brady held a picnic basket, a rather large one, and a cotton blanket. He'd said nothing to Sam back at the mansion about a picnic, but the notion of a picnic enchanted her; she had no desire whatsoever to return to her solitude.

A five-minute walk found them on Gibson's Beach, a long stretch of deserted sand, running north and south with small rollers lapping onto the shore. Sam took off her shoes and let the gentle surf lap her toes.

Brady spread the blanket and opened the picnic basket. Inside he had tarragon chicken sandwiches on fresh multigrain rolls, tree-ripened peaches the size of softballs, fine Swiss chocolates, and a bottle of lightly chilled California zinfandel, Sam's favorite.

Sam looked at the spread, tried to subdue her smile, and said, "My God, Brady, you didn't have to go to all this trouble. The boat ride is more than enough."

"No trouble, ma'am. I mean, Sam." Then, deflecting his own role in this plot, he said, "The boat ride was my idea, but Mrs. Griner put together the picnic basket. She thought you could use a few hours out of the house. What with Jason and Megan being gone all day and your husband away all week."

Sam sighed. "She's so sweet. You're both sweet." And then, swept away by the emotion of it all—troubles with Gunn, troubles with Jason, troubles with her complexion, Brady's kindness, the sun, the sea, the sky—Sam stepped forward and kissed Brady on the cheek. "Thank you so much."

Right on cue, Brady blushed. Another of his many talents: blushing on demand.

They sat on the blanket in the sand and ate their sandwiches. They looked out across Gardiner's Bay to Block Island Sound. Some pipers ran up and down the beach, poking at the wash with their long beaks. Overhead some gulls swooped and squawked, hoping, no doubt, for a discarded crust or a chunk of chicken.

Sam, feeling dreamy and romantic after a glass of wine, wondered if Brady wanted to kiss her. And she wondered also if she would let him if he tried.

Brady offered her a peach. She held the enormous piece of fruit with both hands and bit deeply into the fuzz-covered skin. The supersweet juice burst forth in all directions. It squirted into the sand and ran down Sam's chin. She laughed. Brady laughed. She took another bite. Never in her life had she tasted anything so wonderful. Practically drooling and moaning from the sheer joy imposed upon her taste buds, she said, "I had no idea a peach could taste so wonderful."

She ate the whole thing without once worrying about the bits of fruit and drops of juice on her face and hands and shirt. Samantha Ann Quincy Henderson became one with that peach.

As she neared the end of her sensuous journey, Brady reached over and wiped her chin. She extended her neck to him so he could wipe at will. Then he picked up and bit into a peach of his own. The sugary juice flew. They laughed some more. In fact, Brady, the ultimate control freak, found himself laughing quite naturally, no acting going on whatsoever.

But this frivolous indulgence annoyed him, so he stopped; not laughing, just enjoying it.

Sam did not sense his annoyance. She had no stomach for subterfuge. The world, in her mind anyway, was as it seemed.

Brady broke out the chocolates, solid milk chocolates in the shape of tiny hearts. "Open wide," he said, and she did, despite the blemishes on her face. The chocolate melted deliciously on her tongue.

"Brady," she confessed, after the third or fourth one, "this is all so decadent."

Brady could not believe her naïveté. He poured her another glass of wine. She at first declined, citing a need to get back before Megan and Jason arrived home from school, but when Brady pointed out it was only a little after three, she raised the glass to her lips. She took a sip. And another sip. And another. She soon began to wonder why Brady did not try to kiss her. She wanted him to try. If he didn't try soon, she might just have to try herself.

Little did Sam know that Brady, rarely one to leave events to chance, had pulled the cork on that bottle of zinfandel before he had ever loaded it into the picnic basket. He had pulled the cork and added a generous portion of an ages-old Oriental aphrodisiac, a subtle stimulant to break down the sexual inhibitors, just a little something to help Mrs. Henderson with her shy and delicate manner. It was a lovely little concoction: a blend of ginseng, cantharis, and strychnine, plus a touch of the New World via the coca leaf.

Brady knew he could have kissed Sam, could quite probably have pushed her back onto the blanket and covered her lovely body with his own. He felt certain she would not have objected. But this, he knew, was not the time. Far better to let the emotions simmer. Let her, he told himself as he subdued his physical desires, let her come to me. In her own good time. Much sweeter that way. Far more satisfying.

And so they left Gibson's Beach not long after with little more than a chin wiped and a hand held. But both silently knew they wanted more. The forbidden fruit had still not been tasted.

• • •

Brady had one last thrill in store for Mrs. Henderson. On the ride out he had deliberately puttered, barely pushed the runabout above an idle. But now, as they reached the deep water of Shelter Island Sound for their return trip home, Brady shoved the throttle forward. The big runabout picked up speed. The bow rose out of the water. Brady pushed the throttle, smoothly and confidently, wide-open. The boat leveled and shot across the surface of the Sound. Neither Sam nor Brady missed the sexual connotation of all that speed and power. The engine roared. The wind blew Sam's hair. It made her eyes water. She had to hang on, steady herself for balance.

A shudder raced down her spine. She had no idea if it was a shudder of fear or elation. But she did know she wanted that boat to go faster. As fast as it could go. As fast as the wind. She wanted to be wild. She wanted to be free.

Easy, girl, some other part of her brain warned her, it's just the sun and the wind and the wine. Reality's back at the house, waiting for you. Reality is Jason and Megan and what they did at school today and what they all might do together over the weekend. Reality is Gunn and those lace panties and whether or not he'll come home tonight. And if he does come home will he be sweet and tender or cold and distant?

38 The sexual urge still plagued Sam as Gunn walked through the front door of the mansion just in time for dinner. So acute was her desire that she totally ignored all the ugly and oppositional attitudes her husband had inflicted upon her over the past weeks. She said nothing about those lavender lace panties, not a word about his failure to call home or communicate with her in any way. These trivialities no longer seemed to matter. Sam wanted—make that Sam needed—arousal, sexual stimulation.

Gunn, slipping through the front door looking guilty and sheepish, to say nothing of sexually bamboozled, double-clutched at his wife's smiling face and physical advances. He thought surely it must be some kind of trap. He had fully expected her to be icy and angry and scowling. But no, she met him at the door, kissed him on the cheek, gave him a squeeze, welcomed him home. At dinner she hovered, asking several times if she could refill his plate, pour him another glass of beer. And then, the moment the children fled to the TV room, Sam breezed in close to Gunn's side. Into his ear she whispered, "I think we should go to bed early tonight."

Gunn recoiled, but Sam moved closer, close enough to wet his earlobe with her moist tongue. "I want to fuck you in the worst way."

A shot rang out in Gunn's brain. He wanted to run, make a mad dash for safety. He did not want to touch his wife, much less fuck her. The idea of it actually revolted him. His thoughts blazed away for Nita, for all those smooth curves and luscious lips. He missed her immensely. Monday seemed like years away. But tomorrow, tomorrow he would call her. In the morning. Before Sam got up.

"Gunn!"

Gunn shook off his delirium, looked up, found his wife right in his face, staring at him. "Yes? What?"

"Let's go upstairs."

He put it off for as long as possible: foraged in the

kitchen, lounged with the kids, rummaged through his office in search of a make-believe memo. But eventually he made his way up to the bedroom, hoping maybe Sam had drifted off to sleep. Too bad Sam awaited him, all snug between the sheets, propped up against the pillows, silk negligee draped across her breasts, bare arms showing. "I didn't think you were ever coming."

"Sorry," he managed, "I was still hungry. Then I thought I should spend a little time with the kids."

Sam knew she should say something about Jason's troubles at school, but that, she decided, could wait. "Spend some time with them tomorrow," she cooed as she patted the side of the bed. "Right now it's my turn."

Gunn nodded, ducked into the bathroom, closed the door. He stood over the bowl for quite a long time after his liquids had been vanquished. But finally he crossed to the sink, turned on the water, washed his hands, washed his face, brushed his teeth, flossed his teeth, dried his face, dried his hands, combed his hair—it all took time. Sam called his name. Twice. Both times he ignored her.

In the end, nothing more to do, he returned to the bedroom. Sam had slumped a bit into the folds of the bed, but his appearance revived her. "You're taking forever." She tried not to sound cross.

"Sorry," he said again. "I'm moving kind of slow tonight. It's been a long and exhausting week." Yes, he thought to himself, this sounds good, very convincing. "I'm beat. Like I've been run over by an eighteen-wheeler."

"Poor baby. Come to bed. I'll relax you."

Gunn took off and hung up his shirt and pants with a heaviness of movement. He did his best to appear drained, utterly spent. And when there was absolutely nothing more he could do, he rolled onto the bed. Sam, the hunter for a change, pounced on him in an instant. She knew how to play the aggressor.

Gunn did his best to disguise his disgust. When she made a move for his lips, he turned his head at the last fraction of a second and feigned a hungry desire to kiss her neck. She moaned with delight. Too bad he wanted only to toss her aside, onto the floor would be nice, so he could have the bed all to himself and his thoughts of Nita.

But Sam wanted more. She pushed her breasts against his chest, her hips against his hips. Feeling the onset of rage at this assault, Gunn actually bit his lip to keep his mouth from muttering something venomous. He felt such a terrible tangle of emotions: loathing for his wife, faithlessness against his new lover, anger, fear, confusion, maybe even a touch of self-hatred. But then something quite extraordinary happened: He got an erection. And not just a puffed up, semihard one either, but the real thing: rigid and straight and true. He had no idea why. It could have been Sam's pelvic thrusts. Or his relentless thoughts of naked Nita rolling around in his head. Whatever the reason, Sam did not waste time. "My goodness, Gunn, the beast has awoken."

Gunn had made love to his wife many times, hundreds of times, a thousand times or more. He did his duty; he moved with her rhythm and placed his big hands firmly over the rounded cheeks of her buttocks, exactly as she liked him to do whenever she was on top. And sure enough, her breathing stopped, guttural groans spilled from her lips, her body grew rigid and then damp. "Gunn! God, Gunn!" She only called his name during the most intense orgasms. And then, just moments later, satiated, her whole body relaxed.

Now it was Gunn's turn. But Gunn lingered somewhere between revulsion and arousal. Sam urged him on: sucked his neck, licked the inside of his ear, stroked his testicles. Oh, what the hell, he decided, still hard, I'll just pretend she's Nita.

He began to press, to lift her up and down with his powerful hips. She perched on top of him, a wholesome but naughty grin on her face. Gunn kept his eyes closed in the dimly lit room. Sam had no idea her husband was fucking another woman.

Gunn went at it for quite some time. Orgasm was not about to come quickly in his emotional state, especially after the twenty or so ejaculations he had served up in the past several days. He rolled her over onto her back. He pumped like a madman, the sweat forming under his arms, along his brow. Sam cheered him on, "Harder, baby. Faster." She loved when he got excited like this, when the passion flowed.

But still he did not come.

"You want me to get on my knees?" she asked.

No, Gunn did not want Sam on her knees. He wanted Nita. Beneath him. Legs splayed. Nita could make him come.

Nevertheless, he turned Sam over onto her belly. He grabbed her by the waist and pulled her to her knees. She mistook anger and guilt and frustration for passion. For lust. For love.

Gunn drove it home, and after no small amount of

delay, he finally finished up. Exhausted, he collapsed. He rolled onto his side, closed his eyes, and pretty much shut down.

"I love you, Gunn," he thought he heard his wife whisper his way as he drifted off to sleep. He muttered a couple of cavemanlike grunts in reply.

● ● ●

THE REST of the weekend Gunn did his best to avoid his wife. First thing Saturday morning he pulled on his tennis togs, told her he had a match over at the local club, and then he more or less sprinted out of the house to his neglected Porsche waiting impatiently for him in the garage. He did not go to the club, however. He beelined for the nearest public phone booth where he dialed up Nita at her mother's house in Fort Worth. A man answered, sounded like an older man, maybe her father.

"Is Nita there?"

"Who may I ask is calling?"

Gunn, not thinking real fast on his feet, answered, "Tom Collins."

"Ah, Mr. Collins, I'm afraid Nita's not here right now."

"No?" Gunn felt his own impatience rising. "Do you know when she'll be back?"

"Well, she hasn't even arrived yet. We expected her last night, but she never showed. Probably working. She works like a slave."

Gunn, instantly suspicious, wanted to tell the old coot that they'd knocked off early, but settled for this: "You think she'll be there this morning?"

"Maybe. I expect so. Can I have her call you?"

"Yes. No. I'll call back. Thanks." Gunn hung up.

He drove around in his little sports coupe for hours. He drove all the way out to Montauk, then all the way back to Southampton. Up and down Highway 27 with the engine screaming and the speakers blasting rock and roll. Every hour he stopped and called Nita. The gentleman down in Texas began to anticipate his calls. Before Gunn would even identify himself, the old-timer would say, "I'm sorry, Mr. Collins, Nita's not here yet. I could have her call you."

Gunn said he was on the road, he'd call back, it was business, Creative Marketing Enterprises.

Finally, late in the afternoon, tired and hungry and sullen, he wound his way home. Sam, meeting him once again at the front door, that aphrodisiac a thing of the past, not even the trace of a smile on her face, asked him where he had been all day.

"At the club."

Much of Sam's fear and anxiety had returned. Brady's potion, after all, was not destined to last forever. "All day?" she asked.

"Most of it, yeah. I had a few errands to do afterward."

Sam decided not to mention that his tennis togs looked as clean and white as they had that morning. "You had a call," she told him. "Two calls actually. From the same person."

"Don't tell me," said Gunn. "Reilly?"

"No, not Mr. Reilly. It was a woman. A Ms. Nita Garrett."

Gunn did his best not to jump out of his skin. He could feel Sam's eyes riveted on him. "What did she want?"

"She wanted to talk to you."

I figured that, stupid, he wanted to reply, but, fortunately, didn't. "About what?"

"She didn't say."

A brief but uncomfortable pause settled over the foyer.

"It must have something to do with work," explained Gunn. "Ms. Garrett works for Creative Marketing Enterprises."

Sam stared at her husband, who fidgeted. "I see."

Gunn decided to explain further. "She works for Reilly."

Sam raised her eyebrows. "For Reilly."

Gunn answered, as though Sam had asked a question. "Yes."

Right there in the foyer they had a standoff. Gunn tried not to twitch or look shifty. Sam had to remind herself to keep breathing.

Finally, his offensive nature stepping onto the field, Gunn fetched up the nerve to meet his wife's stare. "Reilly must be on the warpath. I'd better call back. Did Ms. Garrett leave a number?"

"Oh, yes, Gunn," came the answer, awash with sarcasm, "Ms. Garrett left a number."

39 Gunn pulled out late Sunday afternoon, claimed he had a meeting in Minneapolis early on Monday morning.

"When will you be back?" Sam wanted to know.

"Friday night. Saturday morning at the latest."

"Do you think you'll call this week?"

"Do you want me to call?"

Of course she wanted him to call. "I don't really give a damn if you call or not."

"Fine," said Gunn. "Then maybe I'll call, or maybe I won't." And then the breadwinner left; out the door and into his limousine.

Half a dozen or so hours later, his wife neatly swept from his thoughts, Gunn sat beside his sweetie in a dark and romantic Mediterranean restaurant along the banks of the Mississippi in downtown Minneapolis. A glass of earthy red burgundy in one hand, Nita's hand in his other hand, Gunn felt exceptionally well: cool and happy and relaxed.

"Did you miss me?" Nita wanted to know.

"Like crazy."

"I missed you, too."

Gunn couldn't wait to finish the meal and get back to their suite at the Radisson Plaza. "My wife," he said, "was all bent out of shape that you called."

"Yeah," said Nita, all fresh and breathy and radiating sexuality. "Sorry about that. I just needed to talk, hear your voice."

"I know what you mean."

She smiled at him. "I guess you do, Mr. Collins."

Gunn gave her thigh a squeeze under the table. "Hey, that was the best I could come up with on the spur of the moment."

She stroked his fingers. "I hope she wasn't too upset. Your wife, I mean. I told her it was just business."

"She asked a few questions," replied Gunn, "but it was no big deal."

Oh, the little white lies we do tell, even to those we this week love, or at least lust after.

In fact, Nita's sensuous voice coming over the phone line had immediately caused alarms to go off in Sam's head. The way the woman had so casually asked, "Yes, hello, is Gunn there? It's Nita." Not Nita Garrett. Just *Nita*.

"Who the hell is she?" Sam had demanded after their argument had shifted into a higher gear, after Gunn had slipped into his office and tried, again unsuccessfully, to reach Nita on the telephone.

"I told you," answered Gunn, "she works for the company."

"She works for you?"

"For the company, Sam. For Creative Marketing Enterprises. She's like an assistant. Jesus, don't be so damn suspicious."

"Whose assistant?"

Gunn, wanting to head his volatile wife off at the pass, answered, "I don't know. Reilly's, I guess. She's like a peon," he lied, beginning to warm to the task. "A gofer. Go for this, go for that. Get the coffee. Get Henderson on the line." And then, his brain burning, he pounced. "This one, this Nita you're all worked up about, if I remember right, is kind of fat, fat and dumpy—"

Brady, entrenched behind the wall for this scene, had laughed so hard that Gunn cut himself short to see who might be listening. After a quick look up and down the hallway, he finished his description. "—Fat and dumpy with a face like one of those dogs. You know the ones I mean."

"No," said Sam, sighing, dubious, but nevertheless feeling some temporary relief, "I'm afraid I don't know."

"Yes, you do. The ones with the flat, kind of squashed-up faces?"

"Pugs?"

"Right. Pugs. Nita looks like a pug."

"Nita didn't sound like a pug."

Gunn laughed at his wife. "No? And how does a pug sound?"

"Not like this Nita sounded."

Gunn rolled his eyes and shook his head. Maybe he had not satisfied his wife, but he had satisfied himself entirely. "You're ridiculous, sweetie."

Sam didn't think so, but she did not care to discuss it further. At least not right then. Other matters, such as Jason, demanded their attention. They could not, she reasoned, endlessly squabble over their marital problems. But their troublesome son only caused an escalation in their argument. Sam told Gunn about Jason's problems at school. Gunn, preoccupied, told his wife she was making a mountain out of a molehill.

"The headmaster," insisted Sam, "sounded very concerned."

"Those assholes are paid to sound concerned."

"I think Jason's screaming for attention, Gunn. I think you need to talk to him, let him know you're aware of his existence, tell him you love him."

"Christ, Sam, you make such a big deal about everything. The kid's just feeling his oats. So he's fucking around a little at school. Big deal. So what? I say we just let him alone."

"We can't just let him alone. He's our son. He needs our guidance."

"He gets plenty of guidance," the boy's father had insisted. "Just let him escape for a while."

And soon thereafter Gunn had made his own escape; one of the perks of the traveling salesman. For another week or so he had the opportunity to put everything behind him: his bitchy bride, his delinquent son, all the trials and tribulations of domestic life. He was on the road again, out and about with his lovely lady. She had her hand under the table, her long fingers caressing his thigh, her fingertips coming closer and closer to that part of his anatomy they had last week nicknamed Mr. Wonderful.

"Take me back to the room, Gunn," she whispered in his ear, "and ravage me like we've been apart for a year."

So that's what Gunn did. And all went well. They undressed one another slowly, one article at a time.

Every inch of exposed flesh received a kiss from the other's lips. And once naked they lay atop the king-size bed, their limbs tangled and searching. Gunn Henderson worked overtime bringing delight to this delectable dish.

Anyone watching would have seen two people obviously craving one another. They kissed and moaned and held each other tight. Lovers. Only one small problem. Nita, in the more subservient position, stared up at the ceiling as Gunn, his face burrowing between her silicone-engorged breasts, moaned and strained and pumped away. Too bad Ms. Nita looked distracted, bored, even irritable.

40 Early Monday morning, lying in bed, Sam made a decision: She would not just sit around feeling sorry for herself and fretting about her husband. So after having breakfast with Jason and Megan and getting them off to school, after watching Brady swim his laps and practice his dives, she dressed and went down to the kitchen.

"I'm going out for a few hours," she told Mrs. Griner.

Greta tuned right in on this bit of news, but she did not look away from her bowl of cake batter. "Anywhere special?"

"I think I'll go into Southampton. Do some shopping."

"That sounds fun." And then, "Will you be leaving soon?"

"Probably in about forty-five minutes."

An hour later Sam started down the driveway in her Explorer. Up ahead she saw Brady walking along the edge of the drive. She stopped beside him and lowered the window. "Good morning, Brady." She had not seen him since their boating expedition the previous Friday.

"Morning, ma'am. Sam. How are you?"

She met his eyes, but only briefly. "Just fine, thank you. And you?"

"Pretty well," he replied, keeping his distance.

"Going somewhere?"

"Just down to get my truck."

"Your truck?"

"It's in the shop. I've been having some trouble with the transmission. It should be ready by the time I walk down there."

"Walk down where? Downtown?"

"Yes, ma'am. Over to Walker's Garage on Vine Street."

"But that's four or five miles. Why don't I drive you?"

"That's okay, ma'am. I don't want to be a burden. I enjoy walking. It's good exercise and an excellent way to clear the head of all the excess nonsense that accumulates."

"I'd be happy to give you a lift," replied Sam, hoping he'd accept. "It's certainly not a burden."

Brady took a moment to think it over. "Well, I guess if I really want to walk I could walk on the beach later."

"Yes," said Sam, "that sounds like a better idea. I love to walk on the beach."

So Brady climbed into the passenger seat of the Explorer and fastened his seat belt. They passed through the gate and along Old Northwest Road. It was a fine morning in late September, bright and sunny, a slight chill in the air, but certainly not cold.

"I wanted to thank you again," said Sam, "for that wonderful boat ride on Friday."

"Anytime, ma'am. I mean Sam. It was my pleasure. I usually only get out on the water these days if someone wants to go for a spin. It seems like all I do anymore is work."

"More to life than just work, Brady."

Their eyes met, for just an instant. Brady, looking grave, nodded.

They drove into East Hampton and out Vine Street to Walker's Garage, an old brick structure with three bays for repairs and a line of gas pumps out front. Sam pulled up along the side.

"Let me just run in," said Brady, "and make sure they have the old dog ready."

Sam nodded. "I'll wait here."

Brady stepped out of the Explorer and went into the small office in the front corner of the garage. But he did not ask the man behind the desk about his truck. No, he just asked old Ben Walker about his health, about his wife and his kids and his grandkids and whether or not he'd been out fishing and were the blues running south yet and wasn't it delightful to finally be rid of the summer folks. Ben Walker, an ancient and weathered East Hampton native, shot the breeze with Brady for seven or eight minutes. Then

Brady said so long and went back out to the Explorer. He opened the passenger side door, but did not get inside. "Sorry to take so long, ma'am. I'm afraid the truck's not quite ready. They're waiting on a part from Riverhead. It'll be a couple more hours."

Sam was not sure what to do. "That's too bad," she said. "Do you want me to drive you back?"

"Oh no, that's not necessary. I'll just hang around town."

"Are you sure?"

"I don't want to hold you up."

"You're not holding me up, Brady. I was just going shopping."

"Well," suggested the caretaker, his pickup back at the estate, its transmission in perfect repair, "I could give you a little tour of the area. Show you some of our points of interest."

Sam thought that sounded far more interesting than shopping. "Yes," she said, her enthusiasm bubbling over, "let's have a tour."

"And maybe a walk on the beach."

"Definitely a walk on the beach."

• • •

SO THAT'S HOW SAM came to spend the morning and most of the afternoon with the caretaker. With Brady behind the wheel of the Explorer, they cruised slowly through town. On the corner of Long Lane and Three Mile Harbor Road, Brady pointed out an old weathered clapboard house where he said he had lived as a child. "My mother," he told Sam, "lived there until she passed away a few years ago."

"I'm sorry, Brady. What about your father?"

"Oh, he died more than a decade back. A fishing accident off Block Island."

Sam sighed. "You're so young to have lost both your parents. I'm still lucky enough to have both of mine."

Right, thought Brady, Lawrence and May Quincy of 672 Valley Drive, Brookline, Massachusetts. "That's mighty fortunate, ma'am."

Sam nodded and sighed again. "So what happened to the house?"

"I sold her. No choice really. But I got a nice price. Put the money in the bank. I guess it's my retirement. Still, it was tough to sell. That house had been in the family for five generations."

"Five generations! Wow!" Sam was impressed.

"And we've been in the Hamptons for several generations prior to that."

Sam expressed her wonder at this lengthy ancestral line as Brady swung the Explorer out onto Route 27. They cruised through town: passed the Polo Country Store and the Coach Factory Outlet and Mark, Fore, and Strike. At the edge of town stood a large white Presbyterian church with a tall steeple decorated with a rather unusual feature: an enormous clock displaying the correct time.

"My great-grandmother," said Brady, "was responsible for getting this church built. She was a strong, tough, God-fearing woman. All her life she traveled into Southampton every Sunday morning to attend services. But as she got older, the journey became more and more difficult. So she decided the good Presbyterians of East Hampton needed their own church."

Brady knew Sam was a Presbyterian, born and bred;

he might as well make himself one, too. Catholicism had never done him any good.

"Oh, Brady," said Sam, "that's a wonderful story. She must have been a very special woman."

Brady blushed.

Just past the church Brady turned left onto James Lane and parked the Explorer along the side of the road. "If you don't mind, ma'am, I'd like to show you something. It won't take but a minute."

Of course Sam did not mind. She was enjoying herself thoroughly. She loved all this ancestral talk. It gave her a sense of security and continuity. Her own family had lived in and around Boston since back before the American Revolution. She knew about family history. And Brady made her feel so calm and relaxed. Just what the doctor ordered after all the strain and anxiety of dealing with Gunn.

She followed Brady down the street and through a small park filled with towering maples and sycamores. Beyond the trees was a pond, and beyond the pond an ancient graveyard with headstones dating back to the 1600s. In the southwest corner of the graveyard stood the Brady plot. There were nearly a dozen stones bearing the family name, the earliest dating back to 1727. LEVON BRADY, read the epitaph, FARMER, FISH-ERMAN, FATHER AND LOVING HUSBAND. REST IN PEACE.

Brady did not speak. He silently paid his respects. Sam did the same. They did not stay long, just a few moments. But plenty of time for Sam to expand her positive feelings for this strong, quiet, humble man. She thought perhaps she had never met a man who gave off such an aura of confidence combined with modesty, of independence coupled with integrity, of physical power in perfect harmony with internal stillness.

What Sam did not know, and which would, eventually, cause her no end of trouble and turmoil, was that these Brady graves Brady had brought her to see were absolutely in no way related to Brady at all. Brady's father had not been a fisherman. His mother had never for one second lived in that old house over on Three Mile Harbor Road. His great-grandmother had certainly not founded the First Presbyterian Church of East Hampton, New York. She had lived and died in Dublin, never once in all her life venturing beyond County Kildare. His father hailed from Belfast, and had come to America with his wife and children in an effort to avoid the Troubles. Brady's name was not even Brady, for crying out loud, not his first name or his last. Brady's name was Donovan, Carl Patrick Donovan.

As they returned to the Explorer, Carl Patrick Donovan, better known as Brady, turned and asked his companion, "Would you like to take that walk on the beach now, ma'am?"

"I would, yes," replied Sam, "but on one condition. You must, from this moment forward, absolutely stop referring to me as ma'am."

"I've been trying," insisted Brady. "It's just habit. My mother taught me to be a gentleman."

"Well, try harder," said Sam.

Brady smiled shyly and nodded. They drove to the beach, out past the Maidstone Golf Club at the end of Further Lane. They took off their shoes and ventured out onto the warm dry sand. A light breeze blew in off the ocean. Huge, feathery clouds caused the sun to play hide-and-seek.

They walked down to the water's edge, rolled up the legs of their pants, and watched while the surf soaked their ankles. Sam jumped back from the shock of the chilly water. Brady lingered, waded in up to his knees.

They headed east. They walked a mile. Two miles. Talking every step of the way. But quietly, slowly. Listening as well as talking. Mostly about family, growing up, making choices. Sam told the truth. Generally. Brady told nothing but lies, one after another, a flawless procession of tall tales exquisitely linked together. Occasionally he littered his lies with some subconscious psychological confession. Like when he said, "I have always felt a powerful need to preserve the family name, to maintain the family honor." But mostly lies, manipulations, barefaced fairy tales.

All the way out and all the way back Sam kept thinking how pleasant it was to have a friend, someone to talk to, share the day with. She had Jason and Megan, of course, but she nevertheless needed an adult connection, some mature conversation.

She often missed Mandy, their camaraderie. But now she had Brady. Sort of. She knew Gunn would be furious if he knew she was spending the day with the caretaker. He would get it all wrong, instantly become jealous, immediately see Brady as a threat, a sexual threat. And maybe Gunn would have been right to perceive Brady in this light. For as they headed back, the sun warm on her neck, Sam had the urge to take Brady's hand, just grasp it and hold on. She never had the urge to hold Mandy's hand.

And then, at that very second, a little plan popped into her head. Without contemplating the consequences for even a millisecond, Sam put her plan into motion. She grabbed Brady's hand and shouted, "Come on!" And then, their fingers locked together, she led him through the wash. The shallow, salty water splashed up and soaked their pants and shirts. Both of them smiled and laughed; Sam from the sheer joy of a frivolous and playful act; Brady from the perfect symmetry of his calculated seduction.

Although, if the caretaker wanted to be honest with himself, he too felt a certain frivolity that he had rarely, if ever, felt before. Brady liked Sam. And he could tell she liked him.

She did like him. Quite a lot, in fact. At least she liked the man whom she believed Brady to be.

41 Originally Gunn had expected to be gone another fortnight, but on Thursday Reilly called and told him to go home for the weekend, relax, spend some time with his family. Gunn thanked the boss for his consideration, even though he would have preferred to spend the weekend on the road, with Nita.

On Friday night the whole family had dinner together. Gunn felt bored and trapped and antsy. He longed to escape, to pack a bare minimum of essentials and run off with his sweet young thing. Jason and

Megan bickering, Sam scolding them, insisting they behave—Gunn wanted to flip over the table and chuck it all, run for his life.

Near the end of the meal the phone rang. Mrs. Griner answered it in the kitchen. A few moments later she entered the dining room to inform Mr. Henderson that Mr. Reilly was on the line.

Gunn, relieved, pushed back from the table. "I'll take it in my office."

It was not a long conversation. Mr. Reilly informed Gunn that he would be at the house the following morning at nine o'clock sharp. He said they had some business to discuss. And then Reilly hung up after a perfunctory good-bye.

Gunn leaned back in his chair, feet up on his desk, hands behind his head. He knew what Reilly wanted: the sales figures. And he knew also the sales figures were not particularly exhilarating, especially these past couple of weeks, ever since he and Nita had started spending the bulk of their days and all of their nights frolicking and fornicating in various hotel rooms around the country. The memories, despite the lackluster sales record, made Gunn smile. He was, after all, a man in love. And so what if he hadn't sold a Disk in a while? The Disk was a stupid piece of shit. He would just play with the sales figures, do some fancy arithmetic, tell Reilly he had some orders ready to roll. Just stay cool, he reassured himself, everything will work out.

Gunn nodded at his own assessment, then reached into the bottom left-hand drawer, drew out a bottle of very expensive single malt scotch, poured himself a tumbler, took a few sips, and relaxed. There would be no problems. Not here, there, or anywhere. G. Henderson felt confident. G. Henderson had everything under control.

• • •

GUNN'S CONTROL BEGAN to erode rather swiftly the following morning when, at nine o'clock on the button, the front doorbell chimed. In the kitchen, shoveling in some scrambled eggs and crispy bacon, Gunn dropped his fork into the sink and made a beeline for the foyer. At the very same time, his lovely wife, having also heard the chime, left their bedroom and started down the stairs. They both reached the front door at precisely the same moment. Which was just fine with Gunn. A small display of marital unity would no doubt have a soothing effect on his employer.

Gunn, for good measure, smiled at his wife and took her hand as he grabbed the solid brass doorknob and swung open the door. And there, on the threshold, preparing to ring the bell a second time, stood Mr. Arthur James Reilly, smartly dressed in crisp chinos and a navy blue double-breasted Hickey Freeman blazer.

The boss, however, was not alone. Oh, no. Ms. Nita Garrett, the once-described fat, dumpy, puglike assistant, stood at Mr. Reilly's side. She looked good. She looked hot. She wore red. Her blond hair shone.

Gunn's mouth fell open. His eyes met Nita's eyes, big blue beautiful eyes. Their gaze held, if just for a nanosecond, but long enough for Sam to shift her own pretty eyes from him to her and back again.

Before she could accurately assess the situation, mouths began to move, Reilly's mouth in particular.

"Good morning, Gunn. Samantha." Then, without being asked, he guided Nita into the foyer and followed close on her heels. He took Sam's hands in his own, asked her how she was, how the kids were, if all was satisfactory with the house, if there was anything at all he could do for her. He was pleasant and charming. Sam assured him all was well.

Off to the side Gunn struggled to get a handle on his wits. He could feel his heart muscle pounding against his chest cavity. He had no idea what to do, what to say. It occurred to him to run for his life. But no, that simply would not do. He had to stand and fight. He had to keep Reilly from introducing Nita as Nita. That was the key: Nita had to be introduced as Joan or Ingrid or Sally Sue, any name at all would do, just not Nita. He threw a glance Nita's way. His lips silently formed this question: *What the hell are you doing here?*

Nita shrugged, tipped her head toward Reilly, mouthed this reply: *He ordered me to be here.*

And then Reilly, the perfect gentleman, said, "Oh, Samantha, I'm sorry," and he dropped her hands and took a step back. "This is—"

Here it comes, realized Gunn. Do something! For chrissakes, make a move! Sing a song! Have a heart attack! A stroke! Something! Anything!

Too late.

"—Ms. Nita Garrett. She works with us at Creative Marketing Enterprises. In sales."

Now Sam's mouth fell open. Her brain registered the name. Her eyes immediately slapped the fat, dumpy, puglike label right smack between Nita's glorious eyes. She managed to give Nita the phoniest of smiles.

For just a moment this smile gave Gunn a grim measure of reassurance. Perhaps, he hoped, his wife had not remembered his rather inaccurate description of Nita Garrett.

Hope faded quickly. Sam turned to her husband, wiped that phony smile off her face, and gave him a look that said she fully intended to rip his heart out at the first possible opportunity.

And Reilly again: "Nita, this is Gunn's wife, Samantha Henderson. And I'm sure," he added, his charming smile filling the foyer, "Gunn's better half."

They all had a nice little laugh.

Then Nita, gorgeous, confident, stepped forward and reached out her hand. "I'm very pleased to meet you, Mrs. Henderson. I feel like I know you already. Gunn has told me so much about you. He loves to talk about his family."

Gunn, still off to the side but daydreaming of being a million miles away, wished he had the power to make himself small, maybe the size of a flea. Or a missile strapped to his back might be nice, something that could launch him into outer space, make him vanish into the stratosphere.

Sam knew Gunn was fucking Nita. She could feel it in her bones, sense it with every female fiber of her body.

Reilly: "Samantha, I was wondering, might I impose upon you? Gunn and Nita and I have some business this morning. I promise, it won't take all day. But before we get started, I have a few things to discuss privately with Gunn. Would you mind showing Nita around the house?"

So that's how Gunn found himself cornered in his office with Arthur James Reilly while his wife escorted his lover through the mansion. Talk about a loss of control. Almost as though someone had planned the whole thing.

Gunn, his concentration wandering all over the planet, did not do a very good job fudging the sales figures. Not that even on his best day he would have been able to pull the wool over Reilly's eyes. The boss seemed to know the truth, the whole truth, and everything including the truth. And the boss wasn't really even the boss.

"Listen to me, Gunn, and listen good," Reilly began, his face just inches from Gunn's face, his index finger tapping out urgent Morse code messages on Gunn's chest, "I'm not paying you the big money to screw the help. And I don't give a goddamn how good-looking and sexy the help might be. Garrett is a prop, son, nothing but a damn prop. A sales tool. Like a dinner at Antoine's for a very important client. Or a blue Tiffany's box under the Christmas tree. Like I told you up front, she's on the team to make the buyers drool. She's not on the team to fuck up the salesman's marriage, or to keep the damn salesman from his appointed rounds."

"Mr. Reilly, let me assure you, I—"

"Shut up, Gunn. I'm not interested in your assurances. When I brought Nita aboard you assured me you could keep your dick in your pants, but you couldn't do it. That tells me your assurances are bullshit. And now I'm the one suffering. Last week you didn't sell shit, not one damn Disk. I need orders, boy, not excuses. I'd fire your ass on the spot, but I've made a big investment in you already, and besides, your wife seems like a fine and decent woman. I'd hate to see her suffer because of your hard-ons."

Reilly's lusty lecture went on for quite some time, but it all came down to this: no more hanky-panky with the hired help. Period.

While outside on the terrace, Nita cooed over the beauty and the opulence of the estate. "God," she told Sam, "you guys are so lucky to live here. Look at that swimming pool. It's like something a movie star would have."

A dumb blonde, thought Sam, just another dumb blonde. With dark roots. And fake titties. And probably lip implants as well. Hair like a Swede and lips like a Bantu. But definitely not fat or dumpy. Puglike? Not quite. That son of a bitch. I'll kill him. I'll kill both of them.

"So," she asked, phony smile still firmly in place, always sweet and polite just the way her mommy taught her, "what do you do at Creative Marketing Enterprises, Ms. Garrett?"

"Nita, please."

Sam showed her dimples. "I think I'll stick with Ms. Garrett for the time being."

Nita took a double-take on her hostess, then kind of half smiled and shrugged. "It's really the perfect job for me," she answered, sounding far more stupid and scatterbrained than she really was. "Basically, all I have to do is look good."

"Excuse me?"

"I go on calls and to meetings with Gunn, and

pretty much I just make eyes with the clients and the buyers."

"Make eyes?"

"You know, smile at them, flirt a little bit, make them feel important."

"You do this with Gunn?"

Nita nodded. "Yes."

"Sounds like a very challenging position."

Nita shrugged again. "Hey, it's sales. It doesn't matter how you do it, just as long as you get it done. Get them to sign on the bottom line."

That, Sam knew, was straight from the horse's mouth. She had heard Gunn mutter those exact same words a thousand times. She wondered where Gunn and this Ms. Nita did their student-teacher thing: Dimly lit bars? Romantic restaurants? Cozy bedroom suites?

They walked around the side of the swimming pool and entered the rose garden. The last blooms had disappeared a week or two earlier, just the long green stems and abundant thorns remained. Sam wanted to ask the bouncing floozy at her side if she was sleeping with her husband, but before she could muster the courage, Brady entered the garden through the far trellis. He seemed surprised to see the two women. But, of course, the caretaker was not surprised at all; he had been keeping a close eye on events over at the mansion all morning long.

Brady, dressed in denim work clothes, carried pruning shears in one hand and a long-bladed knife in the other. "Good morning, Mrs. Henderson," he said. "I mean Samantha." He tipped his baseball cap to the ladies. His eyes fell on Nita, on her lovely face and luscious figure. But his eyes lingered for not even a fraction of a second. Brady only had eyes for Sam.

Sam introduced them. But still Brady did not stare. He barely seemed to notice the blond bombshell. He stared at Sam instead, even going so far as to tell her how lovely she looked in the crisp, early autumn air.

Sam blushed. And felt extraordinarily fine being complimented on her beauty while in the presence of such a perfect-looking bitch.

42

"Fat, dumpy, and puglike!" Sam screamed pretty much as loud as her voice box would permit. "Fat, dumpy, and puglike!"

Their guests had departed. Jason and Megan had been sent out on an errand with Mrs. Griner. Only Gunn and Samantha remained in the house.

"Fat, dumpy, and puglike!"

And, of course, Brady, who dallied behind the scenes, his lips delectably around a frozen Butterfinger. He tried not to crunch too loud on the chocolate and peanut butter brittle.

"Fat, dumpy, and puglike!"

"Sam," pleaded Gunn, "calm down. Let me explain."

"Explain! Explain what? How fat, dumpy, and puglike can turn into thin, gorgeous, and sexy in the blink of an eye?"

"No, I—"

"I don't think even the master of the cold call can make a sale on this one, buster!"

"Jesus, Sam. You see," Gunn responded, once again aware that the best defense was always an aggressive offensive, "you always do this. You always jump to conclusions before you have all the facts. This whole misunderstanding is because you're so jealous and paranoid and uptight."

"You're pushing it, Gunn."

"No, it's true. You gave me no choice last weekend but to describe Nita Garrett as fat and dumpy and puglike."

"*I* gave you no choice? How do you figure that?"

"Because. You were so bent out of shape just because she called on the phone. I had no choice but to put your mind at ease by making her sound homely."

"Oh, so this was all about you wanting to put *my* mind at ease?"

"Absolutely." Gunn knew she wasn't buying it, but he pressed onward and upward anyway. What choice did he have? Quit talking and the ax would fall. "I don't like to see you upset, especially over nothing. And believe me, Nita is nothing. So I told you she was fat and dumpy."

"And puglike."

"And puglike."

"Gunn, have I told you lately what a truly great guy you are? The extent you will go to protect me; it's touching. It brings tears to my eyes. You lying, stinking bastard! *Fat, dumpy,* and *puglike! Put my mind at ease!* Jesus! You must take me for a complete idiot."

"No, Sam, that's not true. I just wanted—"

"Shut up, damn you. Shut up and I'll tell you something about your cute little Miss Nita."

"What?"

"She's stupid, that's what."

"You're right," agreed Gunn. "As stupid as a stick. Easily the dullest knife in the drawer."

"Duller than Mandy?"

"She makes Mandy look like a rocket scientist. No more brains than a beagle."

"Ah," said Sam, "how witty. Another dog analogy. Don't try to close the door on this thing, Gunn. You're a liar and a weasel."

"A liar? No. I—"

"You didn't say one word to me about her traveling with you, making calls with you. Not one damn word!"

"Listen, Sam, what can I say? That was all Reilly's idea. Send a sexy woman along on the—"

"So you think she's sexy?"

Gunn couldn't help himself. "Well, Christ, don't you?"

"You shit! You lousy two-timing, double-talking shit! You lie and lie and lie, and then you expect me to just sit here and take it. Not say a word!"

"No, Sam, you've got it all wrong."

"No, Gunn, I don't have it all wrong. That's the problem. I've got it all right."

"No."

"Yes!"

"No!"

Brady pulled back. He had heard enough. No need to hear any more. He popped the rest of his Butterfinger into his mouth and headed for the exit. The show was over. Besides, he had to get back to his office on the third floor of the barn. London would be calling. A new buyout was in the pipeline, something right up Graphic Software's alley. Word was out that a small British outfit was developing a Gulf War game with chemical warfare graphics and flaming Iraqis who screamed in Arabic and bowed to Saddam as they died for Muhammad. Brady had read the reports. The game looked like a screamer, but was full of bugs. Brady felt sure if he acquired the property he could work his programming magic, create another mega software hit.

43 Early Monday morning Brady prepared for battle. He took a scalpel and sliced open his scalp where his forehead met his hairline. He made the incision about an inch and a half long, and deep enough to produce plenty of bleeding.

Satisfied with his surgical handiwork, the caretaker stopped the flow of blood with an adhesive bandage. He then covered the bandage with a length of waterproof surgical tape.

Half an hour later, Gunn, Jason, and Megan off to work and school, Brady prepared to swim his daily laps. Standing at poolside, practically shivering from the chill in the air, he glanced up at the second floor of the Georgian mansion. In the window of the guest room down the hall from the master suite, Brady spotted Greta. She gave him a thumbs-up. Thumbs-up meant Sam had taken up her customary position at the window overlooking the pool.

Brady dove into the heated water. He swam half a dozen laps. Normally he swam thirty or forty laps, but the surgical tape covering his wound was beginning to come loose.

Sam, from her window perch, watched the caretaker without much interest. Her eyes moved back and forth across the pool, but her thoughts wandered far and wide.

Brady climbed out of the pool into the chilly morning air. Immediately he began his ascent of the make-believe Matterhorn. The surgical tape had become waterlogged. So had the adhesive bandage. His incision had started to seep. A trickle of blood ran down his forehead. He held his fingertips against the wound to slow the flow.

Sam wondered for just a moment why Brady had swum so few laps. She decided she had missed most of them due to her preoccupation with Gunn and that plastic blond bimbo, the one who had undoubtedly left her lavender lace panties in her husband's suitcase. Sam sighed, then spotted Brady atop the Matterhorn preparing to dive. He looked so calm and graceful up there, a man at perfect ease with himself and his environment. She knew he was the kind of man who would never be unfaithful to a woman. And then she wondered what it would be like to be with such a man. The thought made her laugh out loud. She knew she had been wondering that exact same thought almost every morning all summer long.

The caretaker turned away from the pool and quickly removed the bandage covering his wound. He would have enjoyed performing three or four dives for Mrs. Henderson before setting the accident in motion, but the blood wanted to flow.

He stepped out to the edge of the diving platform and turned, his back to the water. His plan called for a backward two-and-a-half with his head purportedly making contact with the platform during the initial rotation. For weeks he had been practicing skimming the edge of the platform without actually colliding with it.

He reached up and squeezed the incision. The cut opened wide. The blood spurted. But Sam could not see the blood; she was too far away. Brady gathered himself, threw his arms out to his side, and flexed his powerful knees. A moment later, the blood flowing down his face, he launched his body into the air.

Sam loved to watch Brady dive, especially his preparation. He was so concentrated, so intense, but at the same time confident and relaxed. She had her eyes riveted on his muscular body as he dove off that platform.

In midair, Brady began to spin.

A fraction of a second later, Sam heard him scream. A bloodcurdling howl. She jumped to her feet, threw open the window. *My God,* she thought, *he's hit his head! On the platform!* "Brady!"

Brady, under water by this time, did not hear her shout. But he smiled nevertheless, knowing she was on her way.

Sam raced out of the bedroom and down the stairs. "Mrs. Griner! Mrs. Griner! Brady hit his head! Out at the pool! Call nine-one-one!"

Greta, still upstairs in the guest room, secluded behind a locked door, made no move to assist Sam. She knew Brady was okay. Besides, it was in her best interest to just stay out of the way, make herself scarce.

Brady lay on the bottom of the pool. He figured he could hold his breath for at least another sixty seconds. Ninety if necessary. Just a matter of staying relaxed.

Sam, still shouting for Mrs. Griner to call the rescue squad, sprinted through the kitchen and out onto the terrace. Eyeing the swimming pool, she saw no sign of Brady at the surface. Moving instinctively, unthinking, she kicked off her sneakers as she approached the side of the pool. She saw Brady immediately, through the clear water, motionless on the bottom. She dove in and started down. In no time at all she had her arms around his thick chest. Using some previously unknown but deep-seated strength, she pushed off and headed for the surface. The weight of his body barely seemed to register. There was, after all, no choice. Either get him up or he would drown.

Brady, trying hard to suppress his facial muscles from breaking into a grin, made himself as light and limp as possible. He did, however, kick his feet a wee bit when Sam began to run out of steam. His lungs were beginning to scream.

Sam broke the surface and made her way to the shallow end of the pool where she could stand on the concrete bottom. Brady's head floated on top of her hands. The time, he decided, had come for resurrection.

Blood pouring from the self-inflicted gash in his forehead, turning the water red, Brady opened his eyes and began to cough. He coughed and choked for a good thirty seconds.

Sam, breathing hard but clearly relieved, held him

steady. He seemed so vulnerable. She wanted to nurse him, nurture him, hold him close.

Finally, he stopped coughing. His eyes opened wide. He stared into her eyes. "What happened?"

"You hit your head."

"On the platform?"

"Yes."

"I did, you're right. I was doing a two-and-a-half back. I didn't get out far enough. I—" He stopped, grimaced, then reached up and gingerly touched his wound.

"It's not too bad," Sam reassured him. "Just a lot of blood. Let's get you out of the water and into the house where we can get a better look at it. You might need a stitch or two."

They made their way out of the pool and across the terrace. She accepted his weight.

Just before they reached the French doors leading into the kitchen, the caretaker stopped. He turned and looked Sam in the eye. "My God," he said, "you just saved my life. How can I ever repay you?"

Greta, secreted away in her rooms off the kitchen, experienced a twinge of nausea upon hearing Brady's fictitious confession. Still, she was impressed with his acting ability; though how much of it was still an act she was not sure.

● ● ●

LATER THAT SAME MORNING, after arguing over whether or not his cut needed the attention of a doctor, Sam and Brady kissed for the very first time. It was, at least for Sam, a most spontaneous kiss, one filled with both a suppressed longing and a naughty desire. For Brady it was all just part of the plan. At least he told himself it was part of the plan. But he too felt something in that kiss that he had not expected, and was not prepared to feel.

They stood in the small bathroom off the kitchen, the bright overhead light glaring. Sam examined his wound carefully, passed judgment on its depth and breadth. She thought he should go to the doc's; he thought not.

And then, his face quite close to her face, her hands upon his temples as she surveyed the wound, their lips just suddenly touched. No telling who initiated that coupling. She said he did. He said she did. They laughed, and tried another. And enjoyed it. It was so sweet and innocent and playful. At least Sam thought so. Even though she did feel a pang of guilt. But not really that guilty. After all, Gunn was bedding that whore. And besides, it was just a kiss. Just her sad lips upon his lonely lips. What, she asked herself as they tried another one, could possibly be more innocent than a kiss?

His lips felt wonderful: soft and supple and tender. And his breath: like nectar. On the third kiss, she kissed him harder, and made it last longer. He did not resist. She did not resist. There was no resistance at all.

Part Four

THE MOTIVE

44 Down in Dixie the kisses did not flow. At Peachtree Center, at the fancy Atlanta Marriott Marquis, once inseparable lips did not come within smacking distance of one another. Nita, following Mr. Reilly's dressing-down back at the mansion, had cut Gunn off cold turkey.

"But Nita," intoned Gunn, "this is ridiculous."

"It might be ridiculous, but we have no choice."

"Of course we have a choice."

"Mr. Reilly said no more hanky-panky. Any more hanky-panky and he'll fire me."

"He's not going to fire you."

"He said he'd fire both of us."

Gunn stood in the hotel corridor outside Nita's suite. She had the door open but the safety chain hooked. She was not taking any chances.

"He's not going to fire you. He's not going to fire me. He's not going to fire anybody. He just wants us to get on the ball. So tomorrow, first thing in the morning, we're going to hit the streets."

"I think we'd better."

"Don't worry. We'll go out and sell a million of his stupid Disks."

"I don't think he'd like it if he heard you calling them stupid."

"Jesus, Nita, come on, they're totally stupid. Completely idiotic. An utterly useless piece of junk. But who cares? Together, we can sell them. We can sell anything. Look, there's no reason why we can't have our cake and eat it, too. Now come on, baby, unlock the door, let me into the room."

Nita pretended to think it over. "No, I don't think so. If I let you in we both know what will happen. We'll get naked and we'll start making love and we won't stop until like Wednesday or Thursday."

Gunn, the stud, smiled. "Doesn't sound like such a bad way to spend a couple of days to me."

"It's a wonderful way," agreed Nita, her face hidden, "but not right now. Not tonight. We have to be careful."

"Okay, I promise, we'll be careful."

"You say that, but we won't."

"We will."

"Besides," added Nita, upping the ante, "seeing your wife and kids the other day kind of weirded me out."

Gunn, defensive, "What do you mean?"

"I don't know. I mean, like, I don't want to be a home-wrecker."

Even Gunn Henderson had to let a few things slide through his brain before he could respond to that one. But in the end his unyielding male organ carried the day. "Nita, listen to me, Sam and I have been slipping for a long time. Our relationship hasn't been good for a couple of years. Most of the time we're just going through the motions. Meeting you, being with you, has only brought that situation more clearly into focus."

Men, especially horny ones, and really, what other kinds are there—pretty much the scourge of the earth.

Nita, on the other side of the door, sighed. "Oh, Gunn, we need to slow down for a while. My head is spinning."

Gunn sensed an opening. "Just let me in. For a few minutes. I'll hold you. I'll rub your head. You know how you like it when I rub your head. It'll make everything better."

But Nita was resolute. Plus, she had her own agenda. "Not tonight, Gunn. Now go back to your room. I need some time to think. We both need some time to think." And with that she gently closed the door in his face.

●　●　●

NITA GARRETT, real name Louisa May Chance (her mother had loved *Little Women*), crossed to the bed, kicked off her heels, and lay down. Nice and comfy, she picked up the phone. She dialed long distance: East Hampton, New York.

Brady, real name Carl Patrick Donovan, picked up the receiver in his office on the third floor of the old barn on the grounds of PC Apple Acres. "Yes?"

"It's Louisa May."

"Yes?"

"I think it's going to work."

"Of course it'll work."

"Well, thank God," breathed Louisa May, playing

these past weeks the role of Nita G. "If I had to spend even one more night in the sack with him I think I would've puked."

"That bad?" asked Brady, curious.

"Maybe not that bad, but bad enough. He has a great body and everything, but Christ, he's such an egomaniac. A total narcissist. It's like he hardly even knows you're there. It's all about him. He might as well be fucking a hole in the wall."

"Yes, dear," replied Brady, pushing her fragile female buttons, "but in your case, a very luscious hole in the wall." Brady knew Louisa May had a sizable ego of her own. She also charged astronomical numbers for her rather unique services. Louisa May was the only whore Brady knew who had her own agent—no, not a pimp, a bona fide agent, who represented models and actresses as well as high-priced call girls.

"So how long," she asked, "do you want me to string him along?"

"That's difficult to say," answered Brady. "For now just keep him at bay with the work line. Insist the number one priority is to take care of business, sell Disks, make Reilly happy. Then, in a week or two, we'll turn up the heat. By then he'll be on his hands and knees."

"By then he'll be breaking down my door."

"You have to play him, Louisa May. All the way. That's why you get the big money."

Louisa May laughed, while she stroked the nipple of her left breast. She loved her line of work. And she was good at it. A star. She would have had a shelf full of Oscars had there been a category for best female hustler. "Don't worry," she assured the client, "I'll play him for all it's worth."

She really was a delectable and sexy thing to behold. Men the world over would abandon their wives and families and responsibilities for a chance to slip it to Ms. Chance.

"Just make sure you bring him along gently," instructed Brady. "And when the time is right, you'll have to go to him. You'll have to convince him you need him and love him. You'll have to whisper in his ear, tell him you can't live without him for even one more day. One more second."

Louisa May snickered. She loved this kind of stuff. "Sounds like I'll have to fuck him again."

"Oh, yes, dear," said the caretaker, "you most certainly will have to fuck him on that occasion. You will have to fuck him very well indeed."

45 Sam woke up with Brady on her mind. She could not believe she had actually kissed him. Never in all her years of married life had she kissed another man, excluding, of course, her father, her grandfather, God rest his soul, her brother, and her son. But she had kissed Brady, no question about that. Kissed him and enjoyed kissing him. His lips so tender and inviting. So un-Gunn-like. Gunn hadn't kissed her so warmly, so frivolously, in years. No, she decided, lying there, her arms wrapped around a pillow, Gunn had *never* kissed her as sweetly as Brady had kissed her in the downstairs powder room.

Still, she would not kiss the caretaker again. No way. She was a married woman. With two wonderful children. Children she loved and adored. She could not just go out and kiss any man who struck her fancy. Behavior like that led to chaos and depravity. To wrack and ruin. One needed to maintain one's decorum in order to perpetuate civilized society. Sam's father, a gentleman and a stickler for proper social etiquette, had taught her that.

Still, those kisses had been sweet. About the sweetest things to come down the road for Sam in quite some time. And innocent. Perfectly innocent. The innocence, Sam felt certain, was the key. She and Brady had not meant to kiss. It had just happened. Spontaneously. Without a second thought. Or even a first thought. So would it, she wondered, happen again? Could it happen again? Should it? And if so, when? Tomorrow? Maybe today? This morning even?

No, she could not let it happen again. Not today or any day. It was wrong. It was immoral. It was a sin.

Still, her thoughts, and her desires, continued to spin. She imagined Brady strolling into the bedroom, lying beside her on the bed, stroking her leg, kissing her lips. She imagined them spending the day together, strolling through the dormant gardens, one of his big sweaters keeping her warm and cozy, hand in hand, arm in arm. Then, as dusk settled, perhaps down at the boathouse, the waves lapping gently against the dock, the two of them would lie together, his weight on top of her, clothed, of course, but still close. Close and—

"Mommy, are you awake yet?"

Sam, a long way off, heard the familiar voice and snapped back to the present. Her eyes popped open. At the edge of the bed stood young Megan, clutching her stuffed lion to her chest. Sam smiled at her daughter. Megan smiled back, then crawled in beneath the silken sheet. They snuggled. Mother and daughter. Although, for the briefest of moments, Sam fantasized that the little girl in her arms was actually the caretaker.

●　●　●

THE CARETAKER, up in his fully equipped modern office on the third floor of the old barn, conjured up some fantasies of his own. His were not of a romantic nature, however. His fantasies had more to do with seduction and manipulation, conquest and revenge.

The caretaker's fantasies unfolded in living color on his huge twenty-one-inch Sony Trinitron computer monitor. They emanated from his powerful Apple Power Macintosh 9600 with a 300MHz PowerPC with 256MB of RAM saddled with a four-G.B. hard disk and a superhigh-speed CD-ROM drive capable of delivering action in real time. Only the latest and greatest computer arsenal would do for the caretaker.

Running that morning on Brady's Mac was the one and only copy of THE AVENGER, his latest software creation. THE AVENGER was Brady's first computer game aimed directly at the adult market. The game had taken him nearly three years to design and execute. And he figured another year would be needed before the program could be released to the public. Not only did he have more code to write, but the hardware available on the mass market still had not caught up with his potent software. But Brady was a patient and confident man. He knew there was not another programmer on the planet capable of pulling off something as complex as THE AVENGER. He felt certain THE AVENGER would be an enormous success, far outselling anything else Graphic Software had ever marketed. As an entertainment package, THE AVENGER offered the best of all venues. It provided the depth and the solitude of reading, the action and the immediacy of watching a film, and the interactive qualities associated with video games and computers. Plus it was extremely cool. Way cool.

The genesis for THE AVENGER was deceptively simple. When a player, let's call him Bob, first boots up the game, a crisis occurs. This crisis might be something as mundane as some driver cutting Bob off while Bob is cruising home from work, forcing Bob into a ditch and denting the fender of Bob's brand-new Chevy Camaro. Or maybe Bob gets mugged. Or knifed. Or shot. Or maybe some drug dealer gets Bob's fourteen-year-old son hooked on dope. Or perhaps his six-year-old daughter gets kidnapped by some lunatic. Or maybe Bob's father commits suicide after being ruined financially by some greedy and unscrupulous banker.

The point is: One crisis or another will befall Bob the moment he inserts THE AVENGER into his CD-ROM drive. And the one thing Bob can always count on: The crisis will not be his fault. The crisis will definitely be the result of someone else's evil or egotistical action. In THE AVENGER bad things don't just happen out of the blue; someone makes them happen.

Once this crisis strikes, the fun begins. Bob takes control, dealing with the situation in his own personal way. The software does not interfere. It allows Bob to be his own man, to react just as he would in real life. Before too much time passes, either Bob must decide to let bygones be bygones, or he must swing into action against those who did him or his loved ones wrong. If he chooses to let bygones be bygones, a computer-generated voice, sounding eerily like Richard Nixon, calls Bob a gutless wimp and a yellow-bellied loser, and a second later the program crashes. But if Bob chooses to swing into action, he immediately becomes THE AVENGER. He is then welcomed into a wonderful and fascinating world filled with all kinds of psychological intrigue and physical danger. Bob must hunt down those individuals responsible for inflicting themselves on his life. Once Bob locates these individuals he becomes privy to all manner and method of exacting revenge. Only the limits of his imagination hold Bob back at this stage of the game.

The caretaker certainly did not come up short in the imagination department. His imagination knew no bounds. And he knew a thing or two about human nature as well. He knew, for instance, that getting even was one of man's most primal and instinctual motivators. And he believed this need to get even was the progenitor for almost all aggressive action.

The caretaker also believed peace of mind and a secure soul came about only after scores had been settled, only after the psyche had been cleansed of all the filth and ugliness others had heaped upon it. The bad karma brought on by external influences needed exorcising before true contentment could be attained, or even considered.

Oh, yes, the caretaker was a man of very strong beliefs. And he possessed both the intelligence and the resources to bring his beliefs and his desires to fruition. Clearly, having the caretaker as an enemy could be extremely hazardous to one's health.

46 Brady would have enjoyed tinkering with THE AVENGER for another hour or two, but duty called. He had things to do, places to go, people to poison. So he shut down his Mac, pulled on his swimsuit and his sweats, and left his third-floor enclave on top of the barn. The nerve center of Graphic Software, Inc., could take care of business quite efficiently in his absence. The computers, the modems, the fax machines, the answering devices—all worked in unison to keep the information running smoothly. Brady had little to do with the day-to-day operation of the business anyway. He had a partner out in Silicon Valley who took care of those details. New products—the creative end—that was Brady's territory. Over the years his skills had served him well. During its fifteen years of existence, Graphic Software had gone from a basement in Brooklyn to the top of the computer industry heap. Along the way the company's profits had made its founder and major stockholder, Carl Patrick Donovan, a very rich man with homes in Palo Alto, California, and East Hampton, New York. He also kept a little pied-à-terre in the city, on the Upper East Side, a penthouse in one of Manhattan's more desirable buildings.

The caretaker left the barn and cut up through the rose garden to the swimming pool. Mrs. Henderson had not yet arrived, but Brady felt confident she was inside watching, so he stripped off his sweats and dove into the water. The autumn air felt chilly, probably not much above fifty degrees, but the pool maintained a constant seventy-eight degrees, perfect for swimming laps. Which Brady immediately began to do. He swam a dozen or so before Samantha came out through the back door and across the terrace. She had herself all bundled up against the cold: wool jacket, fleece pants, socks and sneakers.

The day before, after their kiss, Brady had offered to show Sam how to do a back two-and-a-half off the platform, "without," he'd added ruefully, "banging your head on the way down."

Sam had reluctantly agreed to come out and swim, and "maybe, but probably not, *jump* off the platform. No way am I diving."

Brady's reply: "We'll see."

Now Sam stood at the edge of the pool: shivering and a little bit scared, feeling a desire to retreat while at the same moment moving forward, confused about her motives but nevertheless certain she wanted to put a little buoyancy back in her life. A little excitement. The excitement of jumping off a platform suspended some thirty feet above the water? Or the excitement of once again being in close proximity to the caretaker? She did not dare provide herself with an answer.

Brady stroked to the pool's edge and emerged from the water in one long, wet, and very deft motion. A moment later he stood before her: tall and lean, water running off his muscles, nothing but that tight bit of spandex covering his most private parts. Sam tried not to remember that she had seen those parts also.

The air was chill. Brady forced himself not to shiver. He imagined himself standing on a beach in Barbados, the hot tropical sun beating on his shoulders. "Good morning, Samantha."

Her breath caught for an instant before she returned the greeting. Then, "God, Brady, aren't you freezing?"

"The water," he answered, still down in the Caribbean, "is much warmer than the air. Come on, let's get in."

Sam had her arms wrapped around her chest. "I don't think I can."

"Sure you can," countered the caretaker. "Trust me, once you get in, you'll love it. It makes you feel alive."

Sam liked the sound of that. She wanted to feel alive. That was the whole point, wasn't it? To feel alive? So she did it. She kicked off her sneakers, pulled off her socks, stepped out of her fleece pants, and unzipped her wool jacket. She stood there for just a moment in her skintight, one-piece swimsuit.

"Here goes!" she shouted, then jumped. She fully expected the shock from hitting the water to stop her heart. But no, once submerged, she relaxed. Brady was right: the water was warmer than the air, much warmer. It felt good. It felt great. Before even coming up for air, Sam decided to join Brady for a swim every morning.

Brady swam two or three laps to every one Sam swam. Up close she could see the raw power of his stroke. He churned through the water. She wondered if maybe she had made a mistake in asking Brady to wear a suit. Her early morning fantasies creeping back into her thoughts, Sam caught a mental glimpse of herself swimming naked beside Brady, stroke for stroke, the two of them diving underwater, embracing, connecting. She pushed the fantasy away, swam another lap.

Brady waited for her at the end of the pool. "Time to dive."

"No way," said Sam. "I can't get out of the water. I'll freeze to death."

Brady grinned, then climbed out of the pool and fetched a large towel and Sam's jacket. "Come on," he said, "you can do it."

She fussed for another minute or so. Brady nearly lost his patience. The chilly air had started to bite into his skin. But just before he snapped, she pulled herself out of the water. He immediately wrapped the towel around her shoulders.

"Brrr," she said, already shivering.

"Think warm," he told her. "Cold is just a state of mind."

She stepped closer to him. "No, it's not. Cold is when it's fifty degrees and I'm outside soaking wet and practically naked."

Brady smiled. And blushed. Right on cue. And then he drew her to him. She came, willingly, partly for the warmth, but also for the intimacy. He put his arms around her back and gave her a good, strong hug. She put her face against his chest. Several moments passed before he relaxed his grip. Her face came up. Their eyes met. And held.

Greta watched all this from the kitchen window. She had mixed feelings about the relationship developing between Brady and Sam. But she knew, in the end, it could be manipulated to her advantage. She just needed patience and resolve.

Brady could have kissed Sam, but instead, because he was about to start shivering himself, he said, "Let's dive."

Sam, reluctance once again snapping at her heels, followed Brady up the make-believe Matterhorn. Sam did not much like heights. Never had. Not as a kid or as an adult.

Brady sensed her anxiety as they neared the summit. "I think the most important thing we can do in life," he told her, "is overcome our fears. Only by overcoming our fears do we have a chance at realizing our full potential."

"It's so high," said Sam. "Much higher than it looks from down below."

Brady reassured her. "It's not that high. And directly below us the water is quite deep. More than fifteen feet. I'll go off first just to show you how safe it is."

Sam nodded. "I know it's safe. I'm just a wimp."

Brady strolled confidently out to the end of the platform. When he reached the end he turned to face Sam. "I'm going to do exactly the same dive I did when I hit my head. I'm scared, Sam, thinking about what happened. And knowing, if not for you, I'd probably be dead now. Drowned. Thank God you were watching."

Sam, embarrassed, shrugged and said nothing. She was shivering again, but not just because of the cold.

"I'm scared," Brady repeated, "but I don't like being scared."

And with that, he raised his arms, flexed his knees, and leapt backward off the platform. He tucked and spun, two and a half times, then pulled out, arched his back, and split the surface of the water with barely a ripple.

Sam applauded. "A perfect ten," she told him as soon as he returned to the surface.

"Well, maybe not a ten, but better than yesterday."

"It looked perfect to me."

"Okay," said the caretaker, "now it's your turn."

"No, I can't do it."

"Do you want to do it?"

"I guess. But there's lots of things I want to do that I don't do."

"This is something you want to do that you can do."

"No, I can't."

"Of course you can." Brady climbed out of the pool and started once again up the Matterhorn. He wanted to help Sam overcome her fear. He really did. He enjoyed Sam. Something about her close proximity made him feel comfortable and at ease. In fact, for quite a while now he had been wondering if there might be some way to complete his mission without her getting hurt. Physically or emotionally.

He rejoined Sam at the summit. "I think you can do this," he told her. "In fact, I'm sure you can."

"Maybe I could just jump."

"Jumping is good. Jumping is the best way at first."

It took a few more minutes, but eventually Brady coaxed Sam out to the end of the platform. He knew he could cause her to slip and fall and drown. But that would be too easy. Besides, though he might not have been willing to admit it, the caretaker did not want Sam to drown. That simple kiss they had shared the day before, the kiss the caretaker had so carefully orchestrated, now had him emotionally off balance. He teetered between his desperate need for revenge and his even more desperate desire for love and companionship.

"Just jump," he told her as he held her hand and squeezed her fingers. "I guarantee you it will all be over in a split second."

"And I'll be fine?"

"You'll be better than fine. You'll be exhilarated."

Sam nodded, but she needed more time. Brady gave her all the time in the world. She could feel his patience, his strength. Gunn, she knew, would have grown cold and sarcastic by this time. He would have called her a chicken and a coward and maybe even have pushed her over the edge. But Brady waited for Sam to gather her courage.

And eventually, she did. And when she did, she simply let go of his hand, bent her knees, and jumped. On the way down she did not even scream.

Plunging to the bottom of the pool, then rising to the surface, Sam felt wild and ecstatic and alive, totally full of life. "My God, that was unbelievable!" she shouted up to the caretaker. "I want to do it again."

"Do it as many times as you want."

So she did. She jumped half a dozen times. She became impervious to the cold. She jumped, climbed out of the pool, ascended the Matterhorn, and jumped again. The fifth time they jumped together, holding hands. And when they returned to the surface, they embraced. And kissed.

After several more kisses they climbed out of the pool and once more started up the mountain. Halfway up, Brady stopped. "Have you ever climbed the real Matterhorn?" he asked.

"In Switzerland?"

"Yes."

"No, but I've seen it. From the valley. From Zermatt."

"You should climb it."

"Have you climbed it?"

"Yes," answered Brady, "I climbed it a few years ago."

"All the way to the top?"

Brady nodded. "It was incredible."

"God," said Sam, "I would love to do that."

Brady knew opportunity had knocked. He looked Sam in the eye. "Then we should," he replied, his enthusiasm running over. And then, an instant later, he dropped his eyes and lowered his voice. "I mean, you should."

Sam wanted to say, "No, we should," but she was too much of a coward to do that.

So they climbed the rest of the way in silence.

At the top Brady said, "I think you're ready to dive."

"You do? Really?"

"Absolutely."

Sam nodded. She trusted him. Her first dive off the high platform was just a simple layout, but she did it very well, and after only a few seconds of procrastination.

When she returned to the surface she could hear Brady's applause.

"A perfect ten," he told her. "Beautifully done."

Sam beamed.

Brady did a one-and-a-half with a twist. He joined Sam in the shallow end of the pool. They kissed again. It might have gone further, much further, but the caretaker said he had played too long. "I have chores to do, errands to run."

Indeed he did. He had to drive up to Westchester and have a little visit with Sam's in-laws.

47

Ms. Nita met Gunn for breakfast in the restaurant of the Atlanta Marriott Marquis. As always, at any hour of the day or night, she looked outstanding. Every male eye in the dining room did the visual Watusi as she made her way to Gunn's table.

Gunn, the gentleman, stood. He'd decided to play along with Nita's desire to think things over. During a long and pretty much sleepless night, he'd realized it would do him no good to get mad or make demands. Women like Nita, in G. Henderson's mind anyway, did not put up with any petty crap from their lovers. He needed to stay cool and patient.

But then Nita sat down, pulled in her chair with Gunn's assistance, and announced, "I have to go home."

"What?"

"I've already cleared it with Mr. Reilly. I'm leaving right after breakfast."

Gunn took his seat. "Your mother?"

"She's taken a turn for the worse. Father had to take her to the hospital last night after her fever shot up to like a hundred and four."

"Wow," said Gunn, sounding right out on the verge of sarcastic, "that's high."

"It's this thing she caught down in the tropics."

"And you really think you need to go home?"

"Absolutely."

"For how long?"

"Hopefully I'll be back in a day or two. As soon as Mother's out of the woods."

Gunn hesitated for a moment, then added, "I understand you have to go, Nita, but remember, you're needed here. You're part of the team."

● ● ●

So Nita packed her bag and went home. Gunn thought she'd gone to Fort Worth, Texas. But no, Louisa May had herself a dandy little one-bedroom apartment on the Upper East Side of Manhattan, right around the corner, actually, from Carl Patrick Donovan's penthouse spread.

Louisa May Chance did not go home to see her mother, who actually lived in Fort Lauderdale, Florida, not Fort Worth, Texas, in a high-rise condo overlooking the Atlantic. No, Louisa May went home to take care of some very important business clients: kinky Japanese automobile executives who threw hundred-dollar bills around like they'd pulled them out of a Monopoly game. Carl Patrick Donovan was fully apprised of the situation. He had, in fact, encouraged it. He thought it would do wonders for Gunn Henderson's libido if Nita disappeared for a while. Make the man even more pliable than usual.

●　●　●

GUNN CARRIED ON in Nita's absence as best he could. Too bad his best was nowhere near good enough. Reilly had a lengthy list of prospective clients he wanted Gunn to see. Normally Gunn set up his own appointments and made his own contacts, but because his liaison with Nita had interfered with business, Reilly had intervened.

"I'll make the contacts," Reilly had told Gunn over the weekend, "you make the call. Sell the product. And I mean *sell,* dammit. It's getting awfully late in the game."

So Gunn found himself in the hot seat. And without his lovely Nita to dazzle the clients.

His calls did not go well. One potential buyer after another more or less scoffed at the whole idea of The Disk. "Ridiculous." "Ludicrous." "Stupid." "I hate to be the one to tell you this, sonny, but Americans are feeling poor these days. They ain't about to throw away good money on a dumb piece of wood inside some chintzy velvet bag."

And so it went, from dawn till dusk and then well

into the evening. Gunn did not get back to his room at the Marriott Marquis until almost midnight. He had made ten calls, eaten three bad meals, drunk at least half a dozen gin and tonics, consumed a quart of Maalox, and worn a phony smile on his face for so many hours he feared he might need a Brillo pad to wipe it off. All this, and not a single Disk sold. Not one damn Disk. Not even the hint of a sale. Plus he found a message from Reilly, three messages actually, all demanding he call back immediately, no matter what the time.

But Gunn couldn't face Reilly. Not right away. So he rang up Nita down in Fort Worth. And due to the wizardry of modern communications technology, that call bounced from Atlanta to Fort Worth, ran into a rerouting signal, and bounced again, straight up to New York City. Gunn's frantic calls a few weeks earlier from the Hamptons to Fort Worth had done the same thing. Only those calls had bounced from Fort Worth to Louisa May's agent on Madison and Forty-second. Rudy Blylock, as per his instructions, had used his best Texas accent to keep the hook in the mark's mouth. Rudy had played Nita's Lone Star daddy to perfection.

"Hello," Ms. Nita answered in a sleepy voice, even as she pressed her finger over her lips to silence the moans and groans of her Nipponese visitors.

"Nita, it's me."

"Gunn. Hi."

"Sorry to call so late. Were you asleep?"

"Not quite. I just got back from the hospital half an hour or so ago."

"How is she?"

"Not so good. They have her sedated."

One of her guests grabbed her right nipple and squeezed. She swatted his delicate little hand away. The Japanese automobile executive, who rarely ever smiled, giggled.

"Is someone there?" asked the ever-suspicious Gunn Henderson.

"Just my father," answered Nita. "He wants to call the hospital, check on Mom."

"Okay, well—"

"Thanks for calling. I miss you. Call tomorrow." And with that, Nita hung up. Immediately, the Japanese attacked. Nita, certainly no shrinking violet, surrendered. Why not? A whole stack of greenbacks, nearly as fat as the phone book, sat on the bureau.

Gunn pulled the receiver away from his ear and stared at it for several seconds. Finally, he set it back in its cradle. He could not believe she had hung up so fast. He wanted to call back, talk some more, tell Nita how much he missed her, but he decided it would be better to just leave it alone. The poor girl had enough on her mind. The last thing he wanted to do was push her.

Then, because he felt lonely, he thought about calling Sam. His wife. But before he could dial, the phone rang. Reilly. Wanting to know the score. Gunn did his best to paint a rosy picture, but clearly, things did not look good. Reilly ranted and raved. Told Gunn he was not performing up to snuff. Doing a lousy job. Letting down the company. Botching up the whole enterprise. Changes could and would be made. Then he ordered Gunn down to Jacksonville first thing in the morning. A whole new schedule of meetings had been set up. A list with times and places would be waiting for him at his hotel. And then click. The line went dead.

Gunn sighed and hung up. He told himself to stay cool, everything would pan out as long as he stayed cool. Then he punched his fist right through the wall of room 604 of the Atlanta Marriott Marquis.

48 Brady waved good-bye to Greta, then pulled out of PC Apple Acres a few minutes before eleven o'clock in the morning. His cargo lay in the bed of his pickup, well protected by a heavy plastic tarp. He checked his watch, did a few quick calculations, and determined he would have no trouble meeting his four o'clock delivery time. No need to rush. No need to break the speed limit. Just relax and enjoy the few hours of peace and quiet. For Brady, an extremely diligent and hardworking individual, these trips up to Westchester County, taken approximately once every three months, were like minivacations.

Vacation or not, the caretaker was not a man who wasted time. Time, he believed, was by far life's most precious commodity. It nauseated him the way people wasted time. They threw it away as though it were a renewable, even boundless, resource. Brady knew different. Brady knew life could be snatched away at any moment. He had seen it happen. Right before his youthful eyes. And he also knew if he managed to live to the age of eighty, his days on earth were very nearly half over. And what had he done with the first half? Not much, in his estimation. Sure, he'd made some money, invented some computer software used all over the world, perfected the three-and-a-half with a twist, cultivated a brand-new type of rose, but still, he viewed himself as a middling success at best. He believed he had much more to accomplish; he had to work harder.

And so, as the caretaker cruised west on the Long Island Expressway, he listened on the pickup's audio system to a series of lectures on Greek history. Brady felt his knowledge of history was severely flawed. He knew bits and pieces about various eras and civilizations, but most of his knowledge constituted nothing but a mishmash of unrelated facts. This annoyed him. So he had determined some time ago to go back to the beginning and slowly make his way forward. Only then could he hope to understand how the modern world had developed. Just as Brady had studied his own life and his own family in grave detail, so he now wanted to study the historical, psychological, and sociological roots of mankind. Time might have been the most coveted commodity in the caretaker's mental arsenal, but knowledge—real knowledge—came in a close second.

Brady crossed the Throgs Neck Bridge at around quarter after one. At one-thirty he passed the Bronx Zoo while traveling north on the Bronx River Parkway. He learned from his tapes that Aristotle spurned Plato's doctrine of ideas, insisting instead that an idea simply of its own accord has no power to produce the corresponding concrete reality. Aristotle claimed an idea all by itself does nothing more than introduce a whole new agenda of complications while explaining absolutely nothing.

"Agreed," said the caretaker, right out loud. "All the words in the world are meaningless and even impertinent until they're followed up with action." And then silently, to himself, he added, "I can think all I want about avenging the destruction of my family, but until I actually do it, I'm nothing but a weakling and a coward."

Brady entered Westchester County and worked his way to the north side of White Plains. In a narrow back alley off North Broadway, he turned the pickup truck into a driveway not much longer than the length of his vehicle. Leaving the engine running, he climbed out, withdrew a key from his pocket, and approached the double-wide garage door. He unlocked the door, took a quick look around, and pulled it open. Then he returned to the pickup and drove the truck into the garage. He shut down the engine, climbed out, flipped on the overhead lights, and closed the garage door.

Everything looked exactly as he had left it three months earlier. The garage was clean and empty except for the white delivery van parked next to the pickup. Across the side of the van, in black letters, it read: WESTCHESTER WATER SOFTENER & SUPPLY. Nothing more. No address. No phone number.

Brady opened the doors at the back of the van. Then he dropped the tailgate of the pickup and peeled back the tarp. It did not take long to move the dozen fifty-pound bags of water softener salt from the truck to the van, just a few minutes.

Once finished, Brady closed up the van and returned

to the cab of the pickup. He fetched a small leather satchel off the floor. Then he walked to the back of the garage where, some five and a half years earlier, he had installed a cupboard with a mirror and a light. Five and a half years: That was how long he had been making these special deliveries. Occasionally the deliveries became a nuisance and an inconvenience, but nevertheless, he never missed one. It was a labor of love, a commitment he'd made years ago to his dead mother.

Brady opened the satchel and pulled out his disguise. Nothing fancy. Just a pair of gray overalls with JOE printed above the breast pocket and WESTCHESTER WATER SOFTENER printed across the back. Brady would be Joe Beattie for the next couple hours. He even had a current New York driver's license that said so.

After pulling on the overalls, Brady attached a fake but very real-looking mustache to his upper lip. He thought he looked good with a mustache, very debonair. Next he slipped on a pair of black frame eyeglasses and a blue cap with W.W.S. scrolled across the front.

There actually was a company named WESTCHESTER WATER SOFTENER & SUPPLY operating out of White Plains. Six years earlier, not long after Brady started making some real money in the software business, he'd purchased the company, with cash, under an alias. He made this purchase as an investment; not a financial investment—an emotional one. He owned the company for only six months. Just long enough to take full and personal control of one particular account: the Henderson account up on Whippoorwill Road outside of Armonk.

Brady glanced at his watch: 3:13. Plenty of time. No need to rush. He double-checked everything, then climbed into the van. The engine, sitting idle for almost three months, needed some coaxing. Eventually it turned over. Brady opened the garage door while the engine warmed up. Then he backed the van out into the drive and locked the garage door. 3:24. Time to roll. When he had scheduled the delivery a few days earlier, he had told Mrs. Henderson he would be there around four o'clock. The caretaker liked to be punctual.

He drove north through White Plains to Mount Kisco Road. Mount Kisco took him north along the Kensico Reservoir. The calm water glittered under a bright afternoon sun. Brady rolled down the window and drank in the fresh air. He loved the smell of autumn.

At the north end of the reservoir he turned off Mount Kisco onto King Street. A couple miles along King, he turned right on Whippoorwill Road. 3:46. He would be a few minutes early. No problem.

The Hendersons' driveway was a mile and a half up Whippoorwill on the left. Brady pulled in. The drive wound for several hundred feet past some stately American sycamores. Most of their leaves had fallen. They lay scattered on the ground and across the macadam.

The driveway split as it neared the house, a large brick colonial with two towering chimneys rising from the roof. Brady knew the value of the six-acre property: somewhere in the neighborhood of 1.3 to 1.5 million dollars. The Hendersons also owned a house in Maine and a condo out in the Bahamas. No doubt about it: The banking business had been very good to Gunn Henderson, Sr. Banking had made him a bundle of money. It was just too bad about his health. He had been having all kinds of difficulties for several years now.

The main drive circled up to the front door. The auxiliary drive led around the side to the garage. Brady took the secondary route. Having been here many times before, he knew the way.

He parked the van and walked around to the back door. All looked calm and peaceful at the Henderson spread. A teenage boy raked leaves in the backyard. Brady did not recognize him, but he waved anyway. The youngster waved back. Probably some neighborhood kid earning a few bucks. Brady rang the bell.

A few moments later, Mrs. Henderson pulled open the door. Gunn's mother, though only sixty-three, carried a cane in her left hand. She needed it to keep her balance.

"Good afternoon, Mrs. Henderson," said Brady as Joe the delivery man, "Westchester Water Softener and Supply."

"Yes, of course. You're right on time, as always."

"We try, ma'am."

Mrs. Henderson smiled at her poisoner.

"So," he asked, "how are you today?"

"Oh, getting along, thank you," she replied. "Getting along."

Brady could see she was not really getting along very well at all. When he had first started his deliveries, Barbara Henderson had been an energetic and vigorous woman. Now she looked bent and weak and weary, closer to eighty-three than sixty-three. Undoubtedly the arsenic. And just in the past six months, since he had increased the dosage, the left side of her face had started to look loose and droopy. Kind of palsied. Probably nerve damage. That could be from either the arsenic or the lead.

"Well," replied Brady, "you're looking well. And now I don't want to make a nuisance of myself, so I'll just start hauling these bags into the house."

"I believe you know where they go."

"Sure do, ma'am. Through that door right behind you and down into the basement." Joe Beattie: the epitome of the polite, hardworking deliveryman.

"If you would be so kind," said Mrs. Henderson, "as to fill the tank with salt. I believe it's getting low, and my husband just no longer has the strength to do it."

I'll bet he doesn't, thought Brady. "Not a problem," said Joe. "I'll take care of it."

"Thank you so much."

Brady began hauling the fifty-pound bags of salt from the van to the basement. He dumped the first six bags directly into the holding tank, bringing the level of salt right up to the top. He knew that would get the Hendersons through the next six or seven weeks. The other six bags he stacked on a pallet nearby. Someone else, perhaps Gunn Jr., up having a little visit with Mom and Dad, could refill the tank. The thought of having young Gunn as an unwitting accomplice made Brady smile. Then he went to work checking out the water softening system. He always made sure before leaving that everything was in good working order. He replaced a filter and several feet of hose. The chemicals had a tendency to eat away at the plastic. Then he cleaned and tightened all the fittings.

The system looked good. It looked as though it was delivering poisons to every spigot in the house with perfect regularity. Just as it had been doing for the past five and a half years. Every time Mr. or Mrs. Henderson turned on a tap and drew a glass of seemingly crystal-clear well water, they were, in fact, getting a low but lethal dose of arsenic and lead. Every single bag of salt that Brady had delivered to the house for the past five and a half years contained the caretaker's very special blend of these two toxic poisons. An amateur but nevertheless careful chemist, Brady knew exactly how to lace the salt to achieve his desired result; that being the slow and agonizing demise of the rapidly aging banker.

For years Carl Patrick Donovan had wondered how best to deal with Gunn Henderson, Sr. All shapes and varieties of pains and tortures had slipped in and out of his brain. Shooting the banker down, slicing the banker's throat, running the banker over with a car (or, better yet, a steamroller) had all titillated the caretaker at one time or another. But eventually he had realized the banker's end must be slow and excruciating. So he read books. And watched movies. And did research. And finally, after years of study, he decided to poison the bastard to death. And what better way to do so than through the water supply?

As Brady climbed out of the basement after finishing his chores, he received an unexpected treat. Often when he made his deliveries he never even got a glimpse of his primary victim. But this time he found Gunn Henderson, Sr., right smack in the middle of his own kitchen. And look at that, confined to a wheelchair, for goodness' sakes.

Gunn Henderson the Elder had long believed in the restorative powers of H_2O. H_2O kept the system clean, fought off disease, even kept old age at bay. And so he drank at least half a gallon of water every single day. And since he lived in an area where the water had an almost legendary reputation for pristine quality and cleanliness, he always took his elixir straight from the tap. For this reason the poisons had affected him faster and more severely than his wife. Just sixty-five years old, Gunn the Elder looked closer to a hundred. Tall, broad, muscular, and ramrod-straight right up until his sixtieth birthday, he now looked thin and frail and twisted.

A look of supreme satisfaction spread across Brady's face the second he laid eyes on his adversary. "I am," he wanted to cry out, "The Avenger!"

But, of course, he said no such thing. He simply tipped his cap and said in a friendly voice, "Afternoon, Mr. Henderson."

Gunn the Elder grumbled something inhospitable under his breath, then demanded, "Who the hell are you?"

The Elder had never been a particularly pleasant or courteous man, except, perhaps, to those he felt were his equals. But the poisons had turned him into a virtual madman. The high levels of lead in his system left him constantly moody, irritable, constipated, and riddled with terrible headaches, heart palpitations, and insomnia. Many nights he could not sleep at all. The man was miserable. He thought often of suicide.

And why hadn't modern medicine fixed him up, straightened him out? The doctors had been trying, for years. Five and a half years to be exact. A wide variety of ailments from cancer to Alzheimer's had been suspected and even treated. But finally, it had been determined, beyond a shadow of a doubt, that both the Elder and his bride had been laid low by a tick. Yes, insisted the medicine men, a lousy little tick was the culprit for all this bad health. The Hendersons had very advanced cases of Lyme disease. After all, the tick-borne disease was endemic in Westchester County. Thousands had contracted it. The Hendersons were just more victims. They had all the classic symptoms. And a few extra ones the doctors were busy adding to their lists.

All this was why Gunn the Elder, slouching in that wheelchair looking very old and sorry for himself, had an IV sticking out of his arm. He had been on intravenous antibiotics for the past several months. The man's entire immune system was quickly going to pot.

Brady gave Henderson a look rife with pity and answered, "Joe Beattie, sir. Westchester Water Softener and Supply."

The Elder grumbled something else that Brady did not quite catch.

Then Joe stepped right up to the wheelchair and presented Mr. Henderson with the delivery slip. "If you would just sign here, sir."

But the Elder could not sign. The Elder was too feeble. He had to call for his wife.

Poor man, thought the caretaker. Then he wished them both a good day and took his leave. On the way back to White Plains he decided one or two more deliveries might do the trick. No need to kill the bastard off. Having him suffer was far more rewarding. But the son, he definitely intended to kill the son. After humiliating him and ruining his career and stealing his wife and turning him into a pauper.

49

So the whole thing was a setup. Right from the get go. Right from that certified letter Sam signed for way back in the spring. Right from that phone call from Mr. Ron Johnson of Creative Marketing Enterprises. That was just Brady calling, disguising his voice, making contact. Same with the weekend up at PC Apple Acres. Nothing but a setup. Sam had thought Mr. Arthur James Reilly reminded her of some actor she'd seen once in some movie. Well, she was right on the money. Reilly was an actor, worked the stage mostly. Off-Off Broadway was his place in the sun. He had the same agent as Louisa May, the inscrutable Rudy Blylock, an old pal of Brady's from their days at Brooklyn College. Reilly, real name Rick Parsons, knew nothing about running a giant corporation. The man could barely balance his checkbook. Brady had watched Reilly's entire performance that first weekend from behind the walls of the mansion, his mansion. No doubt about it, Brady was the main man. There was never any question that Gunn Henderson, Salesman Extraordinaire, would be offered the head salesman's job at Creative Marketing Enterprises. Gunn had that job all wrapped up even before he knew the job, or anyone associated with the job, even existed. Bringing in all those other unsuspecting candidates was just a sham, part of the setup. An exquisitely crafted and perfectly executed setup. One that the caretaker had worked on for years.

Too bad Sam still didn't have the foggiest notion what was going on at PC Apple Acres. Had she known, she surely would have grabbed her children and run for her life.

●　　●　　●

ALL WENT SMOOTHLY at PC Apple Acres for several days following Brady's return from Westchester. Every morning after Jason and Megan left for school, he and Sam rendezvoused at the pool. They swam some laps, then practiced their diving. Sam grew more and more courageous off the platform. As her courage grew, so did her desire for the caretaker. He made her feel relevant and vital. And best of all, attractive. Sam needed to feel attractive.

And he desired her, also; she could see the desire in his eyes. She knew he wanted to make love to her. But he never forced himself, never made demands. If anything, he was a bit more reticent than she might have liked. Not that she was ready to make love to any man other than her husband. But she could fantasize. Fantasies were free. And perfectly innocent.

Twice that week, in a clear indicator of her own desires, Sam invited Brady to have dinner with her and the kids. She did not find these invitations even remotely inappropriate. Jason and Megan liked Brady. Sam thought it was good for everyone to have a man in the house. Gunn, after all, rarely made an appearance anymore.

During these meals together, Sam, naturally, kept her distance from the caretaker. She certainly did not want her children to sense even a shred of intimacy between her and Brady. As for Brady, he played his role perfectly: polite, attentive, even occasionally amusing. He told the kids stories about his own youth. Lies mostly, but his tales kept the youngsters riveted nevertheless.

And Greta McDougal? Better known to the family as Mrs. Greta Griner? The cook watched events unfold from the sanctity of the kitchen. Her kitchen. She did not miss a thing. Her brain sucked it up and stored it away.

•   •   •

THE WEEKEND ARRIVED. Gunn did not come home. He called, claimed he had to work. Reilly's orders. Sam did not believe him, not for a second, nor did she really give a damn. She definitely did not feel like arguing with her husband. There had been enough arguing and ugliness.

In fact, Gunn the Younger *was* working. Like a dog. Night and day selling Disks. Sans Nita, who was still back in the Big Apple entertaining those Japanese execs. Gunn, down in the Sunshine State, worked feverishly peddling those ridiculous pieces of wood. But no one was even remotely interested. He tried, in vain, to explain his frustration to his wife.

But Sam was miles away. She barely heard a word Gunn uttered.

"Fine," she replied when his voice stopped echoing

through the receiver, "I don't care if you come home or not. I couldn't care less."

And with that she gently placed the receiver back in the cradle. No bother. No fuss. Not a single harsh or hostile thought in her head.

50

Sunday it stormed. A big blow out of the northeast. Wind and rain. Thunder and lightning.

Brady, out in the boathouse, paced. Normally he had the patience of a panther stalking prey, but tonight he could not sit still. Nor could he concentrate on his work. His thoughts jumped from one subject to the next, a chaotic jumble of confusion. He wanted to believe his impatience stemmed from the slow progress of various projects at Graphic Software, Inc., but this, he knew in the most rational part of his brain, was nonsense. The stress and strain of business never threw him off stride. No, a woman had the caretaker off-kilter. A woman. Plain and simple. Nothing else in life throws a man's equilibrium out of whack like the slow, steady invasion of a woman's aura. Brady had Samantha Henderson on his brain. No matter how hard he tried, he could not push her aside. Her eyes, her lips, her legs, her scent, her entire being dominated his thoughts. These feelings had been building for weeks, for months. Nothing Brady tried slowed them down.

Too bad the reality of his desire provided the care-taker with absolutely no joy whatsoever. At least no joy he willingly recognized. And so, eventually, after he could take this invasion not one second longer, he decided the time had come to forge ahead with his plan, turn an idea—Aristotle would be proud—into action.

The idea he had in mind had come to him several weeks earlier, but until that stormy night he had been reluctant to act. Reluctant because he did not like to abuse perfectly innocent wildlife. But now, at least partly in response to the impatience and growing annoyance he felt regarding his petty emotionalism, he decided to press forward.

He pulled on a slicker and ventured out into the storm. The wind blew and the rain fell in great sheets. He made haste across the sodden grass to the relative calm of the old barn. Up in one of the locked storage rooms on the second floor, Brady found his captive wildlife alive and well and hanging upside down in the cage he had carefully provided for them.

He had captured the four flying mammals back at the end of the summer when they had mistakenly in-filtrated his work space on the third floor. Initially he had been inclined to open a window and let the furry little fellows go. But at the last second a possible plan involving the creatures popped into his head, so he decided to make them his own, at least temporarily.

Now, wearing a heavy work glove, he carefully re-moved two of the bats from the cage and placed them in a soft suede pouch. They rebelled only briefly with some hissing and wing flapping. Soon enough they quieted down. The caretaker hoped they had not been traumatized.

He left the other bats in the cage and headed back downstairs. To any casual visitor, this barn looked like any other old barn. The first two floors were a collection of rakes and hoes and shovels, tractors and lawn mowers and Weedwackers, crates and ancient fence posts and coils of wire, rusted lampposts, discarded furniture, and cardboard boxes filled with faded newspapers and damp magazines and God knows what else. Only the one-inch electrical conduit pipe running up the main support post in the middle of the barn gave any hint at all that something out of the ordinary might be happening up on the third floor. That pipe protected the dozens of circuits that powered the caretaker's vast arsenal of electric and electronic gadgetry.

He took a moment now to protect that arsenal by checking an emergency switch that allowed his entire office to run on generators in the event of a power failure. The switch was up and running. The caretaker, satisfied, headed back out into the storm, bats in tow.

He crossed the backyard, slipped onto the rain-swept terrace, and crept up to the rear of the house. Through the kitchen windows he could see Sam and the kids eating dinner. Greta stood her post at the sink. They all looked excited, keyed up. Probably the storm, thought Brady. He wished he could be in there, warm and dry, rather than out here, cold and wet. Part of the family rather than the lone wolf.

Men—they never know what they want.

Brady, annoyed with his sentiments, spit, then went

quickly around to the side of the house, pulled open the cellar doors, and slipped into the basement. One way or another, he intended to get inside.

He entered the labyrinth of secret passageways leading to various rooms in the house. His destination this time was Megan's room on the second floor. Her room did not have a secret entrance, so Brady entered through an unoccupied guest room, then cautiously made his way along the hallway. The door to Megan's room hung wide open, but no matter, she would never recall such a trivial detail.

Muffled voices filtered up the back stairway as Brady stepped into the little girl's bedroom. He did not turn on the light. He preferred instead to use the light coming from the hallway. Megan's room was neat and tidy, everything put away and in its place. Brady liked that. He was a very neat and tidy guy. He had bounced Megan on his knee a couple of times over the summer. They had made faces at each other, each time causing the other one to laugh. Brady smiled at the memory as his eyes adjusted to the dim light. He saw the dolls and stuffed animals resting on her bed. He saw the books on her shelf. He saw a little pink diary on her desk. Impulsively, remembering his little sister had kept a diary, he picked it up and carried it over to the door where the light was stronger. He opened to the bookmark. Megan's handwriting was neat and tidy too, each letter perfectly formed.

THURSDAY NIGHT: School was fun today. We learned about plants and listened to a story about a family in Africa. Mr. Brady came for dinner. We had black beans and rice with lettuce and tomato on top. Mr.

Brady told us a story about a whale that once washed up on the beach here. Mr. Brady and some other men saved the whale by pushing it back into the sea.

FRIDAY NIGHT: Mommy fought with Daddy again tonight on the telephone. She was yelling and swearing and scaring me even though I'm sure she didn't think I could hear. I wish they wouldn't fight anymore. They seem to fight a lot since we moved here. I liked it where we used to live better.

Brady sighed. So many complications. He thought about his siblings, his two sisters. One of them dead before her ninth birthday. The other one killed in Londonderry practically right before his eyes. The memory made him kick the door with his damp boot. It crashed against the wall.

Time to act.

In one smooth motion the caretaker returned the little pink diary to the desk, opened the suede pouch, released the two bats, and left the bedroom, pulling the door closed as he exited. Less than a minute later he was back in the basement, his adrenaline pumping. He went out into the night. Both the wind and the rain had grown fiercer. Lightning flashed out over the sound. Thunder rumbled in the distance. Leaning into the wind, Brady made his way back around to the kitchen. Only Sam and Greta remained. Jason and Megan had retired to the TV room.

Satisfied the time was right, Brady retraced his steps to the basement. Back in the utility room he found a flashlight stored in a cabinet. He made sure the flashlight worked, then he crossed to the main circuit breaker box. Over a hundred circuits ran through the mansion and the various outbuildings. Each circuit had its own breaker. But a large double breaker at the bottom of the box controlled all the juice that came in off the street. Brady, flashlight burning bright, reached into the box and flipped that double breaker off. A split second later, PC Apple Acres fell into total darkness.

Brady crossed the utility room and opened a small gray plastic box, the telephone junction box. A vast array of wires and switches occupied the box. He flipped a series of switches, shutting down all of the phone lines coming into the mansion. But the lines running to the boathouse and the barn continued to operate normally. Reports would be coming in from Tokyo. Reports Brady would need in the morning.

The caretaker went back out into the night. He snapped off his flashlight as he exited the basement. Hunched against the cold rain, he strode by the swimming pool, turned, and glanced at the house. The place looked as dark as a tomb. Moving swiftly, seeking shelter from the storm, he retreated to the barn. He needed to let some time pass before he made his move. Eight or ten minutes would do. By then, he figured, Sam would be very glad to see him indeed.

●　　●　　●

A QUARTER of an hour later, Brady, the beam of his flashlight dancing on the raindrops, approached the back door of the mansion. He could see a couple of candles burning in the kitchen, a couple more through the windows in the living room. The upstairs still looked dark.

He tapped on the glass. Mrs. Griner pulled open the door. Greta eyed the caretaker suspiciously. She felt certain all this darkness must be his doing. But they had never discussed a power outage. It made no sense to her.

"Evening," he said. "Storm must have blown down some wires."

Greta, eyes narrowed, replied, "Must have."

Young Megan appeared at Mrs. Griner's side. "Hi, Mr. Brady. The lights went out."

"I see that, Megan. There doesn't seem to be any power anywhere on the estate." Brady still stood outside, protected from the storm only by the narrow overhang above the French doors.

Greta did not seem particularly anxious to invite him inside. She definitely did not like not knowing what he had in mind.

But then Sam arrived carrying a burning candle stuck inside a beautiful brass candlestick. "Brady!" she exclaimed. "Isn't it exciting?"

The caretaker was surprised. Neither the kid nor her mother seemed the slightest bit upset about the power outage. In fact, they seemed delighted with this turn of events. "Exciting? You mean the storm?"

"Yes! I love it when the lights go out."

This was not what Brady had expected. "As I was saying to Mrs. Griner, some lines must be down. There's quite a blow going on out here."

Sam noticed then that Brady stood outside. She stepped forward, grabbed him by the arm, and practically pulled him into the house. "For God's sake, Brady, come in out of the rain."

Greta sighed and rolled her eyes, but forced herself to step back out of the way. Brady slipped past her into the kitchen without making eye contact.

A great weight lifted from his shoulders. Finally, he was inside. Sam was within his reach. He could feel his desire to grab her, hold her tight, smother her with kisses.

Instead, he explained. "I just wanted to come up and make sure everyone was okay."

"We're fine," Sam assured him. "This is the most exciting thing to happen in weeks. It's an adventure!"

Brady, still hoping for some fear and frustration, pressed on. "Sometimes with these nor'easters we lose power for a day or more."

"More than a day," replied Sam cheerfully, "might grow tiresome, but the rest of the night would be just fine."

"Yes," added her daughter, "the rest of the night."

"Well," continued Brady, taking one last shot at saving the day, "I have a couple of emergency generators I could hook up if you—"

"Forget the generators," insisted Sam. "We have to go find Jason."

"Find him?"

Megan clasped the caretaker firmly by the hand. "Jason's hiding," she told him.

"We're playing hide-and-seek," Sam explained.

Brady nodded.

"But no going off the first floor," commanded Megan. "That's the rule."

"Don't worry," said Brady. "I always play by the rules."

•   •   •

THEY PLAYED hide-and-seek for well over an hour. At one point Brady, against his better judgment, showed Sam a hiding place in the formal library behind one of the raised cherry panels. It did not lead to any of the interior passageways; nevertheless, Brady knew he had made a mistake. But he didn't care. He had Samantha, already energized by the storm and the power failure, practically sitting on his lap in that tight, cramped compartment.

"What is this place?" Sam asked. "How did you know about it?"

"Shh," whispered Brady, "someone will hear us." And then, to make sure she stayed quiet, he kissed her on the mouth.

Finally, the hour growing late, Sam called a halt to the game, insisting the time had come for all kids to go to bed. Jason fussed and demanded another round. His mother said no. Jason said yes. No. Yes. No. Yes. Then the caretaker stepped in and told Jason not to argue with his mother. "Love and respect her," he lectured, "but do not argue with her."

Jason argued no more.

Sam beamed at Brady, then she handed Megan a candle. "Go on up to your room, sweetie. I'll be up in a second to tuck you in."

Megan kissed Brady on the cheek, told him he was the best hide-and-seek player in the entire world, then started up the stairs and down the hall to her room.

"She's a great kid," said the caretaker.

"The best," said her mother.

Not too many moments later, Megan shrieked. At the top of her lungs. A full-blown screech echoed through the darkened mansion.

Sam did not hesitate. She hit the first step already at a full sprint. Brady followed close behind. Their candles blew out before they reached the upstairs landing. But Sam did not slow down. Megan continued to howl. Sam groped along in the blackness, her hands searching for the wall.

Brady, always calm, always prepared, pulled a small penlike flashlight from his pants pocket. He flicked it on just before he and Sam reached Megan's bedroom. He aimed the beam inside. Megan lay on the floor, her arms covering her head. Her candle, extinguished, rested on the carpet.

The little girl continued to scream. Sam darted to her side. "What is it, sweetie? What's the matter?"

Megan reached up and threw her arms around her mother. "There's someone in the room," she sobbed. "Someone . . . flying."

"What do you mean, someone flying?"

The bats chose that moment to make their presence known. The tiny mammals flew about the pitch-dark room, their expert navigational skills allowing them to bank and turn and dive with incredible speed and precision. Sam, like her terrified daughter, began to scream.

Brady quickly assumed his role. He stepped forward, gently brought mother and daughter to their feet, and led them out into the hallway. He closed the door as they departed. Jason and Mrs. Griner waited anxiously outside the room, fresh candles illuminating the scene.

"What the hell's going on?" Jason, trying to sound like a tough guy but mostly sounding scared, demanded.

"It's nothing," Brady assured everyone. "Just a couple of bats."

"Bats!" screeched Sam. "In the house!"

Ah, thought Greta, so that's his game.

"They get inside once in a while," explained Brady. "No need for alarm. They're harmless."

"I can't go in my room, Mommy," sniffled Megan, tears still streaming down her cheeks. "There's bats in my room."

Brady squeezed the little girl's hand. "Don't worry, Megan. I'll go in and get them out and everything will be okay. I promise."

●　　●　　●

IT TOOK A WHILE, but Brady did indeed make everything okay. While the Hendersons and Mrs. Griner waited out in the hallway, Brady entered the bedroom armed with a fishing net. Sam and the kids wanted him to kill the bats, but he would not hear of it. He told them bats were perfectly innocent critters, and that these two bats certainly did not deserve to die just because they wound up where they were not wanted.

"But they're so ugly and gross," said Jason.

"And they carry disease," added his worried mother.

Brady told them to stay calm, he would change their minds. He captured both of the bats. One he placed carefully inside the suede pouch. The other one he left in the fishing net. Then he called the kids into the room so they could have a closer look at the bat. Under his flashlight, the beady little eyes glittered.

"You see," Brady said, "they're not ugly or gross. Bats are just mammals with wings. They're like mice or hamsters or gerbils who over the years have learned how to fly."

Jason and Megan stood there in the candlelight and stared at the captive bat. Sam and Mrs. Griner stayed out in the hallway. Greta did her best not to tell Sam what a crock of crap all this flying gerbil business was.

"These bats," continued Brady, "are known, in Latin, as *Myotis lucifugus*. We call them little brown bats. It's one of the most common bats in the world. A perfectly harmless bat. And pretty soon, in just another few weeks, these bats will go into hibernation for the whole winter. And in the spring they'll come out and start feeding on insects. Bats like this little guy here eat millions of insects every single day. Which is good for us because insects can be pretty annoying. Without bats and their ferocious appetites, insects would take over. There'd be so many insects you wouldn't be able to breathe."

Brady talked on and on about bats for a good fifteen minutes. By the time he finished, neither Megan nor Jason wanted to see the cute little bats executed. So the three of them went out into the still-raging storm and set the bats free.

"Fly away, little brown bats!" shouted Megan gleefully. "Fly away free!"

And then the kids went to bed. And Greta, somewhat reluctantly, retired to her rooms off the back of the kitchen to mull over the situation. And Sam and

Brady found themselves all alone in that big, dark house.

"So," asked Sam, after several seconds of silence, "how long do you think the lights will be out?"

Until I turn them on, Brady could have answered, but didn't. "I don't know," he said instead. "A few hours. Maybe till morning. A transformer must've blown."

"The house will get cold."

"Not too bad. It's pretty warm outside actually. In the fifties. But I could build a fire."

"A fire," repeated Sam. "That would be nice."

So Brady built a fire in the huge fireplace in the living room. Sam watched him stack the dried kindling and make sure the damper hung open. A few logs from the previous winter lay beside the fireplace. Brady told Sam he would go out back and haul in another load.

"No," she told him. "You've done enough for one night. We'll just make do with what we already have."

So Brady struck the fire, then went and sat beside Sam. On the sofa. With the storm outside rattling the windows. And the house dark. And silent. Except for the fire crackling and casting shadows on the walls and ceiling.

They very nearly made love that night. It began right there on the sofa: the kisses and the caresses. But before all of their clothes came off, Sam came to her senses. At least momentarily. She certainly did not want little Megan waking up after a nightmare, getting scared, and suddenly appearing in front of the fire. That simply would not do. So Sam led Brady upstairs. Quietly. Neither of them speaking. Each with their own thoughts. Their own emotions. Holding hands. Not to the master bedroom, but to a guest room at the end of the hall.

Sam, excited and nervous and already feeling intensely guilty, locked the door.

They did not even have a candle. Just a faint hint of light filtered through the windows. Storm light. It made them look like apparitions. They sat for a moment on the edge of the bed: the caretaker and the wife of the man he intended to destroy.

But Brady was not thinking about destruction right at that moment. He was barely thinking anything at all. His brain, for once in his life, had taken a much-needed sabbatical. This woman at his side, he suddenly realized, had pulled him in from the storm. Not the electrical storm that continued to rage beyond the windows, but the emotional storm that had consumed most of his life, that had, for so many years, left him an outsider. And so, feeling bewilderingly subdued, he put his arms around Samantha and gently lowered her head to the pillow. He covered her body with his own.

Sam's brain, on the other hand, worked furiously. She felt awkward and even a little bit silly. Awkward because it had been years since she had been this intimate with any man other than her husband. And silly because here she was, a grown woman, forty just a few short years away, and yet she was acting like a teenager, sneaking around the house, locking doors. But so what? she demanded of her guilty conscience. She felt good. She felt fine. She felt attractive. Gunn's obvious interest in that damn Nita had made Sam feel old and fat and ugly. But here was Brady treating her with affection, calling her beautiful and sexy, clearly taking delight in her physical appearance. The attention made her feel wonderful. But she did not want to feel too wonderful, because obviously she knew she should not be lying half naked in bed with another man on top of her. And yet she was doing exactly that. And enjoying it. Especially when he kissed her neck. And ears. And lips. He adored her. She could tell.

It was true. He did. Probably more than he realized. Brady no longer wanted to just have sex with Samantha Ann Quincy Henderson, intercourse with the wife of his hated adversary. No, to seduce her and further destroy her marriage was not enough. Not anymore. He wanted to make love to her. And have her make love back at him.

One thing amid all of this angst is certain: Brady and Sam, after hours of gentle and conservative foreplay, did not consummate their relationship that stormy night. But they did, eventually, slip between the sheets and fall fast asleep in one another's arms.

51 The caretaker's father, Michael Donovan, brought his family to America in the fall of 1961. Michael's daughter, Mary, was five years old. His son, Carl Patrick, had recently turned two. And his wife, Clare, was pregnant with their third child. Michael Donovan had decided to leave their home in Belfast for both economic and political reasons. Unemployment, especially among Roman

Catholics, was painfully high in Northern Ireland. Donovan, a carpenter, rarely had work more than half the year. Also, long-buried animosity between the Catholics and the Protestants had once again started to surface. Violence was on the rise. Donovan decided to pull his family out.

Michael Donovan had a boyhood friend who had immigrated to the States as a young man. He lived in Brooklyn, New York, so that's where the Donovans settled, in the Flatbush section, not far from Prospect Park. In the midst of a building boom, Michael found work, steady work, union work. He earned a good wage, enough to take care of his children and put away some money for that business he hoped one day to own. Donovan dreamed of being his own boss.

In 1965 racial troubles hit Brooklyn. The threats and violence reminded Donovan of the religious troubles back home. He decided the time had come to move out of Brooklyn and buy his own home. Some friends told him to look on Staten Island. So that's what he did. But he needed a mortgage, money from a bank. His foreman at work gave him the name of a guy over in Manhattan, a young guy on the rise like Michael, a loan officer at Continental Bank and Trust. Donovan made an appointment to see him.

The young banker's name was Henderson, Gunn Henderson, Sr.

Henderson and Donovan were both in their early thirties at that time, both married with young kids. They hit it off right away. Henderson, a good English Protestant, had nothing at all against Irish Catholics. After reviewing Michael Donovan's application, he approved the young Irishman for a home mortgage.

So the Donovans purchased their first home. It was a small brick house on a neighborhood street that had thirty or forty other houses on it that looked exactly the same. Donovan didn't care. Number 1503 Hamilton Place belonged to him. Of course, the house really belonged to the bank, but every month, right on time, like clockwork, Michael Donovan wrote out his check to Continental and dropped it in the mail. Never once for almost four years was he even one day late paying his mortgage.

Donovan continued to save his money and dream of starting his own construction company. In the fall of 1967 he got his chance. Several building lots had come up for sale over in the Fort Wadsworth section of Staten Island, not far from the Verrazano-Narrows Bridge. Donovan had saved enough money to buy one of those lots. But he would need a loan to help with construction costs. So he went to see his banker at Continental.

Gunn Henderson, Sr., was now chief officer for home mortgages and small-business loans. Henderson welcomed Donovan like an old friend. And after reviewing Donovan's mortgage history and his construction application, he gave it his stamp of approval. Michael Donovan was at last in business for himself.

He built that first house practically all by himself. Lacking the funds to hire subcontractors, Donovan laid block and framed lumber and hung doors and installed windows seven days a week, eighteen hours a day. His son, Carl Patrick, just nine years old, helped him after school and on weekends. Carl carried bricks and boards, nails and shingles, pipes and cans of paint. And the boy never once complained. He loved being there with his father, listening to him sing, hearing his old man's stories of the Old Country.

Michael Donovan sold that first house for a small profit. He repaid his note in full long before it came due. Then he bought another lot. And received another loan from Gunn Henderson, Sr. He turned another profit. He bought a third lot. And a fourth lot. Each time he borrowed money from Continental. And always he paid the money back. He earned himself and his small company, Donovan Construction, a first-class rating with the bank. And he also had an excellent relationship, even a friendship, albeit a professional one, with the bank's young and very ambitious small-business loan officer.

The trouble began when Michael and Clare's youngest, Iris, age seven, a healthy and robust child, came home one day from school complaining of being tired and hot. Her mother felt her forehead. Iris had a fever, and very swollen glands. Clare kept her in bed for a day or two, but the little girl only grew worse. So they took her to the doctor. That doctor led to another doctor who eventually led to a third doctor. This third doctor was a specialist in childhood diseases. He gave Iris a lengthy examination, then he drew blood from Iris's arm. The blood was tested. Iris's white blood count was drastically elevated. More blood was taken. A whole battery of tests were performed.

And then came the shattering news: Iris had childhood leukemia. The disease had no cure, just some new drugs that might prolong the little girl's too-short life for another year or so.

The Donovans had no health insurance. They had less than a thousand dollars cash to their name. All their money was tied up in their home and in Donovan Construction.

Needless to say, the family fell into a state of shock. Carl Patrick, a quiet and introverted child, watched silently as this terrible drama unfolded. His mother wept constantly. So did his older sister. His father, invariably jovial and accessible, became distant and morose. And his poor little sister, not really able to fully fathom her circumstance, just lay in bed, pale and increasingly weak. Carl Patrick wanted to help, but he had no idea what to do. He felt powerless. So he prayed, just the way his mother had taught him. He prayed all the time. Night and day. He went to church and prayed, five, six, seven times a week. But the days and weeks and months passed and little Iris only grew paler and weaker and sicker. Carl decided praying was a waste of time.

His father missed a mortgage payment. Then he missed a payment on his construction loan. Iris needed medicine and treatment. The pharmacy and the doctor and the hospital wanted their money. So Michael Donovan gave it to them. He stopped going to work. He stayed at home, at his little girl's side. She did not get better. She got worse. The doctor gave her some fancy new medicine. She grew still worse. Another month passed. More payments missed. The bank sent a notice. Michael tried to call Gunn Henderson, to explain, but the secretary insisted Mr. Henderson was in a meeting, at a conference, out of town. More medicine and more missed payments.

After three or four months the doctor told the Donovans the drugs were not working as hoped. Clare wanted to know how long Iris had. The doctor, glum but formal, told the grieving mother it would probably only be a matter of weeks before Iris's immune system broke down and her small body lost its ability to function properly. The end would come shortly after that.

Near the end they put her in the hospital. It took the rest of their meager savings. And still she died. Relatively quietly. In the middle of the night. Her parents at her side. Her brother and her sister asleep on the floor at the foot of her bed.

* * *

THE LETTER of foreclosure arrived in the mail the very next day. The Donovan household was in a deep state of mourning. Family and friends and neighbors had gathered to pay their respects.

The caretaker remembered well. He remembered that day as though it had happened less than a fortnight ago. Brady remembered the little house on Hamilton Place filled with flowers and people weeping. He sat up in his room just staring out the window at a dull gray sky. The postman, a happy-go-lucky guy named Al, whom everyone liked, appeared at the end of the block. Young Carl Patrick watched as Al made deliveries along their side of the street. The postman moved slower than usual, for he, too, was in a state of mourning. Al knew what had happened at the Donovan place.

Carl Patrick pushed up his window as the mailman turned in to their walk. "Hey, Al."

"Hey, kid," replied Al. "Real sorry about your little sister."

"Yeah." Carl Patrick tried to shrug it off, to show he

had his emotions under control. But it was a lie, perhaps his first conscious deception.

"Come on down here, would you, kid?" asked the mailman. "I have some mail here needs a signature. I'd just as soon not bug your folks."

So Carl Patrick went downstairs and pulled open the front door. The mailman handed him a very official looking envelope. Certified. Carl Patrick had to sign for it in two places.

So he signed. Brady remembered signing. And then carrying the letter straight up to his bedroom because he could not face the family and friends wailing in the living room right at that moment.

The boy sat on his bed and looked at the letter. It was for Michael J. Donovan of 1503 Hamilton Place. From Vice-President Gunn Henderson, Sr., of Continental Bank and Trust. After turning it over a few times, he tossed the envelope onto his desk and went back to staring out the window.

Some hours later his parents came in to see him. "How are you doing, son?" his father asked.

Carl Patrick shrugged.

His mother held him while his father squeezed his shoulder and told him, in a not particularly convincing voice, that they would all get through this crisis together, as a family. Carl Patrick nodded, then remembered the letter. He grabbed it off his desk and handed it to his father.

Brady could still see his father's eyes as he opened the envelope, removed the folded pages, and began to read. His father's eyes grew wide. Then, over the next timeless minute, those eyes gave off a whole host of emotions: surprise, shock, annoyance, anger, and finally, although young Carl Patrick did not realize it at the time, another emotion. But Brady had those eyes permanently etched into the back of his brain. And for years now he had recognized that final look in his father's eyes as fear. Sheer terror. It was the first time in his life he'd ever seen his father afraid.

The situation deteriorated quickly. Another certified letter arrived the next day. Again from Vice-President Gunn Henderson of Continental Bank and Trust. The first letter had been notification of foreclosure on the house. The second letter concerned Michael Donovan's latest construction loan. Because of missed payments, the bank wanted the loan repaid, in full, immediately.

Michael Donovan tried to call Gunn Henderson. Several times. A dozen times or more over the next two or three days. But Henderson's secretary kept telling him Mr. Henderson was away from his desk or out to lunch or at a meeting.

Finally, late on Friday afternoon, the day after he had buried his little girl, Michael Donovan turned to his weeping wife and said, "I can't reach him. But I found out from the receptionist that he'll be in tomorrow morning. I guess he works sometimes on Saturday. Anyway, I'm going up there to see him. I'll wait all day if I have to." Michael Donovan put his arms around his wife and gave her a squeeze. "Don't worry, Clare, we'll get this straightened out. I'm sure it's just a misunderstanding. This Gunn Henderson is a decent bloke."

Young Carl Patrick watched this scene from the safety of the stairway. He kept himself hidden behind the banister.

* * *

THE NEXT MORNING Michael Donovan traveled up to midtown Manhattan to see his banker, Gunn Henderson, Sr. He took his young son along for company, and also because he figured having his boy along might make a strong family impression upon the banker. After all, Gunn Henderson had kids of his own.

But what Michael Donovan had no way of knowing was Gunn Henderson's new appendage up at Continental. With the economy sputtering and interest rates on the rise, mortgages and small-business loans were taking a beating. Defaults for nonpayment had reached an all-time high. This statistic did not make the bank's board of directors happy. So they went looking for a man who could be tough, even ruthless, with any delinquent accounts. They found Gunn Henderson. They asked him if he could do the job. Seeing his star rising, Gunn assured them he had the guts and the fortitude to get the job done swiftly and efficiently. So they made him a vice-president. And gave him a nickname: Henderson the Hatchet Man.

Into this environment walked Michael Donovan and his young son, Carl Patrick.

Brady remembered clearly walking into that bank: the revolving doors, the marble floor, the towering ceiling, the hushed voices, the security guards with their revolvers on their belts.

After a considerable wait, during which time he had to sit quite still in an uncomfortable wooden chair, his father took his hand and led him across the lobby, past a line of tellers and another line of empty desks, to a small office up against the back wall. The front wall of the office was made of glass. Inside the office a tall, broad man in a blue business suit sat behind an enormous desk. The big man stood as Carl and his father entered. The big man stuck out his hand. The hand had thick, beefy fingers. His father shook it.

"Mike Donovan! So how the hell are you?" The man's voice sounded as big as he looked. It boomed inside that small space.

"Good morning," said Carl's father, kind of quietly. Then, "I'm . . . I'm . . . well, I'm not so good, actually."

The big man sighed, then glanced at his watch. "Not so good, huh? Okay, then, why don't we have a seat."

They all sat down, Carl Patrick in another hard wooden chair beside his father. The big man had not even bothered to acknowledge the boy's presence. Carl felt invisible.

"So, Mike," the big man asked, while he fiddled with a folder on his desk. "What's up? What's the problem?"

Michael Donovan told the banker his story. He told him all about his little girl getting sick and then, just a few months later, dying of leukemia. He told him the family was emotionally devastated. And that the illness had also been quite a strain financially.

The big man, Brady remembered, listened. Oh, yes, he listened without saying a word, without even changing his expression.

His father had tears in his eyes. Big, wet tears he several times had to wipe away with his fingers. Seeing his father crying, Carl Patrick began to cry also. It was at that moment he finally and fully realized that his little sister Iris was really dead. He would never see her again. Try though he did to collect himself, the sobs spilled from his mouth while the tears ran down his cheeks. He was, after all, just a boy.

And at just that moment, with his father beginning to tell the banker about the funeral, another boy raced into the office. A boy about Carl's age. Exactly Carl's age actually. Born in the same year, just a couple of months apart.

The kid raced in, ran around behind that enormous desk, jumped up in the big man's lap, and interrupted Carl's father in midsentence. "Can I go in the vault now, Dad? I wanna go in the vault. You said if I came to work with you today I could go in the vault."

Gunn Henderson, Sr., did nothing at all to reprimand his son for this rude intrusion. Instead, he swung the lad onto his knee and said, "I'm busy right now, Gunny. But as soon as I get done here, we'll go back and have a look at the vault."

Gunny narrowed his eyes. "How long's it gonna be? I'm bored. I wish I'd stayed home."

Gunn Sr. squeezed his boy's shoulder. "It won't be long, Gunn. Just a couple minutes."

Gunny thought it over. "Is there any gold in the vault?"

Gunn the Elder winked at Gunn the Younger. "I think we'll probably be able to find a few gold bars in there, son, sure."

"Gold," said Gunny, his fist clenched. "Yes!" Then the boy turned and looked at the two people across the desk. "I love money," he informed them. "I have my own paper route. I make almost forty bucks a week. I have my own savings account. I have over a thousand dollars in it. Someday I'll have over a million dollars in it." Then he looked directly at young Carl Patrick. "What about you, kid? Do you have any money?"

Carl Patrick sat there frozen, the tears still running down his face. All he could do was shake his head.

Gunny Henderson stuck his tongue out at him.

Gunn Sr. cut the tension with a laugh, then he set his son back on the floor. "Scoot, Gunn. Go out and make sure the tellers aren't robbing us blind. I'll be along in a couple minutes."

Gunn Jr. started out of his father's office. But along the way he stopped to take a closer look at the kid sitting in the wooden chair. He stopped and stared for several seconds.

Oh, yes, Brady remembered very clearly young Gunn Henderson stopping and staring at him. It remained, even after more than twenty-five years, his most vivid childhood memory.

"What's the problem, kid?" Gunn Jr. demanded. "Why are you bawling like that? You look like a girl sitting there, crying your eyes out. What's the matter? Won't my father give you any money?"

Young Carl Patrick Donovan looked into the eyes of his assailant. He found nothing there but contempt. He wanted to respond, to say something, anything, but words would not come. His mouth would not open. He simply continued to cry as Gunn Jr. stuck out his tongue at him again, then turned and raced out of the office.

Gunn the Elder shrugged. "Sorry about that, Mike," he managed. "My boy gets a little worked up sometimes. A very spirited youngster. But basically a good kid. Harmless."

Michael Donovan nodded while he comforted his son. He said nothing in reply.

"Now," continued the banker, "where were we on this thing? I'd like to get this wrapped up."

52 One month later Michael Donovan was dead. Distraught over the death of his daughter and his financial devastation, he walked the four miles from their home on Staten Island to the Verrazano-Narrows Bridge. It was the middle of the night, two or three o'clock in the morning. No moon. No stars. No nothing. Michael Donovan walked halfway across the bridge, halfway to Brooklyn. When he reached the highest point of the nearly one-mile suspended span, he stopped. He paused. He looked out to sea. Then, quite calmly, his mind clear, he climbed over the rail and threw himself off the bridge into New York Harbor several hundred feet below.

Brady, in a part of his brain that seemed to thrive on repetition, saw his father falling. Over and over again.

Brady sat up in his office on the third floor of the old barn. His thoughts swirled. Too much on his mind. Too many things happening at once. His emotions scattered and volatile. He hated this kind of chaos. He preferred consistency and control.

Not long after his father's death, the Donovan family, broke and facing eviction from their home, moved back to Ireland, to Londonderry. Nowhere else, really, for them to go. They moved in with Carl Patrick's grandparents, his mother's mother and father. Carl hated it there in that tiny, dark house. He hated his grandfather. Sean McDougal was always drunk, always cursing and slapping his wife, his daughter, his grandkids.

A few months after their return, his mother found a job managing a small gymnasium and indoor pool on the outskirts of town. Carl Patrick and his older sister always went there after school. That was where the caretaker learned to swim and dive. He loved it there because it kept him away from his grandfather's cruel hands.

Many times Carl was told he had talent, natural talent. If he worked hard, his coach told him, maybe one day he could be an Olympian. Carl had no problem working hard. He had incredible stamina and concentration.

A year passed. Two years. Carl did well in school, especially in math and science. His teachers wrote notes home calling him gifted, a definite candidate for university. He stayed out of trouble by staying off the streets, by staying in the pool.

Then a new wave of violence swept through Northern Ireland. Protestants were killing Catholics and Catholics were murdering Protestants in every corner of the country.

Clare Donovan wanted to protect her children from the violence, but she had nowhere to turn, nowhere to hide. And then, in the spring of 1972, the violence struck home.

A bomb exploded in downtown Londonderry, a car

bomb. Carl Patrick was there with his mother and his sister. They were just out shopping, spending the day together.

Brady remembered well. He remembered perfectly. He'd just ducked into a candy store to buy some chocolates when the bomb exploded. The explosion knocked the candy off the shelves. The glass in the display counters shattered. Carl raced back out onto the street. He found nothing but panic and chaos. People ran in all directions, screaming and bleeding. Sirens wailed. Horns blared. Up and down the street he saw fires burning and smoke billowing.

He started shouting for his mother. But he found his sister first. Mary had been thrown through the plate glass window of a consignment shop. She was still alive but fading fast. The glass had shredded her skin, turned her face and arms and chest into one massive, bloody wound. She died before young Carl could share a single word with her.

Carl, still only a boy, began to scream. At the top of his lungs. Then he stood and began to run. He ran as fast as he could along the sidewalk, all the while shouting for his mother.

He very nearly tripped over her. She lay on the sidewalk, perfectly still, not moving at all, a jagged and bleeding gash cutting across her forehead. Clare Donovan had been hit by flying shrapnel. Death was close at hand. She barely had the strength to grasp her son's hand.

Carl screamed for help, but no one came. No one responded. Not his father. Not his sister. No one.

Yes, the caretaker remembered. The caretaker could never forget.

• • •

THAT SAME SUMMER he wound up back in the States. He could not bear to live in Ireland. Not with his sadistic grandfather. Not with all the violence in the streets. So he wrote to his father's friend back in Brooklyn. His father's friend invited Carl to come and live with him while he finished high school.

Carl graduated with honors before his seventeenth birthday. The following fall he enrolled in Brooklyn College. The school was in Flatbush, near the old neighborhood where his family had first settled. Brooklyn College was the perfect choice for young Donovan: It was inexpensive and it had an excellent computer science department. Carl Patrick wanted to study computers.

He studied hard, night and day. Semester after semester he achieved a perfect academic record. He kept current on all the latest computer technology, followed the careers of the young pioneers in the field.

And also, in his spare time, he followed the career of a middle-aged banker over in Manhattan at Continental Bank and Trust. And the career of the banker's son, an academic ne'er-do-well serving time up at snooty Colgate University in Hamilton, New York.

53 Brady sat remembering, but trying to forget so he could get back to work on THE AVENGER. In the next week or two he had to go to California and give his marketing boys a demonstration of the new software. But his mind kept drifting: back to Brooklyn, back to Ireland, back to Staten Island.

And back to Sam. Always back to Sam.

Two days had passed since Sam and Brady had spent the night together. That night Brady had slept nearly seven hours straight, longer than he had slept in years. But when he awoke, Sam was gone. He found her down in the kitchen, eating cold breakfast cereal with her kids. Megan and Jason were surprised when Brady strolled into the room. Sam quickly explained that he had slept up in one of the guest rooms because of the storm. The kids didn't really care; they were far more interested in talking about the bats up in Megan's bedroom and the hide-and-seek game and whether or not they could stay home from school.

"No," insisted their indulgent mother, "you cannot stay home from school."

Sam did not let her children stay home from school for frivolous reasons, but also, she needed to speak with Brady, in private. As soon as the limousine pulled out of the driveway, she told the caretaker they needed to talk. Unlike Brady, Sam had not slept much the night before. Not only did she feel fiercely guilty about her narrow escape from infidelity, but she could not believe she had been stupid enough and selfish enough to have another man in the house with her children present. During the night she had become convinced that she had lost all control of her mental faculties. And yet . . . the crackling fire . . . the tenderness . . . the intimacy . . .

She told the caretaker their night together had been sweet and romantic, but it could go no further. It definitely could not happen again. She told him she had made a mistake, a pleasant enough mistake, but a mistake nevertheless. She was, after all, a wife and a mother. She had responsibilities and commitments. She took both quite seriously.

Brady did not object to her decision. He barely uttered a word in reply. He knew better than to raise a ruckus. There were better ways to deal with the situation. Far more subtle ways. And so for two days, almost without respite, the caretaker had been up on the third floor of the barn seeking solutions to his various problems.

THE AVENGER, he concluded, after delving into the Donovan family tragedy one more time, could wait. He had to deal with Sam. He needed to make Samantha Ann Quincy Henderson his own.

For years, ever since his days at Brooklyn College, Carl Patrick Donovan had been plotting to get the Hendersons, both the father and the son. His plot demanded loss and suffering followed by excruciating death. Only then would his family be fully avenged.

Even while he built his company and his immense fortune, he never for a moment allowed his memories to die or even fade regarding the wrongs that had been perpetrated upon himself and his family. It had all started with that foreclosure letter, the one executed and signed by Gunn Henderson, Sr. The caretaker kept that letter nearby at all times. As a kind of daily reminder. At that very moment it lay on his desk, right beside his Power Macintosh.

Avenge, avenge, avenge. It could have been his mantra. Let nothing stand in the way. Not time. Not money. Not people. Definitely not people. Brady did not give a damn about harming the innocent. If old Mrs. Henderson suffered from lead and arsenic poisoning right along with her bastard banker husband, too bad. Tough luck. And little Gunny's family—to hell with them. They would just be more victims. Just as his father had been a victim. And his mother. And his two sisters. Victims all.

But now, without warning, everything had changed. Brady had not intended for it to change, but it had. He had been patient and thorough. He had conceived a plan and put that plan into action with energy and zeal. He had slowly but relentlessly taken control of Gunn Henderson Jr.'s life. He had seduced the man's wife. One by one he had pounded the nails into Gunn Henderson's coffin. But now, with no warning whatsoever, his emotions had intervened. Emotions that had long been dormant, buried deep within his psyche. Suddenly those emotions had come boiling to the surface. Suddenly he wanted Samantha Henderson more than he had ever wanted any woman in his life. He wanted her. And needed her. God, he loved her. And he wanted her to love him back. Truly and openly and without regret. Poisoning the old man, destroying the son, killing them both off, slowly and mercilessly—all of this was still of paramount importance. But just as important, maybe even more important, was full and absolute possession of the wife, the daughter-in-law. As for the kids, he wasn't sure. They might have to go. Especially the older one.

But now guilt, and probably a repressed sense of desire, had driven Sam away. She had claimed their night together had been a mistake. She had insisted it would not happen again, could not happen again. But the caretaker refused to believe or accept Sam's rejection. Rejection did not fit in with his master plan.

But this love thing, swirling around in his head and in his heart, it was new to him. It was making him crazy, driving him mad. For hours on end he paced. Back and forth across his office. He did not work or answer his phone or return his messages. What to do? When to do it? How to get it done? He mulled these questions over again and again as his screen saver flickered and precious time slipped relentlessly away.

Finally, thankfully, his thoughts began to clear. An inspiration slipped into his brain and quickly began to focus.

Moments later he picked up the phone. He called Louisa May Chance at her apartment in Manhattan. The time had come for Nita to get back to work.

54 Gunn lay on his hotel room bed in Raleigh, North Carolina. It had not been a good day. It had not been a good week. It had not been a good fortnight. Gunn had the blues. Plus he had been drinking too much. The man had not sold a single Disk in his last seventeen appointments. No one seemed to give a damn about what only a few months earlier he had deemed the Toy of the Century. Gunn blamed himself. It wasn't the toy. It was him. Something had gone terribly wrong with his sales skills. He had no idea what, but suddenly his ability to soothe and persuade and manipulate had dried up. Never in his almost forty years on the planet had his confidence and self-esteem been so low. He sipped directly from a bottle of Old Granddad.

Reilly, Gunn knew, was pissed all the time now, threatening to fire him if sales did not improve dramatically in the immediate future. That very same night Reilly had told him his failure to sell The Disk had already cost Creative Marketing Enterprises millions of dollars. And many more millions were on the line.

And worst of all: Nita was still back in Fort Worth taking care of her ailing mother. The worthless old hag. Why couldn't she just croak, take herself out of the game?

Gunn belched and sipped his whiskey.

He had called Sam a couple times. But she had been pissy and cold and uncommunicative. To hell with her.

Gunn took another belt, stared at the muted TV, and concluded the whole world sucked.

But then, out of the blue, a tap on the door, and Gunny's fortunes took another turn. "Who is it?"

No answer. Gunn, nothing on but his silk boxers, stood and headed for the door. "Who is it?" he asked again.

Still no answer. Gunn shoved his eye against the peephole in the middle of the door. And there, in all of her sexual glory, stood Ms. Nita, looking red hot in black heels, a black leather skirt, and a black silk blouse tight enough to show the outline of her nipples.

Gunn thought for a moment she must be a hallucination, but no, her naked flesh was soon enough pressed against his own.

They had themselves a swell time that night. At least Gunn did. His blues evaporated the moment Nita stuck her pretty little tongue into his ear and whispered, "God, I missed you. I thought I'd die."

Give that girl a Tony: best live performance by an actress in an original drama.

Gunn, because of the large quantity of sour mash he had consumed, could not offer Nita much of an erection, but she worked her magic nevertheless. That girl pulled out all the stops. She used every trick in the sexual guidebook. Her hands and mouth remained in perpetual motion.

"I love you," Gunn told her every time she bit his nipple or stroked his testicles. "God, I love you."

"That's music to my ears, baby," Ms. Nita breathed in his ear. "I love you too."

So much love in one room.

They slept, awoke around noon, made love again. They made so much noise their neighbors on the left started banging on the wall. Up to their old tricks, Gunn and Nita spent most of the day in bed. The Disk be damned.

Late in the afternoon Nita decided she wanted to go shopping. So they showered and dressed and went to the Crabtree Mall on Glenwood Avenue. Gunn paid for everything. Mr. Big Spender. Nita bought a new blouse. A new skirt. Two new dresses. Some new shoes. A cute little suede jacket. A lovely leather handbag. Gunn just kept pulling out his platinum card.

Then back to the hotel for more frolicking and fornicating. There were three messages from Reilly. Gunn tossed them in the circular file. Back to bed. Later some room-service steaks and a bottle of Dom Pérignon. What the hell? Gunn was happy now. A very happy boy.

Around midnight they lay naked on the damp sheets. Gunn felt entirely satisfied, and whipped to the bone. Nita, still on the job, still focused, rubbed Gunn's chest while she danced her tongue around on his belly.

"Gunn," she whispered, "this is the greatest. I love being with you, being together."

Gunn had his eyes closed. "It's perfect, baby."

"We're perfect." She watched him closely.

"A perfect fit."

"The best fit I've ever found."

He hesitated just a moment before responding. "Me, too."

"I think we should be together all the time."

Gunn's eyes popped open. "You do?"

Nita gave his testicles a squeeze. "I do, yes." Then, "Don't you?"

"You mean be together all the time?"

"Yes."

Gunn's life passed before his wide-open eyes. At the end he found Nita: young and gorgeous and sexy. "Of course I do," he told her. "I want us to be together."

"Then you'll have to tell your wife," she ordered him in her sexiest and most seductive voice. "And soon. I can't stand us being apart. And I hate even thinking about you being with her."

Her big beautiful blue eyes stared into his even as she slid down the mattress and closed her mouth around the tip of his penis.

"Don't worry, baby," said Gunny, "I'm not with her anymore."

Nita smiled softly, then went back to work.

55 Gunn showed up, unannounced, at PC Apple Acres late that Saturday morning. No one expected him. No one seemed particularly thrilled to see him.

Except, perhaps, the caretaker, who slipped into the basement the moment Gunn the Younger walked through the front door. Brady hoped Gunny might have some interesting and entertaining things to tell his wife.

Gunny did. But it took him quite a while to muster the courage.

Gunn headed straight for the kitchen to fortify himself. He consumed large quantities of bacon and fried eggs and white toast and home fries—cholesterol overload. The man might have been preparing to say sayonara to his bride of nearly fifteen years, but he intended to do so on a full belly. If G. Henderson were forced to turn in either his stomach or his phallus, the man would be hard-pressed to make a decision.

After his meal Gunn wandered around the house, both to postpone his date with purgatory and to get his digestive juices up and running. Either the bacon or the home fries had given him a good dose of heartburn. A certain amount of stress probably came into play also.

The caretaker did his best behind the scenes to follow the man from room to room. He had waited years to see Gunn Henderson squirm. No way did he want to miss a moment of it.

Gunn found his son in the TV room tuned into some Saturday morning cartoons. The boy, sprawled out on the sofa, remote permanently attached to his right hand, offered his old man a shallow grunt.

Gunn sighed, shook his head, and said, "Aren't you a little old for this cartoon crap?"

Wile E. Coyote was in hot pursuit of the Road Runner. Wile E., obsessed with the speedy little critter, tried to blow up the Road Runner with several tons of TNT. But, as always, he blew himself up instead. Jason laughed. He had just recently smoked a bone.

"This is what we call relaxation therapy, Dad," he told his father. "It follows a long and grueling week cracking the books."

"Bullshit," Gunn mumbled under his breath. Then, after sticking around just long enough to see the coyote fall several hundred feet into a deep canyon, he turned and left the room. Maybe, he told himself by way of justification, the boy and I will get along better if we don't actually live in the same house.

Gunn, still not quite ready to face his wife upstairs, continued to wander through the mansion. In the small study off the living room he found his little girl sitting on the sofa reading a book.

He sat beside her. Megan leaned over and kissed him lightly.

"What are you reading?" he asked.

"A book on bats," she answered.

"Bats? Like in those creepy things that fly around at night?"

"Bats aren't creepy, Dad."

"No?"

Brady, scrambling through the back alleys of the mansion, arrived on the scene.

"No. Bats are actually kind of cute. And they're very important," added the nine-year-old, "to the ecosystem."

Gunn took a lengthy look at his daughter. "The ecosystem, huh?"

"Yes. They make it so we don't have so many insects."

"I see. I didn't know you were so interested in bats."

"I am. We had bats in the house last weekend."

Gunn tried a joke. He mussed Megan's hair and said, "I think you have bats in your belfry."

Megan smoothed her gleaming hair, so like her mother's. She did not laugh. "Two of them. Up in my bedroom."

Brady smiled as he fished in his pocket for that pack of Necco Wafers he'd bought that afternoon. He found them and popped a couple in his mouth.

"Really? We had bats in the house?"

"Yes," the child repeated, "two bats."

"So what did you do? Don't tell me Mom tangled with a couple of bats."

Megan shook her head.

Brady sucked furiously on his wafers.

"No," the little girl replied, "Brady did."

"Brady!"

"He captured them in a net and we let them go outside. At first Jason and I wanted to kill them, but Brady taught us that bats were really good."

"Brady was here? In the house?"

"Yes. He spent the night."

The smile on the caretaker's face spread from ear to ear. He so enjoyed it when the totally innocent intervened to move the plot forward.

"The night?" Gunn forced himself to stay cool. He needed information.

"We had a big storm," explained Megan. "All the lights went out. Brady came to see if we were okay. Because you weren't here and all."

"So he stopped by to see if you were okay. And then he got rid of some bats?"

"Right."

"And then he spent the night?"

Megan nodded. "In the guest room down the hall from my bedroom."

"And where was Mom during all this?"

"She was here. We played hide-and-seek."

"Brady played hide-and-seek?"

"He was good at it, too. Both the hiding part and the seeking part."

"Christ," slipped from Dad's mouth.

Megan picked up her book. She hated it when adults asked her so many questions.

But Gunn had all the answers he wanted anyway. He exploded off the sofa and headed full-speed up the stairs.

Brady made haste to follow.

Gunn powered his way into the master bedroom. He looked like a Marine coming ashore at Iwo Jima.

"So what's this bullshit I hear now?" he demanded, enraged, utterly oblivious to the fact that he had returned home intending to say *adiós*. "This Brady fuck sleeps in my home when I'm not here!"

Sam stood at the foot of the bed folding clothes. "Who told you that?"

"What does it matter who told me? Megan told me! So where did the bastard sleep, goddammit? Right here," and Gunn slammed his fist against the mattress, "in my bed?"

"Don't be ridiculous."

"What the fuck is he doing sleeping in my house, Sam?"

"My house, chump," said Brady, very softly, as he popped another handful of Neccos into his mouth.

"For chrissakes, Gunn. There was a storm. We lost power." Sam was not sure how much or how little to say. One side of her brain wanted to tell the SOB everything, every last sumptuous detail of her night with the caretaker. But the other side of her brain, and the far more rational side, told her to keep quiet, to say as little as possible. "He came to see if he could help us, then he stayed because it was raining and blowing so hard. It seemed insane to make him walk back to the boathouse in that weather."

Gunn mimicked his wife. "Because it was raining and blowing so hard. It seemed insane to make him walk back to the boathouse in that weather. Little Brady the caretaker didn't want to get wet."

Behind the wall Brady muffled a chuckle by covering his mouth. Then that part of *his* brain that loved repetition dragged out the scene of young Gunn Henderson standing there in his father's office at the bank. *What's the problem, kid? You look like a girl sitting there crying your eyes out. What's the matter? Won't my father give you any money?*

And Brady knew, after he destroyed this man financially and emotionally, that Junior would have to die. Slowly and painfully. Just like his daddy.

"He only wanted to help, Gunn," Brady heard Sam say by way of explanation.

"Yeah, I'll bet. Mr. Helpful. Mr. Help-myself-to-another-man's-wife. I thought about shooting the son of a bitch months ago. Too bad I didn't do it."

Sam glared at her husband. "Nobody's going to shoot anybody."

Gunn laughed, a sick little snicker. "Maybe I'll shoot both of you, take you both out at once."

"I swear to God, Gunn," said Sam, now bitter and angry, "you can be so ugly. So cruel and petty."

Gunn actually paused for a second or two before responding. The real reason for his being home flashed through his mind. He instantly decided this whole caretaker business might work to his advantage. "I'll tell you what's petty, honey. This *marriage* is what's fucking petty."

And with that profound announcement, and a new plan in his pocket, Gunn Henderson turned and strode out of the master bedroom. He went down the stairs and out the front door and straight to his little red Porsche.

"Asshole," muttered Sam.

"Coward," added Brady.

And then the caretaker moved off in retreat. The real fireworks, he knew, would have to wait until later.

●　　●　　●

JASON, sick of cartoons, had retreated, too. He had retreated to the privacy of his bedroom. He sat up there now with the window wide-open blowing his second doobie of the day. Young Henderson loved getting stoned. Just suck some smoke into your lungs and all your troubles slip away. You can just pretend like your asshole of an old man doesn't even exist. Plus it was cool to get high. Very cool. Way cool. All the coolest kids at school blew weed.

Jason had smoked about half a joint when suddenly, almost directly below his window, he spotted Brady emerging from the basement. He had seen the caretaker come out of the basement on a couple of other occasions. He had never given it much thought. But what, he wondered this time, was Brady doing down there all the time?

Jason almost called out, but instead, impulsively, he decided to take a different tack. He extinguished his reefer and shoved it into his pocket. Practically sprinting, he went down the stairs, along the hallway, and out the back door. He crossed the terrace, went along the side of the pool, and through the rose garden. As he emerged on the far side of the garden, he spotted Brady across the tennis court heading in the direction of the barn. Stealthily, the boy pursued. Back up in his room, well stoned, he had decided it would be cool to observe the caretaker from a distance, see what the guy did on a typical Saturday afternoon in autumn. Nothing else to do anyway. Might as well do some sleuthing.

Oh yes, Jason had smoked some pretty potent weed. He had the stoner's grin on his face to prove it. His feet barely touched the ground.

He came through the hedgerow at the far corner of the tennis court just as Brady opened the side door of the barn and stepped inside. Jason waited to see what would happen next. He figured Brady had probably gone in to get a tool, or maybe the tractor, or the leaf blower. But a minute passed, and then two minutes, and three minutes, an eternity to a stoner, and still Brady did not emerge.

Jason crept forward. He reached that side door and very slowly he turned the knob and pulled it open. His head went in first for a hasty look around. No sign of the caretaker. So, high as a kite, his heart pumping adrenaline through his arteries at exaggerated speeds, young Henderson slipped into the musty-smelling, dimly lit barn. Moving slowly, hiding behind walls and pieces of machinery, he searched the first floor for signs of Brady. But the caretaker was nowhere in sight. He'd vanished. Maybe out another door, thought Jason. The cavernous old barn had several. Still, he decided to check upstairs before going back outside.

So up the creaky stairs to the second floor he crept. The ancient treads creaked. Jason knew if the bad guys had been up there with their assault rifles, he would already be a dead man.

But Brady did not have an assault rifle. He did not even have a pistol or a peashooter. The caretaker did not care for guns. Guns took all the subtlety and joy out of life.

Besides, Brady was not on the second floor. He was up in his office on the third floor, already back at work on THE AVENGER. His concentration focused for the first time in days, he had no idea young Henderson, under the spell of marijuana, was hot on his trail.

Jason reached the second-floor landing, took a couple of deep breaths. The second floor had numerous small rooms. Sliding along the walls like he had seen the private eyes do in the movies, he checked those rooms one by one. Still no sign of Brady. But in one room he found a pair of bats, just like the ones in his little sister's bedroom, hanging upside down in a small wire cage. He wondered if they might be sick, if maybe Brady was nursing them back to health.

Actually, Brady, the last time he had gone in to feed the bats, had inadvertently neglected to lock the door of the room where he had the bats in captivity. Undoubtedly he had Samantha on his mind. All kinds of minor details were slipping through the caretaker's fingers. Like allowing Jason to see him leaving the basement. Love can make even the most vigilant and fastidious man make mistakes.

Jason pondered the bats, then stopped to consider his next move. He had never been up to the third floor before. But he knew you had to climb a ladder and go through a trapdoor in the ceiling to get there. The two or three times he had checked over the summer that trapdoor had always been locked. And when he'd asked Brady about it, the caretaker had told him they used to store hay up there, but now it was just an empty space.

Well, just as Jason started back down the stairs, that empty space above him groaned.

It groaned because Brady pushed back his chair and stood up. He needed some notes he had left back in the boathouse, programming notes he needed to proceed with THE AVENGER.

Jason heard footsteps overhead. He froze, then darted into the small room with the bats. He peered around the doorjamb, his eyes riveted on that trapdoor overhead. And sure enough, a second or two later, it began to open. It opened all the way. A pair of feet popped through the ceiling. The feet belonged to Brady. Jason watched the caretaker descend the ladder, pause for a moment or two at the bottom, then turn and head down the stairs.

His heart really roaring now, Jason waited until he heard the door downstairs open and close. Then he raced to the nearest window. He watched while Brady made his way across the lawn in the direction of the boathouse.

Two seconds later young Henderson had his hands on the lower rungs of that ladder. Up he climbed, like a scared cat up a tree. His eyes widened the moment he poked his head through that hole in the floor. Expecting to see dirty hay bales and maybe a rabid rat or two, he saw instead gleaming white walls, sparkling clean windows, and more computer equipment than in his private school's fully equipped computer lab. Computers hummed, screens flickered, modems whirred, fax machines whirled. Jason blinked his eyes several times. He decided he must have smoked far too much dope. The kid he'd bought it from at school told him to be cool with it. "This is like some very potent shit, dude."

But not potent enough to make me hallucinate, decided young Henderson.

He climbed off the ladder. The hardwood floor was spotless, not a speck of dust anywhere. He took a few steps to his right, stood in front of a supercharged Pentium PC clearly in the middle of performing some automated task. He gaped at the screen, saw columns of numbers whiz past. Behind him a phone rang. He jumped. After the second ring some fax tones echoed through the large clean white space. The entire room seemed to buzz with energy. Jason found himself unable to move. Time passed. He had no idea how much time. His feet were frozen to the floor. He felt like an alien invader who had been dropped in some strange and distant universe. He also felt like someone was watching him.

He was right. The caretaker, moving swiftly so he could get back to work, had returned. He stood near the top of the ladder. The instant he spotted young Henderson, he, too, froze. His brain registered a million bits of information in a couple of nanoseconds. He very quickly made a decision on how to proceed with this unforeseen intrusion.

The caretaker did not enjoy unforeseen intrusions. They jeopardized even the best-laid plans. But this, he decided, was different; at least it could be. This he could use to his advantage. After all, the boy's mother might find a simple caretaker a splendid diversion. But no way would Sam throw away her cozy life for a mere diversion.

"Hey, Jason."

Jason just about jumped out of his Nike Airs. He swung around, saw the caretaker coming through the trapdoor. "Brady, I . . . I . . . I—"

"Looking for me, were you?"

"Yes. I . . . I . . . I was looking for you."

Brady took a good look into young Henderson's eyes. He knew right away the boy had been partaking of the evil weed. Not only was the kid's brain fried and his speech muddled, but his eyes looked like firestorms. Plus he reeked of smoke.

"After all this time," the caretaker confessed, "you finally found me out."

"No. What? Found what out?" Jason both looked and sounded bewildered.

"I'm a closet computer nerd," continued the confession. "When I'm not out mowing the grass, I'm up here playing with my computers."

Jason thought he sensed friendliness in the caretaker's tone. "You mean all this stuff? It's yours?"

"Well," lied Brady, "some of it." Really he owned it all. And much, much more.

"Wow. I can't believe I never knew it was here."

"I like to keep it quiet."

"Hey," replied Jason Henderson, "no problem."

"It can be our little secret."

"Right. Don't worry, Brady. I won't tell a soul."

Brady knew that was bullshit. The kid would be blabbing about it by the end of the day. But no matter. He had a plan, a new plan, a slight variation on the old plan, the original plan. As a software developer he had learned the importance of flexibility, of bobbing and weaving when your initial theory proves somewhat unreliable.

"I've been working on a new computer game," he told Sam's son. "Want to try it?"

Of course Jason wanted to try it.

So Brady sat the boy down in front of his Power Mac 9600 and hit the reset switch. The machine began to reboot. A minute or so later THE AVENGER flashed across the screen. Brady held down a series of keys. He did not want the program to choose randomly from its menu of cruel and tragic scenarios. He had something special in mind for young Henderson.

"Just pay attention for a couple minutes," Brady told Jason. "You'll be prompted when it's time to begin."

Over the course of the next two or three minutes, Jason watched as a man on the computer screen broke into his home, tied him to a chair, raped his mother and his sister, beat his father senseless, and robbed the family blind.

"Like wow!" exclaimed Jason. "Unreal!"

Then the time came for the boy to make a decision: Let the authorities handle it, i.e., let bygones be bygones, or roll up his sleeves and go after the filthy son of a bitch himself.

Jason did not hesitate. He rubbed his hands together, glanced over his shoulder at the caretaker, and said, "Let's get the bastard."

Brady nodded with delight.

For the next two hours Jason pursued that computerized hooligan without pause. Stoned or not, his concentration did not waver for an instant. The game, seductive, sadistic, and perfectly programmed, had him mesmerized. He did not have to ask Brady even one question about what to do or how to play. The caretaker had taken care to design THE AVENGER to be entirely intuitive. Even a computer novice could seek absolute revenge.

So Brady just stood back and watched while young Henderson went after the monster who had inflicted himself upon his family. Jason had to work pretty hard to track the monster down. But finally he tracked him to some sleazy fleabag motel in the tough part of town. Once he found the monster, he showed not a shred of mercy. Brady found it extremely interesting that young Henderson did not cease his avenging efforts until the monster had his eyes gouged out, his jaw crushed, his ears sliced off, his arms and legs severed, and his maleness inserted into a Waring blender. Gruesome.

So gruesome the caretaker had to turn away. He found such violent displays distasteful.

Nevertheless, he had enjoyed the show. Watching young Henderson play THE AVENGER with such enthusiasm was all the proof he needed that Graphic Software, Inc., would soon have another hot seller on its hands.

56 Gunn, fortified by several hours of high-speed driving in conjunction with frequent stops at various Suffolk County gin mills, rolled back into PC Apple Acres not long after dinner. He found his family curled up together on the sofa in the TV room.

No one bothered to glance his way. "Hey," he said.

The kids grunted. The wife, irritated, asked, "Where have you been?"

"Out," came the answer.

"We waited to eat. You could have called."

"I could have."

Sam stood and headed for the door. "Bastard," she mumbled in his ear as she brushed past him.

Gunn made way. His legs, unsteady, wobbled a bit. He sighed, looked at his kids. They did not shift their eyes from the flickering TV screen. So Gunn turned and watched his wife march down the hallway and into the front foyer. A moment later he heard her steps on the wide marble stairs.

After a quick trip to the liquor cabinet, where he further fortified himself with a few splashes of single malt, Gunn decided the time had come to lay his cards on the table. Nita, he knew, wanted this done ASAP. He raised the bottle to his lips and took one last pull.

This extra stop gave Brady, who had been up in his office tinkering with THE AVENGER, time to get himself in position behind the wall of the master bedroom suite. He had brought along some caramel chews in anticipation of a splendid evening out.

When Gunn reached the bedroom he found his wife ensconced in the bathroom. He paced for a few minutes waiting for her to come out. The booze had him feeling almost giddy. A certain unreality concerning the events at hand filtered through his thoughts. He felt as though he had sent someone else to take care of the dirty work, to tell his wife the news.

Finally, impatient to get on with it, and undoubtedly fearing his courage might turn fickle, he knocked on the bathroom door. "Sam?"

"Go away."

"I've been out here waiting for you."

"What do you want?"

"I . . . I just wanted to see if you were all right."

"Go to hell."

"Sam!"

"I said, go away."

Gunn paused. His inebriated thoughts swirled. Sweet Nita's cute little ass popped into his brain. And a moment later he whispered those four infamous words of impending doom: "We need to talk."

Sam stood in front of the mirror brushing her hair. Those four words caused her mouth to fall open and her arms to drop listlessly to her side. It took her only a few seconds to recover. She turned, crossed the bathroom, and pulled open the door with a rush of wind. "Oh," she said, "and what is it we need to talk about, Gunn?"

Brady struggled at the peephole. He had a bad angle. He could not tell if she had been crying or if anger had simply flushed her cheeks.

"Well," answered Gunn, "I've been thinking."

"Isn't that swell?" came the sarcastic reply. "About what? Whether to paint or paper the kids' bathroom?"

Gunn retreated across the bedroom. "Listen to me, Sam."

"Oh, I'm listening. I'm all ears."

"Look, Sam, this isn't easy."

"What isn't easy?" Sam demanded. "Being an ugly, mean-spirited, selfish prick?"

Brady smiled, and wished he had some popcorn, with extra butter. Not that he ate much butter. Excluding his sweet tooth, the caretaker followed the food pyramid to a T.

Gunn tried to work the kinks out of his neck. His wife's attitude had him off stride. He struggled to find an alternative game plan. "The thing is, Sam," he said, finally, "you're not happy."

"I'm not happy?"

Gunn nodded. "You're not happy. I'm not happy. No one's happy."

Sam folded her arms across her chest. Every feminine instinct in her body sensed what was coming. "Okay, Gunn, no one's happy. The children are miserable; I'm miserable. So what?"

"So I think . . . well, I think maybe I need to . . . you know . . ."

She had to make him say it. "No, Gunn, I don't know."

"Yes, you do . . . I think maybe I need to . . . you know . . ."

"I don't know, dammit!"

"Well," mumbled Gunn, "I think maybe I need to move out for a while."

So there it was. Out in the open.

Brady felt bad for Sam, but at the same time he patted his own back and popped another chew.

"Oh," murmured Sam, "I see." She tapped her hairbrush against the palm of her hand. "You think maybe you need to move out for a while?" Sam responded with sarcasm, but beneath a very shallow veneer she felt fear and foreboding, and a desperate desire to cry.

"Don't worry, Samantha," Brady wanted to whisper in her ear, "I'll take care of you."

But Gunn had the floor. His words gushed forth. "There's just been so much—ugliness between us lately. So much hate and animosity. So many hurtful things said, so many accusations made. I just think we might benefit from some time apart. It would give us some space, some room to think."

Gunn would have done better to keep his trap shut. Now, with every word he uttered, Sam's fear turned to loathing.

"Time apart," she repeated. "Room to think."

"Yes," replied Gunn, hoping she would see the light and remain calm. "I think it would do us good. Give us a fresh perspective."

"A fresh perspective."

"Exactly."

"I see."

And then, because he had been waiting to say it all day long, he added, "I just need to be alone for a while."

Sam, her face crimson, her anger rising to a feverish pitch, nodded calmly at her husband. Then, in one very deft motion, she raised her right arm, cocked it at the elbow, and let her hairbrush fly. It sailed through the air, end over end, at warp speed. Gunn did not have time to blink. The brush struck him right between the eyes, right across the bridge of his nose.

"Ouch!" His hand moved immediately to his wounded snout. "Christ, Sam! What the hell did you do that for?"

"I wonder."

"It hurts."

Indeed, the hairbrush had drawn blood. And already his smeller had started to swell.

"Poor little Gunny."

Gunn, his vanity already kicking into gear, worried he might have a broken nose. "You're fucking nuts, Sam!"

"And you're a lying, cheating, stinking bastard! You need to be alone for a while. Have your space. Some room to think. What crap! You must take me for a moron. Some cute, ditzy blonde smiles at you, and what do you do? You decide to abandon your family and go off and play house with her. Talk about your classic middle-age crisis. You filthy, disgusting prick! You make me sick! I hate you! Time to be alone. You can't stand being alone, Gunn. Not for fifteen seconds. You constantly need someone around to stroke your swollen ego! So you know what I say? I say . . . I say get the hell out of here! I say better her than me! Go ahead, Gunn, go have your whore and eat it too!"

And with that bit of profundity hanging in the air, Sam exited the master bedroom suite. She slammed the door on her way out.

Gunn and Brady stood there, speechless.

Gunn, impressed with his wife's verbal barrage, felt a twinge of sexual arousal. He wondered if he might be making a very grave error. He had fully expected tears and sobs and a pleading, hysterical woman; a woman it would be easy enough to reject and abandon. And so, in a perfect example of male piggishness, Gunn assured himself he could always come back and make things right. This was, after all, only a trial separation.

Brady just shook his head in sheer amazement. He

had no idea the woman had that kind of temper, that kind of strength. Like Gunn, he was aroused by her performance. It made him want her even more. He wished she would come straight to him that very evening. He would make love to her, finally. Slowly and gently. And tomorrow they would move in together. He would move back into the mansion. He was ready. The boathouse had weeks ago started to feel cramped and lonely. They would make the mansion their home. And then, after the winter, next spring, late May or early June, they would marry. Right out in the rose garden. A big ceremony. After that, a kid or two. Her kids were okay, at least the younger one was, but he wanted a couple of his own.

Oh, yes, Carl Patrick Donovan had gone a long, long time without much love in his life. Years and years. So he leaned against the wall back there in that dark and secret passageway and just allowed his fantasies to run wild.

Sam, however, did not go to the caretaker that night. No, Sam went straight to her children. She sat between them on the sofa for the rest of the evening while they watched sitcoms on TV. She snuggled Megan against her breast. She tried to snuggle Jason also, but the adolescent male, still dependent but seeking liberation, raged within him. He had no choice but to reject his dear mama's affections.

When Gunn dared to show his face in the TV room, she ignored him, pretended the man did not exist. As long as she had the kids at her side, Sam felt safe. And reasonably secure.

And when the time came for bed, she half carried and half herded Megan up to her room. They climbed into bed together. Mother and daughter. Megan fell sound asleep in an instant with her head on Sam's shoulder. Sam lay there for hours, stroking her little girl's hair. She cried, but not too much. She did not really feel sad. She felt numb, as though she had been given an enormous shot of novocaine directly into her brain.

Part Five

THE MURDER

57 A day passed. Two days. Three days. On the fourth day the novocaine finally began to wear off. Sam noticed the feeling returning to her fingers and toes and brain one morning not long after the kids had left for school. All week long she had been moping around the house, head hung low, feeling lost and lonely and rejected. But then, suddenly, out of the blue, while just standing there making the bed, it dawned on her that she hated the bastard who had so casually, almost flippantly, packed a bag and driven away in his hot red sports coupe. Nearly fifteen years, most of her adult life, and that bastard just climbs into his little Porsche and drives off into the sunset.

"To hell with him," Sam told herself out loud. "I'm better off without him." And so, too, are the kids, she decided a few moments later. Gunn was a selfish, rotten father: remote, impatient, utterly self-absorbed. Always yelling and screaming, making demands, telling everyone what to do.

Sam felt herself coming back to life, her numbness

being replaced by anger. She picked up Gunn's favorite pillow and beat the bag of feathers into submission.

She called Mandy. For days she had been wanting to call someone: her mother, her sister, her friend. But she had been unable to pick up the phone and dial. Explaining the dissolution of the marriage that had been the center of her life seemed too difficult, too painful, too stressful. But now she felt ready to push this mess off her chest, heave it aside and get on with living.

They talked for almost two hours. Sam told her friend the whole story, even about the beating she had suffered over the summer, every last detail.

Mandy, seething as the story unfolded, interrupted occasionally to interject her opinions. She threw in such tidbits as: "We should cut his balls off." "I'd like to get a long piece of rope around that bimbo Nita's skinny neck." "Long and painful illnesses for both of them." "Maybe a hit man is in order."

Sam thought this last proposal a bit extreme, but certainly no one ever accused Mandy Greer of being overly delicate or wishy-washy.

As their conversation continued, Sam could feel her strength returning, her courage rising. She knew it might only be temporary relief, but temporary, she reminded herself, was better than no relief at all.

Then, Sam's story told, Mandy moved directly to the nitty-gritty of the matter. "What about money, sweetie?"

"What do you mean?"

"Do you have any money?"

"Of course I have money."

"How much?"

"How much? I don't know. A couple hundred dollars in my purse. Plus the money in the checking account."

"And how much is in the checking account?"

Sam thought about it. "It goes up and down so fast. Maybe two thousand dollars."

"Go get it."

"What do you mean, go get it? Withdraw it?"

"Damn right withdraw it." Mandy sighed. "I swear to God, Sam, you are so naive. You need money, honey. Every nickel you can lay your hands on."

"Mandy, really, I don't think Gunn would—"

"You don't think Gunn would what, Sam? Empty the vaults? Leave you without a dime? That's a nice, trusting attitude, but a week ago you never would have thought he'd come home and tell you he was blowing town for a blond bimbo."

Sam said nothing.

"So this," continued Mandy, "is what I want you to do. And I want you to promise me you'll do it this morning, as soon as we get off the phone."

"What?"

"I want you to go to the bank and withdraw everything. Empty all the joint checking and savings accounts. Cash in any CDs. Stocks, bonds, anything in both your names: Turn them into cash, even if you have to pay a penalty for early withdrawal. And your credit cards, your bank cards, max them out. Either buy yourself something nice, or take a cash advance. Cash is the key here, honey. For the time being, cash is your primary source of survival. You can't count on Gunn. Not right now. Not anymore. He's got his mind on this slut, and trust me, she'll have her grubby little hands in his pockets before you can say, 'Little Jack Horner ain't got nuthin' on me, baby.' "

The caretaker, listening in from his office on the third floor of the barn, chuckled. And decided, once he and Sam had consummated and solidified their relationship, to offer this Ms. Mandy Greer of Arlington, Virginia, a position with Graphic Software, Inc. In what capacity, he did not know, but a woman with that much grit would certainly be valuable somewhere.

"Do you really think," Sam asked, "all this is necessary?"

"You're damn right I do," answered Mandy. "It might already be too late. Now promise me you'll take care of this immediately. This morning."

Sam took a few moments to think it over. It seemed to her like kind of a desperate move. And yet, it might also be the prudent move. Besides, she didn't want a penny to fall into the hands of that home-wrecking bitch, that Nita Garrett.

"Okay," she said, "I promise."

• • •

AFTER THE FINANCIAL PART of their conversation dried up, talk turned to the caretaker, much to Brady's delight. He listened with a smile on his face as Mandy advised Sam forthwith to proceed full speed ahead with any emotional and romantic feelings she might have for the man.

"I almost slept with him a week or so ago," confessed Sam.

"Almost?"

Sam explained about the storm and its aftermath.

"Bury the guilt, Sam," advised Mandy. "Just go for it. Not only because you want to and need to, but because Gunn's a philandering bastard and this guy Brady sounds like Mr. Wonderful."

"He's pretty sweet."

"So? What's holding you back?"

Brady waited.

Mandy waited.

Sam sighed.

"Okay, look," said Mandy, "you have to move on that front when you're ready. I can't make you sleep with this guy. But I can make you come to New York to see me."

"You're coming to New York? When?"

"Tad and I and the kids are going to spend the long Thanksgiving weekend in the city. Why don't you and Jason and Megan join us?"

"We could do that," replied Sam, feeling better with each passing second. "We could definitely do that. The children would love it."

"We'll go shopping," added Mandy.

"Yes, we'll go shopping."

"On Fifth Avenue."

"On Fifth Avenue," agreed Sam.

●　●　●

THE REMAINDER of that day Sam spent on various financial matters. Gunn, much to her relief, had not pilfered the coffers. So she did. She became a woman of action. She squirreled away every nickel she could lay her hands on. She felt as if she had no choice. With Gunn going off half-cocked, she had to think about herself and the children. The children, as always, were her number one priority. Their safety and security had to come first. Gunn had betrayed them: She never would.

The next morning, not long after Jason and Megan departed in the limo, Brady knocked on the back door. Sam pulled it open. She did a mediocre job of suppressing the smile on her face.

"Good morning," he said. "Sorry to bother you."

"You're not bothering me," Sam assured him.

"You haven't been out this week for your morning swim. I just wanted to make sure you were okay." Brady, of course, said not a word about Gunn's ticklish departure. After all, how would he know anything about that?

Sam could hardly believe such a gentleman still existed. "Yes, Brady, I'm fine. Thank you. I've just been busy."

"Well," asked the caretaker, "what about this morning? The air's kind of nippy, but the water's still warm."

Sam took a moment. Why not? she asked herself. I have the right to a life. I have the right to be happy. And maybe, she allowed herself to think for the first time, maybe Brady will be part of that happiness.

"Can we dive?" she asked him.

Brady, the man at least partly responsible for the disintegration of her marriage, gave her a shy smile. "If you want to dive, we'll dive. We'll just have to find a way to keep you from freezing while we climb up to the platform."

"Oh," said Sam, her spirits soaring, "I'll bet we can think of something."

Mrs. Griner, hovering over the sink, smiled with

delight at the romantic overtures between Samantha and Brady. It gave her enormous satisfaction to see things moving ahead so splendidly, now that she had decided upon a course of action.

58 Gunn probably would have pilfered the coffers, but the idea had not occurred to him. He had his priorities out of sync. Normally they ran like this: money, food, sex. But since first copulating with Nita, he had reversed the order. It now ran: sex, food, money.

Sex with Nita was very much on Gunn's mind. And right at the moment he had her not only on his mind but right smack on his chest. Naked.

The dynamic duo had settled themselves, at least for a few business days, in a suite at the Ritz-Carlton across from the Public Garden in downtown Boston. They had come here, ostensibly, to peddle The Disk at a home entertainment trade show over at Faneuil Hall. Reilly had been against the visit to Beantown, but had finally relented.

The aging character actor relented, of course, because Brady told him to relent. This, Brady knew, would be the supersalesman's last hurrah. Soon the ax would fall. The Disk would fail. The Disk had been designed, from the very beginning, to fail. The whole Creative Marketing Enterprises scenario had been a sham, of course, a golden and glittering facade to pull the wool over greedy Gunn Henderson Jr.'s eyes. The company, its past successes, its entire financial record—all fake, fraudulent, phony. Gunn had been sucked in by the big money, the big house, the big dreams of financial glory. And soon he would pay the price for his greed and gullibility. Gunn Henderson would be blamed for The Disk's failure. Yes, the man was extremely close to being completely screwed. In a very short time he would have no job, no benefits, no expense account, no references, no home, no children, no wife, no mistress, no life. The caretaker, after years of careful planning and near-perfect execution, had snatched it all away. Soon, only Gunn's life would be left to take.

But Brady had a soft side. He would allow the destroyer of his youth a few more days of carnal and gastrointestinal delight. Although in truth the caretaker did not do this out of the kindness of his heart. No, he made these few days in Beantown possible because the higher Gunn Henderson soared, the farther the son of a bitch would be forced to fall.

◆　◆　◆

The team of Gunn and Nita did not leave their suite at the Ritz for more than forty-eight hours. Nita only managed to get Gunn to leave the hotel after they had indulged in so much sex that the tip of his penis became too sore to touch. Only then did they grab a cab over to State Street and make a hasty appearance at Faneuil Hall. But even after they had reached the trade show, Gunn made only a couple of very lame attempts to promote The Disk.

"I don't feel like it," he told Nita. "I'm not in the mood."

"Come on, Gunn," Nita prodded him. "We have to sell this thing or Reilly will definitely put an end to our little romantic sojourns. You don't want that, do you?" And with that question lingering on her lips, the high-priced call girl gave Gunn's testicles a nice squeeze. Right out in the middle of the hall. A couple thousand Bostonians milling around.

Gunn, sore and raw, winced and stepped back. "Jesus, Nita. Not here."

"What's the matter, Gunn?" asked Nita. "Don't tell me you're a closet Puritan?"

He took her for dinner at the Bay Tower Room high atop the Sheraton World Headquarters. They sat in front of the enormous plate glass windows, drank expensive Bordeaux, and ate thick slabs of western beef, much to Nita's stomach's horror. Across the harbor dotted with the slowly moving lights of freighters and tugs, they could see the jets landing and taking off at Logan International.

The food, the view, the wine, the woman—together it should have put G. Henderson on top of the world. But the whole scene made him feel anxious and depressed. Not only did red wine have that effect on him, but his dick hurt something awful and he could not stop thinking about his wife. A few years ago they had eaten at the Bay Tower Room. With her parents. And his parents. A big family thing. A celebration. For no particular reason. Just to do it. He had picked up the check, scooped it off the tray before his father or his father-in-law could snag it first. Three hundred and forty dollars, before tip. No problem. He'd whipped out his brand-new platinum card and handed it to the waitress. Oh, yeah, Gunn felt like a big man that night, an important man, a successful man. But tonight, having abandoned his wife and his kids, and knowing that everyone in both families would soon hate his guts, he felt small and inferior.

* * *

THE NEXT DAY Nita wanted to go shopping. Nita loved to shop. So Gunn, very much wanting to please, took Nita shopping. They strolled down Newbury and up Boylston, stopping often to gaze in the windows of all the fashionable boutiques.

At Armani, Gunn bought Nita a small leather handbag that she found "just precious." He paid cash. Four hundred and fifty dollars.

At Banana Republic, Nita found a long black skirt and a white crushed velvet shirt. When she came out of the fitting room wearing the outfit, Gunn could only shake his head at her stunning beauty. Again he paid cash: two hundred and fourteen dollars.

Gunn liked cash. He always kept a large wad in his pocket, folded in half and held together by a monogrammed sterling silver money clip.

As they walked along Boylston, arm in arm and shoulder to shoulder to protect themselves from a chilly north wind, Gunn kept his eye peeled for a bank with an automatic teller machine. He needed to get some more cash. The two purchases had put a sizable dent in his wad.

Near Copley Square he found a bank. He went inside and inserted his card into the money machine. He punched in the proper numbers and requested three hundred dollars from his checking account down in East Hampton. The machine whirred into action. After most of a minute had passed, the digital screen on the automatic teller machine informed Gunn his account contained only seven dollars and thirty-nine cents. He would not be receiving one red dime. Gunn did not know it at the time, but his lovely wife had gotten there first.

So, confused and irritated by what he figured was some bank error, Gunn rejoined Nita out on the street. He said nothing about his failed transaction.

They continued on. Gunn's priorities momentarily returned to normal: money, food, sex. He wondered how his balance could have fallen so low. He knew he had recently made a deposit. A hefty one. Several thousand. Maybe it hadn't cleared yet. Or maybe. Just maybe. Sam . . .

"Dammit!"

"What's the matter, Gunn?"

"Oh," he answered, pulling himself back, "nothing. I just thought of something I forgot to do."

They reached the corner of Boylston and Arlington. Nita spotted the famous Shreve, Crump & Low. She pulled Gunn toward the door. She just had to stop in and browse. Cash depleted, Gunn followed. He hoped she would not be tempted to buy.

Similar to Tiffany's, but also selling fine antiques, Shreve, Crump & Low first opened its doors way back in the early 1800s. For generations it catered to wealthy Brahmin Bostonians. But now anyone with money could walk through the door. Louisa May Chance walked through, and within mere seconds, much to Gunn's displeasure, she found several items she simply could not do without: a pair of sterling silver hoop earrings, a matching necklace, a small hand-painted porcelain bowl made in the Orient, and an antique pillow embroidered with a scene of the Boston Tea Party. Louisa May hated that pillow. She just wanted to see if she could get old sore cock to buy it for her. "I just love," she declared, "anything to do with our War for Independence."

Gunn, stewing pretty good inside, managed to nod in agreement. And moments later, to keep his squeeze happy, he pulled out his platinum card and handed it to the girl behind the counter. She rang up the purchases on the cash register and ran the credit card through the scanner.

Nita drifted off to browse some more.

"That'll be three hundred and eighty-six dollars and forty-seven cents, sir."

"Swell," Gunn grumbled under his breath.

Fifteen seconds passed. Half a minute. Gunn heard a loud buzz emanate from the card scanner.

"I'm sorry, sir," announced the salesclerk, "it appears as though you have used up your available credit on this card."

"Used it up! That's impossible! I have like a twenty-five-thousand-dollar credit line on that account."

True enough, Gunn. But the day before your wife had been very busy. She maxed out both the VISA platinum and the MasterCard gold with either cash advances or straight purchases. Her final purchase, in fact, had been a beautiful leather jacket, five hundred and ninety dollars, at the Polo Country Store right down on Main Street in East Hampton.

"I apologize for any inconvenience, sir," replied the clerk politely, "but I will not be able to credit these items to this account."

Gunn wanted to punch the girl in the mouth to keep her quiet. But instead he slipped her his gold card. She ran it through the machine. Gunn looked over his shoulder. Nita continued to browse. Thank God she hadn't witnessed the failure of his platinum. Or so Gunn thought. Actually, Ms. Nita only pretended to browse. In fact, her eyes and ears were firmly focused on events over at the sales counter.

She watched as Gunn's second card failed the credit test. And then a big smile spread across her pretty face as Gunn pulled out his Creative Marketing Enterprises American Express Card and handed it to the clerk.

Louisa May felt quite certain her boss, C. P. Donovan, would find this particular transaction extremely interesting. At the next available opportunity she would have to call him and spill the beans.

59 Heavy gray clouds hung over the swimming pool the day Sam finally made love to the caretaker. A little more than a week had passed since Gunn had flown the coop. He had called, once, to ask about the kids. But really, Sam knew, he had called to find out about the bank accounts and the credit cards. Sam had assured him the children were doing perfectly fine, then, without another word, she hung up on him.

And now, the temperature just a few degrees above freezing on a blustery mid-November morning, Sam found herself swimming. With the caretaker. Naked.

Yes, naked.

It hadn't just happened. Sam had wanted it to happen. She had even been the first to disrobe. Although, when she did so, it felt like an out-of-body experience, as though it must surely be someone else performing such an exhibition.

But then they were both naked and touching, pressing their lean, wet bodies close together. Sam could not believe how wonderful it felt. The poor girl was starved for physical attention. It had been weeks, months, since she and Gunn had been truly intimate, since back before he had beaten and battered her.

Sam needed love. She needed to be held and hugged and cuddled. Gunn, a selfish and stingy mate, had never given her enough. She always longed for more. But now here was Brady: gentle, patient, completely giving. The exact opposite, thought Sam, feeling a slight pang at betraying her unfaithful husband.

When the time came to head for warmer, drier climes, Sam suggested the boathouse. "I think I'd be more comfortable there than in the main house."

Brady hesitated. He did not want Sam stumbling upon any compromising evidence. But satisfied the coast would prove clear, he nodded. "Yes," he said, "I understand."

They slipped out of the pool. Sam immediately began to shiver. She quickly pulled on her fleece pants, turtleneck, jacket, gloves, and boots. Then she followed Brady through the rose garden. As soon as they reached the wide expanse of lawn, they broke into a run. They ran the rest of the way to the boathouse. But when they reached the back door they had to stop. Brady had to pull out a heavy set of keys, select the proper one, and unlock the door. Sam, still shivering even after their mad dash, pounded on his back to keep warm. She wondered why the caretaker locked the door just to go up and take a swim. But she did not ask; she was happy just to get inside.

Sam had not been inside the living quarters of the boathouse before. It was basically one large room sitting directly over the water garage where the boats were stored. The front wall was made mostly of glass and offered an excellent view of Shelter Island Sound. Whitecaps danced on top of the water that day, while waves lapped against the pilings beneath them.

Sam had most of her attention focused on the caretaker, but she did notice an enormous amount of books. Books everywhere—shelved and stacked, on tables and chairs, even on the floor. Enough books to fill a small town library. But other than the vast array of books, the huge room, divided into an eating area, a sitting area, and a sleeping area, looked clean and neat, everything in its place.

Even the double bed, Sam noticed, was neatly made, with the bedspread smooth and even on all sides. More like how a woman would make it, thought Sam, than a man. And the tiny kitchen, set off by a high counter, looked spotless. Plenty of fresh fruit sat in a bowl on the counter. Sam, still shivering, helped herself to a banana.

"Not to sound forward," she said, peeling the banana, wondering if it looked overly seductive, "but I'm freezing. Mind if I get under the blankets?"

No, the caretaker did not mind. So they took off their shoes and climbed into bed.

The rest of the morning and most of the afternoon provided Sam with some of the most satisfying hours she had passed in a long, long time. Yes, she and Brady made love. They had sex. Twice, in fact. And both times Brady was slow and gentle and sweet. He seemed genuinely to care more for her experience than his own. But the sex, passionate and fulfilling, proved only part of the story. Sam did not spend nearly five hours in bed in the middle of the day just because of the sex. No, she stayed in bed because Brady was warm and giving and extremely entertaining. He sang to her very softly, an Irish lullaby about a sweet lass who every night had to cry herself to sleep because her lover was far, far away. And much to Sam's amazement, and enjoyment, Brady made her laugh with silly faces and stupid jokes and bad impressions of famous actors and politicians. This was a side of Brady Sam had not known existed. But she loved it. She loved to giggle and laugh. She loved it more than anything else in the world. And lately her world had been so serious and grim. She couldn't remember when Gunn had last made her laugh.

• • •

THE NEXT MORNING, and the morning after, every morning that week, Sam rendezvoused with her lover at the boathouse. They skipped the swimming. It was too cold to swim.

On Friday morning Brady told Sam he had to go away for a day or two.

"Where do you have to go?" Sam wanted to know.

Brady hated lying to her, but no way could he tell her the truth. It pained him sometimes to think about all the lies he had told her, and all the lies he would have to tell her forever more. But really, he had no choice. The truth, he knew, would drive this beautiful, loving woman from his bed. From his life. The truth, in this case, would certainly not set him free.

"I have an uncle up in Rhode Island. He's old and sick. I've been putting off going to see him for weeks."

Sam thought about Gunn's parents, Gunn and Barbara Henderson. She had not been to visit them for months. Despite their son's despicable behavior, she still had fond feelings for her in-laws. They had always treated her with love and respect. She squeezed Brady's hand. "Yes, by all means, go see him. Don't put it off any longer."

"I thought I'd leave this afternoon."

"Make love to me again before you go."

So the caretaker did.

●　●　●

THE FOLLOWING MORNING, Saturday morning, Sam went looking for her children. She wanted to do something, go somewhere, get out of the house, at least for a while. She had not slept well. Too many thoughts. Too much confusion. Too much anxiety. Gunn, Brady, Megan, Jason, the future. What should she do? Where should she go? Would Gunn return? Did she want him to return? Was her fling with the caretaker more than just a thoughtless response to her husband's infidelity and desertion?

But before she could answer even one of these questions, a hundred more popped into her head. Could she actually be with Brady? As a couple? Was that possible? How could it be possible? The man had no money, no real home, nothing but that one room in the boathouse. How could they all live there? They couldn't live there. And yet, he was so sweet and tender and amusing. But no, she needed time, time to think, time to sort things out. It was good he had gone away for the weekend. She would have a moment to catch her breath.

Sam found Megan in the kitchen with Mrs. Griner. They sat at the table with a pan of fresh, homemade cinnamon rolls and two cups of hot chocolate.

"Mom!" shouted Megan. "Look what we made!"

Actually, Mrs. G. had made the cinnamon rolls from an old family recipe. But Megan had put them in the oven, watched them through the glass door, and removed them when the cook gave her the order.

Mrs. Griner, maiden name Greta McDougal, had been eating those cinnamon rolls all her life. Her mother had made them for her and her sister when they were children. And later she had made them for her own kids. And for her husband, before the bastard died.

Some months earlier, Mrs. Griner had told Sam that she had been born and bred on the South Shore of Long Island, that she had lived most of her life in and around East Hampton. This story, however, was an utterly fictional autobiography. Greta hailed from the Old Country, from Northern Ireland, from Belfast and later Londonderry, to be specific. She had grown up in a family of tough, violent Irishmen, factory workers mostly, prone to drunkenness and random abuse of their women and children. All through her youth Greta had feared her father, a brute of a man who thought nothing of using his fists. And then she had been fool enough to marry a man, a man who seemed sweet enough at first, but who turned out to have an even worse temper and an even more violent disposition than her father. For years, really until the day he died, Greta had prayed for her husband's demise while she suffered cruelly under his harsh reign.

Sam, unfortunately, knew none of this. She gave Megan a hug and a kiss, then asked, "Have either of you seen Jason?"

"Oh, yes," answered Mrs. G. "The boy came through here like a bolt of lightning fifteen or twenty minutes ago. Consumed two big cinnamon rolls and a cup of cocoa in less time than it took me to answer your question."

"So where is he now?"

"Outside," said Megan.

"Outside? What's he doing outside? It's freezing out there."

"He told me not to tell, but he went to the barn."

"The barn? Why the barn?"

"I think because Brady's away."

"So?"

Megan shrugged. "I don't know. He wouldn't tell me."

"Well," said Sam, "I'm going to go get him. And then we're all going out. You, too, Mrs. Griner, if you would like to come."

Greta fetched Sam a cup of hot chocolate. "I'll go, sure I will. But first take a minute to warm your belly with some cocoa and a cinnamon roll topped with my special whipped cream cheese. You're looking thin and pale, honey. The boy will wait."

For the next twenty minutes Sam sat with Megan and Mrs. G. They made plans for the day: shopping in Southampton, a drive around Shelter Island, a walk on the beach if it warmed up some.

And then Sam pulled on a jacket and a pair of gloves and went out to look for her son. She wanted them all to be together, as a family.

Outside, she could see her breath. She shivered, then set off briskly for the barn. Inside the barn, it felt even colder. What, she wondered, could Jason be doing in here? She called his name.

No answer. Sam took a look around. She had only been in the barn a few times before, usually to look for garden tools. She had never been upstairs, until now. At the top of the stairs she called again. "Jason! Are you in here?"

A few seconds passed. Overhead the rafters creaked. The wind, Sam thought. Chilled, she turned to go. But at that moment Jason pulled open the trapdoor and poked his head through. "Mom, what are you doing here?"

Sam craned her neck. "What are you doing up there?"

The boy, of course, was high. "Nothing."

They went back and forth for a minute or two before Sam decided she'd better investigate, see if her son was up to no good.

All of this Brady had anticipated before his departure. He knew once young Jason got wind of his absence from PC Apple Acres, the boy would make a beeline for that third-floor computer haven. The caretaker had therefore left the padlock off the trapdoor.

Sam began to climb. And like her son's some days earlier, Sam's eyes widened in astonishment the moment she saw that arsenal of electronic equipment. "What is this?"

"It's Brady's."

"Brady's?"

Jason closed the trapdoor as soon as his mother stepped off the ladder onto the gleaming wooden floor. "Have to keep the heat in."

Sam felt the warmth immediately. The heat felt good. She took a moment to relax. Then a thousand new questions bombarded her brain. Several of them she put to Jason, but her son had no answers.

He had, however, led her to the barn. Just as Brady had known he would. Boys, Brady knew, cannot keep secrets.

"Come over here," Jason said, grabbing his mother by the arm and more or less pulling her across the room.

Like something his father would do, Sam thought, with another pang. She followed him nevertheless.

Jason sat down in front of the Power Macintosh 9600. "This is a Mac, Mom," he explained. "Like the one we have over at the house. Only this one is a lot more powerful."

Sam nodded. Her brain was far too active to speak. She merely watched as her son moved the mouse and clicked the keyboard. The large color screen kept changing, but she had no idea what any of it meant.

"Brady," Jason told her, "invented this way cool computer game. I played it the other day. Now I'm trying to find it. I know it's on CD, but I haven't figured out the right commands yet to get it up and running."

That's because Brady had disabled THE AVENGER. Some fairly complex commands were needed to boot the game. Brady did not think for one second that Jason had the brains to figure it out. The caretaker wanted the boy to lead his mother to the third floor of the barn, but no way did he want the kid messing with his latest software creation. Nor did he really want Sam to see THE AVENGER in action; not at this delicate stage of their relationship. It was, after all, a rather violent and disturbing game. She might get the wrong idea.

"Do you have Brady's permission to play with his computer?" The question came despite the fact that Sam had not yet fully comprehended the reality that Brady actually owned a computer, much less a whole roomful of them.

"Of course," lied Jason. "He told me to play with it anytime I wanted."

Sam doubted that, but asked, "And you're sure this is his equipment?"

"That's what he told me."

Sam sat back and sighed. The complexity of the caretaker boggled her imagination.

"Got it!" shouted Jason.

"Got what?"

"I'm in! THE AVENGER is booting even as we speak!"

"THE AVENGER?"

"That's the name of Brady's game."

"And he really made the game up? He invented it?"

"That's what he told me," the boy repeated.

THE AVENGER flashed across the huge screen in bold red letters against a black background.

"Now just watch, Mom. Check this out."

For the next thirty or forty minutes Sam checked it out. She sat there mesmerized, mystified, and, ultimately, horrified, as her son took on the role of THE AVENGER.

The random setup this time was pure terror: A burglar breaks into Jason's house believing everyone is away. But actually Jason's wife and daughter are upstairs sleeping. They wake up while the burglar is busy plundering the house. Alarmed, they both scream. The burglar comes running. In the chaos that follows, he shoots the wife and the daughter dead.

Sam actually cried out when the shots went off. But Jason, an old pro at this now, calmly made the decision to avenge their deaths. "Now," he told his mother, "the fun begins."

"My God," muttered Sam, "that was awful."

It quickly got worse. Jason tracked down the burglar in no time. The burglar was this biker dude who hung around this sleazy bar on the wrong side of town. One night Jason waited outside while the burglar finished his drinks.

"Mom, watch this."

Sam did not really want to watch, she hated displays of gratuitous violence, but she found herself unable to take her eyes off the screen. She could hardly believe THE AVENGER had sprung from the gentle caretaker's imagination. It seemed, somehow, impossible.

And then the burglar emerged from the bar. Immediately Jason attacked. Swiftly and without mercy. First with a tire iron. Then with a spiked ball and chain. Weapons easily selected from THE AVENGER's arsenal.

The burglar's blood began to flow. It flew all over the place. It even splattered against the screen.

Sam recoiled in horror. The blood looked so real she half expected to find some on her wool jacket.

"Good God, Jason! This is absolutely disgusting."

Jason whacked the burglar over the head with the ball and chain. "You're right, Mom. Totally gross. I love it!"

Sam had seen enough. She moved away from the computer. She took a deep breath, then glanced around the room. THE AVENGER may have revolted her, but all the rest of it left her feeling curious. And impressed. She could not wait for Brady to return. Not only did she miss him already, but she had a million questions. Life suddenly seemed exciting again, worth living.

60

Brady did not go to Rhode Island to see his sick uncle, but he did go to New England. He went to Randolph, Vermont. To see Gunn Henderson, Jr.

Gunn had spent the night over on the west side of the Green Mountains in Brandon, Vermont. Alone. Sweet Nita, or so Gunn believed, was back down in

Texas again tending to her ailing mama. Brandon, Vermont, was icy cold. A thin layer of snow covered the not-yet-raked-up leaves. The motel out on Route 7 was old and stark. To save money the owner had inserted forty-watt bulbs into all the lamps. And no matter how high Gunn turned the thermostat in his room, the temperature never got above sixty. Gunny was on his way down. Fast.

After Boston, Mr. Reilly had seen enough. He ordered Gunn back on the road, back to small-town America, back to basics.

"You're wasting my money now, boy," he'd told Gunn on the phone. "And more than anything else, I hate to waste money. I'm sending you north. You're going to cover New England. Like a blanket. Just like you covered the West last spring. One small town, one five-and-dime at a time. And goddammit, at the end of every day you better have something to show for it. Some concrete sales to go in the books."

That one-sided conversation had taken place just a few short days ago. Later that same day Gunn and Nita checked out of the Ritz-Carlton, their last luxury hotel. Ostensibly, Nita flew to Texas, although really she took the shuttle to La Guardia, then a taxi to her digs on the Upper East Side. Gunn went to Hertz, rented himself a Ford Thunderbird, and drove west into the Berkshires. He then started north along Route 7, stopping in such quaint villages as Stockbridge, Pittsfield, Williamstown, Bennington, and Manchester. He ventured into the toy stores and five-and-dimes, but the man's heart was no longer in it. Half the time he walked out without even bothering to introduce himself to the owner or the manager. Gunn had become a salesman without the stomach to sell. He had lost his nerve. And that, he knew in his gut if not yet in his brain, spelled doom.

Outside Rutland he became so agitated and frustrated he threw half his sample Disks out the window of his speeding T-bird. Just lowered the window and hurled the damn things out into the blowing snow.

"Fuck it!" he screamed. "Just fuck it, fuck it, fuck it!"

Things did not improve when he checked into the Brandon Motel an hour or so later. Nor did they improve after a bad dinner at the Brandon Diner. Things got a little worse when he failed to get hold of Nita. And things really turned to hell when he called Reilly.

"Where are you?" Reilly demanded.

Gunn told him.

"Meet me tomorrow morning at ten o'clock at Flo's Diner in Randolph, Vermont. You can find Randolph on the map. It's just off Interstate Eighty-nine. Don't be late."

Reilly hung up.

Gunn went out and bought himself a bottle of whiskey.

●　●　●

GUNN PULLED into Randolph, after crossing the Green Mountains on State Highway 73, right around nine-thirty in the morning. He had no problem finding Flo's Diner. Randolph had only a couple of streets. And virtually all of the dozen or so businesses were clustered together on Main.

Gunn parked out front. He waited in the Thunderbird until about ten of ten. Then he climbed out of the car, locked the door, and went into Flo's. Flo's had a counter with a dozen or so swivel chairs, half a dozen tables, and as many booths lining the front wall. Gunn looked around for Reilly, didn't see him, so he took a seat at one of the booths.

The waitress, a pale and heavyset woman wearing a too tight white dress, came right over. "Good morning, sir. Start you off with a hot cup of coffee?"

"Sure," answered Gunn. "Thanks."

Gunn took another look around Flo's. Not many customers this late in the morning. An elderly couple sat at one of the tables. And a man in work clothes sat at the counter. That was it.

The one at the counter would be Brady. Up from the Hamptons to see how things panned out between Reilly and Henderson. Brady was, of course, in disguise: cap, glasses, mustache. He felt confident Gunny Henderson would not be looking for his caretaker this far north.

The night before he and Reilly had rendezvoused at the Holiday Inn down in Brattleboro. Brady had told the actor how things would go up at Flo's. Then he handed the man an envelope containing twenty grand. Cash. Reilly's final payment from a total of one hundred even. This morning would be the actor's last live performance as Mr. Arthur James Reilly. After this morning, Arthur James Reilly would cease to exist.

• • •

REILLY, dressed impeccably in a blue suit and a cashmere overcoat, walked through the door of Flo's Diner at precisely ten o'clock. Gunn stood. The boss and the employee shook hands. Brady took this opportunity to change positions. He moved from the counter to the booth beside Gunn's booth. The caretaker sat directly behind Gunn. He did not want to miss a word.

"So, Gunn," said Reilly, draping his overcoat over the back of his seat, "I hear you think The Disk is stupid."

Gunn recoiled. "Stupid? No," he told the boss, "I don't think it's stupid."

"I can't have a salesman out on the road who has no faith in my product."

"The Disk is a hell of a product," replied Gunn, but his tone did not sound very enthusiastic. "We're just in a bit of a lull right now."

"A bit of a lull? I haven't seen a single new order in over a month."

Gunn did his best to work himself into this. "That's true, but I don't think it means anything. I just think we're not hitting the right markets."

The caretaker sipped his coffee and smiled. He could hear the edge in Henderson's voice, the uncertainty. The bastard was no doubt beginning to sweat.

Reilly drew a small notepad from the breast pocket of his suit coat. He leafed through the pages. "Tell me, Gunn, this three-hundred-dollar purchase at Shreve, Crump, & Low for jewelry and china, is that part of your expense account?"

Gunn wondered how the hell the boss had found out about his purchase so quickly. "I . . . uh, no . . . I had some trouble with my credit card, so I—"

"I assume you bought this shit for Ms. Garrett. Believe me, Gunn, I know you're fucking her, and I guess it's a free country so you can fuck anyone you want. But don't be buying your squeeze love-goodies on my card. And make no mistake, that is *my* credit card. I am Creative Marketing Enterprises."

The smile broadened on Carl Patrick Donovan's face. The man loved good acting.

"You're right, sir, and I apologize. I fully intended to reimburse you."

The waitress brought Reilly a cup of coffee. He thanked her, then added a spoonful of sugar, no cream. He stirred the coffee for several seconds, then gave the coffee a taste.

"Okay, Gunn," he said, finally, "here's the thing."

"Yes, sir. Whatever you want me to do, I'll do."

"I've heard that from you before, Gunn."

Gunn swallowed his pride. "I've made a few mistakes, but nothing that can't be rectified."

The bastard, thought Brady, is beginning to grovel.

Reilly took another sip of coffee, then said, in a very clear and modulated voice, "Henderson, I'm firing your ass. Effective immediately."

Gunn's mouth fell open. He looked stunned. "Wait. What? You're firing me? What do you mean you're firing me?" Gunn had never been fired before. He had never been fired or laid off or cut from an athletic team or really rejected in any way at all. Ever. "You can't fire me."

"Oh, yes, I can. In fact," announced Reilly, and Brady, who had scripted the line, mouthed it right along with the actor, "I just did, you piss-ass son of a bitch."

"Excuse me? What did you call me?"

Reilly ignored the question. He leafed through his

notepad again. "Now listen up, Gunn, and listen good. I'm only going over this once."

Gunn could hardly sit still. His heart raced. His face had turned an unhealthy crimson.

"First of all," continued Reilly, "there's the matter of your wife. I'm going to allow her to continue living in the mansion for the next few months. At least. I see no reason to put Samantha through hell just because you're an unfaithful scoundrel and a rotten, half-ass salesman."

Gunn's face had now reached the purple stage. His mind was not on his wife. "If you're firing me, Reilly, you owe me money."

Reilly allowed himself a pinched smile, then he returned to his notes. "I don't think so, Gunn. The way it looks to me, I don't owe you one red cent."

"That's bullshit. What about my house? I haven't received a nickel from the sale of my house."

Brady rubbed his hands together. He had to suppress a desire to laugh out loud.

"Creative Marketing Enterprises bought your house, Gunn. Bought it and sold it. Unfortunately, as of today, Creative Marketing Enterprises has filed for Chapter Eleven. The company's bankrupt. And you, friend, are one of the primary reasons why."

Gunn looked confused. "Bankrupt? Bullshit. What kind of crap are you feeding me now, Reilly?"

"Sorry, Gunn, the company has no more assets. Only liabilities. Try all you want, son, but you won't be able to draw water from stone."

And so, just like that, Brady, sitting there with his hands folded on the table, had snatched it all away.

Gunn ranted and raved for several minutes about

stock options and salary incentives and benefit programs. But all his blather was for naught. Reilly placidly pointed out to him that when a company goes south, all the perks fly away with it.

"And now," said Reilly, in conclusion, "as far as that Thunderbird you have sitting out front, I'll give you until the close of business today to get it back to the rental car company. At six o'clock this evening your Creative Marketing American Express card expires. After that, you're on your own."

And with that, Reilly stood up, tossed a few dollars on the table, and pulled on his cashmere overcoat. "I have to tell you, Gunn. The Disk could have been a killer product. But you blew it. You really screwed it up. I'd have to say you allowed pussy to get between you and good business."

Reilly, an actor reluctant to relinquish the stage, waited for Gunn to respond, but Gunn had lost the power of speech. Never in his life had he been so humiliated. So Reilly took the last word, "*Ciao,* chump," and then he left Flo's, climbed into his rented Caddy Coupe de Ville, and drove away.

Gunn and Brady sat there, back to back, for several minutes, only the sound of their steady breathing emanating from their mouths. Gunn wanted to hurt somebody, inflict some bodily damage.

Brady wanted to turn around and say, "What's the matter, kid? Why are you sulking? Did the caretaker take your house and your job and your wife away? Won't the caretaker give you any money?"

But the time was not quite right for that. In fact, Brady was still uncertain whether or not he would ever face Gunn Henderson man-to-man. His pride, of course, wanted him to, but his brain kept telling him to back off, to keep his distance. It would be better, he knew, if Samantha never had a clue about his role in her husband's rise and fall. But that morning at Flo's, the issue had definitely not been resolved. Brady knew it could go either way. So he sat back, and in a voice sounding not at all like his own, the caretaker ordered a large stack of pancakes with real Vermont maple syrup.

61 Brady returned to PC Apple Acres late the following morning, a Sunday. He found Sam, Jason, Megan, and Mrs. Griner all sitting around the kitchen table playing some board game he did not recognize. Board games, except for chess, had never much interested him. In his brief and tragic youth, board games had not played much of a role.

Megan popped up from the table and gave Brady a hug. "Hi, Brady. Do you want to play Careers?"

"Maybe I'll just watch."

"Maybe," said Sam, "we'll take a break. Jason and I have something to discuss with Brady. Isn't that right, Jason?"

Jason, eyes averted, nodded. Already he felt the wrath of the adult world preparing to descend upon him.

"We'll go into the living room," continued Sam.

"Megan, you stay here and help Mrs. Griner fix lunch, sweetheart."

Brady, certain the boy had led his mother to the top of the barn, followed Sam and Jason into the living room.

Sam sat on the sofa. Brady sat across from her in a chair. Jason paced, then, upon his mother's command, he slumped on the opposite end of the sofa.

"So," Sam asked Brady, "did you have a safe trip? And your uncle, how is he?"

"The trip was fine," answered Brady. "My uncle, well, I think he's seen his best days."

"I'm sorry to hear that."

"He's had a good life." Brady was not enjoying this. "No regrets," he added, then grew mute.

"Well," said Sam, "we had a rather interesting day yesterday."

"Oh? What happened?"

"Jason, why don't you tell Brady what happened?"

It took quite a bit of time and fidgeting, but eventually the boy spit it out. "I went up into your room . . . your office . . . in the barn, and, well, I . . . I played THE AVENGER."

Brady needed a moment to let that settle. He decided he must have heard wrong. No way had the kid actually played the game. "You mean you *tried* to play? You *tried* to use my Mac?"

Jason kept his eyes on the antique Persian carpet. "Look, really, I just went out to check. You know, to see if the trapdoor was maybe open. And when it was, well, I figured it was okay. So I went up and played."

"I see."

"Does he," Sam asked the caretaker, "have your permission to be up there? To use those computers?"

Jason gave Brady the briefest of glances. Like his old man, the boy had turned into a beggar. This one, too, would definitely have to suffer. But not right now. Right now Brady needed the stoned-out little pipsqueak.

"Let me just ask you, Jason, did you actually *play* THE AVENGER? Were you able to get the game up and running?"

Jason hesitated, but said, "It took some work, but yeah, I got it going. I got to play a couple rounds."

Brady controlled his desire to lash out. He even allowed himself to be impressed. The kid, he realized, must have half a brain.

"Oh, he played all right," added Sam. "I watched him. But I must say, I found the game rather disturbing. It was so violent. Almost, at times, sick."

Brady felt the anxiety that comes with a loss of control. He definitely had not wanted Sam to see his game in action. Her reaction was exactly as he had feared. "THE AVENGER," he replied carefully, hoping to soften the damage, "is really aimed at the adult market."

"Yes, well," replied Sam, with a small shake of her head, "I really don't think it's appropriate for a boy Jason's age."

"Oh, Mom," whined Jason, "I have all kinds of video games more violent than THE AVENGER."

"Then maybe it's time I took a look at your video games," his mother said firmly. "But really we're getting off track." Sam turned to Brady. "What I want to know is whether or not Jason has your permission to use those computers?"

Brady could see the boy in his peripheral vision begging for affirmation. "Yes," he told Sam, "he does."

A big grin spread across the boy's face. Brady saw that grin and knew he now had the brat in his back pocket. "But in the future," he added, just to set the record straight, "I'd prefer if you only use the computers when I'm present."

"Hey, right," said Jason, "absolutely. No problem."

● ● ●

THE NEXT MORNING Megan and Jason went to school. Sam went to the boathouse. She made love to the caretaker. Their passion, after the long weekend separation, proved undiminished. Sam lay naked in his arms and decided she did not want to think about the future; she just wanted to feel Brady's warmth and affection.

Late in the morning, Sam asked him about the third floor of the barn.

"Most of the equipment," Brady lied, "belongs to Mr. Reilly."

"Mr. Reilly?"

"Yes." Brady had, the night before, put together his explanation. "A few years ago I discovered I had a knack for computer programming. So Mr. Reilly set me up with some equipment so I could try to develop some computer games."

This explanation, he felt, was simple and straightforward. And it allowed for the possibility that he might soon have money, quite a bit of money, enough to take care of Sam and her kids. He decided it would be too big a shock to come out of the closet as the CEO of Graphic Software, Inc. Sam might run for cover.

"Computer games like THE AVENGER?" she asked.

"Yes."

"And so is it finished? Are you going to sell it?"

Brady nodded. "It's almost finished. And hopefully one of Mr. Reilly's companies is going to market it."

Sam smiled. "That's so exciting, Brady." She wondered how much money a computer game like THE AVENGER might be worth.

The caretaker could see the dollar signs in her eyes. But he did not have a problem with that. A woman with two kids needed financial security. And he intended to provide her with all the financial security she would ever need. That and then some. He knew she had fallen in love with Brady the caretaker, not Carl Patrick Donovan the millionaire software developer. Sam was not just some gold-digger out for the cash.

They made love again. They made love all week long.

62 Gunn wound up in New York City with Nita at, of all places, Brady's Upper East Side penthouse. Originally Gunn was supposed to wind up at Nita's much smaller digs around the corner, but at the last second Louisa May balked.

"Look," she told Brady the night before he left for Vermont, "I can't have him here. Not in my house."

"Why not?"

"Because," answered the prostitute, "when the time comes for me to blow him off, I'll need someplace to go, someplace to get away from him. If the SOB's already in my apartment, I'll have nowhere to escape."

Brady immediately saw Louisa May's problem. "Okay, look, when the time comes for you to get rid of him, I'll send you anywhere you want to go."

"That's fine, but eventually I'll have to come back. And he'll know where to find me. I don't want that. We need," Nita insisted, "a neutral site."

Brady thought it over. He needed Louisa May to occupy Gunn for at least a month, longer if possible. The caretaker felt he needed that much time to solidify his relationship with Samantha. "Okay," he told her, "you can use my apartment. Just try not to trash the place."

So when Gunn called Nita from Flo's Diner after Reilly had driven off in his Caddy, Nita told Gunn she was flying from Fort Worth to New York that very morning. She told him she had a place they could stay, a friend's apartment, a friend who was in Paris on assignment for *Time* magazine. Gunn, in need of some good news, thought that sounded great. He jotted down the address, then promised Nita he would rendezvous with her there later that evening.

• • •

So Gunn and Nita set up house. At Brady's place. All went well. For a few days. They frolicked on Brady's bed and on Brady's sofa; they drank wine and stared out the living room windows at Central Park looming far below. "Fuck Reilly," Nita said, shrugging off Gunn's dismissal from Creative Marketing Enterprises. "Fuck The Disk. You're a salesman, Gunn. You can sell anything."

Gunn nodded and grinned and did his best to look positive and enthusiastic, but right behind the grin lurked doubt and uncertainty. Gunn's confidence was all shot to hell. The evidence could be seen in his heavy drinking and his limp erections.

And then, it must have been Tuesday or Wednesday morning, Nita got up and went to work. On her way out the door, Gunn urging her to stay, she said, "Look, I still have a job. And I'd like to keep it."

"But Reilly told me the company was bust."

"Hey, as long as he gives me a paycheck."

Gunn did not want to be alone. "So call in sick. Or tell him your mother's still sick."

Pitiful, thought Louisa May. A real whiner, this guy had become. "I've missed too much time lately already." And then, because she simply could not resist, she added, "Besides, *one* of us has to bring in some money."

And with that, Nita went to work. Down the street and around the corner to her apartment. Most of that day she entertained a Czech diplomat assigned to the U.N. Nita had a pipeline into the U.N. All those lonely and horny foreigners needed a safe haven. Nita liked to tell them she was the Sexual Ambassador for the United States. Her clients found this most amusing.

Gunn, on the other hand, was not amused about anything. He paced around that penthouse apartment like a caged tiger. He tried to put together a résumé, but his brain was fried, he could not concentrate. Plus he had one rather large problem. The last five and a half years of his working life did not look real good on paper. Getting decent recommendations from either Creative Marketing Enterprises or his former employer, the sporting goods giant, who he had run out on with virtually no notice, would be impossible. And without strong recommendations, his job search would be a tough row to hoe.

So what did Gunn do to face these problems? He had a drink. And then he had another drink. By Friday he was drinking before noon.

Gunn had other problems as well. Like money. He had very little money. Less than a thousand dollars cash. And no viable credit cards. He had some investments, investments Sam knew nothing about, but he faced stiff penalties if he tried to pull out his money. And even if he did pull it out, the cash would only be enough to keep him going for a few months, six at the most. He sighed and had another drink.

Then there was his precious Porsche. Parked down on a Manhattan street. No garage. No cover. Just parked out there, a sitting duck for ice, rain, snow, and sunlight. To say nothing of thieves and vandals. At least five times a day Gunn went down to check on his baby. It sickened him to see her sitting there, exposed.

He retreated to the penthouse and poured another drink.

And Sam? He called her several times. Usually Greta answered, and in a rather rude voice she would inform him that Sam was indisposed, then she would hang up. When finally he did get his wife on the line he demanded she cough up some of the dough she had pilfered from the bank accounts and the credit cards.

Sam just laughed in his ear and slammed the phone back onto its cradle.

The next day he called back and told her he wanted to see the kids.

Sam said, "You can see them anytime you want. They have no idea you've abandoned us, Gunn. They think you're off on one of your extended business trips."

"You haven't told them?"

"Why should I?"

Gunn did not have an answer. So Sam hung up. Gunn had another drink.

63

The phone at the penthouse was, of course, tapped. Brady monitored all calls from his office. He was not spending much time in his office these days, however. Sam had the caretaker thoroughly distracted from his work.

In fact, Samantha had the caretaker doing all kinds

of crazy things. Like on Saturday, when he called her after midnight.

Sam had just fallen asleep when the phone rang. A bit groggy, she picked it up. "Hello?"

"It's me."

They had spent the day together. But not alone. Both Megan and Jason had been along for the ride. Intimacy had been impossible.

Brady needed intimacy. In the worst way. For an hour or more he had paced around the boathouse. He wanted to call her, go to her, make love to her. She was all he could think about. Well, mostly all. He had phoned Nita earlier to see how things were going at the penthouse.

"Let's put it this way," Nita had replied, "I'll be glad when this trick is over."

"That bad?"

"This guy's a real pig," she'd said, referring to Gunn.

"Nevertheless, Louisa May," Brady had insisted, "you keep that pig occupied. That's what I'm paying you for."

Nita griped, but agreed to complete her mission.

"Brady?" Sam asked into the telephone, her voice low and sleepy.

"Hi."

"Hi back."

"I miss you."

"That's sweet. I miss you too."

They were like a couple of high-school sweethearts, always whispering sweet nothings into each other's ears.

"I want to see you."

"Now?"

"Yes," answered the caretaker.

"But we can't," said Sam. "It's late. . . . The kids . . . I can't come down there now."

"I'll come to you."

Sam wanted him to come. She knew he would snuggle her against the cold, make love to her slowly and gently. "Brady, we can't. One of the kids might see you sneaking through the house."

"No one will see me, Sam," whispered Brady, his heart beating rapidly in anticipation of what lay ahead. "Just lock your bedroom door."

"Lock it? But how will you—"

"Shh, baby. Just lock it so no one can walk in. I'll be there soon."

"But Brady, wait. I—"

The phone went dead. Brady was on his way.

● ● ●

HE CAME UP through the basement as quiet as a church mouse. Not a single nail squeaked or board squawked as he made his way along those dark and soon no longer secret passageways. He knew in his brain he should not do this, that this was a mistake, a big mistake, but in his heart he no longer cared.

Brady, a.k.a. the caretaker, a.k.a. Carl Patrick Donovan, slipped into the master bedroom suite through a small, virtually impossible to detect panel beside Sam's Georgian cherry bureau. The panel was at floor level, three feet wide by three feet high. Brady entered the bedroom on his hands and knees.

"Brady! My God!" Sam shot up in that huge four-poster bed, her eyes as wide and clear as the white light of a full moon. She felt a strange mixture of fear and excitement. "Where did you come from? How did you get back there?"

Brady did not answer, did not say a word. He covered her mouth with his mouth, kissed her long and passionately. Sam forgot all about her questions. They made love, just as Sam had anticipated.

And afterward they lay there, wrapped together, moonlight flooding through the windows. Sam knew she should ask Brady about his dramatic entry into her room, but she did not want to ask, she did not want to know. Not right now. Sleepy and satiated, she just wanted to lie there in the arms of her lover. She felt good lying there, she felt wonderful. She felt young again, and pretty, like she used to back in college. She felt consumed by the mystery of the man lying naked at her side. Sam did not want to ruin these feelings by asking a lot of questions about why there was a hole in the wall and how Brady happened to know about it. Innocence still soothed her emotions.

● ● ●

WHEN SHE AWOKE she had a much smaller body nestled against her side. Megan had slipped into the room sometime just after dawn and crawled under the sheets beside her mother. Sam, startled, took a quick look around the room for Brady, but the caretaker had vanished. Perhaps, Sam thought drowsily, he had not really come to her during the night. Perhaps he'd been just a figment of her dreams and desires.

Sam and Megan found Brady and Jason down in the kitchen making French toast. "Irish toast actually," insisted Brady, "from an old family recipe."

He cut thick slabs of whole wheat bread, soaked them in a mixture of egg and milk and cinnamon and sugar and vanilla and nutmeg, deep-fried them in a very hot pan of oil, then covered them with the pure Vermont maple syrup he had hauled home from the Green Mountain State. The kids gobbled down several pieces each. And never for a second wondered why the caretaker was at their house so early.

And then something rather rare for that time of year happened: It started to snow. Just before dawn, while Brady arose, put that wall panel securely back in its place, unlocked the door, and exited the master bedroom suite, thick clouds had moved in across eastern Long Island. And now, snow: huge, wet flakes. The excited kids pulled on boots and coats, hats and gloves, and flew out the back door.

Sam and Brady watched through the window as Jason skidded around the slick terrace and a giddy Megan tried to catch the flakes on her tongue.

Brady smiled at the family scene. Sam squeezed his hand.

"So," she asked, "when did you leave?"

"Right around first light."

She looked deeply into his eyes. "Then you really were there?"

"Oh, yes, I was there."

She knew she had to ask. It could not be avoided. "And you really came through a hole in the wall?"

Brady had his answer ready. He had hours ago anticipated the question. "Last night, lying in bed down at the boathouse, missing you like crazy, I remembered the mansion had a series of passageways running behind the walls."

"Passageways?"

Brady nodded. "They were built into the original design to make it easier to get at the air ducts and the plumbing and the electrical services."

Sam, with no knowledge whatsoever of the peepholes that were the real crux of those secret passageways, had no reason to doubt her lover's very reasonable explanation. "That makes sense."

Brady, relieved, nodded again. "I've only been back there a few times, but last night I remembered there was a way into the master bedroom. So, wanting desperately to see you, I decided to use it."

Sam squeezed his hand. "And I'm oh so glad you did."

Brady kissed her lips, then decided it would be wise to change the subject. "I have to go to California for a few days."

"California? Why?"

"To demonstrate my computer game to some of Mr. Reilly's associates."

It was now Sam's turn to smile. "Brady, that's wonderful. You must be so excited. When do you go?"

"In a couple days."

"And how long will you be gone? I only ask," Sam added quickly, fearing she sounded too possessive, "because I'll miss you."

Brady could feel his heart pounding. He felt quite certain he had never been in love like this before. He wanted to postpone his trip. But it had been in the works for weeks. Support staff from all over the country were gathering to get a first glimpse of THE AVENGER. Plus he had promised his partner he would spend Thanksgiving with him and his family.

"Actually," he said softly, "I had a thought."

"What?" asked Sam.

"That maybe you could come with me."

"To California?"

Brady nodded.

"Oh, Brady, that's so sweet." Sam loved to travel. But no, it was out of the question, impossible. "But really, I can't. Not now."

Brady sighed. "You're right, of course. Gunn would—"

Sam frowned. "This is not about Gunn."

"Sam, I'm sorry. I—"

Sam pressed her finger against his lips. "It's Jason and Megan. I couldn't possibly leave them."

"No," agreed Brady. And then he heard himself say, "That's why they'll come, too."

"They'll come, too?" Sam smiled even while she shook her head. "Now that is definitely impossible."

"Why? They're on vacation this whole week. They won't miss a single day of school. We'll all be back on Sunday."

Sam, caught up more and more in Brady's fantasy, actually saw herself on the wharf in Monterey with Megan and Jason and Brady. She imagined the four of them hiking in Yosemite. One big happy family. Without Gunn along to spoil everyone's good time. But, of course, Sam blinked and found reality. She already had plans to meet Mandy in New York. Besides, Jason and Megan, for God's sake, didn't even know yet that their father had abandoned them. And they certainly didn't know their mother had fallen in love with the caretaker.

Sam looked out the window at her children darting

around the terrace trying to avoid the snowflakes, a game she had taught them when they first learned to walk. She knew she must be careful. Very careful. She must protect her children, keep them safe. And secure. Her children were, above all else, her number one responsibility.

◆ ◆ ◆

ON TUESDAY MORNING, Brady left for California. Alone. Armed with two notebook computers and his master copy of THE AVENGER on compact disk.

Earlier, before dawn, up in the master bedroom suite, Brady, after making love to Sam, for what neither of them knew would be the last time, whispered in her ear, "I love you, Samantha."

This was the first time Brady had ever uttered these vital words.

And Sam, terrified but feeling reckless, whispered back, "I love you too, Brady."

No doubt about it: The girl was in way over her head. She did not have a single suspicious bone in her body regarding the caretaker. She trusted him implicitly.

64 Back in the Big Apple, Gunn stewed. Each and every day the boy-man's problems proliferated. Take his hot red Porsche. It no longer had any side-view mirrors. Both had been snapped off by God knows who. Also, a ragged peace sign had been scratched into the engine hood with a sharp instrument. And the passenger window—gone, smashed. In its place—a piece of clear plastic duct-taped to keep out the weather. Inside, the radio had been stolen, along with the gearshift knob, all the manuals, and the fancy Porsche mats.

So much for free parking on the streets of Manhattan.

The question is: Was Brady responsible? Had he hired someone to vandalize Gunn's beloved coupe?

Quite possibly he had, though Gunn never would have guessed it.

Gunn drowned his sorrows in a bottle of Beefeater's. And then he cracked another bottle to escape his solitude. That bastard Reilly kept his sweet Nita working twelve and fourteen hours a day. She left early and arrived home late, usually exhausted and irritable.

Gunn would immediately begin to paw her with his big, sweaty hands the moment she walked through the door. Nita did her best to fend him off, but Gunn proved relentless. So despite the fact that she had already performed sexually on several occasions that day, Louisa May had no choice but to satiate him. The man needed booze, food, and a good fuck before it became even remotely possible to live with him. Louisa May longed for this interminable trick to end. Never again would she take on such a lengthy project. A long weekend was her limit from here on out. No man was fit to live with longer than that.

"Any luck on the job front?" she asked him every night.

"Not a goddamn thing," was usually his sodden response.

Gunn had two very big problems on the job front. First of all, his attitude. The man had a very bad attitude. Consumed by anger and fear and self-pity, Gunn did not at present possess the necessary mettle to seek and land an aggressive sales job. In his state of mind, he probably could not have gotten hired to sell underwear at the local department store.

But this was a short-range problem. Eventually Gunn would get himself straightened out. He certainly would not pout and whine forever. In fact, even now he usually had a couple of decent hours in the morning, before he turned to the booze, wherein he began the search for a viable position. He had talked with several companies and a few hotshot headhunters.

Unfortunately for Gunn, Brady had been in on these

talks also. Behind the scenes, of course. By monitoring the calls Gunn made from the penthouse, Brady was able to keep an eye on G. Henderson's employment prospects. He would then contact these companies, and, acting as Gunn's former employer, Arthur James Reilly of Creative Marketing Enterprises, he would paint a rather negative picture of Mr. Henderson. Descriptive phrases like "unreliable," "uncooperative," and "unproductive" usually caught the ear of the person on the other end of the line. Brady would then expand his critique. "No company loyalty." "Excessive use of expense account privileges." "A serious failure to promote new accounts and make sales." "I would say," the caretaker liked to add as a final tribute, "that Mr. Henderson is definitely not a closer. He might be a good talker, but he's a lousy closer."

That pretty much sealed Gunn's fate. Who wanted a salesman who could not close the deal?

And so Gunn, his confidence and self-esteem slipping a bit further with each rejection, took ever more solace in the bottle. The man was down to two friends in the whole wide world: Jim Beam and the yeoman Beefeater.

65 By late Tuesday afternoon, after just two days of vacation, Jason had managed to drive his mother almost mad. After making his little sister cry, twice, after Rollerblading across the Italian marble foyer, after hounding his mother for a new bike and a new dog and a new big-screen TV, Sam had seen and heard enough. But scolding and threats proved futile. So she tried another tack.

"Brady," she told her son, "tells me the house has secret passageways."

"Secret passageways! Where?"

Brady, of course, had not called them secret passageways. Sam imagined them more as dark, narrow crawl spaces used to perform maintenance. Hands-and-knees kind of stuff. She certainly did not imagine spacious corridors littered with strategically placed peepholes that could be opened and closed at will.

"I don't know," she fibbed, not wanting to tell her son about the bedroom entrance. She wanted him to have to work at it; she hoped for a while. "Why don't you see if you can find them?" Anything, she thought, to occupy him at least until dinner.

It worked. Jason disappeared for an hour. Two hours. Three hours. The house grew quiet and mellow. So much time passed that Sam actually began to worry. But for naught. Just before dinner her son reappeared. He came up the cellar stairs into the kitchen, a small spiral-bound notebook in his hand.

Sam and Mrs. Griner stood at the counter, chopping vegetables for Chinese stir-fry. Megan was busy setting the table. "So," Sam asked her son, "how did you make out?"

Jason, all keyed up, did his best to contain himself. He made a show of studying his notebook before answering. "Let's see," he said, and he glanced at his sports watch. "It's now ten minutes of seven. At thirteen minutes after five, Mom, you went up to your bedroom. You closed the door, took off your sweater and pants, and crawled into bed for exactly seventeen minutes. Then you got up, walked into the bathroom, squatted on the toilet, and took a pee."

"Jason!"

Megan laughed. But Mrs. Griner, immediately concerned about this breach of etiquette, did her best to act like she hadn't heard a word.

"Then," continued Jason, "you washed your face, rubbed some cream on your cheeks, got dressed, and came back downstairs."

Sam scowled at her son. He had her late afternoon R&R down to a T. "And how, may I ask, do you know all that?"

Jason led with a smirk. "Maybe I found those secret passageways."

"Secret passageways!" shouted Megan. "What secret passageways?"

Jason did not answer. He consulted his notebook instead. "Let's see what the little twerp was up to. Yeah, I followed you from the living room to the library to the TV room to the family room, then upstairs to a couple of the guest rooms, and finally to your bedroom where you spent about ten minutes scribbling in your diary."

Instantly young Megan became furious. "How do you know? I never saw you. You stay away from my diary!"

Jason turned to their mother. "Mom, Megan's like some kind of weird pack rat. She has little stashes of stuff all over the house. Coloring books under the couch in the living room. Teacups and spoons in that cedar chest out in the family room. Dolls in the cupboard in the TV room. More dolls—"

"Mom!" screeched Megan. "Tell him to leave me alone! And tell him to leave my stuff alone!"

Sam barely heard her daughter. Her thoughts had shifted to the caretaker, to his romantic midnight entry into her darkened bedroom. It suddenly no longer seemed particularly romantic.

"Mom!"

Sam sighed and turned to Megan. "Yes, sweetie?"

"Tell him!"

"Don't worry, honey. Jason won't invade your privacy anymore."

"He better not!"

Sam wanted to ask Jason exactly what he'd found behind the walls, but decided it might be better to ask him later, when Megan and Mrs. Griner were not present.

But Mrs. Griner, troubled and curious, had some questions of her own. "What about me, Jason?" she asked. "Did you do any eavesdropping on me?"

The cook's somewhat accusatory tone gave Jason pause, but the boy found it impossible to keep his investigative work under wraps. "Well," he answered, "you were in here most of the time. Making chocolate chip cookies. I estimate you ate approximately one out of every three you put in the cookie jar."

Mrs. Griner blushed. Megan laughed. Sam frowned.

"At six o'clock," Jason continued, "you went back to your room. You called Saida and asked her how she was feeling. I guess she's got a cold or something. Then you told her we'd be away for a few days over Thanksgiving if she needed some extra time off . . ."

Sam could see Jason's report was beginning to embarrass Mrs. G. The cook had turned beet red. But Greta was not embarrassed; no, she was furious, absolutely furious, at the caretaker.

"Then you gossiped for a while about some woman who sounds like she's maybe, you know, doing it with someone who's, you know, maybe not her husband, or—"

"Okay, Jason!" interrupted the boy's mother, "that's enough. I can see you've been a busy little bee buzzing around behind the walls. And now I want you to stay out of there so people can enjoy their privacy. What you did was okay to do once. But it'll be ugly and rude if you do it again."

"But Mom, it's so cool. The secret hallways go everywhere. All over the house. You can spy on everyone. It's wild."

"I don't care how wild it is!" Sam snapped. "I want you to stay out of there! Do you understand me?"

Jason knew his mother pretty well. He knew when to back off.

"I'm sorry about that," Sam told Mrs. Griner. "We both know he has a tendency to get carried away."

Greta managed to offer a wry smile. But inside she was seething. Brady had told her early on about the hidden passageways. But he had also told her, assured her, that her living quarters off the back of the kitchen were entirely private, not part of the maze of passages, completely off-limits to any prying eyes. Damn him! she thought. But she kept that soft smile on her plump face and cheerily replied, "No harm done."

A nice response, but entirely untrue. Both women knew an enormous amount of harm had been done.

• • •

BRADY CALLED late that night. Sam, in bed, had been anticipating his call for hours. She needed to ask him about those secret passageways, but she could not decide if she should simply be direct, or if a more subtle approach might be more effective.

Brady whispered a gentle string of sweet nothings into her ear. She did her best to respond, but she was far too troubled for intimacy.

The caretaker could hear the strain in her voice. "Is something wrong, Sam?"

"No," she lied, "not really. It's nothing."

"Something."

She hesitated, drew a deep breath. "Well," she began, reluctantly, "late this afternoon, I was trying to find some way to occupy Jason. He's been pretty wound up. Not enough to do. I told him there was a rumor going around that the mansion was filled with secret passages."

Brady heard the phrase and immediately wanted to slap himself in the head. He never should have entered the master bedroom through that secret panel. It had been an idiot's move, totally asinine. "Yes?" he asked. "So?"

"So," replied Sam, happy now the situation was at least out in the open, "he found his way behind the walls, and then promptly proceeded to spend the rest of the afternoon spying on us."

Brady, annoyed both with himself and with that damn kid, considered a moment, then decided to go with surprise. "What do you mean, he was spying on you?"

"He was spying on us! Watching us! Through the walls!"

"But how would he be able to see you?" asked Brady, calmly, a perfect pitch of innocence in his mellow voice. "The walls are solid. He might be able to hear you, but I don't see how he could see you."

Brady knew perfectly well if the kid found the peepholes, he could see through the walls. But he had to play dumb; what choice did he have?

Sam's alarm softened upon hearing Brady's response. And yet, her suspicion did not disappear entirely. "I have no idea. I haven't been back there. But from what he reported, it certainly seemed as though he was able to see us. Anyone could get back there and spy on us."

The implication hung in the air until Brady responded with, "I don't think that's very likely, Sam."

"Do you," Sam asked her lover, after a brief pause, "ever go back there?"

"Of course not," the caretaker answered promptly, his tone ever so slightly offended. "Unless there's a problem with the plumbing or the heating or the electric."

Sam sighed. She did not really know what to say. But she decided, at least for the time being, not to push it. It might be better to just let things lie. Perhaps she would see what she could find out on her own.

"I'm sure," she murmured, "I'm just being ridiculous."

Brady did not trust this sudden change in attitude, so he said, "Sam, if it will make you feel any better, I'll close the whole thing off as soon as I get home."

"That's not necessary."

"I'll do it anyway."

"No, really, let's just forget it."

"Okay, we'll forget it. But if you change your mind, just let me know and I'll block those passageways off. It's not like they get used very often anyway."

"Okay," she said, keeping up her end of the act. "I'll let you know."

"So when," Brady asked, sounding relieved, "are you going into New York to see your friend?"

"The day after tomorrow. Thanksgiving morning."

"And you'll be back Sunday?"

"Probably Saturday. In the afternoon."

"Hopefully I'll be back on Saturday also. Sunday at the latest."

"I guess I'll see you then," Sam heard herself say.

Brady did not like the sound of that. "I love you, Sam," he whispered.

Sam heard her heart beat. "I love you, too," she said, but wondered if she meant it.

And the caretaker knew it. His lover, despite what she said, was troubled. Suspicion, even if only a thin thread, had definitely slipped into her psyche. He knew he would have to return home early; Friday at the latest, Thursday would be even better. It had been stupid of him to ever leave PC Apple Acres in the first place.

66 The caretaker's instincts were right on target: Samantha Ann Quincy Henderson was definitely troubled by those hidden passageways. What woman even remotely in her right mind would not be?

Sam spent a restless night. Early the next morning, the morning before Thanksgiving, before dawn, she rose, flipped on a light, and pulled on a robe. She stood in the middle of the room and stared at the wall where Brady had so casually entered. Thankful he was on the other side of the country, Sam crossed to the wall and knelt down. So seamless was the panel that Sam could barely tell it existed. But she knew it existed; she had seen it with her own eyes.

A pair of scissors from the bathroom gave her the

leverage she needed to pry the panel open. Sam stuck her head behind the wall, but it was too dark to see. She fetched a flashlight from the hall closet. Then, her pulse racing, she slipped through that hole in the wall.

The first thing to surprise her was the space. She had expected cramped quarters. She found instead a hallway with plenty of shoulder room and headroom. Her flashlight beam leading the way, she ventured cautiously into the dark.

She did not go very far. Half a dozen steps at the most. A very thin shaft of light stopped her in her tracks. The light came through the wall right about at the level of her breasts. Sam bent to have a look.

The hole was not much bigger than the head of a pin, but it gave Sam an unobstructed view of her own bed. She gasped softly.

Something crinkled under her slippered foot. She pointed the flashlight down. And there, on the floor, she saw crumpled candy wrappers: caramel chews, Hershey's Kisses, Butterfingers, a flattened box of Junior Mints.

Her first thought was that Jason had left the litter. But what if Jason hadn't left it? What if those wrappers belonged to someone else? A shudder of fear rippled down her spine. She suddenly felt abused and violated.

For the next half an hour, Sam explored behind the walls. She found peepholes everywhere, looking into almost every room in the house. She was able to look in on her own two dear children, both of them still sleeping soundly, oblivious to this massive and offensive intrusion upon their youthful privacy.

Of course, she had no evidence that the caretaker

had ever once put his eye to one of those peepholes, but she knew without question that he had access to the passageways. And that he had kept the existence of the passageways a secret until one night when he grew horny for her affections.

●   ●   ●

HAVING SEEN ENOUGH, Sam crawled back into her bedroom. She did not bother to put that panel back in its place. Her mind had moved on. She went downstairs in search of Mrs. Griner. In the kitchen she found coffee dripping through the automatic coffee machine and a pan of cinnamon rolls baking in the oven, but no sign of the cook.

So for the first time since Sam had moved into the mansion, she started down the narrow hallway off the back of the kitchen. She knew Mrs. Griner had her living quarters back there, but she had always respected the cook's privacy.

At the end of the narrow hallway she came upon a half-open door. Beyond the door was a small living room with a sofa and chair and a couple of reading lamps. "Mrs. Griner?" Sam called.

The cook did not answer.

Sam entered. She moved slowly, cautiously, like an intruder. On the far side of the living room she came upon another door. This one was also open, but only a few inches. Sam peered inside. Just as her hand went up to knock, she spotted Mrs. Griner, down on her knees, her face just inches from the wall.

Sam did not know it, but the cook was down there on the floor searching for peepholes. Since Jason's invasion of her privacy the night before, Greta had spent several hours combing every square inch of her living quarters. Brady might want to spy on the Hendersons, but no way was he going to spy on her. That was not part of the plan. Already she had located and plugged up one tiny hole in her living room and another one in her bedroom.

But now Sam, worried the cook might have fallen or had a stroke, pushed open the door and entered without knocking. "Mrs. Griner?"

Greta, surprised, lifted her head so fast she bumped it on the table beside her bed. She yelped in pain. Sam rushed to her and helped the cook to her feet. "I'm so sorry! I didn't mean to startle you. Are you okay?"

Greta rubbed the bump on her head. "I'm fine, yes. I was just . . . looking for something . . . an earring."

"I was afraid you'd fallen."

"No." Still rubbing her head, Greta went through the door into the living room.

Sam followed close behind. Greta sat on the sofa. Sam stood. A moment passed. Another moment.

"Did you need something?" asked the cook. "I believe the coffee's on."

Sam looked distracted. "The coffee? No. The coffee's fine. I . . . well, actually, I . . . I wanted to ask you something." Sam wondered if she could trust the cook.

"Yes?"

Sam hesitated. Long enough so that Greta asked another question. "Are you all right, honey? You look as though maybe you hit *your* head."

"No, I'm fine. Really. I just wondered about . . . well, I was wondering about . . . about Brady."

Now it was Greta's turn to hesitate, but only for a second. "Brady? What about him? I know he's away. Until the weekend, I believe."

Sam knew she needed to tread lightly. "I guess I wondered . . . what you knew about him?"

Greta immediately deflected the question by once again rubbing the bump on her head. A bump, by the way, which no longer hurt and had virtually disappeared. She nevertheless did her best to wince, then announced, "I guess I gave myself a pretty good crack. . . ."

"Let me get you some ice," kindhearted Sam said. She headed for the kitchen.

Greta did not try to stop her. She needed a moment to think, to get her thoughts in order. Time was beginning to compress. Decisions would have to be made.

She would certainly tell Sam something. But exactly what? And how much? A fine line of caution was needed.

But right now, Mrs. G. decided, as Sam came back into the living room with some ice wrapped in a dish towel, it would be best to say nothing. Not here in the house. Brady could be watching. Listening. Recording their conversation.

● ● ●

SO WHAT did Greta do? What did Greta say? Greta, who had lived a tough life. Greta, whose life had been dominated by cruel, physical, violent men. Her father. Her husband. Even her own son, who, as a boy, had watched his father treat women harshly and so had grown into a man who behaved much the same way.

Not to mention her nephew, another violent Irishman, a textbook psychopath.

What did Greta do? What did Greta say?

She told a little white lie. She told Sam and Jason and Megan that a flock of great blue herons had been spotted down along the Sound. The giant seabirds were migrating south. Maybe, she suggested, after breakfast, they should all go down and have a look.

So right after eating, Sam and Greta and the kids bundled up against the November chill and headed outside. They crossed the terrace and headed for the water.

There were, of course, no great blue herons down along the Sound. Just cold and wind and whitecaps. The kids, nevertheless, kept looking.

"I don't see any, Mommy!" shouted Megan into the stiff breeze. "Do you?"

"I see some seagulls, but no herons!"

Megan and Jason moved farther away along the shoreline.

Greta waited until the kids were out of earshot, then turned and faced Sam. Her face was very serious. "You asked me earlier about the caretaker."

Sam, shivering from the wind racing through her jacket, glanced at the cook. "Yes. I wondered what you knew about him."

"Well," said Greta, her words chosen with great care, "I just want you to know that I am a woman who tries very hard to mind her own business. My life is difficult enough without getting myself mixed up in the lives of others."

Sam nodded. "Of course. I understand." Her eyes watered from the cold and the wind.

"I will tell you something," continued Greta, "as long as it stays between us."

"It will. Don't worry."

"All right then," said Greta. And then, after a moment, "As far as Brady goes, I think you should be very careful."

For a brief instant Sam looked confused. Then she recovered. "Can you tell me why?"

"Because, Sam, I'm not sure you know who you're dealing with."

"Meaning?"

"Meaning just that."

Sam studied Mrs. Griner's face. It was a full, round face with a few laugh wrinkles around the mouth and at the corners of her dark brown eyes; eyes that gave away nothing, not a clue.

"I have to go back," Greta said suddenly, looking away. "I left something in the oven."

Sam could not recall anything in the oven, but she nevertheless allowed Mrs. Griner to retreat without asking her another question. Then, slowly, she turned and faced the water. She saw Jason and Megan still walking along the shoreline, still searching for those great blue herons; herons, she now knew, they would never find.

And beyond the kids she saw the boathouse, Brady's boathouse. What, she wondered, did Mrs. Griner mean? Why did she have to be careful? Who was Brady? Wasn't he just the caretaker?

Suddenly Sam felt very distant from her old life,

from Gunn and her two children, from their lovely home in Virginia. She felt as if she had turned her back for just a split second, but in that spit of time she had dropped her guard and utterly lost control.

67 For the rest of the morning Sam thought about what Mrs. Griner had said about the caretaker. She thought about those secret passageways and those peepholes in the walls. The cautious side of her demanded immediate departure. Pack up and go, one whole side of her brain kept lecturing. But the other side saw no need to panic. There was no real proof, after all, that Brady had done anything wrong. In fact, since the day she had first met him, the man had been sweet and shy and kind. And later he had been loving and giving and, she thought, honest.

But she could not stop thinking about those candy wrappers. (Jason, under gentle interrogation, had denied they belonged to him.) Nor could she stop thinking about the cook's call for caution. Mrs. Griner's words kept ringing in Sam's ears: *I'm not sure you know who you're dealing with.*

Although, Sam reasoned, her thoughts whirling round and round, Mrs. Griner did not know that Sam knew about the third floor of the barn, or about Brady's computers, or about the caretaker's impending software deal with Mr. Reilly. Surely this was all the cook meant when she counseled caution. After all, Sam asked herself, what else could there be? For all Sam knew, Mrs. Griner might have some hidden agenda of her own, some reason why she wanted to keep Sam away from Brady. It was possible the cook's comments might be nothing more than a means to make Sam paranoid. Unlikely, Sam thought, but possible.

She puzzled over the whole mess while she busied herself preparing for their weekend in New York. She kept telling herself that Brady was not a bad man. No way would she have fallen in love with a bad man. Well, with the exception of Gunn.

The thought allowed her a brief smile. She decided to stop wasting energy on this nonsense. Brady, after all, would be home in a few days. If she had lingering doubts, she would simply tell him.

She bustled about the children's bedrooms, pulling socks and underwear and sweaters from their drawers. Then she went to her closet to search for a dress she could wear to Thanksgiving dinner. Mandy had called a few days earlier to tell her Tad had made reservations "somewhere special. He won't tell me where."

Sam held up her long black dress in front of the mirror. Next she tried on the blue one. Then the gray one. She could not decide.

Suddenly she turned and stared at that tiny hole in the wall. She felt like she was being watched; a feeling, strangely, that she'd had several times since moving into the mansion last spring.

"The blue one," announced an invisible voice. "It goes with your eyes."

Sam, startled, just about jumped out of her shoes. "Jason? Damn you! Are you back there?"

"No," answered the voice, "it's Saint Ralph the Dress God sending you free fashion advice."

"Dammit, Jason! I told you to stay out of there."

Jason chortled. "Sorry, Mom. I couldn't resist. I guess I'm just a voyeur at heart."

Sam felt a dull throb behind her eyes. A sizable headache was well on its way.

* * *

AFTER LUNCH Sam asked Mrs. Griner to watch Megan for an hour or so. Her doubt now running rampant, Sam told the cook she needed to spend a little time alone with her son. She did not add that their time together would be spent investigating the caretaker.

Although, in her own mind, Sam did not classify it as an investigation. No, she was simply curious. She merely wanted to know more about the man with whom she had recently become so intimate. It seemed like the wise and prudent thing to do.

Sam enticed Jason to accompany her by suggesting he might get to play the computer game Brady had invented. What had he called it? THE AVENGER? A title that both intrigued and now troubled her.

"But," objected Jason, "he told me not to use his computer when he wasn't around."

"Oh, right," replied Sam. Then, "Let's go have a look anyway."

Jason was not real excited about venturing out into the cold, but after a bit more prodding, he went along. They found the trapdoor to the third floor of the barn sealed with a padlock. "I guess," said Jason, descending the ladder, "Brady doesn't want me up there."

"I guess not," agreed the boy's mother.

Halfway down the stairs to the first floor, Jason stopped. "Wait a second," he said. "I want to check the bats."

"Bats? What bats?"

But Jason did not answer, not right away. He ran down the second floor hallway and into the small storage room where he had first seen the caged bats. The two bats were still there, but they were now dead; dead from no food or water, dead from neglect. Brady, in his lustful pursuit of Sam, had forgotten all about the bats. Another in a growing list of mental errors.

Jason was visibly upset. "God, Mom! Look at them. Brady just left them in there to die."

Sam squeezed her son's shoulder. She couldn't bear to see the boy so upset. "He wouldn't do that, Jason. You know Brady as well as I do. Do you remember how we wanted to kill the bats that got into Megan's bedroom? But Brady said no, we should save them." Sam glanced at the two limp bats. "I think these guys must have been sick." But even as she reassured her son, her own doubts continued to rise.

They went back outside, back out into the bright autumn sunlight. A cold, almost icy breeze continued to blow off the Sound.

"Let's take a walk down to the boathouse," suggested Sam.

"Why?" whined Jason. "It's freezing. Let's go back to the house."

"Come on, Jason," urged the boy's mother with a smile. "Humor me. Where's your sense of adventure?"

"I don't want to go down there."

"Why?"

"Because it's too cold." And with that, young Jason

took off. He made a beeline back to the warmth of the big house.

And so, somewhat reluctantly, Sam turned and headed for the boathouse alone. She made her way across that windy sweep of half-frozen lawn. Odd how different the grounds of the estate looked now, compared to when she and Gunn had first visited back in the spring. Had her first visit come at this time of year, she thought, she might never have agreed to make the move. Everything looked so barren, so bleak, so cold and forbidding. And it was not yet even December. Sam imagined a long, gloomy winter ahead.

She went directly to Brady's front door. But just as she'd expected, the door was locked. So were all the windows.

She made her way down the stone stairs and out onto the wooden dock. The wind and the whitecaps nudged the dock from side to side. The three large overhead doors, almost twice the size of conventional garage doors, had been pulled closed to protect the boathouse and its contents from the impending weather. But a small door built into one of the overhead doors swung open when Sam pulled on the knob. Sam went quickly inside, out of the wind. She shivered.

The boats had been pulled from the water. The big mahogany runabout hung from a pair of sturdy davits supported by the rafters. The sailboat, the Boston Whaler, the canoe, the kayaks—all of the boats had been hauled out of the water to protect them from the long winter ahead. Everything except for the two Jet Skis bobbing on the surface down at the end of the far bay. Spotting them, Sam immediately recalled the accident that had occurred back in August, when Gunn and Jason had nearly been injured. The memory made her shiver again.

Why had she walked all the way down here? What had she hoped to find?

She slowly crossed the boathouse. The wooden floor creaked with every step she took. She did not want to be here. Not now. Not alone.

A couple of barn swallows suddenly fled their protective cover just over Sam's head. Their noisy exit sucked the breath right out of her lungs. She practically jumped out of her skin. Sleuthing was definitely not her forte.

A steep, narrow stairway led to Brady's living quarters. Distracted and uncertain, Sam climbed those stairs, the smell of salt and canvas and engine oil ripe inside her nostrils.

The back door to Brady's apartment was also locked. Sam wondered if she should break the lock, force her way inside. No, she did not have the courage to do something so rash.

She looked over the railing at the boathouse below. At all those boats and all that equipment. Everything clean and put away and in excellent repair. Brady took care of the boats. Just as he took care of everything on the estate. He was a very fastidious and hardworking guy. And also a decent guy, Sam reminded herself, honest and humble.

Why, she asked herself, had she suddenly become so paranoid about the caretaker? So unsettled? So suspicious? Because of a few candy wrappers on the floor behind the wall? Because of a couple of dead bats?

Because of Mrs. Griner's unsubstantiated cry for caution?

"Nonsense," she muttered out loud. "Total nonsense."

She turned to go. The time had come to return to the house, to finish her packing for the holiday weekend ahead.

Two more swallows suddenly shot out from under the roof rafters the second Sam hit the top step. Startled, she lost her balance and began to fall. She threw up her arms and caught herself on one of the narrow wooden rafters above her head.

Something must have been on top of the rafter because Sam saw it flash past her eyes and bounce down the stairs. Something solid and black. Sam caught her breath, then she went down to see what had fallen.

Sam had no idea, but it was the remote control box for the Jet Ski. Brady had placed it up on that rafter some weeks earlier during one of Sam's first visits to the boathouse. It had been sitting out in plain view on the kitchen counter. Brady had scooped it up, opened the back door, and placed it overhead on top of that rafter. Then, in the passion that followed, he had forgotten all about the black box.

Now, at the bottom of the boathouse stairs, Sam held the black box in her hands. She did not have the slightest idea what it was or what it did. But she nevertheless pressed the Power On button.

A moment later the boathouse filled with a deafening roar loud enough to make the walls rattle. It sounded to Sam like a chain saw or maybe a motorcycle. She wanted to drop the box and plug up her ears.

But then she saw the water in the far bay churning.

One of those Jet Skis was running. The black box, Sam quickly realized, must have turned on the engine, like one of those remote control cars.

Sam did not immediately make the connection between the black box and the accident that had occurred back during the summer. But she did take a more careful look at the box, at its antenna and its numerous knobs and dials. Then she took another look at the Jet Ski. It idled there on the surface of the water, smoke spewing out of its tailpipe.

And then she began to see the connection.

"My God!"

She searched for the Power Off button. She wanted that piercing noise to stop, for silence to return, for suspicion to dissolve. She wanted to get out of the boathouse, now, right now! But her hand slipped. She hit the accelerator instead, the large dial that controlled the speed.

The Jet Ski roared. And shot forward. It moved as though launched from a rocket booster. In seconds flat it skimmed across the water and slammed into the heavy-duty overhead door.

A few moments later, except for that relentless wind and the sound of Sam's breathing, silence returned to the boathouse.

68 Almost midnight now. Sam paced back and forth across her bedroom. Try though she did, she could not clear her thoughts or think coherently. She had the children in bed and the bags packed for the weekend. They would be leaving first thing in the morning. Right after breakfast. For New York. To spend Thanksgiving with Mandy and Tad. Sam knew all this, but somehow it seemed utterly impossible to keep even those few simple facts straight. Her brain kept slipping, losing traction, failing to focus.

Earlier the kids had asked about their father. Where was he? When was he coming home? Would he be there for Thanksgiving? Sam, too much of a coward to tell them the truth, told them what she had been telling them all along: Dad was very busy, working, supporting the family he loved, getting this new job off the ground. He probably would not make it home for Thanksgiving.

The whole mess swirling around her like a dust cloud of confusion, Sam continued to pace. Each time she closed her eyes she saw Brady at the controls of that black box. She saw her husband and her son on that Jet Ski. She saw Brady increasing the speed. She saw Gunn and Jason going faster and faster, unable to slow the machine down. She saw Brady turn the speed up even higher. And then she saw Gunn and Jason abandon ship, their bodies bouncing across the surface of the water. They could have been seriously injured. Or even killed. They could have died.

Sam did not close her eyes. She kept them open. She stayed on her feet. She kept moving, pacing, thinking. . . .

For a minute or more after the Jet Ski plowed into the boathouse door, Sam had stood there in shock, staring at the scene. The door had been cracked and splintered, the fiberglass Jet Ski a fractured mess. It had picked up so much speed over such a short distance. Sam stared at the damage, and then, her heart firing like a machine gun, she dropped that black box onto the floor and fled from the boathouse. Her first impulse after reaching the house had been to gather Jason and Megan and flee PC Apple Acres. But that's when the kids had asked about their father. Then Mrs. Griner appeared and announced dinner would be ready in a few minutes. So Sam struggled to regain her composure. She finally decided to stay until morning. After all, the caretaker was three thousand miles away.

But still Sam paced. Back and forth. The phone rang. She knew it would be him. She did not want to answer it. Yes, she did. She wanted to answer it and demand an explanation. It rang six times before she finally picked it up. "Hello?"

"Hi. It's me."

Who? Sam wondered, almost out loud. *Who are you? Who are you really?*

"I thought maybe you weren't there."

"I'm here."

He was calling from the coast. To tell her he loved her and missed her and couldn't wait to see her.

No way, Sam told herself, listening to that tender and absolutely sincere voice, did this man try to kill my husband and my son on that Jet Ski. Impossible. Ridiculous. Absurd. There is no reason on earth why he would have done such a thing.

But the evidence down at the boathouse told a different story.

She did not tell the caretaker she loved him. Or missed him. No, she simply called him sweet, then asked about the weather.

He sensed immediately something was wrong. Last night it had been the secret passageways. Was it the same thing tonight? Or had she discovered something else to cause her dismay?

"Everything okay?" he asked, as casually as possible.

"Yes," she answered. "I'm just tired."

"Oh, Sam, it's three hours later there. I forgot."

No you didn't, she thought. "That's okay," she said.

"So you're sure everything's all right?"

Sam had never been good at keeping secrets. Even as a child secrets had made her head hurt. It had always been easier to just tell the truth. And so that's what she did now, even though the cautious side of her brain kept shouting at her to shut up, keep her mouth closed, hang up, get her children, and run for her life.

"I had some trouble," she began, "down at the boathouse today."

Brady's paranoia began to twitch. "Trouble?"

"I was out for a walk," she continued. "I went onto the dock. It was cold and windy so I ducked into the boathouse. You know, down below, where the boats are."

"Yes, below," mumbled the caretaker, his mind spinning in an effort to anticipate the trouble.

"So I was inside," explained Sam, "just to get out of the wind . . ." A lie, and she sensed immediately he knew it. "And, well, I found this . . . this . . . this device . . . this black box."

"Black box?" Brady asked the question, but he now had his answer. He did a little pacing of his own, back and forth in his hotel suite. He saw the entire scenario unfold back at PC Apple Acres. He smacked himself yet again on the side of the head for being such an idiot, for not taking care of business.

He had meant to get rid of the black box. Hide it in a safe place or maybe destroy it altogether. Of course he had. But his mind had been elsewhere. He knew where his mind had been.

Sam continued to speak, to draw a picture of what had happened. But Brady already knew what had happened. Sam had somehow found the remote, switched it on, and then all hell had broken loose. Oh, yes, the caretaker could see the damage. The physical damage and the emotional damage. He knew his sweet Samantha must be reeling from this latest blast.

"Accelerated," he heard her say. "Raced forward. Plowed into the door."

Why, Brady asked himself, couldn't she have just stayed out of the damn boathouse, minded her own business? What, he wondered, was Sam really doing down there? What had she been looking for?

"Brady," he heard her ask, "where did the black box come from? What is it for?"

A first-class mind sucked these questions into the vortex of its brain and instantly spit out an answer. It might not be the perfect answer, but it would do in a pinch. It would have to do. He had to say something.

He made his voice sound perfectly calm. "Oh, that thing. I thought I'd lost it." Yes, he told himself, attack the center. No flanking maneuvers now. "I rigged it up over the summer after your husband and Jason had their trouble with the Jet Ski. You remember, when the throttle got stuck."

He knew damn well she remembered. She had undoubtedly been thinking about little else but that damn black box for the past several hours.

But right now only one word penetrated Sam's defense. It was the only word that mattered. She repeated it. "After?"

"Yes," replied the caretaker. "I wanted an easy way to test the operation of the Jet Ski without actually having to go out on the water myself." Brady knew this sounded lame, but he pressed ahead anyway. "By gearing the Ski up to a remote, I could test it just by standing at the end of the dock. It wasn't ideal, but it worked reasonably well. I kind of lost interest after realizing Jason and your husband probably weren't going to use the machines anymore."

Nice touch, he told himself. Good finish.

"Yes," said Sam, after a brief pause, "I see." She did not really see, but she very much wanted, needed, to accept the caretaker's explanation. The alternative was simply too disturbing.

Brady, sensing an opening, took the bull by the proverbial horns. "Listen, Sam, don't worry about the Ski getting busted up. It's not your fault. It's my fault for leaving the remote lying around. I'm just glad you weren't hurt."

Sam did not know what to say. Her thoughts spun in a thousand different directions. Should she believe him or condemn him? Trust him or assume everything he says is a lie? Ask more questions or seek answers elsewhere?

Brady, fully aware of her mental conflict, decided to just keep talking. So for the next few minutes he softly and gently, and extremely persuasively, soothed Sam's concerns. He did the best he could under the circumstances.

And he did quite well. Sam actually bought some of it. But not enough of it to declare her everlasting love as their conversation drew to a close. Instead, before they hung up, she simply asked Brady when he would be home.

The caretaker took a moment to consider his answer. "Saturday afternoon would be my best guess right now. I doubt it will be any sooner."

This was a lie. Brady fully intended to head home immediately. ASAP. On the first available flight. He needed to contain the damage. He needed to get back to PC Apple Acres while Sam was in New York City with her friend. It would give him time to assess the damage, find out if she had uncovered any other nasty little secrets.

Sam, however, had a few ideas about returning home a day or two early herself.

• • •

SAM HUNG UP the phone and climbed into bed. She slipped between the sheets. And closed her eyes. Within seconds she fell asleep. This speedy slumber came over Sam not because she suddenly had all her emotional ducks in a row, but rather because complete and utter exhaustion had finally descended upon her. She was spent. Worn out.

She awoke just before seven. She did not waste time. She did not want to give her brain an opportunity to start mulling over the emotional maelstrom that her life had become.

By eight she had the kids up and showered and dressed. By nine they had eaten breakfast and were ready to roll.

Mrs. Griner followed them to the front door. "Have a good time," said the cook, who would not be cooking the Thanksgiving bird this year; she had been invited to a friend's house in town.

"We should be back on Saturday," said Sam. "Probably in the afternoon."

"That's fine. Enjoy the city."

Then out the door and into the Explorer and down the drive. Sam felt a great sense of relief as she pulled through the gate and made her escape.

• • •

THE CARETAKER, however, had no intention of allowing Sam to escape. She was his now, and he meant to keep it that way.

Too bad the CEO of Graphic Software, Inc., was going nowhere fast. Massive holiday crowds at airports around the country, coupled with early snowstorms in the Midwest, kept Brady grounded at San Francisco International Airport. He waited in relative luxury in the VIP lounge for first-class travelers on American Airlines, but like the teeming masses out in the terminal, he waited nevertheless.

The caretaker, like his adversary Gunn Henderson, did not excel at waiting. He did not enjoy being put on hold. He paced around the VIP lounge, his third cup of coffee, laced heavily with cream and sugar, steaming in his hand.

◆ ◆ ◆

G. HENDERSON was still hanging out at Carl Patrick Donovan's Upper East Side penthouse. With his sweet Nita, of course. Only sweet Nita was no longer quite so sweet.

The once dynamic duo of Creative Marketing Enterprises had been having their share of spats. Nita was sick to the bone of Gunn Henderson and his boozy, arrogant attitude. She could not wait for the man to go away. The sooner the better. Today, Thanksgiving Day, would be just fine with Nita.

And Gunn might have gone, had the man had anywhere else to go. Home was out of the question. Sam, he knew, would spit in his eye, probably kick him in the groin. And he didn't have the dough to go anywhere else. Except maybe to his parents. But they were old and sickly. It would be incredibly depressing to go there. Besides, he would have to spend the whole time explaining the absence of his wife and kids.

So what did Gunn do? He went to the fridge and grabbed a beer. At ten-twenty in the morning.

The loving couple's spat this festive morn concerned Gunn's demanding stomach. Nita did not do much to tend to Gunny's belly. "Nita doesn't cook," was one of Nita's mantras. She didn't shop or clean much, either.

Nita wanted to go out for Thanksgiving dinner. Gunn, broke, wanted to stay in. Nita wanted Thai food. Gunn wanted the traditional Pilgrim feast: turkey, mashed potatoes, gravy, beans, and pumpkin pie.

"If you want that," Nita, ready to blow the lid off this whole charade, told him, "you'd better go see your mommy or your wife, because this girl doesn't do the traditional Pilgrim thing."

Gunn belched and pulled the tab off another Bud.

69 Sam, with the help of several chilled glasses of expensive pinot noir, had a wonderful Thanksgiving dinner at Tavern on the Green. Megan, in a pretty pink party dress, sat on her right, hair gleamy, face rosy with excitement. Jason, looking spiffy in his Jerry Garcia tie and navy Ralph Lauren blazer, sat on her right. Remarkably, both displayed exquisite table manners throughout the marvelous five-course meal. Only near the end did Jason begin to grow restive.

They sat at a large round table. Also present were Mandy, Tad, Tad Jr., and little Danielle. They talked about Virginia and East Hampton and the weather and whether or not life existed on Mars and the menu and the food and the dessert cart. No one mentioned Gunn. They had a fine time.

Before the coffee arrived, Sam and Mandy excused themselves for a trip to the powder room. Once safely away from their families, Mandy asked, "So, Sam, how's it going without the big bruiser around the house? You look tired, honey. Like you haven't slept in weeks."

Sam sighed and thanked her friend for the reassuring words. She then peered into the mirror and tried to hide the dark circles under her eyes with more makeup. It didn't do much good. "Mandy . . . we need to talk."

"So talk."

"Alone. In private."

Mandy understood. "I'll tell Tad to take the kids somewhere. We can talk back at the hotel."

● ● ●

In an effort to reach New York, Brady had to first fly to Houston. From Houston he skipped over to New Orleans. Which was where he sat while Sam powdered her nose and tried to make those black things under her eyes vanish into thin air.

The airline told Mr. Donovan he would have to fly to Atlanta, then north to Nashville, and finally on to La Guardia. Mr. Donovan was not happy about this, but heavy holiday volume made it the only possible route. The ticket agent told him he could expect to be back in New York early the following morning.

"Great," said the caretaker. "Swell." When THE

AVENGER becomes a hit, he told himself, I'll buy my own goddamn jet.

His Thanksgiving feast consisted of dried-out turkey, fake potatoes, and canned peas. The caretaker was not a happy traveler.

◆　◆　◆

GUNN DID NOT fare much better. After his fourth beer he finally agreed to take Nita out. Unfortunately, they did not have a reservation. Every place they went was either closed or booked. They finally wound up at some greasy spoon over near the East River under the tram to Roosevelt Island. Like the caretaker, Gunn did the dried-out turkey, fake potato, canned veg meal. He ate it anyway. Three helpings.

Nita did not eat a bite. The food made her sick just looking at it. "What a feast," she mumbled. "I feel like a Rockefeller or a Vanderbilt."

"Shut up," hissed Gunn, his mouth full. "Quit your whining."

And Nita knew the jig was up. The party was definitely over. No one ever told Louisa May Chance to shut up.

70

"So," demanded Mandy, "what is it? What's going on?"

Sam and Mandy sat up in Sam's room at the Westbury Hotel at Madison and Sixty-seventh. Neither of them knew it, but Gunn and his no-longer-fresh squeeze Nita were passing by the hotel at that very moment. The not-so-loving couple were on their way back to the penthouse after their Thanksgiving feast down along the East River. The couple did not speak. Gunn carried a brown paper bag under his arm. The bag contained a fifth of Jimmy Beam.

"That's the problem," Sam told her friend. "I don't know what's going on. I have no idea."

"Okay, then," said Mandy, who loved a good puzzle, "let's figure it out."

After leaving Tavern on the Green, Tad had taken the kids to Rockefeller Center to hopefully go ice skating as long as two or three million other people hadn't come up with the same post-holiday-dinner idea. Mandy had ordered him not to return to the hotel for at least two hours. "Sam," she'd informed her husband, "needs to talk."

Indeed Sam did. Once she got started, she talked and talked. Practically nonstop for over an hour. Mandy, a pretty fair motor-mouth in her own right, let Sam go.

Sam told Mandy she had fallen in love with Brady the caretaker.

Mandy, a devilish grin on her face, told Sam she was a naughty girl.

"I'm a stupid girl, that's what I am," Sam said, frowning.

"Why do you say that?"

Sam told her why. Sam told her friend the whole story. At least her somewhat fragmented version of the whole story. Sam had a tendency to tell any story in bits and pieces. Continuity was left up to the listener; in this case, Mandy.

Sam told Mandy about the passageways concealed behind the walls of the mansion. About the candy wrappers lying on the floor near the peepholes.

"Peepholes?" asked Mandy.

"Peepholes," answered Sam glumly.

"You're kidding me. Real honest-to-God peepholes like in the old horror movies?"

"Exactly." Then Sam told Mandy about the dead bats lying in the cage in the barn. Before Mandy could ask about the significance of this, Sam moved on to Brady's roomful of computers. And then, barely pausing to draw breath, she launched into a diatribe about this insanely violent computer game Brady had invented called THE AVENGER.

Mandy looked bewildered. "I thought Brady was

the caretaker. Now you're telling me he invents computer games? Sounds like a Renaissance man to me."

"It gets worse."

"Worse than candy wrappers and computers?"

"Mandy, I really don't need you to be facetious."

"I know. I'm sorry."

"This is serious."

"I was just trying to get you to smile, sweetie. Maybe relax a little."

"It's kind of tough to relax when I think the guy I've fallen in love has been spying on me through a peephole."

Mandy could not help herself. Life had left her a cynic. "I can see how that would be pretty unsettling."

"Mandy!"

"Sorry." Then, "You said it gets worse. Tell me."

Sam sighed and moved on. "Do you remember when you came to visit over the summer?"

Mandy nodded. "Of course."

"Remember when we went down to the boathouse to watch Tad and Gunn and the boys ride around on those Jet Ski things?"

"Sure, I remember. Gunn and Jason had trouble with theirs. They almost crashed. It was pretty scary. They had to jump off."

"Yes," she replied softly. "They had to jump off. They could have been killed." And then she launched into her tale of finding the black box. She described in perfect detail what had happened down at the boathouse less than twenty-four hours earlier. She did not leave out a single dramatic element.

And by the time Sam finished her tale, her friend's attitude had changed course one hundred and eighty degrees. Mandy no longer looked or sounded coy; she now looked and sounded horrified. "My God, Sam! This is sick!"

Then Sam told Mandy about her conversation with Brady on the telephone the previous night. She reiterated his explanation.

"Oh, what a load of bullshit that is," declared Mandy, her tone edged with hostility. "He built the remote *after* Gunn and Jason nearly killed themselves."

"So you don't buy it?"

Mandy looked at her friend and rolled her eyes. "Don't tell me *you* do?"

Sam shrugged. She wanted her friend's unbiased opinion.

"You wouldn't buy it either, honey," continued Mandy, "if you didn't have some weird love thing going on with this guy."

"Believe me," said Sam, "I don't buy it. Not for a second. But last night there was something inside me that really wanted to believe him. I mean, he's treated me better than any man has ever treated me. Always a perfect gentleman. Always so sweet and gentle."

"They all seem that way, honey. For a while."

Sam shrugged again. She knew Mandy's opinion of men. "The thing that troubles me," she asked, not really expecting an answer, "is why? Why is he doing these things? What did we ever do to him?"

"Maybe you didn't do anything. Maybe this one is just plain old fucked up. Some kind of psycho."

"I don't know. I think there's more to it than that."

"Hey, there's lots of psychos around these days doing lots of really weird stuff. And nobody knows why. Every time you open the newspaper or turn on the tube there's some nut bird blowing up a building or shoving his wife into a wood chipper."

"Mandy! That's disgusting."

"But true."

Sam shuddered. "So what should I do?"

"What should you do? You should stay the hell away from that man, that's what."

"You think so?"

"Absolutely."

"I don't know. . . ."

"What do you mean, you don't know?"

"I could be jumping to all kinds of ridiculous conclusions. It would be nice to know more before I just dumped him."

"Look," Mandy told her friend, "there's plenty of men out there. Millions of them. Everywhere you go you see them. Lurking. A few of them are even decent sorts. I think it's best to stay away from the ones we even suspect might be psychopaths."

71 Gunn and Nita arrived back at Brady's penthouse in the middle of the afternoon, following their Thanksgiving feast. Gunn immediately cracked open the Beam. He settled down in front of Brady's big screen TV to watch pro football along with Jim, a bucket of ice, a pitcher of water, and a tall glass. By halftime of the Dallas–Washington game, Gunn had punched a sizable hole in that bottle.

Standing up to stretch, Gunn called out to his sweetie. "Nita, baby, come out here and see me."

Nita had herself tucked away in the master bedroom. She had put that bad Thanksgiving meal behind her and gotten on with business. The weeks between Thanksgiving and Christmas were a very busy time for Nita. Lots of people with suitcases full of money poured into the Big Apple. Many of them wanted adult entertainment. So Nita was on the phone, busy making appointments.

Gunn tried to get into the room. Too bad the door was locked. "Nita, open up! What the hell are you doing in there?"

Nita covered the mouthpiece. "I'm on the phone. With my mother."

"Oh the phone! Jesus! Just like fucking Sam. Always on the goddamn phone!" Gunn, scowling, turned and went back to Jim. But after a quick nip off the bottle, he returned to the bedroom door. "Nita, Christ, come on!"

Louisa May did not put up with much lip from men; never had. And she was just about at the end of her tether with this Gunn Henderson. Donovan wanted her to stay with the foulmouthed drunk at least through the end of the year. But how, she wondered, would she ever make it? The man was loud and obnoxious. A total egomaniac. A bum who ran out on his wife and kids the second she squeezed his testicles. Men like Gunn Henderson were the reason Louisa May had decided long ago to never marry. Nice and sweet for a while. Until they got their fill. And then—pigs. Men were the pits. Use 'em and lose 'em. That was Louisa May's motto.

And then the loud, obnoxious drunken bum slammed his broad shoulders into the bedroom door, ripping it right off its hinges. He stood there in the doorway, a great big wise-guy grin on his face. "You wouldn't come to me, baby. So I came to you."

"I'll have to call you back," Nita told the prospective client on the other end of the line. She hung up, then said to Gunn, "You're drunk."

That big grin got bigger.

"And horny," added Nita.

Gunn chuckled and began to disrobe. He pulled off his shirt without bothering to unbutton the buttons.

Louisa May had seen men strut their stuff many times before. She was not impressed.

Gunn kicked off his shoes and unbuckled his belt. Next came the undershirt, exposing his thick chest and powerful arms. Arms, Louisa May knew, that could snap her in half if she was not careful. But she was in no mood for this. She just wanted to get away from the son of a bitch. His bare flesh repulsed her. No way could she fuck him. She would rather puke on him. She could not continue this charade. Not for one more second.

To hell with Donovan, she muttered to herself, I'm outta here. I don't care about the money. He'll have to find some other way to deal with this jerk.

Gunn had his pants off. Only his socks and silk boxers remained.

Louisa May wondered how best to make it through the front door without Gunn getting his paws on her. She knew he was capable of violence. Donovan had told her what he'd done to his wife. And with all that booze flowing through his system, she knew caution would serve her well.

God, she thought, this is the last time I get myself mixed up in something like this. I don't give a damn how much money they offer.

Gunn reached down to pull off his socks. He stumbled and fell. To cover up his annoyance and his embarrassment, he laughed.

Louisa May took the opportunity to make her move. She climbed off the bed and started, not too hastily, for the bedroom door. As she passed, Gunn grabbed her ankle. "Where you heading, baby? Time for a little roll in the hay."

"That sounds swell, Gunn. But first I need to run out for a minute."

"For what?"

"I need something at the pharmacy."

Gunn let go of her ankle and pulled off his boxers. "Everything you need, baby, is right here."

Louisa May thought seriously about kicking him in the balls and making a run for it, but she feared his wrath if her attack failed.

"Take off your clothes, you sweet thing. Lie down on the bed."

Nita thought fast. "I could use a drink."

Gunn smiled and struggled to his knees. "Hey," he said, "now you're talking. Me, too." He stood and staggered into the living room.

Louisa May, happy to escape the bedroom, followed.

After some amount of spillage, Gunn filled his glass with bourbon. He handed the glass to Nita. She took a sip of the foul beverage, then tried to hand it back, but

Gunn waved her off. "You drink that. I'll pull off the bottle. Not much left anyway."

Nita sat on the sofa and pretended to drink the whiskey. What a slob this Gunn Henderson had turned out to be. A real swine. The dregs of the earth. And at first she had actually kind of liked him. He was tall and smooth and good-looking, with a strong, solid body. And he liked to stay in fancy hotels and eat at the best restaurants, order the finest wine. But that was all just surface crap. Underneath it, she knew, lurked a pig who deserved nothing less than total castration.

She wanted to tell him. She wanted to tell him the whole story. She had to tell him. Her ego would not allow her to leave till she had made a few incisions, drawn a few pints of blood. But she had to be patient. She could not just blurt it out. So she waited. She waited for him to empty the bottle. She waited while he grabbed the glass out of her hand and drained it.

He had himself sprawled out on the floor between the sofa and the TV. He lay there naked except for one blue sock he had been unable to remove. He was good and drunk now. Barely able to stand. Damn close to helpless.

Louisa May decided the time had come. Now or never. "Here's the thing, Gunn."

"What's the thing?" he slurred. "Mount me."

"I'm leaving."

"You going to the pharmacy? Why don't you pick up another bottle?"

"I'm leaving," Nita repeated. "And I'm not coming back."

He didn't get it. "Huh?"

"You're on your own."

Gunn took a second to catch up. "What do you mean, you're leaving? You're not leaving." He did his best to rise off the floor, but he only managed to drag himself onto his knees.

"Yes, I am."

He did not even ask why. "Fuck, Nita, I left my wife for you! I left my kids! You're not going anywhere, goddammit!"

Nita was off the sofa, halfway to the front door. She felt reasonably safe, like she could say her piece, and, if necessary, make her escape if Gunn moved on her. "You're a fool, Gunn. A complete and total fool. All this time you've been getting screwed and you didn't even know it. You still don't know it."

Gunn, still on his knees, leaned against the sofa. He had a headache, a dull throb right behind his eyes. And he felt sick. "What the hell are you talking about? The only person I've screwed is you."

Louisa May knew she should keep her mouth closed, utter not one more word. Just grab her coat and go. She knew Donovan would be ticked off enough at her just for leaving. But he would be royally peeved if she actually spilled the beans to this bastard. But look at him, the slob, thinking he's so sexy, so together and charming. Nita had to tell him. She had to blow him out of the water. There was no justice in the world if she kept this secret to herself.

And so, the high-priced call girl opened the dam, and the water came rushing through.

"I'll tell you what I'm talking about, Gunn. I'm talking about a con job. A good, old-fashioned con job. Involving money, sex, and greed. And probably a few other things that I don't even know about."

Gunn, the nausea beginning to spiral through his belly, had his head down between his knees. "What kind of bullshit are you spewing, Nita?"

"This is no bullshit, Gunn. This is your life. All shot to hell because you got greedy and because you wanted some very special nooky. But I never gave a shit about you, you verbose, egotistical asshole. I was just doing a job. Do you hear me? A job. For money."

"Money? What do you mean, money?"

"Money, Gunn. Cash. Greenbacks. Oil of the palm." Nita knew she should definitely nip the rest of it in the bud, but her tongue was happily wagging away. "And I wasn't getting paid by that guy Reilly either. Reilly was just another part of the con."

Gunn struggled to deal with both Nita's insinuations and his growing desire to heave. "Con? What con?"

Nita laughed and pulled on her coat. The time had come to clear out. "Just face it, Gunn, you've been fucked. That's the important point here for you to understand: You've been totally fucked. And believe me, you deserve it."

Gunn lifted his head long enough to glance at her. "Yeah, okay, I get it now. I've been fucked. But by who?"

Nita moved to the door. Soon, she knew, she'd be back in her apartment. Safe and sound. She put her hand on the doorknob.

"Who, goddammit? Who?"

Nita felt a nanosecond of pity for the bastard. "You mean you really don't know?"

Gunn shook his throbbing head.

"Donovan, for chrissakes. Carl Patrick Donovan."

Gunn had to use his hands to lift his head. The man was in a very bad way. "And who . . . the hell . . . is Carl Patrick Donovan?"

Nita laughed again. "Jesus, Gunn, you really are a mess. For a second there I almost felt sorry for you."

"Who is he?" Gunn lifted his aching head high and bellowed. "Goddammit, who the hell is he?"

Nita pulled open the door. She stepped out into the hallway across from the elevator. "I guess you know him as Brady. The caretaker."

And a moment later the door closed and Louisa May Chance slipped away.

72 Sam awoke in the middle of the night. So abrupt and so complete was her arousal that she knew any further slumber would be impossible.

The whole mess came flooding back into her brain. Within minutes she had rehashed the past nine months: from the arrival of that certified letter from Arthur J. Reilly of Creative Marketing Enterprises, to the discovery of that small black remote-control box and the crashing of the Jet Ski into the boathouse door. The entire sequence of events flashed by her wide-open eyes like some kind of superhigh-speed video.

Was that certified letter somehow related to the black box? And if so, how? And what, Sam wondered, was the connection between Brady and Arthur James Reilly?

It suddenly seemed like a good idea to get in touch with Mr. Reilly and ask him a few questions about his caretaker. But she had no idea how to contact him. Through Gunn, she thought, but she did not even know how to find her own husband. Not that she really wanted to find him, the bastard. Maybe she could call Mrs. Griner. The cook might know how to reach Reilly.

Sam snapped on the light. The other queen-size bed was empty. Jason and Megan were sleeping across the hall with Tad Jr. and Danielle.

Sam picked up the phone, got an outside line, and dialed the number at PC Apple Acres. The answering machine picked up after several rings. Sam glanced at the digital clock beside the bed. It was just after four in the morning. Mrs. Griner was undoubtedly still asleep. Sam hung up without leaving a message.

● ● ●

GUNN, just a few blocks away, tossed and turned. He had by now thrown up three times. His head felt like a balloon with far too much air in it. His sheets were soaked through with perspiration. He had no trouble admitting, at least to himself, that he had made a damn fine mess of things.

And so, like his wife over at the Westbury, he picked up the phone and dialed PC Apple Acres. He needed to talk to Sam. He needed to apologize for all his bad behavior and foolishness. He needed to ask her if she would take him back; beg her, if necessary.

What a lowdown, dirty, no-good schmuck.

The phone at the mansion rang and rang. The rings sounded like small explosions in Gunn's ear. Finally, the answering machine picked up. Gunn waited impatiently for the message to stop and the beep to sound.

"Sam, if you're awake, would you pick up the phone." He tried to sound sweet and pleasant, but it proved impossible. Too much booze and too little sleep had him right on the verge of nasty. "Goddammit, Sam, I want to talk to you. I want to see you. Now. Today. I'm coming out there. This morning." He thought it might be wise to stop there, just say good-bye and hang up. But his mouth kept moving. "Dammit, Sam, you better not be with that bastard Brady. I swear to God, if you are, I'll kill him. I'll kill the son of a bitch."

He slammed the phone down after that. And decided he would climb into what was left of his Porsche and drive out to East Hampton just as soon as he was a bit more sober. That way he could demonstrate to his wife, in person, what a swell fellow he really was.

● ● ●

MRS. GRINER heard every word of Gunn's message. She had been asleep, but the earlier call, the one from Sam, had woken her up. She had gone into the kitchen to answer it, but too late. Whoever it was hung up.

On her way back to bed the phone rang again. Who, the cook wondered, could be calling at such a god-awful hour?

The answering machine got to the call first.

Greta listened with amusement to Gunn's snarling voice. So, she thought, the prodigal husband is coming home. And with murder on his mind, no less. That whore, she assumed, must have finally spilled her guts.

● ● ●

AND WHAT about Brady? Where was he resting his head at this early hour the day after Thanksgiving?

On a first-class seat in the front row of a stretch DC-9. Too bad that DC-9 was sitting on the tarmac out at Nashville International Airport. That jet should have lifted off hours ago, but mechanics had thus far been unable to repair an electrical problem.

Brady, however, no longer fussed and fumed. His anger and frustration had dissipated long ago. He felt calm now, in control of his emotions again. He knew what he had to do.

And so he closed his eyes and settled back into that wide and comfortable seat. Within just a few minutes he heard the good news: The captain's voice reported that the problem had finally been fixed and they would be taking off as soon as possible.

Brady allowed himself a momentary grin. Soon he would be home, ready to solve problems.

● ● ●

BY FIVE o'clock Sam could not lie still for one more second. She threw off the blankets and scrambled out of bed. She had to do something. She could not just lie there, passive and inert.

She needed answers. And there was only one way to get them: Go back to PC Apple Acres and start digging. She knew if she stayed away now she might never learn the truth.

She had to talk to Mrs. Griner. She had to search Brady's apartment. And she had to do it now. This morning. Before Brady returned.

Sam quickly washed her face and combed her hair and brushed her teeth. She felt better being on the move. Lying in bed she had felt incredibly tense and anxious.

She sat at the desk and wrote two notes on hotel stationery. The first one was to her children.

Jason and Megan,

I had to go out for a while. I'll be back later.

Mr. and Mrs. Greer are right next door in Room 422. They're in charge. Make sure you do what they say. I'll see you this afternoon.

Love & kisses,

Mom

The second note was to Mandy.

Mandy,

I know you won't be happy about this, but I'm going back to the house. I'm going crazy just sitting here. I need some answers.

Don't worry. I'll be back before dinner. And since Brady's not due back until tomorrow or Sunday, there's no chance of my running into him.

Thanks in advance for watching M. & J.

See you later,

Sam

Sam folded the notes and pulled on her wool jacket and her black leather gloves. She stepped out into the deserted hallway. No one else was prowling around at that early hour. She slipped the notes under the appropriate doors. And then she took the elevator to the parking garage, climbed into her Explorer, and headed east.

Dawn had not yet broken as she sped across the nearly empty Queensboro Bridge.

● ● ●

GUNN WAS on the move also. He crawled out of bed right around the same time as his wife. He took a cold shower and put on fresh clothes. Then he left Brady's penthouse and went downstairs to where his Porsche was parked out on the street. The once snazzy sports car, such a wonderful automotive sight just a few short weeks ago, was a wreck. Some new damage had recently been inflicted. Someone had been jumping up and down on the roof. The trunk had been pried open. Everything in the trunk had been stolen: spare tire, jack, tools, even a greasy rag Gunn used to check the oil.

Gunn climbed in and fired up the engine anyway. She still purred like a tiger. Gunn accelerated away from the curb. Traffic was virtually nonexistent at that early hour. Gunn flew down Park Avenue and within minutes was speeding through the Queens-Midtown Tunnel. He hit the Long Island Expressway doing seventy-five.

Right around the Grand Central Parkway, just a few miles south of Shea Stadium, Gunn blew past Sam in her Ford Explorer. He must have been doing close to ninety by that time. He barely saw his wife's vehicle. No way did he recognize it.

Sam, doing a nice, safe sixty-two, saw the speeding Porsche, but not for a second did she think it belonged to Gunn. His Porsche was always perfectly clean and spotless. This thing was a wreck, a broken-down piece of junk. She forgot all about it even before it zoomed out of view.

Gunn kept the pedal to the metal. He had the speedometer hovering right around one hundred miles per hour when that cop pulled him over out near exit 62 near Farmingville.

And he was still pulled over some twenty minutes later when his wife, still cruising along at sixty-two, drove past him on her way to East Hampton. No way did she think her husband was sitting in that battered red car listening to a lengthy lecture from a bored and grumpy cop.

•   •   •

BRADY CONTINUED to bring up the rear in this race. He still had quite a lot of ground to cover. That DC-9 was somewhere over Pennsylvania, but already the pilot was beginning to make his descent into the New York metropolitan area.

Brady could feel his adrenaline beginning to flow. The limousine would be waiting for him. With a little luck he would be back at PC Apple Acres in a few hours.

73 Gunn surely would have reached PC Apple Acres first had it not been for the speeding ticket. And then, later, a serious lack of fuel. But the New York state cop clocked him doing eighty-six in a fifty-five, and because the Porsche looked like something that had been through World War III, Officer Smythe, grumpy that he had to work a double shift the entire holiday weekend, detained Gunn for over an hour. Only Gunn's smooth-talking charm kept his vehicle from being impounded on the spot. In a pinch, the supersalesman still had it. But his luck was fast running out.

● ● ●

SAM PULLED up to the front of the mansion a little after seven. She left the key in the ignition and headed for the front door. It was, as usual, unlocked.

Standing in the foyer, Sam called to the cook. "Mrs. Griner! Mrs. Griner, are you home?"

Greta was home. Fast asleep. Restless and anxious after Gunn's early morning phone call, she had taken a sleeping pill. It would be at least another hour before she came around.

Sam knew she could talk to Mrs. Griner later. She decided to head straight for the boathouse. Before she lost her nerve. Already an enormous amount of fear and apprehension had started to well up in her chest. She could feel it gathering behind her rib cage, closing in on her heart.

She went out the back door and down past the swimming pool. The water looked cold and uninviting. Sam could not believe she had been swimming just a few days ago. Naked. With a stranger. With the caretaker. It seemed somehow impossible; like something from another life.

She cut through the rose garden, brown and dormant, and crossed to the barn. No, not up to the third floor to Brady's menagerie of electronics, but to the shop on the first floor where Brady kept his arsenal of tools. From the workbench Sam grabbed a hammer and a couple of large screwdrivers.

Marching now, trying to work on her confidence, Sam quickly covered the open ground to the boathouse. She had to break into Brady's home, search his domicile, see what she could find. She had no choice. She had to protect herself. She had to protect Jason and Megan.

The sun had risen, but was obscured behind a layer of gray clouds. A raw wind whipped off the Sound. But Sam had no thoughts about the weather. The cold barely registered in her already overstimulated brain.

The front door of the boathouse was still locked. But this time Sam did not hesitate. She knew if she hesitated her courage would weaken, and then fail.

Sam held one of the screwdrivers against the lock on the door. She struck the screwdriver with the hammer. Repeatedly. Again and again. As hard as she could. It took some time, but finally the lock gave way.

The door swung open. Sam stepped inside and took a quick look around, her fear the caretaker might at any moment spring out mixing with her need to ransack his residence in a search for clues about the bizarre events swirling around her. Trembling, she went to work.

Sam had been in Brady's living quarters before. Many times, in fact, in the past weeks. But she had always been there with her head in the clouds, to make love, to lose herself in the caretaker's sweet kisses and gentle caresses. She had been mostly oblivious to her surroundings.

She was oblivious no more.

She switched on several lights and began to prowl. Her heart raced. What would happen if Brady suddenly arrived? What would she do? What would she say? How would she explain?

Sam assured herself she would not have to explain. Brady was a good man. And as a good man he would understand why she had to break into his home. He would understand her doubt and insecurity. But if he was not a good man, then what? Sam chose to push that possibility aside. After all, he was thousands of miles away, clear across the continent.

A computer sat on the desk in front of the picture window overlooking Shelter Island Sound. A few hints of sun broke through the clouds. The water glistened. Sam thought about that Jet Ski carrying her son as it raced out of control under the direction of that black box. Brady's black box.

Sam wished she knew more about computers. She would turn this one on right now and have a look at Brady's files. Maybe, she thought, I should have brought Jason along to help.

Beside the computer was a stack of Disks. Not computer disks, but the small wooden coasterlike Disks that were supposed to bring Sam and Gunn great wealth and financial independence. Sam sighed, thinking about it, and then she began to wonder what Brady was doing with a stack of Disks. The caretaker had nothing to do with the Disks. Or did he?

She opened the top center drawer. Nothing in there but pens and pencils and paper clips.

The boathouse creaked. Sam jumped. A shot of fear streaked through her bones. She took a deep breath and rubbed her eyes. When she opened them she spotted a wicker wastepaper basket beside the desk. A wide variety of empty candy wrappers lay inside the basket: Hershey's Kisses, Butterfingers, Milky Ways. Sam stopped breathing while she recalled a similar assortment of candy wrappers on the floor near the peephole in the secret passageway behind her bedroom. Clearly, the caretaker had quite a sweet tooth.

Sam, her fear and anxiety on the rise, rifled through the drawers of the desk. Nothing of much interest until she got to the bottom right-hand drawer. And there, under an unopened ream of computer paper, she found a nine-by-twelve manila envelope. Across the envelope it read: G.H. FILE.

Sam recognized her husband's initials immediately.

A connection? Or just a coincidence? Sam pulled the envelope from the drawer and undid the clasp.

◆ ◆ ◆

Back out on the Long Island Expressway, the distance between Carl Patrick Donovan and Gunn Henderson was closing fast. The caretaker's limo cruised smoothly at seventy-two miles per hour. Brady spotted a sign for Patchogue. He figured another hour. At the most.

Gunn, finally released by that state trooper, drove at a nice conservative sixty miles per hour. He did not want another ticket.

Other problems were fast developing, however.

Several miles west of Riverhead the Porsche began to cough and sputter. Gunn gave the engine more gas. But that just exacerbated the problem. It used up the last bit of premium flowing through the fuel injectors. The gauge told Gunn he had almost a quarter tank, but, in fact, there was nothing left but fumes.

Gunn cursed, punched the dashboard, then coaxed the Porsche over onto the shoulder.

Brady's limo bore down.

◆ ◆ ◆

Sam opened the manila envelope and pulled out the contents. It was a typed letter, folded in thirds. Sam unfolded it. The letter was to Michael Donovan of Staten Island, New York. Sam noted the date in the top right-hand corner. The letter was almost thirty years old. The paper had yellowed over the passage of time.

It was the letter of foreclosure to Carl Patrick Donovan's father. The letter was on Continental Bank and

Trust letterhead, but Sam did not make a connection. Not right away. She skimmed the first few paragraphs. She had absolutely no idea this Donovan fellow was the caretaker's father. The letter was boring, nothing but a bunch of legal mumbo jumbo about some poor man who was about to lose his house for failure to pay his mortgage.

Sam very nearly stuffed the letter back into the envelope without bothering to finish it. After all, it had nothing to do with her or her present predicament. Her eyes, however, scanned to the end. And at the bottom of the second page, after the Yours Truly, she spotted the large, bold signature of her father-in-law, Gunn Henderson, Sr., Vice-President in Charge of Mortgages and Small Business Loans.

For several seconds after she spotted that signature, Sam did not draw a breath. Her brain was too busy processing questions to tell her lungs to keep inhaling and exhaling. Who was this Donovan? Why did Brady have his old letter of foreclosure? What did this have to do with Gunn's father? What did this have to do with Gunn? Or with her?

She started to read the letter over. But she did not get very far. Suddenly the door slammed. Sam jumped straight into the air. And screamed. But when she turned around there was no one there. Not Brady. Not Gunn. Not Michael Donovan. Not a soul. The wind, Sam realized, heart hammering, must have blown the door closed.

Still, she thought, the time had come to move on, to continue her search. She tossed the letter onto the desk without bothering to put it away. Then she turned her attention to the rest of the room. She scanned Brady's books. Books on gardening, books on computers, books on history and chemistry and biology and finance. Books on psychology and psychiatry. He was, Sam knew, extremely well read. And quite brilliant. Definitely a tad more brilliant than your average caretaker on your typical country estate.

But what, she wondered, did this all mean? How did it all add up?

Sam felt that she now had even more questions than answers.

She moved to the kitchen area. On the wooden table where Brady ate his meals, she spotted a magazine. Her thoughts random and confused, she picked up the magazine just to see what the caretaker had been reading. It was a computer magazine called *Power Software.*

Without really paying much attention, Sam began to leaf through the pages. A bold headline caught her eye:

ON THE HORIZON

And below the headline a subheading:

GRAPHIC SOFTWARE'S CEO, C. P. DONOVAN, ONCE AGAIN BREAKS NEW GROUND

There was that name again: Donovan. Sam read on:

The reclusive head of Graphic Software, Carl Patrick Donovan, has finally broken his silence. The guru of action games recently told *Power Soft-*

ware that his company's new product will make all other computer games obsolete. Code named THE AVENGER, look for its release sometime early next year.

My God! thought Sam, THE AVENGER! That's the name of Brady's computer game!

And below the text, a photograph. A full-color photograph. Of Brady! Sam's eyes opened wide. She took a closer look. Just to make sure. Yes, it was definitely Brady. A few years younger, but without question it was him. It was her lover. It was the caretaker.

Sam stared at the photograph. She could not begin to get a handle on her thoughts. They raced from one set of stimuli to the next: CEO, GRAPHIC SOFT-WARE, CONTINENTAL BANK AND TRUST, THE AVENGER, THE CARETAKER, MICHAEL DONOVAN, CARL PATRICK DONOVAN, BRADY, GUNN HENDERSON, JR., GUNN HENDERSON, SR., JASON HENDERSON, MEGAN HENDERSON, SAMANTHA HENDERSON.

Sam dropped the magazine. It landed on the floor. She did not bother to pick it up. She needed air, fresh air. She turned and fled.

74 Carl Patrick Donovan's limousine raced past that deserted Porsche parked along the shoulder of the LIE. And a few minutes later it sped past a man marching furiously along the edge of the asphalt. That furious man would be Mr. Gunn Henderson. He needed petrol. But first he had to find a petrol station.

Brady saw neither the Porsche nor its owner. He sat in the back of the limo, his eyes lightly closed in meditation.

● ● ●

BACK AT THE MANSION, Greta rolled over and opened her eyes. Sleeping pills always made her feel slow and groggy, but she knew once she got up and got moving that lethargic feeling would wear off.

She went into the kitchen to make coffee. A cool draft blew through the room. Greta went down the hallway and into the foyer. The front door was wide-open. How had that happened?

She took a look outside before closing it. And there,

in the driveway, was Sam's Explorer. What was Mrs. Henderson doing back? And when had she arrived?

Greta closed the door and called upstairs. No answer. She went up to have a look. No sign of Sam or either of the kids. Where were they? And why had they come home so early?

Greta remembered the drunken message from Gunn. And now, without warning, a day sooner than expected, Sam was back. Clearly, something was up, but what? Her thoughts were cloudy, muddled by that sleeping pill. She decided to have a cup of coffee, think things over, get a handle on the situation.

◆　◆　◆

SAM MADE a beeline for the barn. She had a mission now. Her fear had vanished. Anger, and a desperate need to understand her family's connection to this Carl Patrick Donovan, drove her forward.

Why the charade? Why this intensive effort to pass himself off as some lowly caretaker named Brady? Why all the lies and deceptions? And what about those peepholes and that remote control?

Sam had a hard time coming up with any answers. And an equally hard time comprehending the depth of her own involvement. And the involvement of her family.

She climbed the stairs to the second floor of the barn. Hammer in hand, she scaled the ladder to the trapdoor that led to the room above. Immediately she began to pound that padlock with the hammer. But the lock proved resilient. It withstood the punishment. Sam needed heavier equipment.

She retreated to the utility room on the first floor.

She found a much larger hammer, much heavier, practically a sledge. Adrenaline pumping, she went back to work on that padlock.

After several more solid blows, the lock finally split open. It was not designed for that kind of abuse. Sam pulled it off its clasp and threw open the trapdoor. Seconds later she was in the room. It was warm in there, close to eighty. Too warm for Sam. She wanted to open a window. But the windows were closed. Sealed.

She pulled off her jacket and gloves, stood in the middle of that vast white space, and listened. The room was alive: computers, fax machines, modems. The office, Sam thought, of the future. Or the present.

She crossed to a fax machine, picked up a stack of plain-paper faxes. All were addressed to Carl Patrick Donovan or to Graphic Software, Inc. The faxes came from all over the world: London, Geneva, Hong Kong, Tokyo, San Francisco, Chicago. Computer lingo mostly. Technical stuff Sam could not begin to understand. But she understood enough to know that this Mr. Donovan was clearly an international businessman.

The room was spotless, not a speck of dust or a paper clip out of place anywhere. Something about the antiseptic quality of the room made Sam think of a hospital. And then of death. And thoughts of death swiftly brought back the fear. She felt herself tremble. Maybe, she thought, it would be best to go back to the house, pack a few more things, and leave. Go back to New York. Back to Jason and Megan. Deal with all this later. Perhaps with Gunn. Or possibly even the authorities. There might be more here than she could handle.

The phone rang. Sam jumped. The sound echoed off the walls. Sam looked for the source. She found it on the far side of the room, beneath an expansive window overlooking the estate. There was a bank of phones: four of them lined up like soldiers on a high white table.

The phone rang a second time. And a third time. And a fourth time. And then the answering machine took the call. Sam recognized the voice on the machine. It belonged to Brady. His message was soft, but curt.

"Leave your name and number. I'll call you back."

Sam heard a series of beeps, then the caller's voice came on the line.

"Hey, Mr. Donovan. It's Rick Parsons. Just calling to thank you again for the work. We had a hell of a nice run. I just wanted you to know . . ."

Sam knew that voice, but she could not immediately place it. Something about the accent or the intonation . . .

". . . wanted you to know I'm just a phone call away if you need my services. I'm ready and willing at any time to reprise my role of Arthur J. Reilly, corporate commander and gentleman extraordinaire . . ."

Mr. Reilly! thought Sam. Head of Creative Marketing Enterprises. Gunn's boss. Only . . .

". . . So call me if you need me, Mr. Donovan. *Ciao*."

The phone went dead. The answering machine made a few noises, then reset itself.

Sam, heart thudding, palms moist with sweat,

crossed to the phone. She replayed the message several times. *". . . ready and willing at any time to reprise my role of Arthur J. Reilly . . . ready and willing at any time to reprise my role of Arthur J. Reilly . . . ready and willing at any time to reprise my role of Arthur J. Reilly . . ."*

●　　●　　●

OUT ON THE LIE, Gunn made his way back to the Porsche. He now had a tank of gas in hand. One U.S. gallon.

The kid pumping gas that Friday dawn had offered to drive Gunn back to his vehicle, but he wouldn't be able to do so until someone else showed up for work.

Gunn hated to wait. So here he was walking.

He could see his Porsche in the distance. He figured it couldn't be more than half a mile away. On he trudged, a man shuffling toward his fate.

●　　●　　●

THE LIMOUSINE turned off Route 27 onto Stephen Hands Path. Brady was close now, and getting closer every second.

He figured, with Sam not due to return for at least another twenty-four hours, he would spend his time putting things in order, destroying evidence, preparing for his lover's return.

●　　●　　●

TOO BAD his lover had already returned.

Sam picked up one of the cordless phones and crossed to the computer table where the Power Mac 9600 was parked. She sat down and called the

Westbury Hotel. She had the front desk ring Room 424. Young Danielle Greer answered the phone. "Hello?"

"Danielle, it's Mrs. Henderson. Is Jason there?"

"He's still asleep."

"Wake him up, honey. I need to talk to him."

A couple minutes passed before Jason came on the line. "Mom?"

"Jason, listen to me. I need you to help me with something. I'm back at the house."

"In East Hampton?"

Sam sighed. She did not want to have to explain. "Yes, I had to take care of a few things. I'll be back this afternoon. But first I have to do something on the computer."

"The computer?"

"Yes," she said, "the computer." She wanted to get into the machine and see if she could find out anything else about this Carl Patrick Donovan. But she needed her son's help. "I already turned the power on," she told him.

"Whose computer are we talking about here, Mom? My computer?"

Sam could see this would not be easy. Jason always had to ask a million questions. He had to know everything. "No," she answered, "Brady's."

"Brady's?"

"Look, Jason, I'll explain later. Just help me out here. Tell me what to do. Tell me how to open files and search for information."

"What files?"

Sam told herself not to lose patience. That would only make the situation worse. "Any files."

"Any files, huh? Okay," said her son. "This is kind of weird, but let's give it a try. Tell me what you have on the screen right now."

Sam studied the large color monitor. "There's not really much. In the top right-hand corner there's a little box labeled HD."

"Right," said Jason. "That's your hard drive."

"And in the bottom right-hand corner there's a small trash can."

"Okay," said the kid, "here's what I want you to do. Take the mouse and use it to drag the arrow on the screen directly over the hard-drive icon."

Sam did as she was told. "All right."

"Now double-click the mouse."

Sam double-clicked. But during the double-click the arrow moved. "I did what you said, but nothing happened."

This time Jason sighed. The young man possibly had even less patience than his father. "Try it again," he ordered his mother. "Make sure the arrow stays on top of the icon."

Yes, this was definitely going to take some time. A commodity that Sam suddenly had a serious lack of.

● ● ●

THE LIMOUSINE pulled through the front gate of PC Apple Acres. Brady, rested and reasonably relaxed, stretched his arms and legs. It had been a long journey home from the coast. But now, finally, here he was, back at his estate, his fabulous estate bought with money he had earned with his brains and his toil. He had defied the odds, gone from rags to riches, despite the fact that he had lost his parents and his siblings while just a boy.

Now the time had come for him to move back into his spectacular home. In fact, he intended to sleep there that very night. And if he had his way, if things went well, Sam would soon be at his side in the master bedroom suite. The caretaker felt confident he could convince her it was the right thing to do.

But then the limo pulled into the circular drive and Brady's heart plunged. Sam's Explorer! What was that doing here? She had told him she would not be back from New York until at least Saturday afternoon. A ruse, he immediately assumed. Nothing but a ruse.

Brady climbed quickly out of the limousine, grabbed his bags, dismissed the driver. He crossed to the Explorer and pulled open the driver's door. Sam's keys dangled from the ignition. He pulled them loose and dropped them in his pocket.

A moment later he entered the mansion, silently and suspiciously. He stood in the foyer and made not a sound. A minute passed. Two minutes. Brady heard nothing. Could everyone still be asleep? He glanced at his watch: almost nine o'clock.

Brady went up the stairs and down the hallway to the master bedroom. No sign of Sam. The bed was made up neat as a pin. But there, on the floor! The panel leading to the hidden passageways!

Sam had never put it back.

Brady became instantly agitated. He kicked a hole in the wall beside the door and went back down the hallway. He checked the kids' rooms. They were both empty. Had they all gone to New York in a different car, or perhaps on the train? He went back downstairs.

In the kitchen, the scent of fresh coffee lingered in the air.

"Aunt Greta!" Brady called. "Are you here? Are you home?"

Greta was home. She was back in her bedroom, hiding in the closet. The caretaker might have entered the house with nary a sound, but canny Greta had heard his approach nevertheless. Momentarily startled by his unexpected arrival, she had retreated to her living quarters to make a few calculations. Perhaps her stars had finally come into alignment. There might, she realized, be an opportunity here. And opportunities, she knew, should not be squandered.

Greta told herself to stay calm and collected. Then she went forward to ply the waters of deception.

"Nephew," she said, upon reaching the kitchen, "you're home early."

"I concluded my business."

"And it went well, I hope?"

"I believe so."

"Well," she said, revealing nothing, "it's good to have you back."

Brady hesitated, then asked, "Is Sam home?"

"Sam?" Greta did her best to look uncertain. "I don't think so."

"Her car's out front."

"Then perhaps she is. I don't know. I haven't seen her. But then, I was asleep until just a few minutes ago."

"But she did go to New York? In her own car?"

"Yes. She left yesterday morning."

"Then she's come back. She's here somewhere."

"Did you look upstairs?"

"I did. She's not in the house."

Greta shrugged. She knew where Sam was. And she knew why. Mrs. Henderson was on the prowl. She'd become suspicious. Extremely suspicious. The cat was slowly slipping out of the bag.

"I'll bet she's in the boathouse," said Brady.

Greta offered her best expression of alarm. "You don't think she knows, do you?"

Brady scowled, shrugged, then replied, "I have no idea. She's been asking a lot of questions."

Greta shook her head, as though in disgust. "You never should have fallen in love with her, Nephew. It has clouded your judgment, caused you to lose focus."

The caretaker did not care to discuss it. He loathed criticism. So he turned and headed for the back door. "I'll go find her."

After the door closed and Brady started across the terrace, Greta said, "You do that, Nephew. You go find your sweet." And then she smiled, thinking this day might just make her move to America worthwhile after all.

● ● ●

SAM WAS finally making progress. Jason had showed her how to use the Find File command to search for information on the hard drive. Unfortunately, she had not yet found anything. At least nothing about her family. But she had uncovered some other troubling tidbits. Like the file on Arthur J. Reilly. Real name: Rick Parsons. Parsons's file contained an entire fictional biography, including place of birth (St. Andrews, Scotland), college attended (Oxford), and a long list of companies he purportedly owned. Creative Marketing Enterprises was right at the top of the list.

When Sam typed in "DISK," several files popped up. One of the files was a design program showing the small wooden Disk in various sizes, shapes, and angles: top views, bottom views, and side views. All were signed by C. P. Donovan.

Did this mean, Sam wondered, that Brady was the owner of Creative Marketing Enterprises? Was he the real inventor of The Disk? And if so, did it also mean Gunn worked not for A. J. Reilly but for Brady, for this Carl Patrick Donovan? The possibility unsettled Sam even further; although it also gave her a moment of rather perverse satisfaction.

"So exactly what," Jason asked his mother, "are we looking for?"

Sam decided she had to tell the boy something. "Last summer," she said, "Brady created a file on all the gardens here on the estate. It lists all the flowers and plants that—"

"Booor-ring."

"Well you wanted to know."

"Can I go back to bed now?"

"Just hang on a second." Sam felt better having her son on the line, safer, more connected. After all, it was to protect him and his sister that she had risked returning to PC Apple Acres.

She made several more searches. All proved futile. But then, scanning her brain for possible key words, she typed her middle name into the Find File box: Ann. Nothing. So she tried her maiden name: Quincy.

The hard drive spun. And continued to spin. It

found three matches. Four matches. It finally settled on half a dozen: Quincy One through Quincy Six.

Sam, pulse racing, clicked open Quincy One. The computer needed several seconds to load the file. It was obviously a large file; video files usually are.

And then, right there on the screen, Sam suddenly saw herself. It was a QuickTime video of her up in her bedroom. Nothing very interesting. It must have been shot in the morning. Sam watched herself as she brushed her hair, made the bed, sipped her coffee, studied her reflection in the mirror.

But how, she wondered, had Brady gotten the footage? When had it been shot? Where was the camera?

Brady's hidden cameras. The caretaker's extra set of eyes and ears.

"Mom! I'm sick of this. I wanna go back to bed."

"Just hang on a second. Tell me how to delete a file."

Jason muttered for a second or two under his breath, then he told his mother how to use the small icon of a trash can in the bottom right-hand corner of the screen.

Sam dragged Quincy One into the trash can and emptied it as per Jason's impatient instructions. Then she opened Quincy Two. Several seconds later, she was up on the screen again. This time she saw herself cross the master bedroom to the large picture window. Very slowly she drew open the drapes. And there, outside the window, was the swimming pool and the make-believe Matterhorn. Sam watched herself watching Brady swimming and diving.

• • •

BACK AT THE MANSION Greta replayed the message on the answering machine. The message from Gunn.

"Goddammit, Sam, I want to talk to you. I want to see you. Now. Today. I'm coming out there. This morning."

"So where are you?" asked Greta. "When are you coming out to pay us a visit?"

And then the best part of the message of all. *"Dammit, Sam, you better not be with that bastard Brady. I swear to God, if you are, I'll kill him. I'll kill the son of a bitch."*

Greta smiled and played the message again.

• • •

GUNN WAS HEADING east on Route 27, just north of Hampton Bays. He probably had another thirty minutes before he reached the mansion. As long as he didn't run into any more trouble.

• • •

BRADY SPOTTED the wide-open door of the boathouse as he hurried across the frozen lawn. Assuming Sam would be inside, he slowed and approached with caution. But she was not there. Nor was she downstairs with the boats.

Brady forced himself to stop and assess the situation. Sam had obviously broken the lock on the door to get inside. To do that she must have felt a certain amount of desperation. Was her desperation due to those passageways and that remote-control box? Or was there more?

The answers were in plain view.

The caretaker found the computer magazine on the

floor in the kitchen. He had to assume Sam had seen the brief article about C. P. Donovan. That meant she now knew his real identity. But that was not such a big deal. He felt sure he could put a positive spin on that.

But then he turned and saw the foreclosure notice lying on the desk next to the computer. The caretaker put his foot through another wall.

And then Brady began to pace. Back and forth across the boathouse. Back and forth. Head down. Shoulders forward. Brain spinning like a disk drive. Sorting through information. Scanning for answers.

75

One by one Sam went through the Quincy videos. Videos of her in the bath. Videos of her in bed. Videos of her bruised and battered after Gunn's assault. Videos of her swimming naked with Brady. Each video more disgusting and demeaning than the last. The entire collection made Sam sick. She could not begin to comprehend the disturbed and dangerous mind that would make such videos.

Sam threw the videos in the trash immediately after viewing them. But she was no fool; she knew Brady undoubtedly had copies.

Every few seconds her son asked, "Can I go now?"

"Just hold your horses," she told her son. "I might have more questions."

Jason sighed and grew mute.

Sam typed her son's name into the Find File box. The caretaker had violated her privacy. Had he also violated Jason's and Megan's?

The hard drive whirled. And sure enough, it spit out another video: Jason, lying in bed, looking at a girlie magazine, his young eyes wide and full of wonder.

Sam did not watch the rest of the video. Boys, she knew, will be boys. She dragged the file into the trash.

"Mom, what about I put Megan on the phone so I can go back to bed?"

Megan! Sam's heart twisted. "A few more minutes, Jason, then I'll let you go."

Sam typed her nine-year-old daughter's name into the Find File box. It took several seconds before young Megan filled the screen in living color. Sam took one look, then gasped. There was her precious girl, playing in the bathtub, soaping and rinsing her sweet and slender little body.

Horror and anger boiled up in Sam. She could not believe Brady had filmed her daughter bathing. And then saved it. Preserved it on his damn computer. What kind of a man was he? What kind of an animal? And for the first time Sam knew the man she had been making love to was insane.

Megan drained the water from the tub. Then she stood and stepped out onto the bath mat, just inches from the hidden camera. Her innocence was exposed for all eyes to see.

But Sam could not look. She had seen enough. She dragged the video into the trash and hoped it was the only copy in existence.

"Mom, what are you doing?"

Sam started to respond, but a noise caught her ear. Coming from behind her, from downstairs. She turned and listened, but heard nothing. Nothing but her heart, pounding.

It must just be the wind, she told herself, or this old barn settling on its foundation. But she nevertheless put down the phone, stood, and took two or three steps in the direction of the trapdoor. As she had earlier down at the boathouse, Sam felt maybe the time had come to get out, to make her escape. After all, she now had all the proof she needed that Brady was a psychopath.

"Mom! Yo, Mom! What's going on? Where the hell are you?"

Sam could hear Jason's voice shouting through the telephone line, loud and demanding. Definitely his daddy's boy.

She returned to her chair and sat down. She picked up the phone. "Okay, Jason," she said, "I think we've done enough for today."

"Thank God. So I can go back to bed now?"

Before Sam could answer, a hand grabbed her shoulder. She shot straight up into the air. But the hand held her firm. She dropped the phone. It hit the floor with a dull thud.

"Mom! What the hell was that? Mom?"

Brady bent down and picked up the phone. "Hey, kid."

"Brady?"

"Right."

Jason, oblivious, wanting to sound cool, asked, "What's up?"

"Nothing much," answered the caretaker. "I just got back. Where are you?"

"At the hotel."

"In New York?"

"Yeah."

"With your sister?"

"Yeah, she's here."

"Well listen, kid," said Brady, "I'll take over on the computer now. I think I can lend your Mom a hand."

"Hey, great. That way I can go back to sleep."

Sam wanted to call out to her son, tell him to send help, but she knew it would do more harm than good.

"Right, you go back to sleep, Jason. Your Mom'll call you later."

And with that, Brady killed the call. Then he turned to Sam, who had not moved a muscle. "Computer problem?"

Sam needed several seconds to get her mouth moving. Trapped, cornered, vulnerable—she needed the right response. "Actually," she said, "I wanted to play THE AVENGER."

"You wanted to play THE AVENGER?" His voice was inquisitive, but polite, not at all hostile.

Sam managed to nod, then, "That's why I called Jason. I thought maybe he could get me started."

Brady studied the monitor. Nothing there but the hard disk icons. "So," he asked, "how are you making out?"

"Not too good. I'm kind of a stooge when it comes to computers."

Brady reached out and tucked a strand of hair back behind Sam's ear. "But an extremely beautiful stooge."

Sam forced herself to smile. So, she wondered, is this how we're going to play it?

"I missed you," he said. "That's why I came back a day early."

Sam hesitated, then replied, "I got here an hour or so ago."

Brady nodded. "And why did you come home early?"

"Because," she answered, "I had some things to do."

"You wanted to play THE AVENGER."

His tone, Sam realized, sounded gentle, but there was a menacing quality to it nevertheless. "I was interested in the game," she said. "You were out in California trying to sell it. I wanted to know more about it."

"I guess you did," said Brady. Then, "You must have worked pretty hard to get that padlock off the trapdoor."

Sam swallowed hard. "I didn't think you'd mind."

"Of course I don't mind, Sam. I want us to share everything."

Somehow, she thought, this suppressed innuendo was worse than an open confrontation. "I feel the same way, Brady."

That, of course, was not true. Right now Sam felt nothing but fear. She could feel herself shaking. Intuition told her she was in a very bad place. The key was to keep calm, keep Brady calm, keep him talking. She needed to get out of this third-floor cell, escape to some wide-open spaces.

Brady bent down and kissed her on the mouth. Sam forced herself to kiss him back. Only a few days ago she would have wanted to kiss him. And make love to him. But now she did not even know who he was.

Some pervert who made videotapes of her nine-year-old child taking a bath.

The caretaker kissed her on the lips. He kissed her eyes, her ears, her neck. Sam did her best not to cringe. She feared that at any moment he might hurt her. She wanted to confront him, demand an explanation for the lies and deceptions, for the videos and the violations of her family's privacy. But her instincts told her to keep quiet, play along, show him some affection. And even, if necessary, seduce him.

"So," Brady asked, "would you like me to show you how to play THE AVENGER?"

Sam squeezed his hand. "Show me later," she whispered. "Right now I'd rather go back up to the house."

"You would?" The caretaker sounded surprised by Sam's desire.

Sam did not give him much time to think about it. She stood, pulled on her jacket and gloves, then grabbed his arm and led him to the trapdoor. "I would, yes. Wouldn't you?"

So they went down the ladder and down the stairs to the first floor of the barn. The endless number of things that went unsaid followed close behind. A razor-sharp knife would have been needed to cut the psychological and emotional tension hanging between them. Their brains exploded with plots and subplots, possibilities and repercussions. But they spoke barely a word. And what little they did say contained not a kernel of truth. All lovers lie. But lovers who have grown suspicious twist and distort the truth in unimaginable ways.

They stepped outside. The cold, fresh air and bright light made Sam feel much better, even a bit safer.

But then Brady said, "Mrs. Griner's up at the mansion. Why don't we go down to the boathouse?"

Because, thought Sam, the boathouse is not safe.

She took his hand. "Oh, don't worry about Mrs. Griner. We'll sneak in. She won't even know we're there."

The secret passageways popped into both their brains. They did not, however, choose to make those passages part of the conversation.

"No, really," Brady said, "I'd much prefer the privacy of the boathouse."

Sam wondered if it might be best to just break free. To make a run for it. But she knew she would not get far. Brady, in perfect physical shape, would track her down in no time. So she relented. They turned toward the Sound.

Along the way Sam conjured up a tale about the broken boathouse door, about the condition of Brady's apartment. She would act surprised, as though she had no knowledge whatsoever about this particular situation. A break-in, she would suggest. Someone must have broken in while they were away.

But when they reached the boathouse, Sam did not have to *act* surprised; no, she genuinely *was* surprised. Even shocked.

The front door, which she felt certain she'd left broken and wide open, was closed and latched. And when they stepped inside, nothing, not a single item, was out of place. It looked to Sam as though the Goddess of Cleanliness and Order had descended upon the boathouse sometime after her hasty departure. She breathed a shaky sigh of relief. Until she realized that the Goddess was surely Brady himself. He had already seen the damage she had wrought.

But if so, he uttered not a word about it. He smiled and offered her something to drink: orange juice, or perhaps a ginger ale.

Sam accepted a glass of juice. Her mouth felt dry and cottony. What, she wondered, did Brady have in mind? Why was he being so sweet?

Excellent questions. Questions the caretaker, if asked, would have had a hard time answering. He knew he should take Sam out into the middle of Shelter Island Sound, chain an anchor to her leg, and throw her overboard. She deserved to die, deserved it for not minding her own damn business, for sticking her nose where it did not belong, for uncovering the plot he had painstakingly engineered against her shitbag husband.

Brady mashed his teeth together as he poured the orange juice into two tall glasses. He cursed himself for not finishing off that bastard Gunn Henderson weeks ago. Months. Years. He should have taken out the whole damn family instead of screwing around with this nosy bitch.

But he had feelings for the bitch. Powerful feelings. Intense feelings. He wanted her to be his. But it was all so confusing now. So muddled.

He turned, smiled, and handed her the tall glass of cold juice.

●　●　●

GUNN ACCELERATED as he pulled through the ornate front gates of PC Apple Acres. The cops could not touch him now.

He screeched to a halt directly behind his wife's Explorer. "So she is home," he muttered, stepping out of the Porsche. "Why didn't she answer the fricking phone?"

Gunn, a fair amount of alcohol still flowing through his system, threw open the front door and charged into the foyer. "Sam! Sam, where the hell are you?"

Greta, back in the kitchen, heard the lion roar. Thank God, she thought, the Devil's executioner has arrived.

"Sam!" Gunn, his normally neat and perfect hair all windblown from the long and windowless drive to PC Apple Acres, rolled into the kitchen. He looked like a wild man. He kept shouting for his wife. "Sam!" But instead he found the cook. He did not bother with any of life's little pleasantries. "Mrs. Griner! Where's my wife?"

"Your wife?" Greta made it sound as if Gunn no longer had a wife.

"Her car's out front. She must be here. And where are the kids? Don't tell me they're still sleeping. It's nine-goddamn-thirty."

Greta longed to pluck one of the eyes out of this pig's head, but instead she replied, cheerfully, "I believe the children are still in New York."

"New York? New York City? What the hell are they doing in New York City?"

"They all went in yesterday to spend Thanksgiving with the Greers."

"The Greers! Fuck! So they're still there?"

Greta found her place in this absolutely delicious. "Your children are, yes, but your wife returned," Greta lied, "last night."

"Last night? So where is she? Upstairs?"

Greta took a deep breath and turned toward the refrigerator. "Would you like me to fix you some breakfast, Mr. Henderson? Maybe some eggs and bacon and fried potatoes?"

"Dammit, woman, is Sam upstairs?" Gunn did not wait for an answer. He headed back down the hallway and up the steps, two at a time.

Greta waited patiently for his return. It did not take long, less than sixty seconds. "Mrs. Griner, do you know where the hell Sam is?"

Greta, playing her role to perfection, sighed, then nodded.

"Where?" Gunn demanded. "Where is she? Is she with that fucking caretaker?"

"Mr. Henderson, sir, I'm just the cook. I really don't like getting mixed up in these domestic situations."

Gunn's face had taken on the color of a ripe tomato. He punched the wall with his closed fist. "Where are they? Down in his stinking boathouse?"

Greta shrugged, dropped her eyes. "I would think so, sir," she answered, softly. "They spend quite a lot of time there."

"Quite a lot of time, huh?" Gunn punched the wall again. The blow left a sizable hole in the plaster.

"I know it's hard for you, Mr. Henderson," Greta offered, not much above a whisper, "but they're really very sweet together."

"Fuck sweet," growled Gunn. "I'll show that bastard sweet. I'll show both of them sweet."

And then he turned and went back down the hallway. He slammed through the living room and into his office.

His gun cabinet was locked. He dug his key ring out of his pocket. One by one he fumbled with the keys until he found the one he wanted. He unlocked the cabinet and made a lengthy visual study of his small but nevertheless deadly arsenal.

In the end he chose the Browning double-barrel twelve-gauge shotgun. It would scare the living shit out of his two-timing wife and that son-of-a-bitching handyman.

Plenty of ammo in the bottom of the cabinet. Gunn took out half a dozen shotgun shells. He loaded both barrels, then stuffed the other four shells in his pocket. The weight of the gun in his hand made him feel like a man. After days of sitting around, boozing, doing nothing, taking crap from that bitch Nita, it felt great to be back in action.

Gunn crossed to his desk and opened the bottom drawer. He pulled out a pint of whiskey and took two long pulls. Just to fortify himself. Then he turned and headed for the kitchen. Armed and dangerous.

"Mr. Henderson," gasped Greta, "you have a gun!"

"Goddamn right I have a gun." And with that, he threw open the French doors, stepped outside, and started across the terrace.

"Please, Mr. Henderson," Greta called after him, "be careful. Remember, despite everything, you love your wife."

Gunn growled a string of obscenities under his breath.

Greta allowed herself a little smile. She loved the inevitability of good and precise planning.

Then she grabbed her jacket and her cellular phone. And out the door she went, following Mr. Gunn Henderson at a nice, safe distance.

76 Down at the boathouse, the caretaker, despite his increasingly mixed emotions for Samantha, seemed determined to make love. Sam did not know what to do. She felt trapped inside a spider's web. She told herself to remain calm, to keep her thoughts clear and focused. For the moment, however, she had no choice but to allow this obscene display of affection to continue.

Brady knew Sam could not reject him. She belonged to him now. Some passionate lovemaking would surely make everything better between them.

Of course, he did not know that Sam had seen those videos.

She allowed him to lead her over to his bed. Brady slid his hand under her shirt and touched her breast. Sam sensed absolutely nothing gentle or loving about the caress. She wanted to push him away, to repel his advance, but she feared his wrath. She felt a powerful desire to retch.

Brady took off his jacket, then pulled his shirt up over his head without bothering to unbutton it. And then, tenderly, murmuring her name, he eased Sam back onto the bed. He stretched his body out on top of hers.

Brady covered her neck with wet kisses, then reached down and unsnapped her jeans.

◆　◆　◆

GUNN APPROACHED the boathouse like some freaked-out Green Beret descending upon an enemy command post. Shotgun at the ready, he moved on the front door in a serpentine line. He put his ear to the door, and listened.

◆　◆　◆

BRADY UNZIPPED Sam's jacket, unbuttoned her blouse.

She made herself think about something else. She made herself think about Jason and Megan. She could feel his erection against her thigh.

The caretaker moaned with delight.

◆　◆　◆

HALF A SECOND LATER that moan brought Gunn Henderson into action. He charged the door. It flew open upon impact. Gunn raced into the boathouse, his Browning twelve-gauge leading the way.

Four shocked and startled eyes looked up at him from the bed.

What the hell is he doing here? was Brady's first thought. Then, instantly, he knew something must have gone bad back at the penthouse. Louisa May, that whore, must have blown the whistle.

Seconds later Sam was out from under Brady's weight. She rose to her feet and fumbled at the buttons on her blouse with gloved hands. "Gunn! Thank God you're here!"

The scowl on Gunn's face ran deep and dangerous. He had the gun pointed at Brady, his right index finger itchy on those twin triggers. "What the fuck is going on?"

"He was going to rape me, Gunn. If you hadn't come he would have raped me for sure."

Impulse made Brady laugh. Right out loud.

"Rape my ass!" snorted Gunn. "It doesn't look like rape to me."

And again Brady laughed.

"Shut the fuck up!" Gunn ordered.

"Gunn," pleaded Sam, "listen to me. This man is not the caretaker. His name is not Brady. His name is Carl Patrick Donovan." Sam's words came in a great rush. "He does not work for Mr. Reilly. Mr. Reilly, whose real name is Parsons, works for *him*. Which, I think, means *you* work for him. The whole thing is some kind of setup. I don't have it all figured out yet, but I think it has something to do with your father, with Continental Bank and—"

"You whore!" shouted Gunn. "What the hell are you babbling about? I'm going to fucking shoot both of you—"

"Gunn—listen to what I'm saying! You have it all wrong. You think—"

"I told you to *shut up!*"

Brady stood. He zipped his fly. He looked around for his shirt. "You should listen to your wife, Gunn. You do work for me. Or at least you did until I had Arthur James Reilly fire your ass up at Flo's Diner in Randolph, Vermont."

"Flo's Diner? What do you know about Flo's Diner?"

"I was there, friend. Watching you squirm. I was the guy in the overalls and the fake mustache. Remember? I said so long as you headed out to your rented T-bird."

"What the hell?" Gunn looked confused. The muzzle of his Browning dipped. "But why? Why were you there?"

"Like I said, to watch you squirm."

"He's sick, Gunn. He's a psychopath. He's been messing with us from the very beginning."

Brady smiled. "We both know that's a slight exaggeration, Sam. I think what your wife means, Gunn, is that *she and I* have been messing with you ever since we started our little affair. . . . When was it, Sam? . . . Back in early May?"

"You liar! That's not true. You—"

"No use denying it, Sam. I'm sure Gunn remembers that Friday—"

"Gunn, no, he's lying. He's—"

"That Friday afternoon last spring when he found us lying together in the grass near the garden."

Oh yes, Gunn remembered.

"Gunn, listen to me. He's making it sound like—"

Gunn had heard enough. He raised that Browning and pulled the forward trigger. The shotgun's roar blasted through the boathouse, its echo slamming off the walls. Sam screamed.

Brady fell to the floor. Several seconds passed before he picked himself up. No, he had not been shot, just scared half to death.

The shotgun shell had shattered the picture window

overlooking Shelter Island Sound. As the cold north wind began to blow through the boathouse, all present turned to survey the damage.

• • •

Including Auntie Greta. She stood just inside the doorway. Unnoticed by all.

She was extremely disappointed. She had fully expected Henderson, half drunk and extremely volatile, to blow her nephew away after finding him shacked up with Samantha. But maybe she had misjudged the man. Maybe he didn't have the guts.

Still, there was plenty of time to get the job done. The blast had not brought Henderson to his senses. No, not at all. Look at him. Shoving another shell into the empty chamber.

Greta wanted to cheer Gunn on. She had waited so long for this moment. She had survived an abusive father, and an even more abusive husband. Cruel, sick, foul-tempered beasts. Bastards both. These two standing before her now, Gunn and Carl Patrick, were no better.

Greta just wished Gunn would press on. Quit intellectualizing and start emotionalizing. Point the gun. Pull the trigger.

• • •

Brady turned away from the shattered window. He, too, saw Henderson reload the shotgun. But he definitely did not believe the man had the courage to pull the trigger. Henderson might blow out another window or shoot a hole through the wall, but no way did he have the mettle necessary to fire that weapon into a human being. Henderson might threaten, even injure, but he did not have the balls to kill. The gun, Brady knew, was nothing but a prop.

"Now that you've got that little tantrum off your chest," the caretaker said calmly to Gunn, "I think we can get back to the important issues."

"Meaning what?"

"Meaning your wife and I are in love. Sam's in love with me. And I'm—"

"Bullshit."

"Afraid not, Gunny. Go ahead and ask her. She's a little ticked off at me right now, but I think she'll give you the straight dope on how she feels."

Gunn and Brady turned to Sam. So did Greta. All three waited for her to respond, to say something, anything. But after all that had happened, the roar of the shotgun had been the final blow for Sam. All she could do was shake her head.

"She doesn't love you, asshole," announced Gunn. "She's just pissed off at me because I ran out of bounds for a while. But I'm back now, so get used to it."

Brady took a second or two to consider his options. He decided to show Sam that he was the better man, the stronger man, the more courageous man. He took a step in Gunn's direction.

"Here's the thing," said the caretaker. "You may have the gun, but I've got everything else. I've got money, power, and connections. In the eyes of the world you're just a bum with no job who walked out on his wife and kids for a piece of ass. You've got nothing."

Gunn leveled the shotgun at Brady. "Don't come any closer, handyman, or I'll blow you in two."

"But you won't. You don't have the guts."

"Don't push me, pal."

Brady took two more steps in Gunn's direction. Now he stood barely an arm's length away from the end of the gun barrel. "You're not going to squeeze that trigger, Gunny. You're a coward. A coward who beats his wife."

Gunn shot a look at Sam. Had she told this bastard about what happened up in their bedroom? But Sam stood white-faced and mute. She did not meet his eyes.

"The time has come," continued the caretaker, "for you to do us all a favor, Gunny. Put down the gun and get your ass out of here. With as little fuss and bother as possible. Just turn around and disappear."

"I'm not going anywhere," Gunn claimed, but he did not sound very convincing.

"Oh, yes, you are," countered the caretaker. And then he took another step forward. The barrel of the shotgun pressed against his bare chest.

Sam, certain her lying, cheating, violent husband would once again fire that shotgun, whimpered. Greta mumbled under her breath, "Do it, Gunn. Shoot the bastard."

But Gunn couldn't do it. No way. Not a chance.

So in one swift motion, Brady, as though practiced in the art of hand-to-hand combat, grabbed the barrel of the Browning and drove his knee hard into Gunn's groin. The air flew out of Gunn's lungs. He doubled over and collapsed.

Brady swung the shotgun and cracked Gunn across the side of the head. Half a second later Gunn Henderson lay sprawled flat out across the floor of the boathouse.

And then Brady turned and looked at Sam. In the moment before a soft smile returned to his face, Sam saw the cold and calculating eyes of a killer. A shiver of fear raced along her spine.

"Sorry I had to do that, Sam," the caretaker said, his voice even and apologetic, "but the guy was out of control. I was afraid he'd hurt you."

Sam, her face pale with terror, swallowed hard. After several long seconds, she managed to nod. "Is he . . . is he dead?" she asked.

"No. He's not dead." Brady set the shotgun down on top of the rumpled bed, turned, and looked down at Gunn. Gunn had not moved. He was still out cold. "He's fine. He'll just have himself a little headache when he wakes up."

Greta surveyed the scene. She was not at all sure what to do. She certainly had not anticipated this. So much careful planning, and for naught. Stay calm, she told herself: Another opportunity will eventually arise.

And then one did. Right out of the blue.

Sam stared down at her husband sprawled on the floor. He had started to come around, to move and groan softly. She loathed the bastard for what he had done to her. But she hated Brady far worse. She loathed him and feared him. The way he had so callously deceived her. The evil he had brought to bear upon her family. That foul video he had made of Megan. She would never be able to erase those images of her little girl from her mind. Never.

And so she did the only thing she could do. With the caretaker still turned away, looking down at Gunn, Sam crossed to the bed.

Greta saw Sam reach for the gun. For an instant the

two women made eye contact. Sam expected Greta to call out, but no, Greta gave Sam a subtle nod of encouragement.

It was all Sam needed. She picked up the shotgun. She stepped back.

Brady, sensing movement behind him, turned.

Sam raised that Browning double-barrel and pointed it at the caretaker's chest. She had never fired a gun before.

"No, Sam. No." Brady shook his head.

But Greta, in the background, murmured very softly, "Do it, Sam. Shoot him. Shoot him now."

And Gunn, his throbbing head rising off the floor: "Sam—wait!"

But Sam had waited long enough. She had seen too much. The caretaker had done too much damage. Threatened everything she held dear.

So she closed her eyes. And squeezed the trigger. The shotgun roared. Sam pulled the other trigger. It roared again.

Brady, just a few feet away, literally flew into the air. He hung there, for a split second, then dropped like a rock through the shattered window.

• • •

THE BLAST threw Samantha flat onto her back. Firing that big twelve-gauge was like discharging a cannon.

Greta did not waste a second. She slipped outside, closed the door, and fired up her cellular phone. She dialed 911 and reported domestic trouble at PC Apple Acres. She informed the police dispatcher that Mr. Carl Patrick Donovan had been shot. Murdered.

Then she turned off the phone and went down to the dock.

The Hendersons stood there staring at the caretaker's broken body floating on the surface of the water. The water around him had turned a murky red.

Gunn tried to take his wife's gloved hand, but Sam, Greta noticed, pulled sharply away. A snake of blood stained her shoe.

Confident now, Greta crossed the dock and stood in front of the Hendersons. She did not mince words. "Here's the way this will work," she informed them. "You're going to take the fall for this, Gunn. I'm going to tell the police I saw you do it. An eyewitness. After all, your prints are all over the murder weapon. Sam has gloves on. She won't show a single print. Plus, I've got you on tape threatening to kill Mr. Donovan."

Terror began to work its way along Gunn's spine as the cook's words reached his brain. He remembered the phone call he had made earlier that morning, the enraged message he'd left Sam, the message in which he threatened to kill the caretaker. Somehow the cook had heard that message. And she now had it in her possession.

Sam shook her head. "No, I'll just explain. I'll tell the police everything. The whole story . . ."

"It won't do any good," said Greta. "You don't know the whole story, Sam. You don't know the half of it. Besides, there's a dead body here. A body blown to bits by a shotgun at point-blank range. Take a look, honey. A man has been murdered. An extremely wealthy and very powerful man."

Sam, trembling, continued to shake her head. "No,"

she whispered. "They'll understand. I know they will. He was after us. He wanted to destroy us."

"Believe me, Sam, you'll never be able to prove a thing," Greta informed her. "The authorities won't believe a word you say. They'll think you and Gunn conspired to kill him. So pull yourself together and listen to me. I'm willing to help you out, honey. I'll help you pin this on that useless scum groveling at your side."

"No," Sam said again, but less forcefully. The reality of what she had done had started to take hold.

"Trust me on this, Sam. Do you want to face murder charges? You have to think about your children. Who will raise them? Who will care for them when you end up in prison? This worthless scrap of human garbage?

Sam slowly shook her head.

"He'll take the fall for this," continued Greta. "You'll walk away, Sam. Walk away and start over. You and Jason and Megan."

Sam stared down at the caretaker's bloody body, lifted by the glittering waters of Shelter Island Sound. She thought of Brady, diving naked outside her bedroom window. She shuddered. Then she raised her eyes to her husband.

Gunn tried, but failed, to hold her gaze.

In the distance, a police siren wailed.

"Sam," Greta asked, her voice urgent now, "are you with me on this? It's your call. The police will be here any second. There's no more time to talk this over. It's very important you make a decision and stick to it. Do you understand?"

Sam, terrified of what she had done, but even more

terrified of what could happen in the future, kept shaking her head. But she was not a stupid or foolish woman. She knew what she must do. Not for herself, but for Jason and Megan.

A moment passed. Sam looked down at the blood-ied water. A tremor shook her. Then she looked into Greta's eyes and nodded.

"Yes," she whispered. "I understand."

Epilogue

HENDERSON FOUND GUILTY

By Mike Jones
Newsday Staff Writer

(May 23. EAST HAMPTON) Gunn Henderson, Jr., 40, of Armonk, New York, was convicted to-day in the murder of Carl Patrick Donovan, multimillionaire software developer and CEO of Graphic Software, Inc.

The verdict came quickly from the jury of nine women and three men. The trial lasted just six days. The jury's deliberations lasted less than five hours.

Evidence presented by the prosecution clearly showed that Mr. Henderson murdered Mr. Donovan in a jealous rage. Mr. Henderson shot Mr. Donovan twice in the chest with a double-barrel shotgun.

Estranged from his wife, Samantha Henderson, Mr. Henderson became infuriated when he learned his wife was involved romantically with Mr. Donovan.

Samantha Henderson, who last month filed for divorce, refused to testify against her husband. There was, however, an eyewitness to the homicide.

Greta McDougal, 63, of East Hampton, New York, Mr. Donovan's aunt and sole living relative, testified that she saw Mr. Henderson shoot Mr. Donovan immediately following a heated argument.

Pending his appeal, Mr. Henderson remains in custody.

Greta sat at the head of the table in the lavish dining room of that vast Long Island mansion. She finished reading the article, then she folded it, very neatly, and set it on the table. It did her heart good to see the verdict down in print. A verdict that closed the circle.

She lifted her glass and sipped the fine French champagne. A champagne breakfast. She had waited a long time for her own champagne breakfast. Now she planned on doing it regularly, several times a week.

The telephone rang. Greta went into the kitchen and picked it up. "Hello?"

"Ms. McDougal?"

"Who is this, please?"

"Mike Jones. From *Newsday*."

Greta knew the reporter from the courthouse, always hanging around, asking questions, frantically taking notes. He was a small, thin, aggressive man with bugged-out eyes.

"Yes?" Greta asked, politely. "What can I do for you, Mr. Jones?"

"I was wondering if you had any comment on the jury's decision?"

"Just that I'm glad it's over. It was extremely stressful."

"You were a very convincing witness for the prosecution. You definitely helped put Henderson away."

"It wasn't Henderson I was interested in, you idiot," Greta would have enjoyed telling the reporter. "He was just icing on the cake." Instead she settled for this more modest response: "Mr. Henderson put himself away."

Jones produced a soft, but cynical laugh. "Yeah, I guess he did. But what about all the accusations Henderson leveled against your nephew?"

Greta, her grieving aunt routine down cold, replied in a most somber tone, "The desperate ramblings of a desperate man."

"So then there's nothing at all to any of his accusations?"

"What would you have me say, Mr. Jones?" asked Greta. "Would you like me to confirm Mr. Henderson's wild fantasies? Would you like me to say, yes, my nephew plotted to destroy Gunn Henderson and his family? And would you like me to tell you that I helped him do it?"

"It would certainly make for an interesting story if you did."

"Perhaps it would, Mr. Jones. But I'm afraid what you suggest is utterly ludicrous."

"What about your nephew's millions?"

"What about them?"

"The money will go to you."

Greta stiffened. "Some of it, yes."

"How convenient."

"What are you suggesting now, Mr. Jones? That *I* killed my nephew for his money and pinned the blame on Gunn Henderson?"

"That's front-page material."

"I'm afraid," said Greta, "you give an old lady far too much credit."

"Do I?"

Greta smiled. It had been so easy, so ridiculously easy. A man with a vendetta can be so easily manipulated. Even a man as brilliant as her nephew Carl. With nothing more than a delicate nudge and an occasional shove, Greta had led him to believe that his life was meaningless unless he fully and finally avenged the deaths of his parents and sisters. And after that, well, after that Auntie Greta was able to take little Carl wherever she wanted him to go. Straight down the primrose path to his own damnation and demise.

"I did not shoot my nephew, Mr. Jones. Nor did I force Gunn Henderson to shoot him down in cold blood."

"No need to get defensive," countered the reporter. "I'm just doing my job, asking a few questions."

"Yes, I suppose you are."

"Have you heard about Mrs. Henderson?"

Greta's ears perked up. "Have I heard what about Mrs. Henderson?"

"She's pregnant."

"Pregnant?"

"Almost seven months now, the way I hear it."

Greta's brain went to work. She decided it would be best to get off the phone. Immediately. "I hadn't heard about the pregnancy, no, but quite frankly, I don't really care. Mrs. Henderson's condition is of no concern to me. And now if you will excuse me, Mr. Jones, I have things to do."

Greta hung up quickly before the reporter could ask another question. This news was a great distraction. She needed time to think, to mull it over.

Greta returned to the dining room, picked up the newspaper and her glass of champagne, and went into the library. On top of the plush Oriental carpet was a family photo album. But this was not your typical album of mom and dad, brothers and sisters, aunts and uncles, growing up and growing old. No, this was Greta's special album.

Greta took a pair of scissors and carefully cut out the article from the morning edition. She put a dab of glue on each corner of the article and pasted it firmly into the album, right next to the full-color picture of her nephew lying dead on the dock taken right after the police arrived to begin their investigation.

While the glue dried, Greta leafed back through the pages of the album. There were other pictures of her nephew, both dead and alive, as well as various articles about his accomplishments and his tragic end.

And further back in the album were pictures of Greta's son, her husband, her father. Pictures of them alive and pictures of them dead. Articles about their lives and their sudden deaths. Her son, drunk at the time, had perished in an auto accident. His brakes had failed. Her husband, also drunk, blind drunk, had fallen down the stairs and broken his neck. And her father, hungover early one Sunday morning, had shot himself in the head with a revolver.

Bad brakes? A fall down the stairs? Suicide? Greta's only regret was that she had not acted sooner. It would have saved so many people so much pain, so much grief.

On her fifty-first birthday she'd had a revelation, a kind of religious call to do good deeds. For a dozen years now she had been doing her duty, slowly and meticulously ridding the world of all male members of her immediate family.

It had been hard work, demanding all of her physical and mental prowess. Always she'd had to stay one step ahead of the psychotics. But it had been extremely gratifying, especially when things went well. And things had certainly gone well this last time. Not only had she managed to take out the last male in the family line, shutting off the bad gene pool, but she had also gotten rid of that philandering bastard Gunn Henderson. And inherited a tidy sum of money along the way.

But now this news of Samantha Henderson with child. And a good chance indeed that Carl was the daddy. What to do? How to take care of this sordid little detail? She could not risk another male child growing to adulthood. There could be no more men in her family, spreading evil to whatever they touched.

Greta sighed and finished her champagne. Clearly, the circle remained open. There would be no more bubbly, no more champagne breakfasts, at least not for a while. There was business to take care of first. Family business.

Greta did not waste a second. She moved directly to the phone. The time had come to call Sam, living up in Massachusetts now with her children and parents, just to see how Mrs. Henderson was getting along.

About the Author

THOMAS WILLIAM SIMPSON is the author of four previous novels, including *This Way Madness Lies,* which has been optioned by Paramount Pictures. Mr. Simpson lives in New Jersey, where he is at work on his next novel, *The Hancock Boys.*